PF
THE

KJ MACMILLAN

TYPESET IN BASKERVILLE

EDITING, DESIGN, TYPESETTING AND PUBLISHING BY UK BOOK PUBLISHING

WWW.UKBOOKPUBLISHING.COM

ISBN: 978-1-914195-87-7

ACKNOWLEDGEMENTS

I would like to thank my amazing wife Lesley for her encouragement and putting up with my "I am going to write a book one day" comments. My brother Malcolm for not only teaching me to read but also the value of reading. And to LKH for working through my early drafts and brainstorming ideas.

ONE

Louise Stewart had one objective: poison a Russian General with a Russian strain of Novichok and get out alive. If she got caught, she would never be seen again. The big Russian machine would just make her disappear, buried in a woodland somewhere just outside of Moscow in a shallow grave. It added a certain amount of spice to the situation. She thrived on it. The mystique of living a lie and being deep undercover in a foreign country with limited back-up in place. To make things even more interesting, the General was the commander of the FSB, the Russian Intelligence service. Not only could what she was doing lead to a death sentence in Russia, it would be a political disaster for the UK Government and would make a mockery of their holier than thou attitude they cultivated across the globe.

In her mind Louise still saw herself as just a wee girl from Glasgow who had had a tough upbringing. She was not one of the victims in life, she believed that life makes you who you are. The good bits you enjoy, and the bad bits are where you learn; and the in-between bits, well, they are just life's highway to the next good bit. She smiled to herself as the bad bits don't feel like a learning experience at the time. They generally kind of suck at the time; it isn't until afterwards when you are sitting with a glass of wine or a pint of beer that you look back and try to rationalise it.

Louise was born on the kitchen floor of a two-bedroom flat in a council estate on the outskirts of Glasgow. She had been bullied, abused and outcast from school, just one of the kids that was just written off at an early age by a system set up to stream middle class kids for university. It wasn't that she was not intelligent – she was off the charts in intelligence – she just had different learning opportunities in life and that meant she had gained a different set of skills to the ones they teach you in formal education. The bullying and abuse made her mentally and physically resilient, the system writing her off made her all the more determined to succeed. When life put her into a tough spot where it is easier to lie down and let go, she would remember the smirk of derision on her guidance teacher's face as he told her she should stick in at home economics so she could make a good homemaker. Fuck you, Mr Smith!

That was the mantra she used whenever it was easier to give up than go on. She did not even have to think about it these days, it just came instantly into her head: "Fuck you, Mr Smith".

Louise had been working undercover as a waitress at the Bolshoi Theatre in Moscow for a little over three months. These operations take a long time in the planning and even longer to carry out. Any westerner in Russia was under surveillance, most often electronic but sometimes physical as well. She took her time to set up a routine, one of banal mediocrity, work, commute and exercise. Her way of saying to the intelligence agency, nothing to see here please move along. It was important to maintain a façade of aloofness from her colleagues at work and with the other tenants in her block of flats.

Despite everyone's best efforts, a back story can only go so deep; letting someone in too close was a risk. That meant banal mediocrity was the weapon of choice. At work Louise was chatty when required but kept a sensible distance, and when asked out on social engagements, she politely declined citing a jealous boyfriend. It was really just about being an employee that was eminently forgettable, she did not want to stand out from the crowd. How many times do you see it on TV when the neighbours say the suspect just kept themselves to themselves, but they seemed polite enough? This type of job suited introverts better than extroverts. They were more comfortable in staying below the radar and just quietly setting up the routine and working through every detail of the job in hand.

It took about six to eight weeks to get the work, commute and exercise routines properly established. Once her agent in charge, Edward, was happy everything was in place, he sent word of a Secret Intelligence Service (SIS or sometimes MI6 as they are known) asset within the FSB. A middle-ranked man in his early forties who, despite being married with a family, had developed an affection for dalliances with random young men. A couple of years earlier London set up a specific team to carry out a sting operation to get compromising photos of him with a young male lover. As far as Edward was concerned, they were not exploiting the target for being gay – leverage was leverage no matter what it was. It was about finding someone's weak point and using that. It could be a married man who visited prostitutes or had a gambling problem, it could be a film star who had done porn films when they were younger. It did not matter what the weakness was, it was all about could they use it to force them to do what the intelligence service needed. In this case being gay was just a normal part of society so what SIS were exploiting was how difficult it still is to come out of the closet when you are married and have children. In Russia, very often your house or flat was linked to your government job and although being gay was tolerated more now than it ever had been, it was not allowed in the security services like the FSB. In this instance, not only would the target lose his wife and children, but he would lose his job and his flat.

Edward always felt blackmail was such an ugly word; he much preferred exploitation or active encouragement. It was how every intelligence agency across the world operated, they would use any lever they could to get you to do what they wanted including in this case a sting operation to take compromising photos.

It started with a good-looking person sitting down next to you that they knew would interest you. Of course, they already knew your type, whether it be tall, short, blonde, brunette, it did not matter. They always knew what would tempt you. Then they would ply the target with alcohol and drugs, sit, and once your guard was down the *"why don't you come back to my room"* request did not seem unreasonable.

That was the trick in the intelligence game, no single request was unreasonable, it was all about the next request building on the first and before you knew it you were in over your head. Unfair, yes; despicable, yes; it could even be described as grotesque, but in the intelligence game nothing was off the table. They would be told just do this one thing and your debt would be repaid; however, the asset would never be rid of their indiscretion. It would be there forever, and they would be asked to deliver more and more information at greater and greater levels of risk. The words spy or secrets were never used, it was I just need this small piece of information or I just need you to find out who is running this project. There would be rewards, of course, just to make sure the asset did not give up in despair and stupidly confess or commit suicide. Either one would set the service back months, sometimes even years.

The name Edward had provided Louise for the asset was Sacha. It was not his real name, of course, but for the purposes of the operation it would suffice. Sacha was a family man with a pretty young wife and two sons of primary school age. In a lot of ways, he was living the Russian dream and he was the model FSB operative. A family man who had attended state school and over the years created an excellent reputation for himself for academic excellence. He had attended Moscow State University and graduated with a first-class honours degree in Mathematics before being recruited into the FSB and starting a promising career.

Having read the file provided by Edward, Louise could not quite figure out the attraction of risking both career and family for a quick tumble with some random stranger. The fact that Sacha was bisexual was a non-issue for Louise. Louise herself had over the years had lovers of both sexes and really, she was attracted to the person irrespective of their gender. Sacha had a weakness for random gay liaisons. Like a lot of taboo things, they started as every year, then every six months, three months and just before he was targeted it became as often as he could get. Despite Russian society being more liberal than it had been in the last 100 years, it was still frowned upon.

Edward had known that a same-sex liaison would not really have been enough to blackmail Sacha into providing information to SIS. Edward liked the term providing information: it was a much less emotive description than spying. The end result was the same, of course, and over time it would end up as spying. However, for these things to be successful they started off as a request for something that was perfectly reasonable. Each further step was just a small extension of the previous request and each time it would appear reasonable. Before long poor Sacha would end up in so deep, he would have no way out but to continue. Oh, SIS would dangle the carrot of ripping up the photos and statements of "we will take care of your family" but, it would be years before Sacha was allowed out of the no-walls prison that he had created for himself.

Edwards's research had shown that Sacha had a distinct type, so for the sting he had recruited a particularly handsome looking man, tall with dark wavy hair, olive Mediterranean looking skin and who dressed very smartly. He had perfectly formed white teeth and although old enough to be perfectly legal, Edward engaged a makeup artist who made him look underage in all the photos.

Nobody wanted even the sniff of an underage liaison anywhere near them. Prison was not somewhere that Sacha ever wanted to be and being known as a paedophile in prison meant a life sentence of hell.

It just made everything so much more difficult to explain away and therefore created a stronger case to exploit Sacha for what they needed. The threat of photos being provided to the wife, her family, friends, and neighbours, as well as the FSB internal affairs team, were enough to persuade Sacha that the path to redemption would be working for British Intelligence.

Under Edward's direction, SIS had tailed Sacha to his favourite pick-up point on an island at a bend on the Moskva river called Serebryany Bor (Silver Wood). The wooded area was a well-known gay cruising joint. The young man SIS had recruited to play the part of an underage victim was very well paid and took Sacha to a room rented by the hour and which Edward had set up to provide very graphic images of the liaison. The end result was that Sacha was now an asset for Edward within SIS.

Louise had received word from Edward that the information they had been waiting on was now available and would be passed along at a specific dead drop that Edward had set up for Sacha. The dead drop had been live for some time. Louise was heading to the nominated place at a bench in Vagonoremont Park near the Dmitrovsky District in the North of Moscow. Edward had insisted that they use old school spy techniques to keep them off the radar of modern Russia. It keeps everything off grid and is more difficult to track. Nowadays digital footprints are easier to track than people think so keeping things old school made sense on this occasion.

Louise was comfortable either way and each one had its merits. As this was old school, each time she was going to a meet, Louise would leave the flat dressed in her normal attire and somewhere along the route would change into a disguise – it could be a public toilet, a changing room or if it was a simple change just an alleyway. She was that practised at it she could enter an alley as a smart young office worker and at the end of the alley walk out as a frail old woman pulling a shopping bag on wheels. Sometimes it was a down and out, sometimes a high-class woman walking with a wiggle. Today she was a jogger, tall, black poker-straight hair in a ponytail that reached just below her shoulders, a grey baseball cap, grey sweatpants and a grey crop top to make the most of the glorious weather. It was finished off with a small black rucksack that contained a quick change of appearance in case she had to shake a tail.

She had run for five kilometres constantly looking for tails, turning corners and looking in car mirrors. This always put her on edge, this could be the time she gets caught. Adrenalin was coursing through her veins, heightening every sense to the maximum. She was confident she had not been tailed but like every previous time she was being extra cautious. She entered the park and slowed her pace to little more than a gentle jog.

She took her time and circled the park. It was a glorious day in Moscow, not a cloud in the sky, which in summer meant another hot day. She passed the dead drop bench seat, which had an elderly gentleman sitting on it, reading a newspaper. It was a local newspaper, only really read in Moscow. He was pretty unremarkable and dressed as most of the local old men were. As she ran past him, he did not even look up from whatever article had grabbed his attention. That was a good sign. If he was an operative, he would be more interested in the people around about him than in the newspaper itself. Was it just a coincidence he was sitting at the dead drop or was it something to worry about?

She decided to do another lap of the park to check it out. It was a park with lots of open spaces, tarmac paths circling the park and crisscrossing it at intervals. It was a haven of tranquillity in an otherwise concrete jungle. Plenty of locals took the chance of spending some time in amongst the trees and grass when they needed some alone time or just to empty their head of the rest of the causes of stress that affected their lives.

There were other characters that caught her eye. The man sweeping up litter on the north side of the park. This man was young, dressed head to toe in local council grey overalls which were sweat-stained and grubby, having been used over a number of days. His shoulders were slightly hunched and he swept with the long strokes of someone who knew what he was doing. She discounted him as a genuine worker. Coming from a working-class council estate background, she appreciated the blue-collar worker and the work they did.

The last person of note was a woman, sitting on the bench, overdressed for the area in a calf-length red dress, shoes meant for show rather than walking, shiny, dark curly hair that had obviously been washed and styled specifically for today. She was sitting forward on the bench looking all around her anxiously, her head continuously moving and scanning the people walking in the park. She did not look at the people who were stationary or actually working, only people coming towards her. She was making Louise uncomfortable.

Just as Louise was going to leave, she saw the woman stand up and wave at a young man striding purposefully towards her and looking anxiously at his watch. He was obviously late for their rendezvous. They hugged and kissed and headed off hand in hand in the direction of the underground.

Louise let go of her anxiety and focussed on her second circuit of the park. Nothing else stood out to her and as she approached the area near the bench, she pulled up a few metres short. She spent a couple of minutes stretching. First her calf muscles by standing on a kerb and dropping her heels a few centimetres before crossing her legs and touching her toes, holding for 60 seconds to stretch her hamstrings, and then crossing her legs the other way and repeating. All the time she was watching the people nearby.

She moved to the bench to continue the stretching, foot up on the seat and fingers pulling her torso forward, stretching out the hamstrings further. She did not acknowledge the gentleman reading the newspaper – making eye contact made you memorable and this was something she tried to avoid. All the time she was checking for something that was out of place, anything that didn't feel right, and she would simply jog on. She double checked everyone in view; once again she viewed the street sweeper who was totally focussed on keeping the park clean, the retired gentleman having a coffee on the next bench who was immersed in his newspaper and enjoying the fresh air, the other runners in the park out in ones and twos. Had she seen them before anywhere? An exceptional memory in the espionage and assassination business was everything. She was looking for patterns of behaviour, a way of walking, a hairstyle or familiar hat, anything that would set off her sixth sense. Louise had scored off the charts when she had been tested for pattern recognition.

Over the years she had learned to trust her senses. When you were bullied and abused as a child you learnt to live on your instincts. If it did not feel right, it usually wasn't.

She sat on the bench and rubbed her calf muscle, just taking an extra few seconds to make sure everything was clear before reaching under the bench and taking out the package. It was the size of her thumb and she kept it in her hand as she continued to rub her calf and wincing as if she had picked up a minor injury. She would not read the message until she was back at the flat; she had to be extra cautious. Her nerves were tingling and senses on high alert as she took in every detail of her surroundings before taking one final stretch and jogging on.

She did a further full circuit of the park just at jogging pace. Every fibre of her being was screaming at her to leave the area immediately, to get away from danger and into safety. It took all her will and determination to carry on as if everything was normal.

On exiting the park, she sighed inwardly as it was back to the heat-soaked concrete jungle streets; a little bit of her mind regretted leaving the grass and trees and more importantly the tranquillity. As she ran past shop windows, she checked the reflection for anything unusual. Had she seen that face before, or the way someone walked? It wasn't just about behind her, it was also about the other side of the road or someone she would pass. Busy streets were easier to hide in, but they also made it easier to be followed. She changed direction onto side streets and round corners and finished by running round the block of the dingy one-bedroom flat she was living in.

The term nowadays is safe house – in her experience the words 'safe house' really meant total dump. It was all about ingress and egress. How quickly could she get out if she was discovered? This flat had four different escape routes if she needed them, a go bag stashed on each route with money, false passport and change of clothes that could disguise who she was. Three of the routes had been planned in meticulous detail with the backup team. Everyone knew each other's routes, apart from one which they all kept secret in case a member of the team got caught.

The safe house was small and rented quarterly in advance. Moscow was an expensive place to live and as a waitress she could not afford anything more than shabby. Her life had to be believable – if a typical waitress could only afford a dive, then that is the way Louise needed to live. Any other way would attract unwanted attention.

Like most cities the centre of Moscow is lavish, built during the time of the Tsars and the Russian empire. Stunning architecture built by architects and builders at the top of their game. However, away from the city centre were, in architectural terms, the concrete monstrosities built by the Soviet machine that housed millions of people in shabby little flats. There was nothing in the local area that stood out. The flat was in dire need of renovation. Painted woodwork that had mellowed from pristine white to a vague beige colour due to years of cooking and scrubbing and under investment dulling it down. Wallpaper that had come unstuck in the corners where dampness intruded into the flat. Louise was undecided if it was dampness or condensation, but the result was the same: a horrible dark mould that crept up the walls and gave rise to a dank stale smell. There was only single glazing which meant in the winter months the windows constantly streamed with condensation, so maybe she had just answered the condensation v damp question. The curtains were a limp brown colour and there were no carpets, just bare floorboards with an occasional threadbare rug in the centre of the room and four chairs that creaked due to dried out joints and had generally seen better days.

Russia had some of the richest men on the planet with the Oligarchs but the normal everyday blue collar workers were still barely making enough money to survive. It was a common theme the world over: the rich getting richer and the poor at best standing still.

Before entering the flat Louise checked the signs she had put in place at the front door to ensure no one had been inside. A hair seemingly trapped in the paint went across between the door frame and the door. It was still in place as was the matchstick perfectly placed to fall near the bottom of the door that was placed specifically in a groove in the door for just that reason.

Only when she was completely happy the door had not been opened did she step inside. If she felt the door had been opened, she would have headed for one of the escape routes and simply called the hit off.

Once safe in the flat, she made a bug sweep. The tool she was using was looking for usage of a radio frequency being transmitted from the flat, it could be piggy backing on the flat WiFi or using a hard-wired transmitter. The listener of the devices would need to be holed up somewhere nearby like one of the flats next door or a van in the street as these types of bugs had a limited range. All of this detail was a chore, but she would complete all the checks any time the flat was left unattended. These things don't need to be sophisticated, and they didn't cover every eventuality, but they tipped the odds of survival in your favour and that was all you could do.

Only once she was happy everything was cleared did she open the package. It contained one line: Bolshoi 7pm Friday. At last, she thought, and felt a sense of elation, the boring routine was finally coming to an end. The intelligence source had stated that tonight her target General Andropov was to attend a production of the Nutcracker at the Bolshoi Theatre unannounced. The target was the commander of the FSB, and his mother had been a ballerina before she met his father who had also been a General in the military before his death five years previously.

British Intelligence hoped that at some stage he would take in a show due to a love of his mother and a love of the Ballet. People are creatures of habit and eventually everyone gives in to it. The General had a fondness for the ballet, pretty young ladies and for Vodka.

Louise knew that this was a revenge mission for British Intelligence. General Andropov had ordered the hit on UK soil in Salisbury using a nerve agent called Novichok and this would be payback. Louise knew this was personal for Edward, as his reputation had taken a hammering for not knowing it was being planned.

Louise opened her laptop and navigated to a specific server housed on the dark web. It had been set up by British Intelligence some months ago for this specific assassination. It was unattributable to SIS and was housed in the same way as the other dark sites. The dark web tended to be used by Criminal gangs and Paedophiles as it was notoriously hard to navigate. There was no search engine which meant you could not just type in *www.secretrouter.com*. It was sometimes referred to as the TOR network which translates to The Onion Router. Each layer of the "onion" had its own layer of encryption, which made it almost impossible to track users. I say almost impossible as it can eventually be done, and the intelligence agencies had put a lot of manpower and resources in place to get on the front foot.

The team's messages would look innocuous to anyone but the intended recipients. To the uninitiated it would just look like she was moving a piece on a virtual chess board. To the support team and to Edward, they knew the status of the assassination had changed. In essence the team had four codes. Everything ok was moving a pawn; something concerning me was a major piece move, i.e. a Knight or a Rook; get out now was moving the King. The last code was moving the Queen which translated to "I have news, we need to meet". Louise tagged Queen to Queen's knight four.

The team would assemble in four hours' time. They had to follow the same strict security protocols that Louise did in checking for tails and being ultra-cautious. That meant Louise had time to re-energise and she lay down on her bed, closed her eyes and allowed her mind to drift.

Louise had been one of the poor kids at school. From an early age she learnt to accept the teasing and lack of friends, she did not need the fake barbie doll type girls in her life whose only challenge was what outfit to wear with their new shoes. She learnt to stick up for herself. It might have been easier to become a victim and accept the bullying and intimidation as a part of life but that was just not how Louise was. She did not take the easy path; it was just not in her; she was one of life's fighters.

A few girls tried to make her life a misery, taunting her, teasing her, pushing her around in a circle, stealing her stuff. A girl named Bethany was the worst and was the ringleader; she was tall, heavyset with brown curly hair and a permanently angry look on her face that showed she hated the world.

Carla, Alison, and Lizzie were the followers. They were similarly built; however, they did not have that permanently angry look, more of a permanent frown. To be honest, Louise didn't really care about the words they used, they meant nothing to her – they were not friends or family, and she therefore did not care what they said about her. Louise knew she was poor, and she knew that her mum tried her best, and in Louise's mind that is what counted.

One day all that changed. Louise was walking to school with her younger brother Jaimie when Bethany and the others started calling her names and trying to make her fall over by clipping her heels together. Louise could normally take it, but this time it was different, her brother was with her and she was highly protective of him. He was such a loving, innocent boy who was always asking questions about how things worked, and his love of the word "WHY" could sometimes wear her down. He was one of those boys who could never walk anywhere, he just seemed to bounce along doing cartwheels or jumping off walls. He had a genuine love of life and Louise just loved him to bits.

Jaimie wore grey shorts to school. Her mum said it was because they were in fashion, but Louise knew it meant she did not have to keep buying long trousers when he grew out of them. Her mum said that Jaimie just ate, slept, talked, and grew his way through life, which was pretty accurate from what Louise had observed.

Bethany pushed Jaimie so hard in the back that he fell to the ground, his hands hitting the ground hard, but it saved his face smashing on the pavement. He sat up and started to cry, tears of pain and bewilderment running down his rosy-red cheeks. As he stood up his leg had blood streaming from a cut on his knee and the palms of his hands all grazed with small bits of sand and dirt embedded into the torn skin.

"Oh look, junior smell is here today, let's teach them both a lesson," shouted Bethany to her three sycophantic friends.

Something inside Louise just snapped and she faced into Bethany, looked her straight in the eye and said, "Leave Jaimie alone, he is just a boy, why don't you try picking on me instead?"

"Hahaha and just what do you think you are going to do about it?" Bethany retorted with a smug, superior smile on her face.

As Louise turned to confront the other three bullies, instead of anger, she felt a strange calmness take hold, an incredible focus where everything seemed to slow down and become more vivid. Louise kicked Bethany hard on the outside of the knee and watched in satisfaction as the knee bent inwards at a horrible angle and she let out an agonising scream. As Bethany bent down to grab her knee, Louise punched her across the side of the nose and just smiled as she watched the nose move sideways with a snap and pour with blood. As Bethany's friends engaged in the fight, Louise kicked and punched with a speed and power that caught the bullies off guard. Using fists, feet and elbows just as fast as she could, she made sure each one landed and used her bodyweight to add power to each one.

With calmness and focussed aggression, she took them all on. They landed a few of their own, but with adrenalin flowing through her body she registered the hit, though there was no pain, at least not yet.

As Bethany started to rise, Louise turned as fast as she could, and round house kicked her across the face, forcing her to hit the ground hard in a mixture of tears and blood.

Louise's confidence grew and grew, and as she turned to the others, she instinctively knew she only needed to take one more and the other two would run. Alison was a fat redhead with a temper and grabbed Louise from behind, trying to hold her so the others could teach Louise a lesson. As she grabbed hold, Louise moved six inches to one side, just enough to bring her elbow back hard into Alison's solar plexus. It forced its way through her rolls of fat like a hot knife through butter and Louise could hear the wind rush out of Alison's windpipe. As Alison let go, Louise brought her elbow up and drove it back hard at head height and heard it hit Alison's jaw with a satisfying crunch. She let out a scream and as her hands headed up to her face, Louise punched hard upwards, catching Alison on the already damaged chin and watched with a glowing sense of satisfaction as her head whipped backwards and she slumped to the ground.

With two assailants on the ground in a flood of tears and blood, Louise turned to face the two that remained standing. She looked them both in the eye, exuding a confidence that was disconcerting. She took two steps forward towards them and let out a fierce Celtic roar and watched in satisfaction as they turned and ran, just as her instincts told her they would.

Louise gingerly took her brother's hands in hers, kissed them and headed to school to get him cleaned up; she had a few bruises on her face and her ribs felt tender, but the satisfying glow made up for it all.

Jaimie looked at his older sister in awe. A look of total amazement bordering on worship.

"Where did you learn to fight like that? You were amazing, punching and kicking and spinning. They never stood a chance. I bet you are the best fighter in school."

When Louise looked up onto the hill, the old man who lived next door to them was watching. He never waved nor acknowledged them in any way, but Louise could tell he had seen everything. Louise got that sense of dread in her stomach as she knew she would be in trouble for this. She sighed quietly to herself, thinking her life was just about to get a lot harder. It wouldn't be the first time. She was a bit of a tomboy and trouble seemed to follow her about. It is what happened when you had a bit of an attitude. She did not see it as an issue. She was never a fan of people applying gender to all aspects of life and she was more than happy to do stuff that wasn't feminine. She railed against the "girls just should not do that kind of thing" statement.

It turned out her neighbour seeing everything was a blessing in disguise. After taking her brother to the nurse to get his cuts cleaned and appropriate plasters applied, she headed off to class and shrugged off the attentions of the school nurse for her own bruises and facial swellings. Louise took her usual desk at the side of the class out of the way of the teacher's pets. She focussed on completing the Maths questions written on the white board. She found Maths easy, but she hated being the centre of attention, so she made sure she got a few wrong even when she knew the answer. She was extremely intelligent; however, she did not like being in the limelight.

There was a knock at the door and one of the Administration assistants entered the room and spoke with Mrs Lightbody, the Maths teacher.

"Louise, the headmaster would like you to go to his office immediately."

As Louise got up and headed out of the class with the Administration assistant, the rest of the class started to grin and chant.

"You are in trouble; you are in trouble."

Louise was escorted up to the Headmaster's office. He was a stern man in his late fifties, short with a full head of grey hair, almost bordering on white. He was stocky with a ruddy complexion, which suggested he liked a whisky or two.

He had a booming, deep voice which he used to great effect as he yelled and pointed and banged his desk and told Louise she was good for nothing, a liability to the school and an embarrassment to her poor mother. Louise genuinely felt she would get expelled but instead she got a two-week suspension.

It turns out that the neighbour called the school and told them what he had seen. Not many witnesses would have done that, and it saved Louise from the wrath of the school as Bethany and her cronies had made up a story that Louise had assaulted them and tried to steal their lunch money. The suspension was for not reporting the bullying, which allowed it to become physical.

When Louise arrived back at the Maths class there seemed to be genuine shock that she had not been expelled both by Mrs Lightbody, the teacher, and from the pupils. Their looks of disbelief still made Louise smile. Louise packed her books up from her desk and walked back home, along past the roads with the red sandstone tenement flats, in through the park where she just loved sitting watching people going by and guessing what they did for a living and where she thought they would live. Did they dress like they had money in bright, newly coloured clothes or were they wearing worn, washed out clothes like Louise. Louise looked up to the block of flats where she lived – there were thousands of them in Glasgow built in the 1950s and 60s. The government built these concrete monstrosities and packed people in. They left communities where everyone knew everyone else and were packed into flats that were soulless and where community spirit just did not exist. They did, however, have internal toilets which was a step up from the previous housing. Louise had never known anything else; she had always been poor and had always had to take on more than other kids her age. She had been into care homes on a couple of occasions when her mum struggled with drugs and alcohol. As long as Louise and Jaimie were together, she could deal with whatever life threw at her.

When she got home, Louise knocked on the neighbour's door. She felt nervous as she had seen him a few times, but they had never really spoken. He generally kept to himself, and their block of flats never had any of the drugs gangs hanging about like other flats in the area. She had seen him talking quietly to any who tried, and you just didn't see them coming back. He seemed a genuine type of person from what she knew and what the other neighbours said.

"Thank you, it was very kind of you to phone the school on my behalf, not many people would have done that and especially not for someone like me."

"That's ok, dear, I could tell what type of girls they were. I have seen their type before, bullies and liars that think they can do what they want. I was impressed that you stood your ground against four bigger girls, they were a good bit bigger than you and that took some guts. I thought for sure you were going to take a kicking. Your technique is a bit ragged, but it worked. You should be proud of how well you did."

"Thank you, I don't really have a technique; I just did what I thought would work."

"Mmmmmm, that won't really do, my dear. If you are going to get into those kinds of scrapes then we better teach you to do it properly."

"You mean like train me?"

"If that is what you want, but I am a hard disciplinarian. I am ex-Army, you see, and if you want to get anywhere in life you need discipline."

They sat talking for about an hour about what the training would entail and that if she missed a session, she would end up doing double the next time.

It turns out his name was Mr MacPherson. He was a bull of a man, about five foot eight inches tall, broad shoulders and a deep chest that bulged with muscle under his black t shirt. His arms and legs look equally muscled. He had shoulder-length black hair which Louise suspected was dyed, with a black goatee beard. Despite being older he obviously still worked out. Apparently, he had joined the Royal Corp of Signals when he left school and he had served with 22 regiment SAS of the British Army for 15 years, whatever that was. He had piercing blue eyes that seemed to look right through you to the point where they knew what you were thinking before you did. There was a calmness about him as if he knew how to deal with life and what it sent his way. For some reason, Louise knew that this relationship would set her on a different course in life. Little did she know just how different.

Louise slowly brought herself back to the present and sat on the floor, crossed her legs and went into a meditative state; she used it as a technique to sharpen her focus and mentally review the plan devised by the whole team. Within the depths of her mind, she imagined an underground tunnel with lots of different rooms coming off it. The tunnel was well lit but went off into the distance with no obvious end. In some ways it was like an underground hotel corridor. Each room that came off the tunnel was labelled and they each contained different things that she needed to remember. Tonight, was a red door with the words "*Moscow assassination*" typed in black onto a gold nameplate that was screwed onto the gothic wooden door. In her mind she opened the door and stepped across the threshold into the room, gently closing the door behind her. The room was furnished with a single high backed Edwardian chair with a number of large pin boards attached to the picture rails on each wall. Louise sat on the chair and focussed on the board immediately to her right. Each board was a storyboard outlining the timeline of the assassination, detailing photographs of buildings, bus routes, stopping off points and changes of direction. The plan on the boards went from right to left and outlined what each member of the team would do from the time they left the flat to when they left Moscow. Every detail was on the wall. Each night as the plans were firmed up, she would build the picture in her mind of what was now within the room. Multiple large colour maps of Moscow detailing escape routes, photos of key players in the assassination game and everything she knew about them. Mentally checking each part of the plan, did it all still make sense, taking into account any new information? In this game, planning and preparation were everything, yes you had to be able to react on the night to a curve ball, but the more you kept within the plan the more predictable the outcome.

A sharp knock at the door brought Louise immediately back to full consciousness and back into the real world. Her heart was racing, this was when danger crept in. Louise was relying on the other team members having the same vigilance as her. She had a lot of faith in them as they had been together for the last three years. Despite that, there was always a sense of danger as an operation came to fruition. All it took was one careless comment or someone having a bad day and the team could be compromised. A knock on the door could be anyone and she was relieved as the team arrived a few minutes apart. One bringing food but each one bringing their individual go bag as they would never go back to their own accommodation. Each flat would by now be forensically wiped down to make identification of the occupants as difficult as possible. The idea was to be the vanilla neighbour no one remembered.

They were a four-man assassination team, though the word man these days was pretty redundant – their team comprised two females and two males, but like all good teams, they could not be arsed with all that political correctness nonsense. In fact, their sense of humour bordered on the scandalous at times and if overheard could easily be misunderstood.

The two guys were Hairy Dave and Mac, with Storm and Louise the females. They each had a general skillset in killing people with their own particular specialities over the top of that. They had been in a number of scary situations over the three years they were together, and that unique bond would never leave them. You would not call it a friendship; it was so much deeper than that. When your life was literally in someone else's hands and you knew they had your back no matter what, you developed something special, and words just could not do it justice. It almost became supernatural, you knew how someone would react in a situation, what their next move would be and what you could do to support.

Storm was the communications queen. She knew everything there was to know about secure communications. She was doing a final check to make sure the comms they were going to use during the hit were working. There was a discreet earpiece for Louise, which was good, but it did have a limited range. Each of the others had an earpiece that was hard wired to a transmitter hidden in their jacket. The range was better for them and the wire did not matter as much as they were outside the theatre. Comms were one of the most vital parts of any mission and they had all seen missions fail because the comms did not work. Each item was thoroughly checked, and each member of the team carried a spare battery pack concealed about their person in the unlikely event they would be needed. Storm would keep a full additional kit just in case something failed completely. Better safe than sorry.

With the comms check complete, they went through the plan one last time, pedantic yes, detailed yes, but this was not only about the hit itself, it was about doing the hit and getting away. Some would say living to tell the tale, but in this business that wasn't true. It would never be talked about. During the Second World War the saying was loose lips sink ships but, in this case, loose lips just got you a severe case of dead. The people they assassinated were powerful and they could reach across the globe with unimaginable resources, so you took the stories to your grave. It was not just about the members of the team, it was also about family and friends.

Louise took the lead. "We will leave here at 15-minute intervals and head to the vicinity of the Bolshoi Theatre by different routes, Op sec rules are in play, extra vigilance from everyone. I will be the only member of the team operating inside the target location, I will arrive at 17:30 in time to get everything ready inside the theatre. I have the Novichok nerve agent in my bag and I will engineer an opportunity once there. I have a number of options but will flex as needed. Outside we have Hairy Dave on overwatch, making sure we do not get ambushed and there is an escape route free. No shots to be fired unless lives are in danger and it is a last resort. Storm will patrol the theatre square just outside the theatre with Mac further out. If we see more than the expected amount of FSB or Police, we abort and look for an alternative. Once the nerve agent has been deployed, I will leave the Bolshoi as quickly as I can. Mac will boost a getaway vehicle and we get the hell out of Dodge. Any questions?"

On this job Louise was calling the shots, but she was only as good as every other member of the team. Everyone else's role was equally as important, they made sure the routes in and out were free. They also made sure that if something kicked off that they had her back. It was vital that the team talk through the plan for the final time, challenging each point as if it was the first time they had been through it. There were no egos at this point, each challenge was accepted, explained and then you moved on. New knowledge could have come about that would change it. The worst thing you could do was assume last week's plan still stayed solid today. The plan was signed off by all and the team went into their own routines of checking weapons, checking go bags and making sure their own individual tasks went to time and were successful.

Over the space of the next hour each member of the team left the safe house and made their way to where they were meant to be. Operational Security measures were first on the agenda. Check you are not being followed or compromised, check again and then check some more.

Louise could feel her anticipation level rising – people that say they don't feel nerves are lying, some people say that nerves are a bad thing and something to be avoided; however, they have never been on the front line. It doesn't matter if you are in school sitting exams or doing a presentation in front of 200 people, the nerves are the same. You just face into them, accept them for what they are and use them to spur you on. Nerves are what give you the edge, they bring your senses to the fore and as an Assassin they made Louise comfortable, kind of like a warm blanket. She was expecting them and welcomed them like welcoming a lover.

TWO

Louise was five foot eleven inches tall and a UK size 10. She was naturally a brunette but as with all assassins at the top of their game she would change her appearance at a moment's notice. She had large blue eyes and lashes that most women would die for. Her mother used to joke that she had two looks: a model and homeless. She had strong cheekbones and large full lips. Her nose annoyed her, a nose she must have inherited from her dad, whoever he was; it certainly wasn't from her mum who had a button nose like Jaimie, her younger brother. It was bigger than she would have liked but as an overall package it fitted in with her other features. Her skin was typical of the Celts that dominate the population of the west coast of Scotland. She would tend to freckle in the sun rather than tan and like most Celts her base colour was a whiter shade of blue through to white and then freckles.

Through sheer hard gym work her shoulders were well muscled and, in some ways, took away from the classical model look, but on the right occasion when she wore make up, a long black dress and wore her hair other than in a functional ponytail, she drew appraising looks from every eye in the room. Tonight, she was dressed for work wearing a functional white blouse, a black skirt just above the knee, black stockings, and flat black comfortable shoes. The shoes that waitresses the world over craved when you were on your feet all day.

Louise left her flat at the allotted time and set a sensible pace in making her way to the Bolshoi Theatre at the heart of Moscow. It was about a mile from the Kremlin to Theatre Square and the place was buzzing with tourists and Muscovites alike. Tourists were great cover, but they provided the same opportunity to anyone wanting to carry out counter surveillance on her. She therefore took the usual Op Sec precautions.

From the flat she got a bus part way, sitting at the back of the bus where she could watch the other passengers get on and off. She paid close attention to anyone getting on and off at the same stop as her. What were they wearing, how did they walk and were they only interested in themselves or were they taking a more detailed than expected interest in fellow passengers? She walked to a different bus route and on the way went into and out of three different shops. In one she spent time browsing and even tried on a nice red dress, in a second it was just a quick in and out as if the shop held nothing of interest and the third, she queued for some artisan bread just to check if anyone waited about for her to exit.

Of course, surveillance was not about spotting one person as very often they would use a team of four where they would rotate in and out to make it more difficult to spot. Some things were more difficult to change so she looked out for the way someone walked, the shoes they were wearing and the shape of an ear. Such a strange thing but ears were very distinctive.

She planned to arrive at 17:30. This gave her time to set everything up but not too much time that being early would attract unwanted attention and make her stand out. Tonight, more than ever, she needed to blend in, just another waitress earning minimum wage to help feed a family. Five minutes early at 17.25, she stood outside the Bolshoi Theatre, taking it all in – it is one of the most incredible buildings in the world. From the outside it was almost Romanesque with eight mighty columns reaching up to a roof with a charioteer and four magnificent horses. The building itself had been built, burnt down and rebuilt a number of times. The outside can only be described as magnificent but inside it was breathtakingly opulent and so it should be after its $850m refit. It had multiple tiers of balconies rising up into the Gods. Individual columns supporting each tier and filled with Imperial red and gold. In the centre of the ceiling was the most amazing chandelier that brought all of the other artwork together. The building was the pride of the people of Russia and, like the Sydney Opera House, St Paul's Cathedral, and the White House, it was one of the standout buildings around the world.

After pausing outside to take in the architecture for the last time, Louise entered the theatre and headed downstairs to the female staff changing room. Once there she unlocked the padlock on her allotted locker and placed her jacket inside. She had been using the same locker since starting work there a few weeks earlier. It was a basic metal locker, the type that are seen in changing rooms everywhere. She quickly checked all parts of the changing room to ensure she was alone and taking a deep breath opened her rucksack and put on a pair of clear latex gloves, the kind worn by health professionals and lab workers all over the globe. She then took out a small glass bottle that looked like a miniature perfume bottle. She left it inside the clear sealed plastic bag as she had been instructed by the chemists, placed it in her apron pocket and donned white cotton gloves over the top of the latex ones. With the preparation work complete, she placed her rucksack in the locker and closed it over. Not to be too dramatic but the additional precautions she was taking were kind of essential if she was not going to die tonight. Edward had sourced a Russian strain of the nerve agent Novichok which could not be traced back to the UK. Each strain had a signature that could be tied back to place of manufacture and the last thing they needed was this to be traced back to the UK Defence laboratory at Porton Down in the Southwest of England. I am not sure sourced was the right wording. In essence they had retained a sample from the Salisbury poisoning carried out in the UK in March 2018. The Salisbury hit had been orchestrated by General Andropov, the same General who was the assassination target tonight. That kind of deed could not go unpunished, even if it did take months or years to complete. The British Government could not accept Russian assassins operating with impunity on British soil.

Louise had been told that there were two reasons for using a perfume atomiser bottle – it could pass inspection should Louise be stopped for any reason (keeping it under 25ml meant it would not raise suspicion going through airport or building security scanners) and you could apply it to a surface you wanted the target to touch without actually touching it yourself.

Louise, confident she had everything in place, walked up the stairs to the bar area and went about her normal waitress duties. In the lead up to the performance, she would be serving patrons of the arts champagne, snacks, cocktails, and vodka.

She just needed to blend in. In the same way as she wore the grey jogging gear in the park, tonight she was wearing a standard white blouse and black skirt to allow her to blend in with the other employees. People rarely noticed the waiters and waitresses, or if they did it was only to order drinks. The trick was to avoid eye contact, stare at the notepad to take the drinks order and simply slip away. Eye contact made you memorable.

The ballet was normally a sell out and tonight was no different, a large crowd was gathered in the Foyer, looking blankly at their tickets and up to the various doors in front of them before being directed to their seats by one of the four ushers employed for that very job.

Louise kept herself busy and focussed on providing a great service to the customers already at the theatre. There was nothing else she could do before she got word that the General was arriving. Keeping busy also distracted the brain and that was a good thing. She was very practised at knife skills and various other means of assassination; however, this was the first time she had used a nerve agent and that in itself was disconcerting.

Hairy Dave left the flat second at 15:00 and headed for the bus stop nearest the flat. He was built like a brick shit house, one of those guys that just looked like they worked out for four hours before breakfast. He was wearing a hat pulled down low over his ears and keeping his face low, not quite peering at the ground but making sure he was not looking directly at any cameras or passengers. Today he was wearing baggy clothing and trying to not look like a security guard. He preferred tight white or black t-shirts that showed off his muscles. He had put a lot of work into his physique and was rightly proud of it. It was a fine balance though between carrying all that body builder weight and ensuring he had the level of fitness required with this team. Not only did he need to be able to carry a full Bergen which weighs 25Kg, he also had to be able to carry it over the distance of a full marathon. The fine line of strength and stamina was important, and Dave knew he fell just on the right side of the line.

He hated the nickname Hairy Dave, but like most things when you have come from the Army it stuck and there was not a damned thing you could do about it. Once it landed you just had to accept it with as much grace as you could muster. He gave an involuntary shrug of the shoulders and focussed on the job at hand, several changes of buses and a change of appearance later, Dave walked into the reception of the Art Hyatt hotel dressed as a maintenance worker from a local air conditioning company. It would give him unrestricted access to the roof area.

The hotel was in the ideal location to be able to look out over Theatre Square with an unobstructed view of the front of the Bolshoi. It was also far enough away not to draw unwanted attention. Dave walked up to the concierge desk and smiled at the concierge on duty.

"Good morning, I am here from Tito Smart Air Conditioning to service your system."

"Let me just get the Duty Manager for you. Do you have any identification?"

"Oh, yes, certainly, I have my company ID badge and an appointment letter that was sent out to you two weeks ago. Is that sufficient?"

"I will just pass this along to the Duty Manager who will be with you shortly."

Dave was tempted to say 'Thank you but don't call me shortly', but sometimes his sense of humour missed the mark, and he did not want to be remembered as the creepy guy.

The Duty Manager arrived and stated, "I don't seem to have an appointment in the diary for today, are you sure it is the right hotel?"

"Yes, sir, it is definitely this hotel, the name is just there." Dave pointed to a line on the letter.

"Perhaps one of the other managers forgot to put it into your appointment book?" stated Dave, trying to be reasonable when all he wanted to do was tell the guy to stop being a dick.

"Yes, perhaps that is it. What exactly will you be doing as I don't want any unnecessary noise that may affect our guests, this is a very prestigious hotel?" asked the Manager.

"Just some routine checks, air flow, inlet and outlet temperatures and replacing some filters. Nothing that will concern your guests, you have my personal guarantee on that. It is important work, though, as air temperatures will start to rise significantly as we head into summer and we at Tito Mart Air Conditioning want to ensure the system works perfectly during your peak season. We would not want an outage when you need it most."

The Duty Manager thought for a couple of seconds. "That is fine but please stay out of the public areas, we don't want worker types in view of the customers."

Dave went to reply, but the manager had already turned on his heel and was stomping back to his office obviously displeased he had had to deal with an unexpected interruption.

Dave made his way down to the cellar area and opened his tool bag to show that he was indeed working and after 20 minutes of inspecting the air conditioning pumps, he made his way up to the roof area, settled in, set up his Lobaev SVLK-14 S sniper rifle and started to scan the crowd. The Lobaev had cost a little over £30,000 from an arms dealer in the UAE. It was the pride of the Russian army and claimed to be the deadliest sniper rifle in the world. If you were good enough you could hit targets a little over two miles away. Of course, only a handful of snipers could kill at that range and that in itself made you memorable. The target on this occasion was a little over 300 yards. Far enough to be away from the crowds but close enough that it would not narrow down the list of suspects beyond a few thousand. Using the local brand of rifle used by the Russian military would also deflect suspicion.

Dave spent some time ensuring his sights were set up properly, and took out a wind meter. Dave had to calculate the set-up of his telescopic sight. The rule of thumb for the level of inaccuracy was 2.5cm for every 100m, so at 300m Dave had a potential inaccuracy of 7.5cm. It was Dave's job now to minimise that inaccuracy. There were four main variables: wind, gravity, distance and air humidity. Dave did not have charts of calculations. The hours and hours spent in the shooting range gave Dave the edge he needed to improve the accuracy of any potential shot. Ideally you would shoot from 600m out and the boom of the shot would not be heard by the target as the bullet slows down as it travels and is sub sonic by the time it hits the target. In a city environment, though, it just wasn't possible with all the buildings.

Dave looked through his sight to a flag he had tied to a post in Theatre Square so that he could estimate wind speed and make the relevant final adjustment. He was confident now he was set up for success if he was required to take out a target.

Dave's job was overwatch, keeping the team informed of what was happening from a bird's eye view and to take out anyone that would stop a clean getaway. Dave needed to be in position early, adrenalin was a sniper's curse as it made you jittery and he needed to let any adrenalin from the op sec routine of getting to the hotel drain from his system. He lay in place and focussed on the task at hand. Using the telescopic sight, he worked his way through the crowd at the front of the theatre in the square. He was looking for people out of place, anyone loitering too long or who looked like they were FSB, the Russian Intelligence service. He was looking for people in the square displaying op sec behaviours, trying too hard not to be noticed or anything out of place that might suggest the team were walking into a trap. Everything was clear as far as he could see, and he forced himself to relax.

Storm was in Theatre Square, doing a similar job to Hairy Dave but from the ground – sometimes seeing things from a different perspective made all the difference. She had long brown hair that was plaited down her back. Her big brown eyes were enough to lure you into a false sense of security. People constantly underestimated her as she had a real innocent look that she used to her advantage when she needed to. It was her job to approach anyone who looked suspicious from the bird's eye view and see if they were anything to worry about. With a nod and a disarming smile, she was confident she could charm her way out of most situations.

She smiled inwardly at being called Storm – it came from the X-Men. When required she was like a force of nature, harnessing an inner aggression and frightening speed to front up to whatever was in their way. Hand to hand combat, a knife fight or close quarter gun fight and she was someone you definitely wanted on your side. It takes real courage to take the fight to the enemy, it went against all instincts and most times it caught the enemy cold and they backed away. She had supreme confidence in her abilities and that in itself put people on edge.

Storm was five foot seven, with broad shoulders, and had that stamina you need to make it in this profession. If she had to, she could carry an injured teammate for miles. It was a strange thing to say, but to be successful in this game you had to accept the pain, own it and push through it. Nothing fazed Storm; like all the team she had some troubles in her past. The troubles made you stronger, if you could harness them. These things could be a chain to the past or a springboard to the future and she chose the latter.

Today she was dressed as a theatregoer. No point in being a down and out in this environment, nothing was more likely to bring unwanted attention in this district, so tonight she was a middle-class theatregoer. Moscow was warm during the day but cold in the evenings at this time of year, so she was well wrapped up in a light woollen coat, a smart dress underneath, but flat fashionable shoes in case she had to run. She did like a nice pair of heels, but on a job like this they were useless.

She worked the square methodically using her own experience to look for potential trouble. She could see nothing out of place so started winding up Dave to relieve the boredom.

"Hey Dave, we should set up a spa day when this is all over, maybe a back wax or something."

"Hahaha you're such a comedian, Storm, I am up for it as long as they can do you a moustache wax, you better make sure that they have extra wax ordered in for that."

"Leave my moustache alone, Dave, it has taken me 25 years to grow that."

Despite her best efforts she subconsciously raised a hand to her top lip, and she heard Dave chuckle in her ear. She knew then Dave had been watching her – the fucker felt he was one up. She put her hand behind her back with the middle finger extended and she heard another chuckle from Dave.

Just then an official-looking black SUV arrived and they all heard Dave whisper in their ear.

"Standby, standby" followed 30 seconds later by "Principal arrived, four CPO in standard formation."

A CPO was a close protection officer, the type that would make up the Secret Service or accompanied state officials all over the world.

The Principal in question was General Andropov. There was no fuss as the lead CPO got out of the SUV, took 10 seconds to look around and assess any potential threat before opening the rear door for the General to exit the vehicle. The four accompanying guards fell into formation and he swept into the front door of the Bolshoi Theatre.

"Principal entered the premises. Zulu one, the ball is in your court."

There was no message of good luck, it was taken as a given, if they had done their planning properly, they hoped luck would not come into it. They all had call signs, Zulu one to four. It was unlikely their radio transmissions would be overheard, but just in case it paid to be extra cautious. No point in using real names, especially on a job like this. Louise's body was alive with adrenalin, the naturally occurring fight or flight drug was coursing through her veins. Despite all the planning and operational walkthroughs this was the sharp end, unexpected things could happen. She was now in her element and she loved it, thrived on it. The past few months of being a waitress was torture for someone like Louise. If you embraced adrenalin often enough, you got that you craved it like a narcotic, you became an adrenalin junky. This was a high unlike anything you could get in civvy street. Life or death, it genuinely was that binary.

Louise spotted the General as he breezed in through the front door of the theatre. She was a bit disappointed if she was honest – he was distinctly ordinary looking, dressed in a navy-blue suit, white shirt and red tie. He was about mid-forties in age, greying hair although relatively young for a General. He had been a rising star in the FSB and he walked with a confidence, one could almost say arrogance, of someone who knew every eye in the room was on him. As he entered through the front door it seemed like there was magic in the air as a circle of space automatically appeared around him. The FSB still had an aura of fear around them and here right in front of them was the head of the FSB. They could rename the organisation; however, the old stigma of the KGB just followed.

He took a minute or so to look upwards and take in the majesty of the Bolshoi, the opulence and grandeur of what is arguably the home of ballet. If you took the time and looked closely at him, you would see the glassy eyed look of someone who felt like they had come home from a long trip and they had forgotten just how important home was to them. When you loved the ballet and the Bolshoi, even the good and great never tired of drinking in the breath-taking views and the excited, expectant atmosphere.

The General looked round the room and spotted a pretty waitress called Natasha and from the briefing file she looked exactly the General's type. She was a six-foot blonde with shapely legs that went on forever. The type the ladies wanted to be and the guys wanted to be inside. She knew she was the General's type; you could see it in the way she flicked her hair and giggled at his jokes. The General leaned in close to Natasha and whispered something to her. All the time his eyes were taking in the room, who were the people that were close to him, who was hanging back, and even who was in his path towards the door he would use to climb to his box.

Louise took it all in and took an instant dislike to this man. He screamed misogynist and narcissist, only interested in himself. He was shallow and had those dead eyes of someone who had inflicted intolerable pain on another human being and enjoyed it. If there was a definition of evil, this man had to be close to it. His file outlined his predilections for inflicting pain and narcissism. It is hard to understand sometimes what you read on paper and translate it into a person, but this man was Mr Creep of Creepsville in Creep County.

As the General moved though the foyer, nodding and smiling at people and occasionally stopping to talk to various members of the Moscow hoi polloi, Natasha headed to the bar to fulfil the drinks order of one of Moscow's most infamous men.

Louise watched Natasha move behind the bar and saw a gilt-edged opportunity to progress her mission. Natasha was making up some drinks, namely a Moscow mule in a copper goblet and four bottles of water.

"For someone special, Natasha?"

"That General that just came in, Andropov, he is very powerful; I need to make this just as he likes it. He is dreamy, don't you think? I do get turned on by men with power."

"Anything I can do to help?" asked Louise.

"Can you get me some ice for the Mule, Irina?" Irina was how Louise was known at the Bolshoi.

"Of course, Natasha, he will love you, you look hot tonight."

Natasha smiled in that arrogant way that barbie dolls do. A smile that said of course he will, they all do.

Louise took the copper goblet over to the ice bin, picked up a few cubes of ice and placed them inside the goblet. With her back to the customers, she then carefully got the atomiser out of the sealed plastic bag in her pocket. There were two ways she could do this.

Spray the ice and then put it into the drink; however, she was worried this would dilute it as the ice melted and there was no way to determine how much of it the General would drink. It was also possible he would taste it as it was slightly oily and if it floated to the top, he would surely see it. Too little and he would be at death's door, but they could bring him back.

The second option was to spray the copper goblet. All it needed was a few seconds' contact time through the skin and he would not make it back even if they did get him to a hospital. Louise sprayed all around the goblet with as much of it as she sensibly could without it dripping down the side and being obvious.

The best way to apply it was not something she could achieve tonight, which was to spray his underwear with it. It would have meant only he would touch it and would create prolonged exposure, but that would have meant gaining access to his residence in Moscow.

"That's the ice in the drink, Natasha, good luck with the General, maybe he is a keeper." Louise gave Natasha a thumbs up and a beaming smile.

Louise would just have preferred to let Dave take the shot as the General walked up the steps to the Bolshoi, but Edward insisted the assassination should be by Novichok. Death was not instantaneous; it would come on over a couple of hours and that meant that in theory it would give the team time to get the escape plan into action before the FSB (Russian Secret Police) took control and the inevitable interrogations started. There were rumoured to be 50,000 FSB throughout Russia, which is more than some countries' armies.

Louise watched Natasha put the final touches to the Moscow mule and leave with the goblet and four bottles of water on the tray. Every part of Louise's mind was screaming to get out of there right now, but she had to be sure he got it and he lifted the goblet. Louise picked up a tray and some drinks and headed up the stairs on the opposite side of the theatre. She wanted a vantage point where she could see the box of the General.

She entered the amphitheatre and took a few seconds to work out where the General's box was located. Initially she struggled to see which one it was when suddenly, she could see Natasha's blonde head nodding as she served the General. She could see him with the copper goblet in his hand. Satisfied she had completed her task, Louise headed back down to the bar area.

Natasha seemed to take an eternity to return, and Louise was thinking about her exit strategy as Natasha walked into the bar area with a huge self-satisfied, superior grin.

"I told you he would want me," she said as she licked her lips. "I could take him all in," she said with a wink. "He had to hold onto the drink with both hands as I pleasured him. He asked me back to his flat after the performance. This could be my day."

Ten minutes later, Louise went to her locker, and using a spare clear latex glove she removed both the outer and inner gloves, placed them in the sealable plastic bag beside the atomiser, sealed the bag, picked up her stuff and simply walked out the door.

"Elvis has left the building."

This was the code to the rest of the team that Louise was on the move, and they had to invoke the escape and evasion phase and disappear.

THREE

T he obvious escape and evasion tactic for most people would mean heading back to the flat, gather their belongings and head to the airport as fast as they could. That, however, was what the Russians would be expecting and was therefore not only the fastest way to get caught but was also the fastest way for this to be traced back to London. With 50,000 FSB resources available, they had to assume that a significant portion of them would be put to investigating the assassination and the team had to expect that they had someone tailing them at all times.

Louise turned left as she exited the building, with Hairy Dave continuing to provide overwatch.

"Clear so far," stated Dave.

"Roger that," Louise replied.

She kept walking for two blocks, walking past Storm without any acknowledgement. Storm took a final look around the square to make sure they did not have a tail, crossed the street and walked diagonally behind Louise to ensure there was not a team in place following them that she had missed in the square.

"Get you at the rendezvous," declared Hairy Dave as he packed up his rifle and headed out of the fire escape from the Art Hyatt hotel.

Louise turned a corner and Mac pulled up beside her in a black SUV. She got into the back seat as Storm went to the passenger side front seat, with her Glock pistol sitting on her knee in case of emergency. Mac signalled, and spotting a gap in the traffic pulled out into the steady stream of cars. He drove another block to where Hairy Dave was waiting and jumped into the passenger side back seat after stowing his rifle in the trunk.

"Let's get a fucking move on, Mac," said Dave.

Mac knew where he was going, he had practised it at this time of the evening on a number of occasions. He took a few additional turns to make sure there was no tail. Some left turns and some right, making sure he had to stop before crossing oncoming traffic. Any tail would have to do the same and very often it would flush out anyone following.

"Everything go to plan, Louise?" asked Dave as he looked across at Louise in the back seat.

"No dramas, he was drinking Moscow Mules as the file said he would, and I sprayed the copper goblet. I think one of the waitresses will have touched it as well, which is unfortunate."

Mac entered an underground carpark at the North end of the city, parked up and the team took out some bleach wipes and wiped it down – steering wheel, handles and seats. They wanted to remove all trace of being there. They had to assume the FSB would be red hot on their tails and if they could not tie them to the area, they had plausible deniability on their side. Mac led the way out the side entrance and crossed the road to an adjacent car park, avoiding CCTV surveillance capture. Once there, Mac boosted a white sedan before paying for parking and heading out into the busy traffic. Once out of the city he pulled off the main drag and swapped number plates, the team changed clothes and dumped anything that could be traced back to the Bolshoi. Louise took out some lighter fluid, soaked the backpack in the field adjacent to the layby and set it on fire. They did not want someone accidentally picking it up and touching the atomiser. It was one of the basic errors the FSB assassins made in Salisbur,y resulting in multiple innocent deaths. Simple things can make a difference in escaping or getting caught and the details mattered. In Moscow if you were discovered and not out of the city within 30 minutes you were probably going to get caught. This is Russia, they can shut the city down. Although you might get more complaints now than they would have during the Cold War, the regime did not particularly care. An overt attack on the state meant a fast and harsh response. The team binned all technology, smart phones had SIM cards removed, the cards cut into pieces and disposed of separately, hard drives removed from laptops and smashed, again disposed of separately. It seems pedantic to do all of that but since 2013 the Russian cyber units had massively improved their technology and their ability to track a digital footprint across the globe was as good as anything in the Western Hemisphere. It seemed the sensible thing to do. It might be a coincidence that a well-known American whistle blower took refuge in 2013 in Russia and since that date their abilities have significantly improved, but experience has taught the intelligence agencies never to believe in coincidences. No such thing as a free meal as they say.

To slow down the inevitable digital search, they had purchased air tickets to Amsterdam with KLM and also train tickets to Berlin. All they were trying to do was divide the enemy into different searches and dilute their resources. It wouldn't hold them up for long, but you need a lead in a chase, and this might just tip it in the team's favour.

FOUR

General Andropov left the Bolshoi having enjoyed the Nutcracker, he had drunk a few cocktails and was in a buoyant mood. It was a Ballet he had seen many times before, but it never failed to delight. His security team held him in his box until the official car was at the front door. He stepped into the foyer and headed toward Natasha and asked her to join him for a night cap. The lead CPO frowned in consternation as it was not on the plan; however, he had learned not to voice his concerns and just accept the change. He stood outside the theatre for that vital few seconds to survey the crowds exiting the theatre and gathered in the square, and seeing nothing untoward allowed the General and his unexpected guest to exit the building with the other guards in formation. The General took his seat alongside Natasha in the official car with two guards in the driver's and passenger seat, while another two guards took their positions in a following vehicle. The cars swept through the city, neither stopping at lights nor queuing traffic. It eventually stopped outside his official residence in one of the more salubrious suburbs. He walked up the stairs to his front door, put his key in the latch and waved Natasha inside before he dismissed his security detail. Unlike Louise's safe house, this official residence was anything but a dump. Beautiful high ceilings, ornate plasterwork on the ceilings, polished wooden floors and Persian rugs. Beautiful pieces of art by Viktor Vasnetsov hung in the hallway, Ivan Tsarevich riding the Grey Wolf. Natasha was mesmerised by the opulence of it. She was just a working-class girl with high hopes of landing a rich husband, which was why she accepted the poor wages in the theatre – it allowed her to meet the good and the rich. In Russia the haves tend to have everything and the have nots have nothing.

Andropov noticed Natasha looking at the painting and moved to stand beside her and told her the story of the brave Prince and the tired frightened princess riding the grey wolf through some dark and mysterious Slavic woods. That it was at this moment the pair fell madly in love and he talked Natasha through the story of the Prince's arms holding the princess protectively on the wolf and how close together they were.

Natasha was fascinated and watched the General as he went to the drinks cabinet and poured two large vodkas, one for Natasha and one for himself. He invited Natasha to sit beside him on a superking-sized four poster bed.

"How long have you worked at the theatre for, sorry what was your name?" asked the General.

"I am Natasha, I have been at the Bolshoi for just over two years now, I enjoy the arts and I get to meet some really interesting people. I wanted to be a model, but work is scarce, and I need to pay the bills."

Andropov reached out a hand and gently stroked Natasha's face, his thumb caressing her cheekbone as he smiled at her.

"I struggle to believe you don't find good modelling work, you have such delicate, beautiful features. Maybe I can help with that. One phone call and I can give you everything you dream of."

Natasha smiled a winning smile. This was what she had worked at the Bolshoi for. A patron to help her ambition.

"Oh, that would be amazing, General, I would be ever so grateful."

"I am a very busy man, Natasha so I would only make the calls to the right people for someone that does things for me. You scratch my back and I scratch yours. What would you be willing to do for me?"

Natasha unzipped her dress so that she was standing in front of the general in matching black lacy underwear. She removed her hair tie and allowed her blonde hair to cascade down across her shoulders, her black underwear accentuating her curves. She tentatively approached him and felt triumph as she saw the greedy look in his eyes. This could be the one night that would change her life forever. Natasha put on her most seductive pose and looked forward to a night of passion and intimacy. She twirled before him before bowing as though she was in front of a Prince.

"I can see that you like what you see, General. Let me help you make this a night we will both remember."

The General lifted his hand to the side of Natasha's face once more, but this time he had a cruel smile on his face and instead of stroking her he grabbed a fistful of her hair and twisted it painfully. He pulled Natasha close to him and drank in the scent of her hair and whispered in her ear.

"Oh, you won't forget this night, Natasha, I can assure you of that."

With his free hand he grabbed Natasha's throat and squeezed until she struggled to breathe. The look of fear on her beautiful face urged him onwards and made him want her even more. He threw her onto the bed and ripped her underwear from her body as she cried out in terror. He forced himself on her and dominated her for what seemed like hours. When Natasha felt it was finished, he came back and went again. Each time more painful and horrendous than the one before. The more she cried and called out, the more awful it became. It seemed to motivate him to find even more creative ways to inflict pain. When at last he was finished, Natasha rolled off the bed and grabbed the dress she had casually thrown off hours before, threw it over her beaten and bleeding body and fled from the flat. Her makeup smeared down her face and blood flowing freely from her lip, she sobbed uncontrollably as she hailed a taxi and fled to the sanctuary of her home. She stepped inside and immediately went for a shower. She wanted to scrub herself clean. As she approached the shower she collapsed, convulsing, until she lay dead on her bathroom floor.

As Natasha left the flat in tears, the General poured himself another vodka. He had enjoyed the waitress running crying from the apartment, she had learnt what it meant to owe him a favour and he would call on her again in a few days' time. He would make good on his promise to help her modelling career and had a dossier on a high-profile modelling agency he could use for leverage. After all, he was not a total monster; it was the waitress's fault for waking the beast within him. It certainly wasn't his fault.

He took a seat on the chaise longue, and was enjoying a Cuban cigar and the afterglow of the evening when he started to feel unwell, his chest felt tight, and he was struggling to breathe. His heart started racing and his temperature must have been up as he was sweating profusely. He stood up and staggered to the bathroom and only just made it as he started to vomit. Surely this could not be the alcohol – he had drunk a lot more on previous occasions and not felt this bad. He started to shake all over as his body convulsed. He knew then something was badly wrong, and it was possible he had been poisoned. He crawled back down the hall to his bedroom to get to his mobile phone and picked it up, but he was now shaking so badly, and his vision had blurred that much that he could not use the fingerprint scanner to unlock it. He quickly fell into a coma from which he never woke up.

The Novichok had done its job. It is a nerve agent that attacks the heart and unless you are doing a robust toxicology test as part of a post-mortem it could easily be put down as a heart attack – which was what Louise and the team were hoping for. Unfortunately, in Russia, every senior official that dies unexpectedly undergoes a full autopsy with a detailed toxicology screen and within 18 hours the FSB knew one of their own had been targeted by an assassin and that made it personal.

FIVE

Mac, as well as being an integral part of the assassination team, tended to take on the role of the driver; he was ex-military intelligence from his days in Northern Ireland. He was the oldest by some distance in the group, five foot eight, thin and came from the Leith area of Edinburgh. He had what can only be described as a 1960s' porn star moustache. During the "Troubles" he had carried out multiple undercover operations and being of Catholic mother and Protestant father he could play both sides. To be honest, he could be a bit of a bastard and if something got in the way of the job he just dug in and took it out. He fitted right in, in Northern Ireland. He was also mentally as tough as they come. You lived on the edge in that job. One slip up, one wrong word and you would quite simply become one of the disappeared. The Provisional IRA had no conscience and were well known for just making people who were a threat simply disappear, never to be found again. There were never any witnesses, no one saw anything, ever. Part of it was support for the cause and part of it was simple fear. People did not want to become part of the disappeared. It was a difficult time in British history – the British Army hated the Catholics (or Fenians), the Catholics hated the Brits and the Protestants just hated everyone.

The Brits had to be seen as a stand-up Government with significant world standing and could not be seen to murder civilians. They therefore used the Protestants to carry out the hits that they could not be seen to have a hand in. It was all very complicated and very messy. Mac remained tight lipped about the whole thing, some of it from that professionalism where you just kept your mouth shut, and part of it from self-preservation as the Tory Government were giving in to pressure to conduct witch hunts on what were government sanctioned hits, although with no paper trail the only people being prosecuted were the squaddies that set up the work. Mac was the quiet introspective type; you could rely on him to give 100% every time. Nothing fazed him, whether you were in a fire fight or hand to hand combat, I have never seen him give an inch. He was one of those guys that, looking at him, you would underestimate; however, he was genuinely hard as nails. He also appeared to have no conscience. It was simple in his mind: the job was the job and if you got in the way then you deserved what was coming. Mac was a guy you wanted in your corner. He did have one annoying trait, however: he was a cheeky motherfucker and constantly out to take the piss out of anyone.

"Hey Mac, how long till we get out of this shit hole?"

"You were at the same briefings as me, dipshit, you should have paid attention."

It took 30 minutes to reach the edge of the city, and the first target was always to get beyond the city limits within those 30 minutes. It was a tense time for everyone other than Mac, who just seemed to have ice in his veins. The challenge was not knowing how long the nerve agent would take to act – it all depended on exposure time and that was outwith the team's control. Control the controllable items and mitigate the risks was the normal mantra. Louise took some time to enjoy looking at the architecture of Moscow. Such an amazing city, at least in the centre, the outskirts not so much as you saw the concrete monstrosities of the social housing projects. It was no different to most capital cities really. People migrated there from the countryside with no real money and needed housing. If the state did not provide it, you ended up with the shanty towns like South Africa or India. To Louise it was no different to Easterhouse or Nitshill in Glasgow.

Hairy Dave commented: "This is fucking depressing around here, what a shit hole."

To his surprise it was Mac that went into a rant and stood up for the Soviets. "It is no different to where I grew up in Muirhouse in the North of Edinburgh. In the 1980s it had the worst heroin problem in Northern Europe. This was Thatcher's Britain and Scotland got the worst of it. Unemployment was in excess of 10% and in the under 25s it was 70%. People like me joined the army as there was nothing else. The only choice was between taking the Queen's shilling or join the dole queue. I have friends and family that ended up addicted to heroin and it completely ruined them. Some died of blood poisoning from dirty needles and some from overdoses; the ones that got clean were never the same and even now have that haunted look in their eyes and are either fitness addicts or turned to religion – in essence they have swapped one addiction for another. The car manufacturers shut down which cascaded in through the shipyards, the steel industry and finally the coal mines. The sons of Thatcher in the investment banks might slag off Russia for being poor, but at least the state looks after its own. Communism might not have worked the way they wanted but at least everyone gets an education, food on the table and accommodation. When you look at the streets of Edinburgh and the volume of homeless people sleeping rough, can we really say the same?"

"Jeez, Mac, when did you become such an old man? Oh, wait, you are old, in fact were you not in school with Mary Queen of Scots?"

"Fuck off, Dave, you are only annoyed because Charles Darwin thought you were that Hairy you were the lost link between Apes and early man."

"Don't you think they sound like an old married couple, Louise?" commented Storm. "Are you sure you guys don't have something to tell us?"

"Well to be fair, Mac is more feminine than you, Storm, you make Atilla the Hun look positively cuddly?"

Just like that the tension was broken and the usual banter and bickering broke out.

At the city bypass they took the E105 to St Petersburg rather than the M11. It would take just under three hours longer but fewer traffic cameras and toll booths where your movements can easily be tracked. The journey would be 10 hours with staying under the speed limit and as they did not want to attract attention that is exactly what they would do – 706km of Russia back roads trying to become ghosts.

Hairy Dave was sat in the passenger seat and at six foot tall he had to move the seat slightly back to make room for his legs. He was one of those guys that the ladies would call handsome, and the guys looked at with jealousy. He was well muscled and barrel chested; he did not think of himself as a body builder, more like a gymnast. It was typical of the armed forces that he could have been nicknamed the Bull or Pretty boy but no, he was the hairiest guy the team had ever seen. When he stripped off it was like a wolf pelt so, naturally, he got called Hairy Dave. He hated it and of course that meant the name stuck. Hairy Dave's premier skill and that one that made him stand out was being a top sniper, which was why he provided overwatch during the operation. Keeping the team safe and making sure they did not get in too deep. Dave was a *"geezer"* from the East end of London, with that real Cockney accent. He had had a troubled youth with a father that beat him and his mother – his father was fine sober but when he got drunk, he was a real piece of work. Dave joined the army just to get away from it all and keep out of the gangs. His family had history with the local gangs, and his grandfather told lots of stories of knowing and working for the Krays. No one knew if it was true or not, but to the team it did not really matter. A troubled background was not uncommon when it came to agents in the special forces / Black Ops – most have a history of some sort. There were a lot of Jocks (Scottish) in the UK Special Forces, not a surprise really as they can be a belligerent lot with a Socialist background and an us-against-the-world mentality. Dave loved to play on the English v Jock rivalry that had lasted hundreds of years. Dave served Queen and country, a proud Englishman, but the Jocks, well they were in it for each other, that clan mentality never left them. The good thing was when you were adopted into their clan there was no stronger bond, and they would walk over hot coals to get you out of trouble. Hairy Dave was a quiet lad, tall for his age, which meant he was a target for older lads out to show just how tough they were, and he had a hard time when he went to the senior school. His grandfather took him to join a local boxing club when he was 12. It was always his grandfather that took an interest – his father was more likely to be in the pub spending what little money they had on beer and cigarettes. He went into puberty earlier than most and was hairy even in those days: he had a full moustache at 12 when most boys were still as smooth as a baby's bottom. He took to boxing like a duck to water, he loved the discipline and the 6am start to get some gym work in before starting school. The cardinal rule was never raising your hands out with the club. As he got stronger and fitter, he quickly rose up the amateur rankings, boxing for the local team and made it into junior English championships. Three rounds of three minutes each. It did not sound like much, but the training to get to that point and to be able to inflict pain on an opponent while defending yourself took an incredible amount of work. The problem was when the gangs saw how strong and powerful he was as he reached 18. They were starting to court him to get into the protection racket. They also had all the right connections, and they would make sure he got into professional boxing. He talked to his grandfather about it who told him to stay out of it – once you were in their pocket you would never get away and there were no such things as favours from those guys. One day Dave had some time to himself, which was unusual, when his dad came staggering in from the pub. Dave guessed from the look in his eye, he had spent all the money for the week on booze and was itching for a fight to ease his guilt. His dad starting ranting at him, telling him he was worthless and would end up in jail like his worthless friends. His dad just picked the wrong time on the wrong day as Dave had just split up with his girlfriend and was in no mood for the verbal abuse. Dave shook his head in disgust and went to walk past his dad to get out of the flat. Dave had that dead eye look of 'who are you calling worthless, you sad old drunk'. As he went to walk past, his father moved into his way with a lopsided grin on his face and that was when his father made his mistake – he went to slap Dave with the back of his hand, Dave ducked under the clumsy hit and as he rose back up all the energy from his hips and shoulders channelled through three inches of trained fist which landed on the side of his father's head. His father landed hard on the living room floor like a sack of potatoes. Hairy Dave just stood over him and without raising his voice, which made it even more chilling, said:

"Touch me again, you fat drunk cunt and it will be the last thing you ever do; and you ever lay a hand on my ma and I will hunt you down."

With that Dave went to his bedroom, packed a rucksack with the little belongings he had and marched out the door straight down to the army recruiting office. His mother crying at the door of the East End flat shouting for him not to go.

"I have to go, Ma; I will end up killing him if I stay here. Don't let him hit you, Ma, he is just a drunk and you are worth so much more than putting up with him."

His father staggered to the doorway and shouted:

"You will never make it in the Army, too fucking soft, we will see you back here within six months, just another fucking failure."

And that was that. Dave signed up to join the parachute regiment; he kind of fancied himself in the red beret. Dave took the train to ITC Catterick in the North of England, excited, nervous and determined to make it succeed: he would show his father who the failure was. Dave thrived, he loved the physicality of it and the RSM screaming at him just reminded him of his dad and it just washed over him. He was always at the top of his intake, but it was as a marksman he excelled. He could judge the wind, the elevation and make the necessary adjustments in his head. The numbers just made sense to him. It was as if the sniper rifle was just an extension of himself.

Louise brought him out of his thoughts. "Dave, stick some tunes on, babe, 10 hours of Mac whinging about roads isn't something I can do."

"How about some Biffy Clyro?"

"Perfect, babe."

It amused Dave that Louise called them all babe. There was no romance in it, just one of those little idiosyncrasies that she had.

Louise closed her eyes in the back seat, listening to Biffy Clyro's 'The Captain' and let her mind drift. One thing she had learnt over the years was take the rest when you can get it as you never know when you could be three days and nights on the move. Her thoughts turned back to her youth.

Mr MacPherson, it turned out, was the devil incarnate. He rented an old lock-up and started Louise's training. Her day started at 6am and she had two hours before school. She had to drag her sorry ass out of bed to make it down to the lock-up on time. If she was late, she had to do a forfeit. Her mum never really noticed anything as she was permanently high or out trying to get her next fix, but she hated lying to Jaimie and she didn't want anyone to know. It was perhaps a bit silly in retrospect, but she was young, and, in those days, she did not like to give anyone ammunition to give her more grief. She would run for miles with Mr MacPherson cycling behind her on an old pink girl's bike, whistling along to himself as Louise puffed and panted and spewed her guts up. There was never any sympathy.

There were constant phrases like "No, no, no, Louise, I want shorter faster strides, if you keep your stride that long you will end up with injuries like shin splints", or "no pain no gain, Louise, get up and get moving". Her least favourite was "Finish up being sick, Louise, we still have more to do."

When she got back from the running it was straight into stretching and toning exercises with weights. According to Mr MacPherson, athletes who only run are missing out on a potential 20% gain. Her shape was changing, she lost some curves but gained muscle. Her shoulders were becoming broader and her thighs and bum bigger but more toned. She now had muscle rather than fat. She even had a six pack. Mr MacPherson made sure she had a rest day every week – he said it was important to prevent gym burnout. There was a fancy Latin name for it, but gym burnout was the term she remembered. It took six months of physical training before he even started to talk about self-defence training. It started with Tai Chi, which was very graceful with nice long, open moves. Louise just didn't get it and after another two months was starting to get frustrated and decided to confront him.

"Mr MacPherson, when will I do real self-defence? All this Tai Chi stuff is very pretty but how is that supposed to help me in a fight?"

"Ah, Louise, I was wondering how long it would take you to reach that conclusion. I know this may seem innocuous but there are two reasons for it. The first one is about wiring the brain; you have never trained your brain for this kind of thing and Tai Chi is the best method of wiring the brain about the shapes and flows you will need, not only for defence but turning that defence into attack. You have to be able to react to what is in front of you without thinking about it. If you have to think about it, the winning opening is lost, or you have already been hurt. The second one is about seeing how much you want it. If you were happy with what we had been doing I would have left it at that. It is good to see you want more. On Saturday we will bring in some other things and you will see why Tai Chi was the best springboard."

And so, they embarked on what Louise classed as proper training, oh he still made her do all the physical stuff, she needed to be faster, stronger and with more stamina than potential competition, but he introduced loads of other fighting techniques. The running became running with a rucksack filled with sand, the fighting became knives instead of sticks, he taught her how to use what was available, pots, pans and even rolled up magazines. It was amazing how devastating a rolled-

up magazine was in the right hands and how easily it would break ribs or shatter a nose. Looking back, Louise never really understood what progress she was making; when you are doing it every day the gains are marginal, and it is difficult to understand the progress. The training was good, and she knew she was stronger than before, but unless you are competing you never really know. She was about 15 and had been training for 18 months when one evening she was coming back from training. She could not afford nice training stuff, just an old baggy sweatshirt and cheap Yoga pants. She was about a block from her flat when a group of three boys turned the corner in front of her. She sighed inwardly as she recognised them. They were trouble and thought they owned the neighbourhood. Louise just put her head down and went to walk past when the biggest one stood in front of her and was pushing her back.

"Hey Louise, what's the rush, why don't you come hang with us, I can sort you out." His two friends laughed as he grabbed his crotch.

"No thanks, I am just heading home for dinner."

"Your mom isn't in; she must be turning tricks in town."

With that his town friends burst out laughing again and started to push her about.

"Are you a whore like your mama, Louise? Can I get a freebie? ~I can teach you a lot with this?"

The leader stepped forward and tried to push Louise to the ground. As he leaned in to put weight behind it, Louise dropped her hip as she turned 180 degrees and brought him right over her shoulder to land hard on the ground flat on his back. The air left his lungs with an audible whoosh, and she stomped down hard with her right foot hitting him hard on the collar bone, breaking it. With him on the ground and out of the game for a couple of minutes, Louise turned to face his two pals with a dead pan look of confidence on her face. They split up, moving 5m apart and went to rush her at the same time. The one on the left was marginally ahead and made a grab for Louise first. She easily brought her arm round to block the lunge and followed through with a sharp punch to the solar plexus; as he doubled up, she brought her left leg through in a round house kick taking him across the side of the head. He fell to the ground on his hands and knees, dazed. The last one standing grabbed her from behind, his forearm across her neck in a chokehold.

"I got you now, bitch, now we are all going to get a piece of that tidy ass."

Louise surprised herself and did not panic, even though in a straight strength contest guys would win most times; she just shifted her weight sideways and using one arm to push the other back hit him three times in the stomach with her elbow. As his grip loosened around her neck, she brought her fist sharply backwards, her knuckles smashing hard into his nose. As the grip loosened further, she ducked and spun free. Before he could regain his balance and once again become a threat, she stepped in and struck two quick open-handed blows to his eye. His natural instinct was to rock backwards away from the threat to his eye. Louise waited until his weight was coming forward again and as it did, she turned sideways, dropped her shoulder and brought her foot up as quickly as she could and caught the side of his nose with a roundhouse kick. His nose exploded and blood rushed everywhere. He just dropped in a heap shouting "my nose, my nose".

With the three assailants on the ground, Louise disengaged and simply walked away. If she inflicted further damage, then it would move beyond that point of self-defence into assault and that was the last thing she wanted as she would lose her training with Mr MacPherson. She had dealt with three thugs with ease and as she walked back to her mum's flat, she felt that glow of knowing she could properly defend herself. She got a swagger in her step that she would never lose. She told Mr MacPherson of the fight and how she had dealt with it.

"So, let's analyse what you did and why you chose the moves you did, Louise."

"Why did you use a Judo throw on the Leader, followed by a kick to the collarbone?"

"I could see he was off balance and I had an opportunity to put him down. The kick to the collarbone was to keep him out of the fight."

"OK, so what were the potential risks in that approach?"

"Well, I suppose I had to turn my back on him to throw him and he could have resisted my throw and he would have held me from behind."

"Good, now thinking about it now was there a better way to deal with it?"

"I could have used a sweep to get him on the floor, targeting his load bearing leg and then followed up with the kick to the collarbone."

"Good, it is important to analyse wins as well as defeats. Don't assume that just because it worked it was the best move – against a stronger, more experienced opponent will it still work? I have to say I am really proud of you, lass; you have come on leaps and bounds."

SIX

General Andropov had a younger brother in the FSB, Colonel Josef Andropov. He was young, dynamic and a real stickler for detail. Nothing escaped him and he kept his team on their toes. Josef was a fiery redhead and kept a tidy goatee beard – behind his back he was called Lenin, who also sported red hair and a beard. Red hair was not unusual in Russia and in particular near Volgograd (formerly Stalingrad). Like Lenin he was only five foot five inches tall and thickset. He was not someone who ruled by stature but by intellect. When word came through that they had found his brother dead in his apartment and the waitress he had taken home later found dead in her own place, he swiftly took control of the situation and ordered an immediate autopsy. The autopsy on his brother took priority, the waitress was of less interest as she was just his latest pick up. He knew of his brother's weaknesses and he also knew he liked to treat them rough. He was not that way inclined himself – he refrained from pleasures of the flesh as he felt it gave his enemies opportunity and the risk was too great.

Josef was ambitious and he had a reputation for walking over anyone that got in his way. He had greatly admired the American J Edgar Hoover, who had founded the FBI decades ago. Not that he ever told anyone of his admiration – that kind of thing did not go down well in his beloved communist Russia. His admiration was restricted to one main thing: knowledge was power, and he had files on all his main rivals within Government and he had no compunction about using anything that came his way. He had a fabulous network of informants that kept him at the forefront of internal politics.

"Colonel Andropov, my name is Aleksandr Popov, the consulting pathologist at the Kremlin Hospital in Kuntsevo, Moscow and I have had the sad job of carrying out the autopsy on your brother, the General. I would like first of all to pass on my condolences at this sad time. The physical examination showed significant heart damage and under normal circumstances and for anyone else I would have put it down simply as a myocardial infarction death or in layman's terms as heart failure. However, when I looked at the lungs, I could see internal bleeding and significant damage. It was also apparent on the brain tissue I examined as well. While it is unusual for there to be issues in all three, it is not unheard of, so I wanted to complete a full toxicology screening beyond what we would normally test for. Colonel, the blood work has shown evidence of a pathogen called Novichok. Colonel, this is highly unusual, and I cannot think of legitimate reasons he would be exposed to this substance. Colonel, I need to get Defence-level scientists involved to understand why that particular pathogen would be in his blood and if there is a risk of wider public exposure."

"Mr Popov, have you worked on the waitress yet that came in at the same time?"

"Yes, Colonel and the results are similar, although she was exposed to a lower dose of the pathogen."

"Thank you, Mr Popov, leave it with me and I will start a full Defence inquiry."

Josef sat in his office and pondered the conversation he had just had. Novichok was not widely available even to the world's intelligence services and it was severely restricted in Russia. It was manufactured and stored at only one location and that was at the Defence research facility in Shikhany near Volgograd, about 1000km to the South East of Moscow. It was not the kind of place his brother would just happen to be passing through. This had all the hallmarks of an assassination, although whether it was internal to Russia or an external agency was the ultimate question. Internal politics was aggressive in Russia and if someone had seen the General as a threat then it was possible it was someone clearing their own path to the top.

Josef picked up the phone to his assistant. "Karine, I need my brother's whereabouts over the last four weeks, and I need a war room set up within the next 30 minutes with the heads of departments for the FSB. My brother, General Andropov, has been assassinated."

As the war room was being set up, Josef sat back in his chair and pondered the problem, looking at it from different directions and working through in his mind if it was possible this was accidental exposure, an attack directly on his brother or less likely but possible an attack on Josef by taking his brother out. The war room was set up at the other end of the corridor from his office. It was normally a conference room used by the Heads of Departments. They were housed three floors underground where any meetings they had could not be overseen by prying eyes. There were no windows or even internal glass. The walls of the conference room were lined with a fine metal mesh, effectively encompassing it in a Faraday cage to prevent electronic eavesdropping. No mobile phones were allowed into the room and any laptops were hard wired into the LAN as WiFi did not work. All laptops were fully encrypted, and communications went through dedicated encryptors that only highly security checked engineers could touch.

Across every Russian embassy the communications equipment was not allowed to be fixed by local engineers; instead, a trained secure engineer was flown out from Russia. Any replacement spares had to come from the FSB storeroom in Moscow. Nothing was sourced from local suppliers. It might come across as cumbersome; however, secure communications in the Cyber security age was vital. The room slowly filled up with the various FSB Heads of Department. There was a buzz of anticipation as Josef rarely invoked the war room status and it indicated something important had happened. Josef waited until they were all in and seated before he made his entrance – it was a powerplay thing, it was good to let them wait for him.

"Comrades, as some of you may already know, my brother General Andropov died alone in his apartment last night. He had dismissed his protection team as he was entertaining a young lady whom he met during his visit to the Bolshoi Theatre. The young lady was later found dead in her own apartment about three miles away. I have just spoken with the Consultant pathologist and the physical autopsy suggested heart failure; however, his blood work has shown significant signs of Novichok poisoning."

At this there was a collective intake of breath. How on earth could that have happened?

"There are only two likely scenarios. He was in Shikhany and had some sort of accidental exposure, or he has been deliberately targeted."

"Are you suggesting, Colonel Andropov, that he was assassinated?"

"I am not suggesting anything, Vassily, we will be led by the evidence; I am merely stating the possibilities. My assistant has sent me my brother's diary over the last four weeks, and there is no diary entry highlighting a visit to Shikhany, at least not in an official capacity. Here is what I need from you all."

- "I want a copy of the visitor logs from Shikhany research centre."
- "The last person he was with was some waitress from the Bolshoi, who was she, how long had he known her and other than the obvious, what is her connection to my brother?"
- "If this was an assassination, who has the capability to deploy Novichok both within Russia and external intelligence agencies? Better also check if known terrorist groups have access to it."
- "I want to know who produced the particular strain used in the attack; let's get it traced back to its origin."
- "According to the General's diary, he attended the Nutcracker at the Bolshoi Theatre last night. I want to know who else was there,

where are they from, every guest, every employee. I want all CCTV footage from inside and outside the theatre. In fact, from a three-block radius."

"Ladies and Gentlemen, this is now your highest priority, this is an attack on the General, the FSB and on Mother Russia; we do not rest until we have the answers. I don't want excuses, I want results, we want results. Do not disappoint me! We reconvene in 90 minutes."

The various heads of department filtered out of the War room, heading up to the main office before frantically making phone calls and getting the massive FSB machine moving. Manpower was not an issue but if this was an assassination, time was not on their side. They had to find out if it was internal Russian politics, foreign intelligence services or terrorism. It would not be the first time that a political opponent did something outrageous for a gain. Novichok, though, was another level of complexity. If discovered, it was always going to attract attention. Josef went back to his desk and made a call to the interim FSB Director. It was a call unlike anything he had experienced so far in his career and one he hoped never to repeat. Once that one was over, he had to phone his family – there was not much he could explain other than his brother had died suddenly, and the autopsy was suggesting heart failure. With a sigh of frustration, he picked up the phone and made the calls. The frustration was not about the content of the calls, more that they were an unnecessary distraction from what in his mind had already become a manhunt for the perpetrator or perpetrators of this outrageous assassination.

SEVEN

As Josef was reaching his conclusion about this being an assassination, the team had arrived at the outskirts of St Petersburg. The drive had been uneventful, no roadblocks or police cordons, just 10 hours of careful driving along the back roads so as not to attract attention. The plan now was to dump the car in a busy car park. Somewhere random where it would take the FSB time to find it, where there were cars parked overnight and if they were lucky, it would not be found for a few days. Mac picked a long stay car park near Pulkovo airport – the E105 was within a couple of blocks of the airport so it did not really add much in the way of additional time and a car sitting there for a few days would not attract attention. Giving the car a quick wipe down, mainly for fingerprints, the team split up and headed into the city.

Tonight, they would stay at a cottage on the outskirts booked over the internet for a week by two sisters with their husbands. It was unlikely they would be discovered this early, but it made sense to avoid the normal hotels in the city centre. They booked for a week even though they only expected to be there for one night. It was really just about slowing down any search, but it was also difficult to book a cottage for any less than a week during tourist season. The plan was overnight at the cottage and to catch the first train to Helsinki at 06:25 departing from the St Petersburg Finnish railway station. In total it takes three and a half hours with a stop at passport control at Vyborg. By mid-day tomorrow the team would be back in the West and safe.

They took two separate taxis into the city centre from the long stay car park, walked to a different taxi rank and then took two separate taxis out to a location about a mile from the cottage. They did not want any one person knowing where they were staying and keeping the cottage location unknown. Tired after the long drive it was not something they wanted to do however when you were tired you were more likely to make mistakes, so the extra precautions were worth it. One night's lack of sleep for the team was not a big drama though they trained for it and it only really started to become an issue on the third night. They walked the last mile to the cottage, took the key from a numbered keylock on a wall near the front door and scouted round the cottage, followed by a scout round the extensive well-kept gardens. There was a tree line about 30 yards from the cottage on three sides which meant a good kill zone. The fourth side contained the driveway with a low concrete block wall topped with a black railing. It provided a good view over the access road. Thinking that way was a bit dramatic perhaps, but thinking that way was just second nature. Storm did a bug sweep in the cottage; it would not be a surprise if the FSB had planted bugs in a cottage expected to have foreign tourists over the summer months. Having found nothing, the team started to relax. One more night and they were home free.

The team sat down in the living room and after a few minutes of silence Mac started talking. "Do you know much about St Petersburg? It is a strange city; did you know it was the capital city of Russia when it was ruled by the Russian Tsar and his family, and not Moscow? The palaces are amazing, full of gold, art and general opulence. The Tsars in many ways were very much like the Royal Stuarts in the UK, you know like King Charles the 1st, the one that Cromwell had executed. They believed, like the Stuarts, that they ruled by divine right and that they were superior in every respect to the general populace. Like a lot of the European monarchs, they taxed the poor, not to pay for healthcare and housing but to pay for their opulence and self-indulgent lifestyle. When you think about it, it was really only a matter of time before they were overthrown. It is more of a surprise that it happened so long after the French revolution. They just did not learn that you cannot have the common people starving whilst you sit in a golden palace eating five course meals with your cronies. In the UK, when they brought back Charles the 2nd to take over the crown after Cromwell's death, they did so with significant restrictions with the King only allowed to rule through the will of parliament."

"Wow, Mac, how did you know all that?" asked Louise.

"Oh, I read in my downtime and I read a book about the monarchs of Europe a few years ago. It was interesting to see which ones cared about their people and which ones just felt entitled," replied Mac.

"Not a surprise that the Jocks want a republic," snarled Hairy Dave.

Mac just ignored Dave – he wasn't in the mood for the usual banter. "It isn't all glitz and glamour for St Petersburg though, it is now the heroin capital of Russia and possibly Europe. Since the end of the Cold War and Russia engaging in capitalism, the gangs have taken control of the poorer, less developed parts of the city."

"Sounds like a great place to hide out in," laughed Storm. "Oh, and Dave, stop being a dick, no one likes a smart arse when we have been up all night."

"We need to get back in touch with Edward and let them know the exit plan is still in play and we will be on the 06.25 to Helsinki tomorrow. We need to get some burner phones."

"Louise and I can do that while you guys get other bits," said Dave.

Dave and Louise headed into the city centre first and grabbed a quick bite to eat. Nothing memorable, just a burger and chips. Something to provide energy and where they had a high turnover of customers so they would not be easily remembered. After food it was time to buy the technology, they needed to get back on comms with London. It wasn't difficult to buy mobile phones – they were on sale in a lot of shops – however, despite speaking good Russian it was clear they were not locals and buying phones in multiple shops meant there was a dilemma between not being conspicuous and memorable from buying four phones in one shop or being in four different shops which meant talking to more people. They had decided the four shops was less of a risk.

After purchasing cheap smartphones, they went looking for security cameras. They had to be HD, wireless and internally powered. They found them in two different stores and also bought an over the shoulder holdall. Just a cheap olive canvas bag used by armed forces all over the world. Something big enough to take the items, non-descript and thick enough not to be able to see what they had bought.

Mac and Storm went to the other end of the city centre and headed into the less salubrious part of the city. They wanted knives, not fancy ones, just something concealable but deadly in the right hands.

The streets were busy, a real bustle as tourists found their way around the various museums, theatres and palaces. The usual tourist shops selling utter rubbish that would go in a drawer as soon as they got home. Perestroika under Mikhail Gorbachev certainly opened the Russian market up and although you can't say it ended the Cold War, it certainly thawed it substantially. The streets, once away from the tourist centre, had a menacing feel about them. Any city with a substantial drugs problem had a hard underbelly, a group of people who craved their next fix and did not care how they got the money for it.

Mac and Storm decided to take a short cut through an alley which like a lot of alleys in cities stank of piss and rotting food. Storm wrinkled her nose in disgust. Although not a stranger to the seedy side of the world and sleeping rough during surveillance, it still stank, and it still made her skin crawl. It was the type of smell that clung to you for days.

"Thanks for this, Mac, I am going to stink of this now."

"It saved us five minutes by not having to walk around the block."

Although Mac was defending it, he did look a bit sheepish as he stood on a half-eaten burger. Just at that they heard a step behind them, just that out of place sound that you picked up on when you were out of your comfort zone.

Storm looked round. "We have some company."

"Anything serious?" asked Mac in reply.

"Nothing we can't handle but let's just get it out of the way." With that they turned in unison and confronted the two would-be assailants. They had a large kitchen knife each and looked the way junkies very often do, that skinny, haunted look in their eyes telling the story of their bones feeling as if they are on fire. They weren't really a threat for the skills of Mac and Storm; however, they could still be dangerous as they had nothing to lose, and everyone can get a lucky strike in.

"Money, jewellery," the larger of the two stated in a strong local Russian accent that screamed that they were the only English words he knew.

Mac just stood his ground, planted his feet and brought his balance up onto his toes. "No, look, mate, you really don't want to do this, I am going to have to hurt you if you don't walk away. I don't have money and I never wear jewellery, so you will just have to find some other victim."

The leader turned to his partner with a 'did you understand that' puzzled look and both Storm and Mac swung into action. The look to his partner was the distraction they needed, and Storm instinctively took the one on the left, swung her foot hard into the side of his knee. The knee collapsed at an unnatural angle indicating significant cruciate ligament damage.

As the unfortunate would-be robber leant down to grab the side of his knee with an anguished cry, Storm put her weight onto the other foot, swung her shoulder towards the ground and spun. The momentum of the swing brought her foot crashing onto the side of his head with the force of a car smashing into a tree. His head flopping to the side and his eyes rolling back in his head, he dropped to the ground unconscious. With the impact, the kitchen knife spilled onto the ground beside him.

Storm turned to try and help Mac, conscious he was older and a bit slower than when he was in his prime, but she need not have worried. The robber stabbed the knife towards Mac and quick as a flash Mac grabbed the knife hand, spun into an arm lock and with a quick flex of his muscles broke the assailant's arm. With the knife out of the way he brought his elbow full force into the head of the robber, knocking him unconscious. In total the fight must have lasted less than 10 seconds.

"Not bad for an old guy, Mac, not bad at all. I was worried you might have slowed down but you did all right."

Mac turned to look at Storm with a serious look on his face. "I can still teach you a thing or two, ya cheeky bitch," retorted Mac.

"I do love a good scrap though." Then as if nothing had happened Mac started walking the rest of the way through the alley, whistling happily to himself.

Storm just tutted, shook her head and smiled. She loved Mac's irrepressible attitude to life.

The scrap, as Mac called it, had put them both on high alert. On this occasion it had been a couple of junkies, but it could easily have been something else, an armed FSB team looking for them, for instance. The part of town they were in was, as some would call it, down on its luck. It was tired looking, shops and offices that needed paint, neon signs that had letters not working, hookers on street corners with pimps lurking about in the shadows.

The cars were mostly old European cars that were no longer fit for the European market, paintwork dulled with lack of polish, wheel trims scraped and scratched and bodywork full of dents. In this part of town Mac and Storm would be potential targets, so they kept themselves vigilant. As well as the old bangers, there were a few nice cars about, BMW 7 series with darkened windows, Mercedes E class and Range Rovers. However, they were obviously owned by the drugs kingpins and gangland chiefs. They definitely wanted to stay off the radar of those guys.

They found a shop with knives in the window. From the outside it looked tired, just like the rest of the neighbourhood. It needed painting and some render replaced. Times were tough away from the city centre. More often than not, it was Russian internal tourists that bought items in these shops as they cost less money and were classed as better value than the tourist items in the city centre proper.

Inside the shop was just as dated, but it was clean and tidy. The shop owner took pride in it. The decor was mid-1990s as if it had last been done during Glasnost as the Russian economy woke up. Storm looked quietly about and nodded at Mac as she found what she wanted: a slim blade that looked like a commando knife. The blades were ideal for concealment and as a last-ditch method of escape they were just what the team needed. She bought four blades and put two each in the inside pockets of their jackets.

Next on the agenda was to get some basic provisions so they headed to get some food in. Cereal for breakfast, noodles, stir fry veg and some chicken for dinner. Having got what they came in for, they headed back to the cottage in a taxi and again stopped about a mile short and walked the rest.

When they arrived back at the cottage, they saw that Louise and Dave had arrived before them. They opened the front door and made their way into the kitchen where they found their colleagues sitting at the table with their purchases spread out before them. Four burner phones and six security cameras. Mac and Storm added the commando knives and the groceries for breakfast and dinner.

They took stock of their purchases before Mac and Dave headed out into the garden with the cameras and placed them strategically around the house, facing the trees and front driveway.

Storm fired up the burner phones, connected them to the cellular network and the house WiFi. She then downloaded the software to get the cameras to connect with the phones. The phones would get an alert if motion was detected from any of the cameras and they could cycle round the cameras as part of general surveillance. It wasn't a professional installation, but for under 24-hours it would do the job. The three of them worked together to get an interconnected network of cameras to ensure there were no dead spots.

Louise watched the guys out in the garden and said to Storm, "I will check in with Edward, and make sure everything is ok from their end."

Louise left the cottage and after about a mile she felt she had enough distance between herself and the cottage. If the phone call was tracked, they would only get the general area of the call rather than the specific location. She continued to walk as she dialled a number she had committed to memory and checked in.

"Brixton holidays, Sam speaking, how can I help you today?"

"I am interested in a company holiday, perhaps a cruise?"

"Do you have a particular cruise in mind?"

"No, but I would like a presidential suite."

"Let me connect you to our cruise expert now."

A very cultured male voice came on the phone, very Kensington / Chelsea sounding. The senior management in the government agencies had a tendency to come from the well-educated Oxford and Cambridge University types.

"Louise, it is good to hear from you. It has been a while. I have heard from a regional friend of mine that he has had a death in the family. They and their large family are trying to find some lost friends. Is the family well? Did you find some suitable accommodation as part of your holiday plan?"

"The family are all fine, thank you, Edward. We are at the holiday village tonight waiting on a transfer to a cruise first thing tomorrow. Once we arrive, we will check into the company hotel."

"I have been instructed by my Cruise Director to let you know that there has been a slight alteration to the itinerary. You need to stay at the holiday village for an additional 72 hours. It is outwith my control, I am afraid; it was a Director override, and I can only apologise. While you are waiting, they also want you to pick up a package and bring it home. It has landed a bit faster than they were anticipating, I'm afraid, but it does have some significant value for the company and as you are already there it would be awfully nice of you to help out."

"You better be fucking joking, Edward; our family only take particular types of holiday and a cruise with a baby-sitting facility is not the type of holiday we go on. Which Director are we talking about?"

"My immediate Director. I won't give out names on an unsecure line. I understand your concerns but the small print on the cruise contract allows for some minor changes to the itinerary. I will give you some time to brief the family on the change. This package has information crucial to preventing a particular type of financial problem back home. Why don't you call back tomorrow at 4pm and I will give you the details of the changes?"

"Just fucking marvellous." Louise's reply was dripping sarcasm.

Edward was a decent guy, but he could not deal with conflict and you could almost hear him wince. He knew she was going to make him pay for this. She wasn't sure who the Director was, but he sure knew how to make crazy decisions. She would ask Mac who he might be when she got back to the cottage as he knew that world inside out.

Louise switched off the phone, took the battery out and walked back to the cottage. The team were not going to like this one bit. Twenty minutes later she arrived back at the cottage and gathered the others around the kitchen table.

"I have some news from Edward in London; Moscow was a success, but the FSB are actively hunting us, they don't know yet where we are, but they know we exist and from what Edward said they have every asset looking. The challenge is that Edward's management team have changed our plans and we need to stay in play for another 72 hours. Edward has a package that has particularly valuable information that will prevent some sort of financial crisis and needs to be taken out of the country. I know we don't normally do this, but we are it. Oh, and the other good news is it is a high value package so that could cause quite a stir."

"Good news about Moscow, we put a load of effort into it. On the package removal that is a chore – not only will we have all the FSB on our tail over Andropov, but now we will have the rest of motherfucking Russia as well. London are such a shower of ivory tower wankers. I would like to see one of those office jockeys out here taking an extra 72 hours." Dave was not taking it well.

"Look, it is what it is, we need to work our way through it. Let's get planning and make sure we know what we are facing into. The last thing any of us want is a mad dash for the train and we get caught as we didn't work through the detail. Mac, the decision was made by Edward's immediate Director – any idea who that is?"

"It's a guy called George Williams, one of those dictatorial types, I have come across him before, total idiot in my view," replied Mac.

"Well, he is not my favourite person right now," stated Louise.

The team spent the next hour brainstorming the situation, teasing out the risks and how they could mitigate as much of the risk as possible. The biggest risk was the lack of firepower if they were cornered and had to shoot their way out of trouble. They also needed to scout out the train station. Louise wanted the team to be out and about each day. If nothing else, it gave them the chance to do counter surveillance. To do this successfully, the team needed the ability to change their appearance quickly and potentially while on the move if they did encounter trouble.

They also needed a plan to abandon the 72-hour holding pattern if it became too hot. Edward might not be happy, but it was better than being killed or captured. The basic plan was this:

The train to Tallinn was the easiest option so that would be classed as plan A. Plan B was Mac and Storm to steal a 5-seater car, something plain, like a grey sedan. They would prefer an SUV but it would potentially stand out, so the sedan would do. It needed to have some power under the bonnet as well. Plan C was a cruise ship, not ideal to be honest as they took too long to get out of Russian waters, but it would do in an emergency and might well get overlooked by the authorities. Plan D, which in truth wasn't really a plan, was just reacting to whatever was in front of them at the time and to just do the best that they could and keep the package in one piece.

The first order of the day was sustenance. In any kind of intelligence or armed forces, you could be cold, you could be wet, and you could be hungry. Being all three was a real chore.

"I will make some grub, chicken stir fry, a good mix of protein, carbs and vitamins," said Mac.

You could tell Mac was a dad of four kids – he loved to take any opportunity to cook, especially when it was not the usual armed forces rations. First, he diced the chicken into roughly 2cm cubes. It was best if they were all roughly the same size as it meant they all cooked through at the same pace. Next, he placed it into a frying pan on a high heat. This browned the outside of the meat, keeping the inside nice and moist and full of flavour. With the outside nice and brown, the heat was turned down and a splash of water was added to enable the meat to cook slowly, allowing it to be nice and tender. Last he added the veg and a touch of salt and pepper he had found in the cupboards, which gave it some bulk, flavour and importantly much needed vitamins and carbs. Mac allowed it to simmer for just under 20 minutes. At the last minute he added the noodles.

The team were hungry, and you took the opportunity of grub when you could. It would have been better with some soy sauce, ginger and garlic but these things are not always available. So, they just had to do with it as it was.

"Grub's up, come and get it," shouted Mac. The team sat round the table in silence as they ate dinner.

"Awww, Mac, that was fabulous, babe. You are wasted doing this assassin shit; you should have been a chef." Louise loved it when Mac cooked. Storm and Hairy Dave noisily agreed, and Mac got a couple of high fives.

"What age are your kids, Mac? They must love your cooking," asked Louise.

"Oh, my kids are all up with families of their own these days, and with my wife dying ten years ago I was happy to stay doing all this stuff. Not sure what I would do without this. They do love it when I am back home, the sun is shining, and I do a BBQ," replied Mac.

"Can't beat a BBQ in the sun with a couple of cold beers, my friend. What is your go-to dish?" asked Dave.

"I went on holiday a few years ago and I had mini sliders they called them. They were like mini burgers so you could eat different ones. I make a variety. Pork and apple are good, lamb with a bit of cumin, coriander and chilli, and the last one is beef with red Leicester cheese, fried onions and a special home-made sauce."

"Crikey, Mac, I need an invite to your next one," said Storm.

The team spent the next 30 minutes discussing the best food they had had around the world before they focussed back on their current situation. Mac went out with Storm into the garden to look for the best place in the treeline for an overwatch. They would take it in turns during the night in two-hour intervals. With the four of them it meant they would get the chance to grab some sleep over the course of the night and on an Operation, sometimes that was a luxury. About 20 minutes later they came back in, having found the best spot – it wasn't ideal, but it would do the job. With the added security of the cameras, it gave them some confidence they would get enough of a heads-up to make it out in one piece before any armed response units could get fully set up.

"I will take first watch," said Mac.

Louise knew there was a reason she loved Mac. He genuinely thought of everyone else before himself. It made her sad that he had lost his wife a few years ago and all the kids were grown up. It must be lonely at times and she fully understood why he continued to do what he did, even at his age. The others didn't get undressed, just lay down on the beds and slept with their boots and gear on. Sleep is important in escape and evasion – take it when you can get it. Without it, eventually you start making mistakes. In the elite units like 22 SAS and Marine Commandos, they trained for it. They kept you awake for days on end and forced you into making decisions. The idea is you need to recognise the signs of exhaustion, so you know you need sleep before you make that last fatal decision that sees you dead or captured.

Louise was normally one of those lucky ones, head on the pillow and was out like a light; however, tonight was one of the exceptions. She was uncomfortable with the change to the mission, and she had a nagging, bad feeling about it. She was vaguely aware of Dave tossing and turning on the other single bed, but just tried to shut it out.

After about an hour she drifted off into that dreamless sleep shared by angels and psychopaths. She guessed which camp she fitted into. With the work she did she remained unemotional and detached so getting to sleep was rarely an issue. Dave, on the other hand, had a conscience; it is easy for the bosses and psychologists to talk about keeping emotion out of the job and remaining detached but in the quiet times your brain does its own thing and that is when the demons come to haunt you. With the job they were in there were plenty of demons and it was hard to shut them out. Many operatives took to drink during home time to quieten the demons. It was one of the reasons so many ended up divorced.

Louise awoke with a start and lay awake, listening intently to the wind outside. She could not hear anything out of the ordinary and had no idea what had woken her, so she just lay on the bed and drifted into a light memory-filled REM (random eye movement) sleep.

Louise's mum had been a heroin addict for years and as she lost her jobs and thus her income, she turned in desperation to prostitution, but she was still Louise's mum and despite everything was her world; Louise would do anything for her and to be honest when her mum was high, she frequently did. Prostitution was the only way she could feed her habit and feed both Louise and Jaimie her younger brother. Jaimie was three years younger, and Louise had looked out for him since the day he was born. Her mum had been a real looker in her day but by the end the heroin had taken her looks, she ended up skeletal thin and had that haunted look so often seen in people with a habit, whose only thought was where the next fix would come from. She had tried her best, but her best was getting lower and lower.

Social Services were frequently involved, and her mum got regular visits from them. They must have been classed as a high-risk family as they got visits most weeks when other families Louise knew had infrequent visits. To Louise it seemed a pretty ordinary life; she and Jaimie went to school most days and, on the way home, she stopped at the local supermarket to steal something for dinner. She did buy things as well, so the security guards did not follow her round the store. When she got home, she would make dinner and wait for her mum to get out of bed to serve it up. When she says make dinner, it was really just heating up whatever she had stolen.

Often her mum looked like hell as her last fix from the night before had worn off and she had the shakes. After dinner Louise would do some homework ready for her mum to head out and earn the money she needed to feed her habit and what little there was left she used to feed Louise and Jaimie. Now in her early teens, Louise was now at that age when she was fully aware of what her mum was and was embarrassed. She knew what she did and implored her to stop, to get clean and she had tried on a few occasions, but it just wasn't in her, the heroin had taken her and would never let go.

Louise remembered the fateful day she met John Slater, the social worker. She had just come home from school when he met her and Jaimie on the doorstep; he instantly gave her the creeps. There was just a look about his eyes that felt as if you needed a wash by the time he looked away. That day would forever haunt her, as Louise and Jaimie turned into their street, they saw a police car outside their block of flats. They climbed the stairs as the lifts were out of order again and the Police and John Slater were at the door of their flat.

"Why are you in our flat, is my mum ok?" asked Louise, sounding anxious.

"Come in and sit-down, Louise, we need to have a talk," answered Slater. With that he turned and walked into the living room and took a seat on one of the threadbare chairs. Louise and Jaimie sat on the sofa and waited anxiously for Slater to talk.

"Your mum was found dead this morning, Louise, when I came to do the weekly social work visit, so I called the Police. I will put you and Jaimie into a care home

tonight before I find more permanent accommodation for you."

Later that afternoon Louise and Jaimie headed off to a care home for kids and waited to find out what would happen with them full time. The next day Slater arrived at the care home and asked for Louise to come out for a walk with him, leaving Jaimie in his room.

"I want us to be friends, Louise, I like you and want to do the best by you and Jaimie, because care homes can be awful places. There is no telling what might happen if you run into the wrong person. I may even have to put you and Jaimie into separate care homes, and anything could happen to him if you are not there to protect him." Even his voice seemed oily, what a creep.

"Why would I not be there to protect him?" asked Louise innocently.

"Well, it is all on my recommendation, of course, but it is probable he will go into a separate home, one where you would never see him and he would be all alone with some real bully types, you know the ones, drug dealers and that type."

"You wouldn't do that, though, would you? He is my little brother; I have always looked out for him." Louise's voice was getting high pitched as she was starting to panic.

"Well, anything is possible, of course, but if I do something for you, Louise, it means I need something in return. I would like to keep you and your brother together, Louise, I honestly would, but it is really difficult and would take a lot of work. It can be unsafe for little boys in care, I know some men pay good money for access to little boys if you know what I mean. To keep you both

safe I would need you to do me certain favours to keep him safe. Would you be up for doing me some favours?"

Louise was stunned and suddenly felt sick – not only was she feeling instantly emotionally drained, but this sicko was also threatening to send Jaimie to be with a paedo ring. Louise started to panic and in her head was saying "Shit, how do I get out of this and keep Jaimie safe?" – he was the most important thing she had left in the world and she could not let anything happen to him.

"What kind of favours do you mean?"

"Just the same kind your mum used to do for me, we will start off nice and simple, just some straightforward sexual favours. You are a pretty girl. Afterwards we can take it from there. I have friends who also used to get favours from your mum."

"Why would my mum give favours to your friends?"

"For the same reason you will, Louise, because it will keep your little brother safe. If you tell anyone, and I mean anyone, your teacher, a neighbour, a friend, I will sell your brother to the highest bidder. No one listens to street tarts like you anyway. I have friends all through law enforcement, I have judges and police chiefs who pay me to find them some fresh young talent. Just play the game and I will keep Jaimie safe."

Louise felt trapped with no way out, this guy gave her the absolute creeps and she felt sick even looking at him. She could not see a way out and felt she had no choice but go along with what he wanted. She just sat there, tears running down her face, that sick feeling deep in her stomach with her mind turning in on itself as panic started to set in. She had to think on a way out, but she needed to find some space to do it.

"Do you promise to keep Jaimie safe if I do your favours?"

"Of course, I will. You just make sure you keep your mouth shut and he will be fine. Take this phone and when it rings you meet me where I tell you to. Do you understand?"

"I understand."

And so, it began, that plunge off a cliff face into desperation that meant you had to do things you would not otherwise do, the darkest chapter in Louise's life she had buried deep, never talking about it, which in turn became her own motivation. The well she could tap into when all else fails. A deep-seated anger and hatred that she harnesses when she has nothing else. She had to get time to think, she had to find a way out that protected both her and Jaimie. Having drawn a blank Louise decided to confide in Mr MacPherson. She left school and headed to her old flat instead of heading to the care home, and knocked on Mr MacPherson's door.

"What are you doing back in this block of flats, young lady, too many bad memories for you here?"

"I am in trouble, Mr MacPherson and I have no one else to turn to." With that she broke her heart and just sobbed and sobbed.

"Come here, lassie, it can't be that bad."

With that Mr MacPherson hugged her tight in that fatherly way only older men can do, he said nothing and just let her get it all out. He was intrigued and saddened that such a lovely young lady felt she was in that much trouble. He sensed her desperation, and he was determined to help in any way he could.

"OK, talk me through it, what has you in such a state?"

Louise talked through the discussion with Slater, detailed what he was asking her to do. She told him even the way he looked at her just gave her the creeps, that she knew he had visited her mother and that he always left before she got home from school. She showed him the mobile phone and how she had to wait for a phone call and show up at a designated time and place so she could show Slater and his clients a good time.

"How do I get out of this, Mr MacPherson? I need to protect Jaimie, the police would never believe me, and all I would do is put Jaimie at risk. Maybe I should just do what he wants."

With that Louise burst out sobbing again and Mr MacPherson just gave her another hug.

"Just let it all out my girl. I am here to help you; we will come up with a plan together. Let me make a brew, everything is always better after a brew," said Mr MacPherson.

"Ok" answered Louise trying to hold back the sobs.

Mr MacPherson headed off into the kitchen to put the kettle on, whistling away to himself. It was what he did when he was thinking. Louise wasn't even sure if he was aware he did it. It made her smile even in the midst of her crisis. He just seemed to have a calming influence, nothing ever seemed to faze him. Ten minutes later he appeared back, carrying two mugs of tea. It wasn't fancy tea just what her mum would call builders' tea. A nice strong brew.

"Here you go, Louise, you will feel better after this. I have added two sugars for you. The sugar helps after a shock, so drink it all up."

They sat for a couple of minutes in silence, just enjoying the mug of tea.

"I think we need to look at the options available to us. We have a number of options. Firstly we can go to the police, outline what was said and show them the phone. You will need to provide a written statement and put it all on the record. You can't be the only person he is doing this to so it might open an investigation and there would be other people come forward. The problem with that is there were no witnesses to what Slater said. With your mum's profession they would question your reliability as a witness and so far, you have not had any text messages. We would need to catch him in the act and other witnesses might be too scared to come forward.

"If he does not get convicted, it means you would be at his mercy going forward. You also said he has judges and people like that as his clients so the whole thing feels too risky.

"The second option is that I can pay him a visit, intimidate him, and make him understand I know everything. I can make sure he understands that unless he backs off, he will be in a lot of pain. The downside is like option 1 that if he has law enforcement contacts as you have said, then I would get dragged into a cell, charged with some made up charge and if I end up in prison then you are back to square one and on your own.

"That leads us to option three, we wait until he texts, you turn up at the allotted time wearing a concealed recording device. We get the required evidence by recording him outlining what he wants, we get him actually asking you to do these favours. I arrive after he has outlined it, let him know of the evidence we have and that it will go to the Police and online if he does not back away. I then give him a physical reminder that touching young girls has consequences.

"The last option is that we take him out permanently. It is really extreme and not something I would recommend as the consequences would be far reaching and could change the whole course of both of our lives if we get caught. I think we hold that back as a last resort. What do you think?"

Louise smiled a shy smile of a young lady trying to appear in control, but internally her head was going round in circles.

"I don't want you getting into trouble because of me, Mr MacPherson. I think we need the evidence before we do anything else. I am scared that if I meet him, he can just rape me. What if he has friends with him? What do I do then?" asked Louise hesitantly, trying to appear calm.

"What do you think of going with the recording device and see if we can get him to back off. It is the simplest option and very often that is the best one. You can deal with this scum bag if he tries anything. You have it in you and have shown it against three and four assailants before. What we will do, though, is get you a weapon. Something hidden that gives you that bit of extra protection. I will be just outside so all you need to do is buy me a few seconds to get inside and I can deal with it from there. It is your decision, Louise; I will back you on whatever you decide to do," said Mr MacPherson in his calm voice.

Louise took some time to consider the options before responding. "I will do the recording. I just want Jaimie to be safe."

"That's fine, let me work through some detail and get a suitable recording device and weapon. You need to head back to your care home for a day or so. Come back

and see me in a few days and we will be ready to go. Finish up your brew and I will walk you back."

"Thank you, Mr MacPherson, I really appreciate it."

Louise spent the next few days on edge, waiting on her mum's funeral and dreading a text message telling her where to go and meet up. She had since learned that the waiting and inactivity is the worst part; the brain makes up scenarios and generally overthinks the situation. However, for Louise, she was still a young girl who had just lost her mum and just had an empty void inside. She was pleased Mr MacPherson had agreed to help, but the 'what if' questions just played over and over.

By the time her mum's funeral came round three days later she had not slept and felt like a spider's web on a windy, wet afternoon. Paper thin and ready to break. The care home found a basic black dress that had seen better days, but thinking back on it, Louise was not in the position to care. She had always been poor and hand me downs were the norm. They found Jaimie some black trousers that were a bit too short and a white shirt with a black tie. The woman from the care home came with them and held their hands at the crematorium. It was a surreal experience and Louise felt she watched it through someone else's eyes. It was hard to believe her mum was gone. She might not have been the greatest mum, but she was their mum, she had done her best and now they had no one.

There were only about 20 people there including the lady cop, Mr MacPherson and some women Louise did not recognise but they said they worked with her mum. Louise expected that it meant they were prostitutes as well. Louise stood there dry eyed throughout the ceremony. In retrospect the time with Mr MacPherson probably had her all cried out. She stood as the coffin went down into the floor of the crematorium with an arm around Jaimie who was sobbing his heart out. Louise just stared forward, wishing she could be with her mum so that she wasn't all alone.

At the end of the ceremony Louise turned to leave and saw Slater standing at the back, hands by his side, wearing a dark coloured suit and a raincoat. As she walked past Louise looked at the ground, but she saw him standing there with a smarmy knowing smile and he winked at Jaimie. Louise raised her gaze, stopped briefly and just stared right through him with that dead eyed stare of someone who has nothing. Slater saw a vulnerable girl who was going to be the latest part of his and his friend's enjoyment – what he should have seen was a girl who had fought against the regime all her life and now had nothing to lose.

Mr MacPherson saw the interaction, walked forward and put a protective arm around Louise and Jaimie before ushering them outside to the waiting cars. It was one of those miserable grey Glasgow days where the rain swept in sideways, and it took all his self-control not to walk back to confront Slater and deck him there and then. He knew Slater's time was limited; he would make sure of that. One way or another, he would take that smug bastard out of Louise and Jaimie's lives. Slater just did not know it yet. Louise and Jaimie went back to the care home and Louise sat with Jaimie and asked him if he was ok. He had that haunted look of someone whose world had been blown apart and did not know what the future would hold.

"Mum has gone, Jaimie, and it is just you and me now. Mr MacPherson will help us when we need him to, but we need to be strong and work it through together. We can be anything we want to; we just have to make it happen. No one else will do it for us, but we are as good as anyone else. What do you want to be?"

"I want to have a computer and save the world from bad people," said Jaimie with the enthusiasm of a child.

"Then that is what you will be," said Louise.

At that Jaimie settled down and fell asleep leaning on his big sister. In his mind he now had a plan. For Louise she still had some tough times ahead to make sure both her and Jaimie did not become playthings for Slater and his band of paedophiles.

It was three days later when a text came through from Slater. The buzzing from her bag had Louise confused for a few seconds until she realised what it was. She had never owned a mobile phone; they did not have any spare money for anything other than food and occasionally, if they really needed it, clothes. The text was requesting a meet at a house in the southside of Glasgow. Louise did not know where it was, she had never travelled more than a mile or two from her house. She never had the money to go on the school trips. She was one of the ones left back in the classroom when virtually everyone else headed off all giggling and excited on a bus trip to a museum or the zoo.

Louise walked to see Mr MacPherson that afternoon and they went through several scenarios together and how they could deal with anything unexpected that might happen. Louise was starting to get frustrated, as in her mind it was just as simple as turning up with the recording device and then showing Slater that they had the evidence, and he would just back off. Mr MacPherson patiently highlighted that a plan is just a plan, and it would give you 80% to 90% of what would happen, but it was important that Louise understood that she would have to react to whatever the circumstances threw at her. What if there were others present, what if Slater panicked and attacked her, what if they had a gun or other weapon?

Mr MacPherson had bought a digital recording device which was small and not easily seen. Louise also had Slater's mobile phone so Mr MacPherson could listen in. If Louise got into trouble, she was to say, "life just isn't fair" and Mr MacPherson would force his way into the house. As a back-up, though, he had bought Louise a switch blade knife. It was nothing fancy, but he had spent an hour sharpening the six-inch blade so that it was as sharp as a razor; he even joked he might keep it himself as it was better than the disposable razors he had been using.

Over the next two days Mr MacPherson trained Louise even harder, not on the running or fitness stuff but on defence and attack techniques using the knife, hands and feet as weapons. There was no point in taking a knife and not knowing how to debilitate someone and, if needs must, how to kill. Just as importantly it was vital she did not freeze and could let her body flow. Special forces trained to make sure that did not happen, you had to make sure you could deal with a situation as if you were on a shopping expedition. Louise trained harder than ever, determined to protect Jaimie and to make Mr MacPherson proud of her.

Late afternoon on the day of the meeting Louise headed along to Mr MacPherson's flat. Looking at the *front door of their old flat was a poignant moment, and she had a lump in her throat as she knocked on Mr MacPherson's door. He answered promptly, taking a quick peek outside to see if anyone had watched Louise enter the flat. It was more out of habit than anything else. They went through the plan one last time and Mr MacPherson had made a plate of lentil soup.*

"Do you fancy a plate of soup, Louise? It is freshly made by my fair hand and even if I do say so myself it is positively fantastic."

"No Thank you, Mr MacPherson, I am not hungry, I feel a bit sick if I am honest."

"Ach, that is just the nerves, lass, it is nothing to worry about. We all feel nervous at some point. Nerves are a good thing; they make your body alive when you need it. Adrenalin is your fight or flight drug, and the body makes it so that you are ready if you need to either fight or run away. What you need to do is just accept them, hold them to you and give them a big fat cuddle."

That made Louise laugh, and she relaxed just a little bit.

"That is better, lass, now I know you said you did not want any but here is some soup, get it down you. You will need it later tonight and there is plenty more in the pot if you want some more."

When the time was right Mr MacPherson hailed a cab. He did not want to book one upfront. That meant it was a black hackney as they were the only ones that could do a street pick up. It would cost a couple of pounds more, but the anonymity was worth it. They got the taxi to a point about a 20-minute walk from the target house. Mr MacPherson knew that would mean they were within a mile of the target and if caught they could talk their way out of it. They did not want to be dropped off just outside the house in case something happened, and the taxi driver recognised them on the news. Mr MacPherson did a final check of the digital voice recorder and Louise called Mr MacPherson's mobile phone. Mr MacPherson had headphones on so he could listen in and positioned himself a few doors down in case Louise needed him urgently.

Mr MacPherson took Louise's hands in his, looked her straight in the eye and in a calm reassuring voice, said, "You have got this, Louise, you are an incredibly intelligent, gifted young lady. There is nothing they can throw at you that you can't deal with and if you need me, what do you say?"

"Life just isn't fair," said Louise, a bit subdued.

"Look at me, Louise and tell me you got this."

"I got this."

"Louder," demanded Mr MacPherson.

"I got this."

"Louder," demanded Mr MacPherson.

"I…Got… This."

"Yes, you do, and I am just outside. Go get him, lass."

Louise marched confidently up to the door of the posh house in the Southside of Glasgow, near Bellahouston Park. Louise rang the doorbell and waited anxiously until Slater answered the door.

"Ah there you are, Louise, right on time." His creepy voice made Louise want to vomit.

"Have you told anyone where you are, Louise? How did you get out of the care home?"

"I told them I was studying at a friend's house and would be back before curfew," answered Louise as she

looked at the floor. She was trying to appear shy and intimidated, but in reality, she was avoiding eye contact so she would not get caught out in a lie.

"Very inventive," said Slater, his voice dripping sarcasm.

"First door on the right, head on through," said Slater, anticipation now apparent in his voice.

Louise entered the door as directed and once inside she found another two men, three including Slater. A fat bald guy that talked in a very posh accent – Louise felt he was a lawyer or a judge by the look of him; the other one had the feel of someone who was in the old bill, high up perhaps but he screamed Police. They all knew each other really well and laughed and joked as they offered Louise champagne. She politely declined, stating, "I am only 15." At that they just laughed and said they made the law and pushed the glass back toward Louise. Louise got the feeling there was something in the champagne that they wanted her to drink, Rohypnol maybe. When Louise refused again, the cop grabbed her by the throat and in a grim voice said, "You need to learn to play nice, little girl, and do as you are told, or we will need to teach you what the consequences are if you don't."

Slater grabbed Louise from behind and the judge tried to pour the drugged champagne into Louise's mouth. Louise spat out the champagne into the face of the cop. She did not have the time to say her 'I need help' phrase. Louise knew she was in real trouble and in too deep. The three of them were getting red in the face with rage. What was supposed to be an evening of fun with a compliant 15-year-old had degenerated into a farce. Slater was embarrassed in front of his high-

power friends and reached into a drawer and pulled out a length of rope.

"I will tie her up and teach her some manners," said Slater, and he looked meaningfully up to the ceiling. Louise followed his gaze and noticed that there were two eye bolts in the ceiling. This was not the first time they had done this to an underage girl obviously. Louise got a sinking feeling that they were not only going to rape her, but they were going to hurt her in a really bad way.

Louise knew she had to get on the front foot and flexed her shoulder muscles to free up her right wrist, just a fraction but enough to take the switch blade out of her sleeve; she pressed the button to make it flick open with a satisfying click. With a marginal pause to grit her teeth and steel her nerve she pushed the blade backwards into the cop's groin and pushed it back and upwards sharply. The blade sharpened to a keen edge by Mr MacPherson cut open the cop. He let out an animal scream and as he let go of Louise, he looked down to see she had severed his femoral artery. The blood was coming out in bursts, he tried to add pressure to the wound with his hands to stem the bleeding and Louise quick as a flash spun on her heel and stabbed him three times hard and fast in the chest with a final cut across the side of his neck. The cop's eyes opened wide in disbelief as if to say how did she manage to do this.

The judge, never a man of action, suddenly realised the danger he was in and made a grab for Louise. Unfortunately for him, he was fat and out of condition and that made him far too slow for a trained young girl with lightning quick reflexes. Louise just brushed aside the feeble grab attempt, stepped forwards and pushed the blade direct into his eye just as hard as she could. Instead of waiting to see the result of her action she immediately withdrew the blade, then stabbed him twice in his left side puncturing his lungs. By now the Judge was screaming at the top of his voice, asking Slater for help, Louise moved half a step to her left and thrust the knife hard and fast into the Judge's windpipe and through into his neck, severing his spinal cord. He dropped to the floor, his legs caving in from underneath him and Louise glanced down. He was no longer a threat and she moved towards Slater. He was paralysed with fear and looked on in horror – what should have been a fun night with his influential friends had turned into a horror show.

"I am on your side, Louise, I only wanted a bit of fun, some girls actually like it rough." With that he turned and made a dash for the door. Slater was too old and too slow and was simply not fast enough to get away from girl on a mission to protect her little brother. Louise stabbed him in the back just where Slater's kidneys would be. Slater slowed to a stand-still, howling with the considerable pain and as Slater said, "I am sor…" Louise grabbed him by the hair, pulled his head back and slit his throat from ear to ear, the arterial blood spraying all over the walls. Louise turned away, rather than watch him die in front of her.

Just as that happened Mr MacPherson burst in the door. He had heared the commotion but by the time he got to the door it was all over. The room looked like an abattoir and Louise just stood there covered in blood from head to toe. Louise dropped the knife as the reality of what she had just done hit her like a truck.

Mr MacPherson looked about the room, quickly taking stock of everything. He took a rucksack from his back and from it he gave Louise a bag of alcohol wipes to clean the blood from her hair and skin; all he needed to do was make her look presentable until he could get her home. From the rucksack he took out an old hoodie, joggers and trainers for her to change into. He picked up Louise's blood-soaked clothes, the knife and the alcohol wipes and placed them into a plastic bag and then inside his rucksack.

"What all did you touch, Louise?"

"Just that champagne glass and the door handles and I sat on that leather couch."

"Ok, time to leave, I will come back later and do a clean."

With that they calmly left the house and went to a flat of a friend of Mr MacPherson's that was away on holiday. Louise went for a shower and Mr MacPherson told her to wash her hair at least three times and use conditioner. When Louise finished, she was told to put her hands into a basin of distilled water and scrub under her fingernails. Blood when it comes into contact with distilled water bursts and the DNA is contaminated. It is a good forensic counter measure when you have nothing else. Mr MacPherson sat Louise on the couch.

"How are you feeling, Louise? That was a tough ordeal for anyone to go through."

Louise replied, unnaturally calmly, "I am fine, honestly, they were scumbags who preyed on young girls. I do not feel sorry about what I did."

Mr MacPherson looked at Louise for a few seconds trying to gauge the truth of the statement. Seemingly satisfied he just nodded and said, "I am going to head back to the house and make sure they cannot trace it back to us."

He put on his jacket, took the rucksack with him including the clothes Louise had changed into and headed out. Louise sat in front of the TV and just stared at it, not really taking it in. She must have dozed off as about three hours later, Mr MacPherson returned, smelling of petrol and smoke. He went in for a quick shower and changed his clothes. Louise thought this friend must be more than a casual acquaintance and more like a friend with benefits if he had a change of clothes at the flat. Mr MacPherson walked Louise back to her care home, making sure she arrived before the start of curfew, which would trigger all the wrong sorts of enquiries.

The next morning it was all over the local news about a suspected gangland hit on law enforcement, three senior officials dead and the house set on fire. Louise half expected the cops to come bursting through the door at any minute, but it never happened. A few days later and a female social worker arrived and told Louise that her and Jaimie would be moving into Foster care. They were a decent sort of family and loved Jaimie to bits, but Louise was seen as a bit of a handful. Louise kept in close contact with Mr MacPherson, and he took her and Jaimie on days out. Sometimes it was fishing, sometimes shooting for rabbits. Everything had a reason with Mr MacPherson. He kept a close eye on them during the two years they were in foster care. The foster family were more in it for the money than anything else, but Jaimie and Louise were safe, and that was the main thing. Mr Macpherson never mentioned the incident, it was what he called a code of silence – you did not talk about it ever and Jaimie must never know.

In the blink of an eye Louise turned 17; she wanted to leave school and wanted out of Glasgow. It had lost its shine and the world seemed an awfully big place full of excitement compared with the humdrum of a 9-to-5 job in a city she no longer loved. Mr MacPherson said he would talk to some government people and see if he could get her into an Intelligence training academy. She had shown she could handle herself in difficult situations, did not panic and just as importantly afterwards could maintain her silence. Not only that but she did not get caught up in the world of remorse. The one thing she was worried about was Jaimie and said she would turn down the academy to look after him. Mr MacPherson sat both Jaimie and Louise down and told them that he had filed for adoption of Jaimie.

The adoption process took six months for everything to work its way through the system, but it took that long for the Intelligence academy to have another intake. It did not seem that long when Jaimie, Louise and Mr MacPherson were standing in Central Station in Glasgow saying a tearful goodbye and Louise promising to phone and visit every time she could. Louise would miss them both, but this was now her time. Little did she know that her life would become about taking out bad guys for a living. Louise headed to platform one, took her allotted seat on the train and took the chance to sleep.

Back at the cottage, Louise opened her eyes and got ready to get up and take her turn at overwatch.

EIGHT

I n Moscow the FSB were relentless, Josef was back in the war room.

"Ok, people, what do we know? Let's get it up on the story board."

"We know the waitress was called Natasha and worked at the Bolshoi Theatre, we have been to her flat and we have all of the contents in the warehouse and are going through them, we have all communications coming from that flat and are getting every website and message from the internet provider as well as every text message from the phones in that block of flats."

"Excellent, I want to know every aspect of her life including who her family and friends were and if they have any political connections or foreign contacts," replied Josef, with some excitement in his voice.

"We know the General was never at Shikhany, the visitors log is clear, and the Head of Security has stated he was never there, so it is unlikely this was accidental exposure."

"OK, that makes sense and ties into what we expected. Good, good. What is the CCTV telling us?" asked Josef.

"Natasha arrived at the theatre alone – having interviewed the others at the theatre, that was normal. She arrived at the theatre alone most days. Occasionally she would bump into other employees just outside the theatre, but nothing specifically arranged."

"Ok, so we need to know if Natasha is involved in this mess or not. Was she accidentally poisoned as she carried out the Novichok poisoning on the General, or was she an innocent who was just unlucky and in the wrong place at the wrong time? Let's make that a priority please."

"There is one other interesting piece of information we got from the interviews, Colonel. We have a waitress missing since the assassination. She did not turn up for work and there has been no contact to say she is ill. Maybe we have another fatality and maybe she could be involved somehow. We have her address, but she is not there. We have all her belongings in the warehouse as well, although the flat was very clean, almost forensically clean. Her name was Irina Lebedev. Worked there for a few months, kept herself to herself. We are just working up a profile."

"Ok, let me summarise where I think we are. We have General Antonov visiting the Bolshoi at 7pm, watching the Nutcracker and leaving with Natasha, a waitress, in tow. He allowed his security detail to leave after he entered his apartment. Both the General and the waitress were found dead in the morning. Natasha worked in the Bolshoi, nothing screaming at us from her history although not yet fully cleared. We have a missing waitress from the Bolshoi named Irina Lebedev, although she has no obvious link to the General, but it is suspicious she is now missing."

"Anyone got anything in addition?"

"Right, I want her stuff gone through with a fine-tooth comb, does she have credit cards, has she paid for anything else recently, let's get a social media work up and let's find her on CCTV, how did she get to and from work, did she meet anyone. We reconvene in one hour, get to it, people."

Josef had that feeling he got when he was on the right path – this girl was the key, he could feel it. The question in his mind was motive, why his brother and why Novichok? That was no coincidence, it felt like a message, but what? He went back to his office and made a phone call to the Director.

"Good evening, Director, we have a lead, a waitress that is missing. It has all the hallmarks of an assassination, but we don't yet know why. I need access to my brother's personnel file, what has he been working on. It feels personal."

"Let me make a call, Josef, you will have it within an hour; but Josef, everything is classified "In the National Interest". You reveal nothing that is within those files to the wider team. I am providing it to guide your investigation."

"Yes, Director, understood."

With that he put the phone down. The Director knew something, something his brother had been working on at some point. He felt alive, like a wolf chasing down a stag.

"Colonel, I have the missing waitress's credit card – she booked a flight to Amsterdam, leaving this morning."

"Get onto border control at the airport and get the CCTV footage, I want to know if she made that flight and get someone to Amsterdam airport, I want her followed as soon as she lands."

I will chase you down no matter how long it takes, Josef thought to himself. He went back into the war room and analysed the storyboard, photographs, places, credit cards, room contents. String connecting the items as the FSB worked to get the further details. What was strange was the lack of internet traffic, only some encrypted traffic which they could not yet trace. Sometimes you need to stand back, and if a pattern is not emerging you need to look at the lack of a pattern against normal behaviour. Josef had a hunch and called the cyber team.

"Have you got the missing waitress's social media profile yet?" he asked.

"We have, Colonel, but it is very light, nothing much in it. If I am being cynical, it is as if she did not exist beyond 12 months ago."

"Thank, you. That is very helpful."

"No problem, Colonel, any time."

Strange as it may sound, the lack of a social media profile made more sense than it should. The lack of a pattern, the lack of a social media history, a flat that was too basic as if it wasn't lived in for long and had been forensically cleaned. He could almost tell the CCTV would give up very little. This screamed a professional, almost Intelligence Agency level or large criminal gang level hit. Just what had his brother gotten himself into?

Was it revenge or a pre-emptive hit? Was it political by an internal opponent or something else? He knew time was against him, with this level of planning and operational security, they would either be out of the country or just about to be. He walked along the length of the war room to a map of the world. Moscow is here, the obvious exit would be the airport, but it was too obvious, and this girl had been meticulous in her planning so far. Although there was a flight booked to Amsterdam, it had been too easy to find, almost as if she wanted them to find it, like a false trail. Trains were an option. For intelligence agency bases it could be Berlin, London, Paris, China, Eastern Europe. China did not feel right, North Korea would follow China's lead, so if China was out so was North Korea. America, CIA possibly.

He had to get ahead of the game. He did not need full details to cast out a net and see what he could land.

"Get me the field commanders on the Phone for Europe, America, Asia and let me see, I want St Petersburg and the other potential exit points covered. I want boots on the ground checking foreigners in all hotels, guest houses, car hire firms and checks on any car stolen within Moscow."

"Colonel, that is a huge amount of information."

He let the silence build until it was uncomfortable. It was an amazing tool in getting what you want.

"I will get on it right away, Colonel."

He could feel the excitement of the chase building, adrenalin coursing through his body. That butterflies in his stomach and slight tremble to his hands. His breathing was faster than it should be, and he closed his eyes to block out the room and just bring himself back under control. He needed to be clear minded, not in a state to rush decisions and make mistakes.

He needed to plan for the phone call with the FSB Regional Heads. He needed their help, and they were people with large egos. He needed a clear timeline of events, then outline his strategy followed by a clear ask to each of them. He quickly got to work. In these situations, detail was the enemy as they would mentally just switch off, so it was about finding the balance between enough detail to set out why he needed them and high level enough that he did not bore them.

Within an hour he had some of the most powerful Intelligence personnel on the planet on an encrypted video conference. At the end of the war room was a 90-inch screen, set up so that it looked like an extension of the war room table. Almost as if the Regional Heads were sitting in the war room. They sat there looking supremely confident in their capabilities, bordering on arrogant. Josef took a couple of seconds to take it in. He started off by summarising the plot to kill his brother, the detail of the search so far and the reasoning behind the view that there is a high probability of this being a foreign intelligence agency assassination. He then outlined his view that the person or persons responsible were either now outside Russia or soon would be and that he wanted to drive them across Europe, let them know via the media they were being hunted and get them to make mistakes.

"My ask of you is to get your people monitoring airports and ferry ports that we think would be the most likely points of entry back into their host countries. The suspected agencies are the main world players in this space, SIS (UK), DGES (France), CIA (USA), BND (Germany) and Mossad (Israel); however, I would like to extend it to RAW (India) and CSIS (Canada). I want boots on the ground asap and I want to pull in your informants across the globe, someone somewhere either knows who did this or is seeing the senior people in those organisations in a flap. Any unusual behaviour in the organisation and I need to know, and we can focus more attention there. Let me know when you have your assets in place."

Josef cut the call and sat back pondering the call and how it had gone. He needed their cooperation. He could, of course, go to the Director to ensure he got it, but it always looked better if you got it yourself and Josef was ambitious. Optically he wanted it to look good.

NINE

Outside the cottage in St Petersburg, Mac was the unlucky one on stag duty; another ten minutes and he would hand over to Louise. It was raining, that low level drizzle that seemed innocuous but later when you started to get cold you realised you were wet through. So far there had been nothing to report. It was quiet and there was no noise from the surrounding neighbourhood. It was at times like this that Mac's mind would turn in on itself. For some reason he had never really figured out it was always during the small hours where the memories would start to surface. Some good and, if he was being honest with himself, some of them, he would rather forget.

Mac was born in a small town on the West coast of Scotland but moved to Edinburgh when he was still a toddler. He lived in a council estate on the North of the city. His mum was a force of nature and worked in projects helping the local community, his dad worked with one of the local utility companies. It seemed a good life until one day his dad upped and left to live with another woman. Mac was devastated – he idolised his father, the whole thing was tough to take. He realised his father was selfish and a bit of a dick, and at a young impressionable age it has a big impact on who you are.

After that, money was tight and he grew up with his mum alone. The streets of the estate were tough, unemployment was high and hard drugs were easy to find. In his early teens Mac regularly saw teenagers and adults in their early 20s shooting up with heroin, or smack as it was called on the streets. Used syringes and needles littered the hallways and parks of the estate. Edinburgh had a huge drugs problem in the 1990s. With no work and little prospect of finding one, drugs were the easy way out for many.

If you were an incomer in these places, they were dangerous, and you could easily become a target of the locals addicts needing fast cash to pay for their next fix or just needing some cash to pay for food and rent. In fact, if you were unlucky, you could even get a kicking just because you were there, and you did not fit in. Mac became a boisterous teen, always looking for adventure and was happy to go with his friends shoplifting into the city centre to make a bit of extra cash. The stuff he stole he sold round the doors and at Christmas time he would steal to order, computers, TVs stereos, shell suits. They all sold; however, you did have to pay a tax to the local gang to be allowed to do it.

That was where Mac went wrong – he was good at shoplifting, quick hands and he looked innocent, which was half the battle; however, he got greedy and started to short-change the gangs. They got hold of him one Friday afternoon, tied him to a chair and gave him what they lovingly called a punishment beating. He was lucky to survive, and he knew if he did not get out, he would end up dead before he reached 20.

He had developed good survival instincts living life the way he did, and they were telling him to run. Which was why when he turned 18, he joined the British army. He did not just want to be a squaddie but wanted something that would set him up once he left, so he joined the Royal Corps of Signals. One of his mates had been a big fan of Citizens Band radio (CB) and had built his own set up in his mother's house. They would regularly stay up until 4am talking to random people around the globe from Germany, Brazil and even Russia. He found it exciting and the prospect of working with radio in the army appealed.

He struggled during basic training. Taking orders was not a natural thing for Mac and he rebelled against authority figures, especially the Sergeant Major that for some reason had taken an instant dislike to him. Mac being Mac just could not keep that sarcastic mouth of his shut and it cost him most days. Regular punishment details of moving boulders, keeping them above his head, press-ups with them on his back and sit ups by the thousand.

He never did lose that smart mouth, but he did manage to control it, and in the process, he became hard as nails. The extra punishment meant he was fitter, stronger and leaner than the rest of the intake and when it came to the physical side, he excelled. In the classroom he was the top dog. He was naturally very intelligent; however, growing-up he just hated school. He could not see the connection between school and real life. In the army he could see the connection and it drove him on with a fire he did not think he had in him.

On graduation from basic training, he joined the Royal Corps of Signals. He got a job at the base in Hereford working alongside 22 Squadron who are normally called the SAS (Special Air Squadron).

They are the meanest, most talented sons of bitches the army has ever produced. They are one of the world's leading quick reaction teams and were made famous by the Iranian embassy siege in London where they stormed the embassy in full view of the press and freed the hostages and eliminated the terrorists, all without any friendly casualties. The fact the terrorists all died meant that there was a court case around the significant use of deadly force used on the day. One of the soldiers giving evidence behind a screen was asked why he shot a terrorist 13 times and he casually replied, "Because I ran out of bullets." It was that which made them stand out. It is rumoured it takes £6million to train each SAS soldier but that is why they are successful; nothing is left to chance.

There is something about the Scottish mentality that makes them ideally suited to this band of brothers. It might go back to the clan mentality of blood before death, but whatever it is Mac loved to be around them. He knew he would fit right in as there are always a disproportionate number of Scots in the SAS.

Mac watched them train and took it on himself to go for SAS selection. It took a year of training to get himself in the physical shape to believe he could make it through. It is still one of the most gruelling selection regimes in the world and has on occasion resulted in the death of individuals taking part. It is designed to be deliberately brutal and potentially deadly to only select individuals with a tough enough mindset to never give in and think on their feet. Mac went through it three times and failed each time.

The first time, despite all the training, he had underestimated the physical and mental toll it takes.

He was just not prepared enough; that in itself was not unusual, and the selectors liked the fact he came back for more.

On the last occasion Mac had made it all the way through including escape, evasion and eventually capture. He was excited as they pulled him into the room at the end expecting to be told he was successful. It came as a complete shock when they told him he had not been successful and he left the room totally dejected – this had been his sole focus for the last three-four years of army life. As he left the room, head down and a slow anger starting to build, a Major stepped out of the shadows and called him aside. Mac recalled that meeting vividly. The Major was probably the most unremarkable man Mac had ever seen. When he spoke, it was with a very cultured Southern English accent.

"Mac, why don't we go for a walk? I have a kind of proposition for you that I would like you to consider. I have been watching you over the last couple of years and pulled your file. I like what I see and think that we could help each other. I need people like you, people who do not stand out in a crowd and know their way around the streets. As you can imagine, people with my accent can make me stand out a bit too much in certain situations, but I think you have what I need. Your SAS selection progress shows you are mentally tough and don't crack under pressure. What I am about to offer you is a solo life, mostly undercover and at times extremely dangerous, but your country needs you, I need you. What do you think? Have I piqued your interest, old chap?"

The chat continued over the next two hours and Major Smith (Mac never did find out his real name) outlined the work. It would be undercover in Northern

Ireland during the troubles, working both sides of the Catholic / Protestant war with the British Army smack bang in the middle. Mac's mind went onto the times he was personally responsible for the capture of a number of high-ranking officials in both the IRA and the UDF. Controversially, his work also included the assassination of prominent figures on both sides, as well. Illegal perhaps, necessary certainly, and something he would never ever talk about.

In this day of war crimes tribunals, you just kept your mouth shut and remembered nothing. It was a trick learnt from the interrogation of IRA members at Castlereagh in East Belfast. Depending on which side of the line you were on, it was called torture or enhanced interrogation. If you were the recipient, the trick was to stare straight ahead, say nothing, react to nothing and don't give them a way in. The downside to this approach was it could lead to stronger interrogation techniques being used as the interrogators lost patience with you.

Mac had been gathering low level information for several months and was making friends with active participants. Mac became more vocal in his anti-British rhetoric and how he could really help the cause. His Scottish accent gave him an edge as there were terrorist sympathisers all over Scotland so it helped him fly under the radar.

He still had nightmares about the time he was grabbed off the streets of Belfast by the IRA Brigade commanders and brutally interrogated over two days. He was proud to give them nothing of note. Of course, he talked but he only gave them his false name and back story that allowed them to check up on pre-planned information about him so they could corroborate his version of the truth. The worst part of it was the simulated drowning, which was learnt from the South African Police during apartheid. Luckily it had been used on him during SAS selection. It was important he already knew how it felt and it allowed him to deal with it without panicking. All along he was just thinking I hope the hell they know what they are doing. The worry was the IRA were a bunch of amateurs and if they got their timings wrong Mac would end up in a shallow grave like so many other IRA prisoners that had gone before.

After the two days they cleaned him up, brought him to a pub with secluded booths near the Falls Road in Belfast. There he met two individuals whom he had seen mug shots of in briefing sessions as suspected IRA participants. He was told he had passed the test and was to meet senior Brigade commanders the following week. Mac left the meeting puzzled but excited – he had made a major breakthrough in his undercover work but the danger he was now in was more than ever.

He thought back to that feeling of constantly living on the edge and the toll that it took on his mental health. The bad dreams and the deaths that haunted him. Not so much the ones he carried out, but more the ones he failed to prevent. The young squaddies or the RUC policemen that died because he did not get enough intelligence, or even worse, when he knew they were going to happen but to make it known would blow his cover wide open. He was not naive enough to think that the IRA did not have its own sympathisers and informers in the British Government and the local Police / army units. That was the worst part of it – what do you hand over and what do you keep secret.

The other bit was you started to build a relationship with the "enemy". Their beliefs started to get through to you and you could start to see both sides. The IRA commanders were not daft young boys, they were university lecturers, teachers, politicians and local businessmen. Yes, the thugs very often carried out the atrocities, but the "senior management" were educated, considered and methodical. Mac became one of the most important Military Intelligence agents over a 20-year period.

Of course, the whole Northern Ireland landscape changed in the late 1990's. American funding was starting to dry up and faced with throwing rocks at the British or finding a political way forward, the IRA reluctantly entered negotiations with the British and the Good Friday agreement was born. It also meant a complete change for Mac as he drifted somewhat unexpectedly from MI5 and into SIS. From there he moved into the black ops assassination units working across the globe on the unofficial requests from SIS. He still avoided Ireland as a country, he stayed off social media and where possible avoided having his photo taken. There were bound to be people who would remember him for the wrong reasons and although the peace process still holds, grudges in that part of the world last forever. Since that time, he had lived a strange life; work became false passports, new teams and assassinations he did not always approve of. He hid that part of himself that did not approve – he had to assume that he was fighting on the side of the righteous. It was the only way you dealt with what went on. When he spent time at home with his wife and family, he buried his work as deep as it could go. Not necessarily healthy, but it was his way of doing it. As he thought about his wife, her death and his kids, he started to wonder if he had been in this game too long – was it possible he was starting to hold on too tight?

As Mac lay low in the undergrowth remembering his past, Storm was lying in bed doing the same.

By comparison to Mac and Louise, her background was different. Born into a middle-class family in Manchester, she was an only child. She was gifted in school and was an amazing problem-solver, excellent at maths and languages. She won a scholarship to Cambridge University where she studied mathematics with French and Russian.

She came to the attention of SIS after she graduated with a first-class honours degree and won the medal for being top of her class. Having briefly considered staying on to complete a PhD she eventually decided enough was enough and wanted out into the real world. SIS appealed and after joining she was based initially in the SIS building on the South bank of the Thames in Vauxhall as an analyst on the Russian desk and the growing threat of Cyber security warfare from within that country.

There was a strong tie-in with Cuba as Russia were the arm around the shoulder and protector of that regime. It became tedious after a time and like almost any occupation, the profession eventually became a job and she craved excitement.

It became known by the seniors that she wanted into the field and an opportunity came her way to train and work in several Embassies across the globe. She excelled in cultivating relationships, but she had a tendency to create a maelstrom of destruction and quickly she was given the nickname Storm. She decided to own it and entered the world of black ops where she created a name for herself.

Like everything in life, it became a double-edged sword and she found herself not wanted for the more delicate operations that required a light touch and she fell into working with the assassination teams. Storm had worked with the current team for the last few years and had grown to like them. She became the expert on communications and explosives within the team. She was frequently the spotter for Dave when he was on overwatch or doing a hit from a distance. The speed she could work things out was almost superhuman and the team loved it.

She also had an amazing ability to see patterns well before anyone else. A pattern of behaviour, a pattern of communication or even the lack of a pattern which in itself could be a line of inquiry. People by nature stick to patterns and it takes a real effort to stop doing it and that in itself could be a clue. Very little in nature is purely random. Funnily enough, there are mathematical equations that govern a lot of what happens in nature.

Her first assassination assignment had been in Libya during the Arab Spring where her target was a tribal warlord that had leanings toward Al Qaeda. She followed him home from a coffee shop in Tripoli, and 200 metres from his house she bumped into him as he turned a corner. Just as he turned to carry on his journey, Storm spun round and slit his throat. She paused and turned to make sure of the kill with a quick dagger thrust to the heart before calmly walking on. He was found an hour later when his family became concerned. No matter how many assassinations followed, she always remembered her first one. Perhaps it was the adrenalin-high that etched in onto her memory, she no longer counted how many it had been. It was kind of depressing to keep count.

After Mac's two-hour stag, he was replaced by Louise. Rather than sleep, Mac went into the living room where he met Storm making a coffee and they talked through what cars they had seen around the streets that would make a suitable getaway car. They decided on one of the more non-descript ones, rather than the flashier drug dealer type ones which would be more conspicuous and would potentially be subject to random stop and search by the local cops.

As they were not tired, they decided they may as well start now and go out for a reconnoitre and see what was about. The streets were significantly quieter in the deep of the night. Night life in St Petersburg felt even more dodgy in the outskirts of town than it did during the day, and by looking at Mac Storm could tell he was feeling the same. His eyes seemed to be everywhere checking every person out, looking to see where the next threat would come from.

They headed into a residential district where they could find cars parked overnight and if stolen around 10pm it could potentially give them a 10-hour head start before they would be reported to the local cops. It doesn't sound like much, but they could make it to Helsinki or Tallinn within that time. They looked about for the best part of three hours and found four vehicles that would do the job. They broke into each one, checked the fuel load, and under the bonnet to make sure the engine looked maintained, no oil leaks and there were no warning lights. They then locked them back up and noted the addresses. They would take nothing parked in a cul-de-sac, only from a location with an easy connection to the main routes out of town and places where there were not loads of kids hanging about late at night who might recognise the vehicle.

Job done for the night, they headed back to the cottage to get some sleep. Neither of them liked the babysitting a package, it would just slow them down and place them in more danger than they were already in. It wasn't the 72 hours wait that was necessarily the problem, they were used to waiting. An awful lot of time in the Intelligence and armed forces is spent waiting. The frustration was in not knowing the package, how much additional risk it would create and how they could mitigate it. There was nothing else they could do tonight, so they headed back to the cottage in time for Storm to take the next rotation of stag. Once there, she settled in on the edge of the undergrowth so she could hear the street noise. Nothing untoward happened, just the usual city noises of traffic, police sirens and the occasional shouting of drunk locals on their way home.

Early the next morning, Hairy Dave and Louise headed out, scouting out the train station and getting together some basic items they felt they might need now that the op was being extended. They did not yet know who or what the package was, but some items were common to most jobs. Four LED torches and four roles of black electrical tape. Sometimes a full beam was too much, and the electrical tape could tone it down to just the right amount of light. Some trail mix for food that was easy to eat and provided a mix of carbs and protein. Bombay mix was similar, but the spices meant you could smell it from a few feet away and in a tight spot you did not want that. Some bin bags containing dry clothes – no point in being cold and wet if you did not need to be. Over the counter painkillers, paracetamol and codeine were the best. You had to avoid aspirin or the other non-steroidal anti-inflammatory drugs as they thinned the blood and if you were shot it increased the chances of bleeding out. Ladies' sanitary towels and tampons. The team did not have medical dressings, and these were the next best thing. You had to stop the bleeding and keep any wounds clean. A length of rope about 5mm in diameter that could be used as a tourniquet. More ammunition would be good but too risky asking about blindly in a city you did not know, so they would have to deal with what they had and hope they did not get pinned down in a prolonged fire fight. Compression bandages, needle and thread and forceps. They all had basic field triage training. It was not about major operations, but it was about stabilisation. Stopping blood loss was the key. They would let the medical experts worry about blood poisoning and wound infections. If you stemmed the blood loss the experts would prevent the other issues.

I mean, it isn't ideal, but in a field situation where you are fleeing a determined enemy it was the best they could do. More groceries were needed, and they picked up some basic stuff. Pasta, potatoes, chicken and veg. Just enough to get them through 72 hours. Supplies bought, they took a circuitous route back to the cottage. The Ritz it was not, but it was out of the way, cheap and not the kind of place that attracted attention.

Louise was feeling a bit grubby and went to freshen up. Unfortunately the cottage only had a rather pathetic shower rather than a bath – the shower had terrible water pressure, but it was all they had. Louise sighed to herself about life having no standards and went for what can only be described as a tepid shower. It did the job in getting her clean, but it was not relaxing and not what she actually wanted. Enjoying the clean feeling, she turned on the TV and flicked through some channels, but it was just local TV stuff and she tuned out.

At 3:30pm Louise went for a walk so that she was away from the cottage for the 4pm follow-up call with Edward. She did not like the posh, educated types; they just came across as entitled and portrayed a feeling that the assassination teams were just pawns on a shadowy chess board. Only there to do the agency's bidding and ultimately expendable.

She was proud of what they did, taking out enemies of the state, but she was not naïve. In a tight spot she knew there was a possibility they would be cut adrift to fend for themselves. If it became a political embarrassment for the Government or the SIS hierarchy, they would be gone; not only that, there would be no guilt on the part of the spooks. In Louise's view they were a complete shower of Oxford / Cambridge wankers.

Louise went through the same two-factor authentication process on the telephone where there were follow-up questions and not just the one. They had to remember the phones were not secure, so details had to be sketchy and there would be no real detail on the package and why they had to be moved so quickly out of Russia. Frustrating but necessary.

"Everything ok with the holiday camp?" asked Edward.

"Best accommodation we have ever had, it's like a 5-star hotel, jacuzzi, 75-inch TV in the cinema room and amazing views over the city. It must have cost a small fortune. It is very kind of you to think of us and give us a break before coming back. Thank you."

"You are joking, yeah?"

"Oh no, it is amazing; the team can't thank you enough."

Posh boy did not know if Louise was joking or not – he lived in a parallel world to the workers. A bit flustered from not knowing how to take Louise, Edward carried on.

"I will post details onto the notice board on how to meet the package, store it and take it out of the country. You will meet tomorrow at an agreed location ready for exfil."

"One problem, we smashed all the hard drives and binned the laptops from Moscow. We could not take the chance of being caught with anything from that time," noted Louise.

"Ah yes, sensible precautions. Please take a note of this number and one of the Cyber team will talk you through what we can do to remedy that. We can't do it over this open line. 020 xxxxxx, give me an hour to set it up. Louise, I am concerned we have a leak in London, somewhere in my chain of command. I need you to take this off the books, I will set you up with new passports but don't use the usual escape routes or safe houses. I am sorry I got you involved in this. I think they are trying to get you caught and interrogated."

"You have to be fucking kidding me, Edward. Can't we just abandon this fiasco?"

"No, there is a major drama about to hit a number of financial institutions and the package has information that can stop it. Let's get him out in one piece. As an additional bonus the information we get could give us incredible access to Russian Cyber security."

An hour later Louise called the number and followed a similar two-factor authentication methodology.

"I need help in getting secure comms in place quickly. Can you help?"

"Hi, my name is Tim, just for info. Right, I want you to type in the following IP address into the browser on the phone and when it asks if you want me to take control just say yes. It is faster if I do it rather than me talking you through it. 2.19.159.xxx."

"Yup that's it."

"Excellent, ah there you are, just click on the yes box and we will get you sorted in no time." The engineer just hummed tunelessly away to himself for a few minutes before replying, "Right, that is you sorted; I have set you up with a VPN, that's a virtual private network. I have also downloaded encryption software onto your phone which means it will have 256-byte encryption on all traffic. It also means that your voice over IP phone calls will look like they originate within the UK. As a bonus, the encryption on your phone means if it falls into the wrong hands, it will be undecipherable at least for long enough for it to no longer matter. You can now download your instructions from the following IP address I have just pinged you. The file will delete itself within 24 hours so memorise it please; under no circumstances should you print it. The other thing is the encryption takes up a lot of memory, so your phone is going to be pretty slow. Oh, and when you open up the phone it will need your fingerprint, a passcode which is, blwckP4wn2R%0k4. I would not normally put such encryption on this type of handset, but needs must and all that. Just type 2.20.95.xxx. into your browser and you will get a connection. Once on it, click on the file Operation Stranger. Any questions?"

"No, I got that, thank you for helping."

"Not a problem, ehhhh when you get back to the UK why don't you look me up and I can buy you a drink."

"Thanks, Tim, I will bear that in mind."

Louise downloaded the file and headed back to the cottage. She was intrigued with who / what the package would be and the way they could get it out of the country. Once back at the cottage Louise gathered the whole team into the living room and opened the file on her phone.

"The package is one Dimitri Antonov, who is the Russian Head of Cyber Security; now that is going to cause a stir right enough, bloody hell. He is single, only child and both parents dead, so no additional baggage. He does have a security detail though, so that will be a challenge. He is in St Petersburg tomorrow night for a cyber security conference, so we need to grab him, extract him from the conference and get him the hell out of Russia. The good thing with him being Head of Cyber Security, his online footprint is small, and he avoids media attention so his face will not be well known. Comments?"

"What is the information he has that will protect the financial institutions?" asked Storm.

"From what we have here there is going to be a coordinated cyber security attack on the main Western financial institutions that will prevent them trading. This isn't about stealing money, more about bringing the finance centres of the West to a standstill. We won't be able to pay for gas from Eastern Europe, transfer money within the UK for any institution. Within 10 days the food trolleys will be empty, and there will be riots on the streets. Total Armageddon."

"And this guy can stop it?" asked Dave.

"Apparently so," replied Louise.

The team brainstormed a plan – 24 hours was short for an operation like this, although in the current circumstances they preferred it that way. It felt short sighted of London to use a team already in play rather than a team who specialised in extractions and who had the proper time to prepare, rather than throw something together at the last minute. They would make their views known during the Operational debrief when they got back to London. The reaction to the mole in British Intelligence was one of resignation rather than anger. It did not change much other than avoiding the usual routes out of Russia and safe houses. The rest remained the same.

- Pick up passports for all from a contact in a pole dancing club St Petersburg tonight at midnight.
- Scout the Kongressnyy Tsentr Petrokongress venue where the conference was being held – it was on an island at the harbour. According to Google maps, there were nine ways off the island so a quick exit was achievable, but

they had to be quick as the lockdown by the security forces could be done in under 15 minutes. That was tight.

- Steal a car which would take five plus baggage and have a bit of power under the bonnet. If you steal it too early, it will be on the Police scanners, it you try and leave it to last minute you might not find anything decent.
- Get to the venue early enough to spot the FSB guards so they can be avoided.
- Grab the package.
- Exit St Petersburg in one piece.
- Exit Russia.

The tasks for today were the top three. All four would scout the venue late afternoon into early evening and then split up. Mac and Louise would head to steal the car while Hairy Dave and Storm would hit up the pole dancing club. It wasn't the normal pairs they split into, but Storm fancied the pole dancing club, and Hairy Dave, well he was never going to turn down that kind of opportunity… the girls just looked at him with withering looks as he sat there with a huge grin across his face.

Mac, on the other hand, had the resigned look of being the wheel man and knew he was first choice for boosting a car. That and the fact he had scouted them out the previous night. They headed out into a very wet evening in the city centre. Rain was good – most people walked with their head slightly down so it was less likely they would be noticed. Still, scouting a venue in the rain was always a bit of a chore. They went tooled up each with a Glock 17 and one of the Commando knives recently purchased. The idea was not to attract attention, so it was a last resort thing.

They headed to the conference centre and split up to walk round the venue separately, Mac and Storm took the distance approach and walked round the outskirts of the squares nearest the venue. Louise took the close-up streets nearest the venue and Hairy Dave took the inside. London had provided blueprints of the layout, but they were a few years old and some things might have changed. Dimitri would exit the conference centre via the front door and would feign losing his briefcase and would head to an exit at the rear of the centre where he would be greeted by the team. Well, that was how it looked on paper, but in reality nothing is ever that simple and the team needed to plan a number of different scenarios including an abort one. Edward would not like it, but no point in them and the package being killed.

After the allotted two-hour scouting trip, the team met up at a small café bar which overlooked the venue to discuss what they had seen that they could use to their advantage and what the risks were that they needed to eliminate, manage, or just accept.

When they entered the café, they took a good look around, picked a table that had a good view of the door and was away from other patrons. Subconsciously they looked for other ways out, scanned the other patrons for anyone trying too hard not to be noticed or who did not seem to fit into the tourist vibe. This was not a café for locals. The waitress headed towards them and Louise automatically looked at her shoes. You could tell a lot by someone's footwear. Simple black shoes that had seen better days and were scuffed meant she looked right. They were the type of shoes you wore all day every day and when you got home you threw them in a cupboard under the stairs, so you forgot about them until the next day.

They ordered some basic tourist food and a strong coffee and just tried to blend in with the normal customers the café saw day-to-day in the summer months with the cruise ships and flocks of European middle classes that wanted to see how the Tsars lived. Like most tourists they went ooohhhh and aaahhhh over the opulence and ignored the fact that to achieve that opulence the Tsars overtaxed the populace to a point where they could not afford to eat. Any ruler who believes they have a divine right to do what they want has a tendency to be self-absorbed and feel they deserved whatever they wanted, and it was the poor workers' job to make it happen.

As they waited for the drinks to arrive, they took turns to outline the pros and cons of what they had seen. Storm took notes and they each raised questions as they came to light. Every angle of this had to be explored, nothing left to chance. These types of events would have FSB in the audience just mingling and checking out those in attendance. Both internal Russian and foreign. After they had eaten and talked through all the information they had gleaned, they headed back into the area and did it all again, but this time they swapped roles. Louise and Hairy Dave took the outskirts, Mac took the close up, and Storm took the inside. It might sound sexist, but Storm might pick up other things on rest room layout or where the queues would be. There are never enough female rest rooms in venues, and they inevitably build up a queue, especially in-between the speeches.

Surveillance completed, they headed for a different coffee bar further away from the venue. They went back through what they had seen, and a few additional items were raised. Some clarification questions from the previous session answered and they now believed they had seen enough to formulate a plan. The inside would be tricky as access to backstage would be strictly controlled. Each entrance would have security, and although they were unlikely to be FSB, they did tend to be big and handy in a fight. Storm had boosted a security guard's pass when she feigned falling over and flashed him her best can you help look before limping out of the venue. So, the team could get one member of the team inside and backstage. It was risky as a new face might stand out, but it was worth the risk. Outside, the alley had a couple of down and outs sitting in it drinking cheap vodka – with the right disguise one of the team would fit right in and be in control of the alley, which was essential in getting the package out and away. The trick was to ensure they had a disguise for the package so that by the time they walked the length of the alley he would be unrecognisable from the Head of Cyber Security. Men in grey suits looked the same the world over.

Mac would park the getaway car the in the street near the venue and stay with it. Not necessarily in it, but nearby. There were no CCTV cameras nearby and other vehicles in the area would make it blend in. No point in being in a multistorey with a single exit when you needed to be away sharpish. There was no obvious overwatch point so they would have one outside the venue scanning police frequencies and scanning the crowd. They wanted to get the package and get away with no fuss. Weapons in this circumstance were a defensive option only. Hands before knives and knives before guns. They were comfortable with the venue, the plan around it and getting the package to the car. It was now 9:30pm so Mac and Louise were heading to steal the getaway car and Hairy Dave and Storm were heading to scout out the pole dancing club.

"Have fun, you two, enjoy the show," said Mac with a slight twinge of bitterness in his voice. Storm just giggled and winked at him.

"Right, Louise, let's head out of the city centre and see which of the vehicles we saw last night we fancy the most."

With that they headed out of the bright lights of the city centre and into the shadier areas of St Petersburg. There was always an element of danger in this part of an Op. It just took some junkie getting lucky and you picked up an injury. With the added complexity of the package, they did not need a last-minute hitch. They headed through the back streets and just did a few checks to make sure they were not being followed. They avoided the alleyways, having learnt their lesson from the last couple of nights. There was no need for shortcuts or taking unnecessary chances.

It took about 45 minutes of walking to get to where they wanted to be, and they checked out three of the vehicles they had scouted out previously. They fancied an older BMW 7 series. It was black, tinted windows and had a 4-litre engine and new tyres. It was a reasonable indicator it had been well maintained. Mac went to work on the driver's door while Louise stood watch. It would have been easier if they knew where the owner lived, and they could use a key sensor extender to fool the car into thinking the owner was unlocking the car.

There were two issues with that approach, unfortunately. One, it was parked near a block of flats so the key extender would not extend that far, and two, it was an older model with a different lock. This one you used your knife to put a hole in a tennis ball. Put the tennis ball to the lock and hit it hard. The air pressure from the tennis ball forces the locking mechanism. In the hands of Mac, he was in the car within five seconds, only marginally slower than the owner would be with the key. Nice and natural. He then took a screwdriver out of his pocket, smashed off the plastic housing and forced the lock to start the car. In Edinburgh as a youth, stealing cars was just part of growing up. They were not sold for profit really, but just because you could – the thrill of joyriding was what it was all about. There had been a few close encounters with the law, which was why he now only took cars with powerful engines, even if they were that bit older.

As the car started, Louise jumped into the passenger seat and they sedately headed off down the road in their new vehicle. They drove about a mile and Mac pulled over and was lying under the vehicle checking each wheel arch, the boot, under the front dashboard and popped open the bonnet to check for a tracking device. It looked like a pimp's car so he doubted he would find one, but he did not want to take a chance. He dropped the car off at the cottage and put an old tarpaulin over it and some rubbish so it would not be seen easily from the road and made it look like it had sat there for months.

They then went to steal a second car. Nothing powerful this time, just an old run about.

Mac wanted to head back to the conference centre and drive about. You got a different view of the city from a car and he wanted to be comfortable in a car chase he could navigate his way out of the city. They checked out the bridges off the island the conference centre was on and rated the routes on how fast they would be able to move, and the risk of each route being blocked by the law. From the list they picked their top three. They then went back along each route one at a time etching them in Mac's memory, so driving them would be second nature, before dumping the car and heading back to the cottage.

Whilst Mac and Louise were stealing cars and driving about, Hairy Dave and Storm picked a bar near the pole dancing club. Remarkably, the club was near the city centre and not in some dive in a shadier part of town. They did not want to go too early as you would stand out if it was quiet and that made you memorable. They ordered vodka and coke and sat nursing their drinks. They wanted to blend in but not end up impaired by alcohol.

At 11:45 they entered the club, giving a nod to the doorman and hoping they did not get into a fight with him later on. He was massive, well over six foot six inches and barrel chested. In a city of gangs and drunk tourists, it paid to have a deterrent on the door. The guy could have been a pussycat; however, the bent nose and scars around his eyes told a different story.

As they entered the club, they did so slowly, taking in the carpet their feet stuck to and the neon lights on the various small stages where ladies in various stage of undress did their pole routines. They had been told by Edward to reach out to a girl, mid-thirties with blue hair, going by the name of Sky. Sky blue, it made sense I suppose in a sex industry sort of way. Hairy Dave and Storm sat in a corner booth, ordered some beers which were massively over-priced and watched Sky do her routine.

"That's impressive, you know; it takes a really strong core to do that kind of routine," commented Storm.

Dave said nothing as he was mesmerised by Sky. Storm smiled and by the look of the bulge in Dave's trousers she knew Sky had a new fan. Sky finished her routine, saw Sky and Dave sitting in the booth, came over and sat down.

"First time in the city?" enquired Sky.

"No, but it is our first time in the club," replied Dave.

"Did you like the routine?"

"Very dramatic."

The pass phrase completed, Sky told them the envelope was stuffed down the back of the chair. Dave reached back and retrieved it, quickly checking it contained five passports. Once he was happy all five were there, he relaxed.

"Whereabouts in the UK are you from?" Sky asked in a broad Manchester accent.

"Fuck me, I thought you were a local," replied Dave. "I am a London boy me, Cockney through and through."

"I am finished here at the end of the season and will be heading home, look me up next time you are up North, here is my number – oh and I do like a guy in a navy-blue jacket."

Sky passed across a scrap of paper with a number on it and went back to work. Storm and Dave stayed for a few more minutes and slowly made their way out of the club, checking to see if anyone was giving them undue interest. It was difficult to tell as Storm seemed to have a fan club of her own as she got admiring looks from the men in suits who were frequenting the club. Storm clicked that this was why SIS would have an asset in such a club in Russia – drunk men in suits paying for pole dancers were an easy target to charm for information and with the Conference centre nearby they would not only be locals but from all over Russia. There would not be military secrets to be had here; however, Intelligence these days was also about Industrial espionage, political power and Russian gangs trying to sell drugs into the West. These days it was more about stealing computer logins, mobile phones and just getting access to IT information.

Intelligence agencies had other ways of doing that, but it only worked to a certain extent. When people downloaded stuff off the internet, they were full of spyware, some from criminal gangs but other stuff was from intelligence agencies. When you thought you were downloading the latest film or the latest game, very often you were also downloading spyware that could access your location, all your files and every keystroke you made. People always were the weak link in cyber security and with laptop computers and mobiles that would not improve anytime soon. It was well known that Intelligence agencies across the globe tried to access power grids, IP Network providers and Transport agencies. In some instances, they have been very successful and if you did not keep your laptops, phones and network elements fully patched you were very vulnerable. That is why Government agencies use 256-bit encryption software – it kept their communications secure from prying eyes.

Hairy Dave and Storm headed back to the cottage with their new passports, taking a circuitous route and making doubly sure they were not being followed. It would be a disaster at this late stage.

TEN

Meanwhile in Moscow, Josef was in a bad mood – they did not have anything solid as yet and it was starting to get to him. The next war room briefing was just about to start, and he had his fingers crossed that they had something to go on.

"Ok, ladies and gentlemen, what do we now have? I will go round the table, keep it brief and high level unless I ask you to go into detail."

Josef pointed to the grey suited gentleman sitting beside him.

"Colonel, we have followed up on the flights and train tickets that we traced using the waitress's credit card and they are a dead end. No one checked onto the flight and no one matching the description of the girl boarded the train. We stopped the train and did a full search from one end to the other and she was not on it. There were four people who did not turn up for the flight so we should assume there are at least four of them – by the names it looks like two men and two women. We have the passport numbers from the pre-flight information; however, we do not know if they are genuine or not, I suspect not. That is all."

Josef pointed to the next along.

"We checked all the CCTV from a five-block area surrounding the Bolshoi and we traced a black SUV seen in the area to a parking lot a few blocks away. It had been wiped down, removing all fingerprints, and that in itself makes it suspicious. We do have a photo of the front passengers from a traffic camera, but it was old equipment, and you cannot make them out clearly. It is very pixelated. We don't know if they left on foot or swapped vehicles. We are currently checking all vehicles parked in the car park at that time and which left within a one-hour window. I have taken the liberty of checking the other nearby carparks as well, just in case they changed car parks. A bit of a long shot."

Josef continued along the table checking in with each department chief in turn before carrying out a quick summary at the end and allocating the next set of actions.

"We now believe we have four targets, two male and two female, who left the scene in a black SUV that was abandoned within the city limits. We know they did not leave by plane or by train so that makes it highly likely they swapped vehicles either in or nearby the carpark," summarised Josef.

"Actions, ladies and gentlemen:"

- I want all vehicles checked in the area surrounding the car park everything in and out of that area.
- I want to know if they split up or they are still together.
- I want to know which direction they were travelling in, either together or separately.
- I want photos – some camera somewhere will have caught them either on bridges or toll

roads, but there will be one there so let's get
on it please.

"Next update in 60 minutes," stated Josef as he eye-
balled each member of the team. They were starting
to look jaded. He needed to be careful – drive them
too hard and they would get tired and make mistakes.
Mistakes happened in life, but in this investigation, it
would cost him valuable time.

Sixty minutes later and they had the lead they
needed: a camera caught the waitress leaving a car
park in the passenger seat of a sedan, just a normal car
but they now at least had something. They then got
another photo heading north towards the E105. The
only question now was: is it a false trail or were they
heading to St Petersburg?

"How long does it take to get to St Petersburg?"
asked Josef.

"About seven hours by the most direct route,"
replied one of the department heads.

"That means they have quite a lead, people, they
might even be out of the country by now. Let's get on
it. I want that car found in St Petersburg asap. Let's get
all camera footage along the route and into the city,
and get me photos of the other three accomplices asap."

With that, Josef left the war room. He was gaining
on them but not fast enough; he knew he was going
to need some luck to get ahead of them. With that, he
had a thought – rather than luck maybe he changed
the playing field to one of his liking.

"Get me the FSB officer in London on a secure
line."

"Right away, Colonel."

"Michail, thank you for taking my call, did you hear about my brother?"

"I did Josef, most unfortunate, my condolences. How can I help?"

"What assets do we have in SIS?"

"Why do you ask?"

"We have evidence this was an assassination on my brother, and we are tracking them towards St Petersburg, but they are too far ahead. I want to get ahead of them and see what information we can glean from SIS. They hit one of ours, Michail. They have to pay."

"Let me see what I can get. It usually takes time to verify what we are getting is genuine as I prefer to get information from three sources. What I get will have to be unverified if it is this time constrained."

"I understand the risks, just get me what you can."

ELEVEN

B ack in the cottage, the team worked out a detailed plan of what they needed to do both inside and outside the conference hall. It made them relax knowing they had a way to make this work. With the planning complete, they wanted a summary before taking turns at stag during the night. As they stayed in one place it only increased the risk of them being found and an FSB armed response unit capturing them.

Russia did not sign the Geneva Convention, so if you got caught you were in for a rough ride. Not that the Geneva Convention had any teeth – it was really just a standard for how prisoners should be treated. As the US showed in Afghanistan and Iraq, even if a country did sign it, you could still be tortured or, as it is sometimes called, you would face enhanced interrogation. They could call it anything they wanted – to the individual it really just meant a world of pain. Even if you did give them the information you had they would torture you until they were convinced you were not lying. In essence that is how the US killed Usama Bin Laden. A whole host of prisoners faced enhanced interrogation until they got enough leads to get a location. The debate around torture versus saving lives is one that will never be solved as it really comes down to the individuals running a country at a particular moment in time. For the team in St Petersburg, it really came down to one thing. Don't get caught.

"I am concerned about the potential leak inside SIS. If the FSB are aware of this Op, it could be a trap," stated Mac.

"Yeah, that has been nagging at me as well," replied Dave.

"I get that, but we still need to get the package out of Russia. Is there a way we could adapt the instructions from Edward so we get the package, just in a different way?" answered Storm.

"What do you have in mind, babe?" asked Louise.

"So, the only bits London know about are where we get Dimitri at the rear of the conference centre and our route out of St Petersburg up to Helsinki. We could change one or both of those. Views?"

"Ok, there was a fire exit to the side of the stage that opens out into an alleyway. We allow the package to complete his talk and leave the stage, but I intercept him and get him to head to the rest room near the fire exit. We neutralise his security detail quietly and we leave via the fire exit. He would then just step out into the alley into the welcoming arms of the team and disappear. He wouldn't be ready for it, but we could get it to work. It would mean two people inside the conference centre. Me to intercept him and get a message to go to the restroom and out the exit and Dave to be there to deal with his security detail. We leave the escape route as it is and just hope we get the jump on them and get over the border before they work the rest out," stated Storm.

"Sounds to me like it would work," replied Mac.

"Dave, you have the inside, you will need to get yourself a security guard uniform and boost an extra pass. Is there anything from the layout surveillance you think you will need?" stated Louise.

"I will get some duct tape, cable ties and a taser. Anyone gets in my way and they will be dealt with hard, fast and silently. I just hope the package knows what he is doing and hasn't set us up for a fall," answered Dave.

"I will be in the alley in disguise – of all of us, I am the most likely to be recognised from the Bolshoi so a good disguise would be helpful.

"Storm, that means you are with Dave inside the centre. Mac, that means you are on wheels duty and pre-meet overwatch if you can find a spot."

The team split up the following morning with Dave and Storm heading into the city to get what they needed to look the part. Dave needed to fit in as a security guard so everything black, and Storm needed a good disguise to make Louise look homeless.

Dave went to a basics shop and bought black cargo trousers with good deep side pockets, black polo shirt, black cap and black blouson jacket. He would steal a branded jacket and cap at the venue to ensure he blended into the rest of the guards. The disguise was just to avoid scrutiny as he arrived at the venue and to get inside initially. He just needed to find someone his size on arrival. Dave then went looking for a Taser and found one in an army surplus store. Nothing fancy and handheld rather than the ones that shot out wires. If he needed it then it would be up close and personal.

After Dave completed his look, Storm went shopping – an old wool coat that was threadbare from a charity shop, old trainers that were scuffed and she would make look even older with a rub of sandpaper back at the cottage. An old fur trappers' hat that she would pluck a lot of the fur from to make it look old and scabby, and a grey wig that she would brush through with melted beeswax. Last she wanted an old shopping cart filled with blankets and empty plastic bottles.

Even in this day and age, people rarely looked closely at the homeless. They would struggle to give a description beyond the obvious clothing, even height and weight were difficult to judge as most homeless people stooped, might well walk with a limp, and with layers of old clothes judging weight was almost impossible. Storm was very particular with disguises and detail counted – a well-groomed person with an old coat on just would not cut it; it was important to look the part and, on this occasion, to smell the part as well. Once back at the cottage she would get a bottle and fill it with urine so she could spread it around the area she was sitting in. Hopefully not to get too much on her but if she did, she did, it was just one of those things. She also bought cling film so she could take a shit, wrap it up and take it with her to the alley. Just another smell to spread that would deter anyone wanting to arrest or move her. The small details provided that level of authenticity she required. Sometimes her attention to detail would frustrate the team, but it had kept them out of trouble on a number of occasions.

Back at the cottage, Mac and Louise were cleaning it down, all the rooms wiped down to reduce the risk of fingerprints and DNA. It is impossible to be forensically clean when you have stayed somewhere for a few nights, but it would pass an initial look. Suddenly they got an alert on Louise's phone that one of the cameras in the garden had picked up an intruder.

"Mac, get your ass over here, we have an intruder," whispered Louise.

"Shit, have we been found?" asked Mac.

Louise shared the video feed streaming over the cottage WiFi to her phone. The camera was facing the trees on the RHS of the property near to the stolen car. The intruder was not moving, but was using a monocular telescope to watch the house.

"He is wearing a camouflage jacket and hat to make sure he is not easy to spot in the undergrowth. His face is obscured by a monocular telescope and is covered in camouflage body paint. This is not the look of a casual peeping tom and unlikely to be a gang member looking for the car. They would not dress like that. Looks like he recently moved position to get a better view of the front entrance to the cottage and that is what triggered the camera."

"We need to check the other angles and make sure he is alone before one of us slips out of a window at the back and circles round behind him. We need to get him alive as we don't know if he is up here on a punt or if this is a precursor to a fully armed raid."

"You take the back and LHS, and I will take the front and RHS."

They spent 10 minutes checking every bush, tree and blade of grass, looking for an outline. They used black and white vision scopes as it is easier to pick up an outline in black and white than it is in colour.

"Looks like a lone wolf, Mac. You slip out the back and circle round and I will make an appearance near some windows to keep him interested. How long do you need?"

"Twenty mins max – it isn't the circling round that takes time, it is the creeping up behind."

With that, Mac exited the cottage from a rear window and made a dash for the nearest bushes on the exact opposite side to the target. He slowly circled round through neighbouring gardens until he was directly behind the target. The last bit was the hardest – he needed to creep up without being heard and that took time. The fear was the target was in radio contact with a backup team and had already radioed in that he had found them, and the backup was on its way to apprehend them. Mac carefully made his way through the undergrowth in a commando crawl, delicately moving twigs likely to snap out of his way before moving forward. He was conscious of the time, but stealth was more important. He needed to take the target alive but quietly, and that meant being up close and personal. His commando crawl took him to within 20 feet, from which he had an unobstructed view of him.

The target was lying in the prone position and in camouflage gear head to toe. This was definitely a planned operation and that probably meant a Government agency. Unlikely to be the local Police as they would just drive up and knock on the front door. It was more likely local FSB; the big question was whether he is operating under local command and this was just checking on foreigners not doing the normal tourist stuff or was this on the orders of Moscow.

"I have a gun pointed at your head, place your hands behind your back where I can see them."

"Don't shoot, I am unarmed."

"Stand up, keep your hands behind your back and move slowly towards the cottage. If you so much as twitch in the wrong direction you will be dead before you can blink."

Once inside the cottage, Mac kept aim on the intruder while Louise tied him to a kitchen chair. Hands tied behind his back and feet tied to the front chair legs. He was about five-foot eight inches tall, slim build, receding brown hair and approximately mid-thirties in age. He looked nervous as his blue eyes darted about the room. He knew he was in a whole lot of trouble. His nerves suggested this was a new experience to him and he had not undergone interrogation before and that could play to the team's advantage.

"What is your name and why are you here?"

"I am Adrian Yahontov of the FSB."

He was looking carefully at Mac and Louise, trying to judge by their reaction if being in the FSB was a good or a bad thing.

"Thank you, Adrian, where are you based?"

"I am based here in St Petersburg."

"Why were you watching the cottage, Adrian?"

"Orders came from Moscow to look out for four people that may have come from Moscow and committed a high-level crime in the city."

"Do you know what that crime was and why you were watching us?"

"I am just an agent trying to do my job, I don't get told such things. There was a report of an assault in an alleyway a couple of days ago by a westerner that took on two local gang members and left them unconscious – they still had weapons and cash, so it piqued my interest. I checked out local holiday rentals looking for an anomaly and after asking neighbours they told me there were four adults renting this cottage. I was just following up a lead. I am ambitious and with Moscow involved this could be a good career break for me."

"Who else knows you are here, Adrian?"

There was a slight pause and Adrian looked away and to the right before responding.

"I told my superior I would be here; he is expecting a call from me within an hour."

"You are lying to me, Adrian, why are you lying to me?"

The team needed to know for sure. Louise looked at Mac who nodded to a bucket in the corner and Louise disappeared from the room and filled the bucket full of water and came back carrying a thick hand towel. Mac tipped Adrian's chair backwards so it was leaning on another chair and Louise pulled the towel over Adrian's face as tightly as she could. Adrian was squirming and moaning and trying hard to break his hands and feet free from the chair. Mac picked up the bucket and poured the water over the towel that Adrian was holding. Mac counted slowly for 30 seconds and Louise released the towel allowing Adrian to breathe. Thirty seconds was the minimum and after 10 seconds the technique was repeated, this time for 40 seconds. With the head tilted back water ran into the nasal cavity and you felt as though you were drowning. At that point they let Adrian sit upright and he vomited up water and continuously coughed, trying to get the water out of his airways. Adrian looked helplessly around the room, eyes darting everywhere.

"Adrian, I need you to answer this question truthfully or we will need to do all this again. Do you understand me, Adrian?"

"Yes, please don't do it again, I don't want to die."

"Just answer the question truthfully, Adrian, and it can all be over."

"Who did you inform that you were coming here today to watch this cottage?"

"I did not tell anyone; I am here alone." Adrian had a tone of someone who feared he was going to die alone and there was no one coming to save him.

"How do I know you are telling me the truth, Adrian? Maybe I need to do the water again. Do you want me to do the water again, Adrian? Are you telling me the truth?"

"I am telling you the truth, I am here alone, I told no one. No more water please."

As Mac picked up the bucket of water Adrian began to sob uncontrollably, and his bladder went as he pissed himself in fear.

Louise put her hand on Mac's arm.

"I don't think we need to do it again; look at him, he isn't holding anything back."

They moved into the other room and discussed what they needed to do.

"We could kill him and eliminate the threat," suggested Mac.

"We could but the gunshot would alert the neighbours and that would just arouse more suspicion. We are out of here this evening – we could tie him up, gag him and put him in the boot of the car. He recognises us now so we can't let him go before the package arrives."

"It makes sense to me, but let's wait on the others and talk it through with everyone. We all need to be on the same page on this one."

An hour later, Dave and Storm arrived back from their shopping trip. As they walked through the door, they saw Adrian strapped to a chair, hooded and gagged.

Mac beckoned them all into the other room and in low voices they discussed how they had found him, who he was and the enhanced interrogation to get to the truth on who else knew he was here.

Dave kicked off the discussion on what to do with him.

"There is no real benefit to putting him in the boot of a stolen car. It actually makes it more likely he will be discovered than leaving him here. The only other option is we slit his throat."

"Storm, views?"

"I am not up for slitting the throat of someone tied to a chair – he has seen two faces but that is it. We have another three days of the lease here so it is unlikely he will be discovered before then. I vote we leave him here tied to a chair and we carry on with getting the package out of the country this evening."

There were general nods of agreement around the room. They moved Adrian to a cupboard in the centre of the house and barricaded the door. That way he was away from prying eyes and in the unlikely event he managed to get rid of the gag it was equally unlikely his cries for help would be heard.

They parked the problem of Adrian from their mind and went through the plan one final time, watches synchronised and bags, guns, knives and taser all checked one final time. Dave checked the Lobaev SVLK -14 S sniper rifle they had for the Moscow job. There was no reason to suspect something had happened to it, but he would rather know for sure.

With that they left the cottage, locked all the windows and doors and headed to the car in the driveway. Mac took the old tarpaulin off the car, started it and they headed into town at a pace that was legal and would not attract attention. Mac turned a number of corners and checked his mirrors for any sign of someone following, but everything was clear.

In the cupboard, Adrian heard them leave and was trying desperately to break free, but his hands and feet remained stubbornly tied.

TWELVE

Josef had taken a 60-minute nap sitting in his office chair and woke groggily and looking a bit guilty as there was a knock on his door.

"Colonel, we have a lead, a strong one at that, the team are gathered in the war room, waiting for you."

As Josef entered the war room, he could tell there was a mood of optimism; the jaded body language had lifted.

"Gentlemen, I believe we have made some progress, who is leading on the update?"

"Colonel, we have found the car they used to escape Moscow in St Petersburg, they did not follow the E105 as we thought they would and our cameras never picked them up. It looks like they took one of the back roads to deter surveillance. We found the vehicle in a long stay car park near St Petersburg airport. It has different number plates on it, but we are sure it is the same car."

"What make you so sure?"

"The number plates are for a red version of the same car, not grey, and there are no fingerprints within the vehicle, at least from the initial check – we have still to complete a full forensic examination of the vehicle. No car that has travelled for 10 hours has no fingerprints – it has clearly been wiped down."

"What about flights from St Petersburg, trains, cars?"

"That is the strange thing, we have been through CCTV footage from the airport and the waitress has not boarded a plane. We have checked car rental companies, trains and she has not left the country by normal means. I don't really understand, but it looks like they are still in St Petersburg, holed up somewhere."

Josef was pacing up and down the room as he processed the information and working it through in his mind. He was not someone who verbalised half ideas.

"I want checks with the local police on stolen cars, recent crime, stolen guns etc, anything involving foreigners to be fully reviewed by local FSB and entered onto our database we are using to coordinate this investigation. Recheck all flights out of the country, car hires and trains. Also get the local police to look into any false passports from their gang activity. They are holed up in St Petersburg for a reason. I want all internet activity and mobile calls. There is no way they are working this alone; they have to have been in contact with handlers."

"Colonel, the local FSB are already checking out recently booked accommodation by foreigners."

"Excellent, let us not assume they are on foreign passports – if this is state sponsored, then they may well have fake passports so let's widen the search. We can draft in help if we need it. I want every hotel, Bed and Breakfast, rental property and campsite phoned and logged on the database asap. Someone in St Petersburg knows who these people are and potentially why they are still there."

With that Josef left the war room and headed back to his office to once again reach out to the FSB contact in London.

"Michail, have you managed to find out anything for me yet? I know I am pushing hard but this is critical to our investigation."

"Ah Josef, it isn't like you to push this hard, you are normally like a chess master and moving your pieces quietly across the board and assessing their import to your overall strategy."

"I know, Michail, but these are unusual times and they demand unusually fast results."

"My source has revealed that there is an operation underway, there are loads of closed-door meetings in the lower levels of the SIS offices, the ones used to keep prying eyes away and conference calls with GCHQ who have put additional resource on the Russia desk. I do not have specifics yet, but they are working on it. We have to strike the right balance between pushing hard for answers and the risk of burning an asset when the assassination has already taken place."

"I understand, Michail, I would prefer more information when you can get it before they get the chance to leave the country. We can get them and interrogate them before parading them in front of the world's press. I will reach out to Mossad and CIA as well, rather than assume this is the operation they are referring to."

"One other thing, Josef, they are picking up chatter about a defection in the offing. They don't know at what level or from where. Probably not connected but I thought I would throw it into the mix. I need this kept between us, Josef. It cannot get into your investigation records. The defection could be someone within that room and this would burn our source."

"I agree, Michail, thank you, and see whether you can get a location from your source."

Josef sat down in his worn leather chair and pondered what he had just been told. He could not afford to burn a source in SIS. They took years to cultivate and longer to get them into a position of power where they were really useful. SIS were stung in the 1940s and 50s by the Cambridge five. Of course, times were different then. There was empathy with the Soviet Union and perhaps communism was seen as extreme, but socialism across Europe was growing. Although the Soviet Union has gone, Russia remains a dominant player in world politics and is still seen as a disruptor.

Something did not feel right about the team staying in St Petersburg. As a chess player you get a feel for how your opponent plays, whether it is their opening moves or how they consolidate in the middle; you could start to recognise the patterns. In intelligence it was all about the patterns; it might be the digital age, but the patterns were still there. A hit team got out of the country as fast as possible, it left the smallest footprint and was therefore the most difficult to track. Josef could understand going north to St Petersburg rather than getting a flight out of Moscow as airports had security galore and you could track suspects across the globe, but to stay in St Petersburg was just wrong on every level. No hit team would do that. Something else was at play here, something unusual.

Whoever was running this operation in London looked to have made a mistake. Josef was a good enough chess player to look at any opening or potential mistake with suspicion, especially one that stuck out the way this one did. He decided to let his subconscious work the problem and walked along the corridor into the war room to look at the story wall that had all the information they had gathered so far, with links drawn in green where they either knew for a fact they were links or in red where they were suspected links.

As he was looking at the wall, he followed a red link line to an FSB operative in St Petersburg who had been red circled.

"Who can tell me why this man is circled in red?"

"He is missing in St Petersburg. He left the office to follow up on a couple of tenuous leads that the rest of his team had discounted. He is seen as one of those types who can't look at the bigger picture."

"Get me his personnel file and find out what the tenuous leads were asap."

Josef did not like things that stood out, the outliers in an otherwise normal pattern, but what he had learnt over the years was rather than just dismiss them as an outlier he should investigate them. Something about this man going missing was bothering him. He could, of course, just be having an affair and was with his mistress during work time, but it could be something linked to his investigation.

Thirty minutes later he had the personnel file, and he knew this was not someone having an affair. Adrian was detail conscious, meticulous even and him going missing was very much out of character for someone who turned up to work an hour early and left mid-evening, every evening. He might not be the best guy to sit next to in the pub, but he would know his city inside out and which gangs led which district and who the key players were. Josef went striding back along to the war room, a real spring in his step. He knew he was onto something.

Within the hour he had five addresses that were being investigated by Adrian.

"I want eyes inside each of these dwellings asap; how do we storm five separate buildings in St Petersburg simultaneously? We have to assume each building contains the assassin and their team, that they are heavily armed and extremely dangerous. We probably need five teams of eight agents, so that is 40-armed response agents. How many do we have in St Petersburg?"

"Colonel, we have 20 at any one time in St Petersburg, so we need to supplement the local teams with ones from Moscow and we will need local agents prioritised to each dwelling to back up the armed response agents in order to interrogate and document everything they find at each dwelling."

"Flight time is 75 minutes, so I want boots on the ground and ready to execute within three hours. Take whatever units you need in St Petersburg and prioritise them onto this, people."

Josef left the war room excited and pensive at the same time. He had a nagging feeling that he had missed something, his chess brain was firing a warning shot that somewhere in all of the information he had missed something vital, some small piece of information that he would look back on at a later date and wonder how on earth he had missed it. He was well aware, though, that someone's biggest asset could easily be their biggest weakness. A man blessed with patience could be seen as indecisive. A strong decision maker could be seen as hasty. For Josef the only bad decision was the one you failed to make.

THIRTEEN

Mac parked the car in a multi-storey car park, away from prying eyes and unlikely to attract attention. The team got to work without conversation. The time for chitchat was over and it was time for game faces. Storm was dressed as a homeless tramp – long greasy grey hair, an oversized woollen coat over multiple layers of jumpers, walking boots and grubby fur hat that came down over her ears. She had a pensioner's shopping cart filled with odds and ends and covered with soiled looking blankets that had a distinct odour of piss and alcohol. Inside the cart she had a bag she would give to the package as he left the conference centre to change his appearance.

Hairy Dave was top to toe in black security guard garb, black steel toe capped boots and baseball cap including earpiece, ID pass and black backpack. Mac was dressed as a tourist, nothing flashy or memorable, greys, beige or blues. Mac had a basic camera around his neck and a bottle of water in his hand. Those inside or just outside the venue had to be the most convincing and took the most time to make sure they looked and walked the part.

Louise took on a meek shuffle and walked with head down avoiding eye contact as those who are at the mercy of the world do. If you avoid eye contact, not only do you get noticed less but people in general tend to leave you in peace. Other than law enforcement, who seem to have a hard on to make life difficult around the world for those who need help the most. Hairy Dave walked with an arrogance and confidence of those in the security business.

"You didn't really have to practise that walk, Dave; you were born to play a self-important wanker." Mac grinned as he winked at Louise.

"Awww, thank you, I would like to dedicate this award to my dad who I used as my role model for this part and to my current team who I met at Wankers Anonymous at the start of this particular world tour."

"Hahahaha, you are such a dick," laughed Louise.

The team split up as they headed to the car park exit. Mac heading to a coffee shop near the venue to carry out initial surveillance at a distance. Louise moving slowly past the venue before eventually moving to the alley at the side of the venue, and Hairy Dave and Storm wandering towards the venue at a sedate pace. They did not want to get there too early. They split up, Dave the security guard heading directly to the venue and Storm as a delegate dressed in jeans and a t-shirt, wandering around near the venue making sure nothing was amiss.

As Dave approached the venue, he noticed another security guard dressed in back but with his ID on his belt and a black baseball cap with an embroidered company logo on it.

Dave put on a quick jog and targeted the other guard and hit him hard and ensured the poor chap fell to the ground. Dave apologised profusely, extended his hand and helped the chap to his feet. As he did so he put his hand on the victim's waist as he patted him in apology, retrieved the ID from his belt and then bent over to pick up the chap's baseball cap, with sleight of hand swapping it for his own non-branded one, and then placed it on the chap's head.

"I am so sorry, my man, can I buy you a coffee as a way of apology?"

"No, it's ok, just a bruised ego and a couple of scratches."

"I insist, it is the least I can do. How do you take it?"

"Just white, thank you."

With that, Dave headed to a street vendor selling hot coffee and ordered two white coffees as his ID theft victim stood there waiting, none the wiser to the crime and thankful of the offer of a coffee on a chilly evening.

Dave appeared back grinning, with two coffees in hand and passed one to the other security guard and they both headed into the venue.

Dave chatting away with ease on how a cyber security conference would be his idea of hell and why did a bunch of techy geeks need physical security anyway.

Mac finished a coffee and wandered close to the venue, trying to pick out FSB within the crowd. The local police stood out in their uniform, but it was the local FSB that concerned them more. Mac picked out two, but he was expecting significantly more, and this troubled him. His experience in Northern Ireland was invaluable in this situation. You could tell people with a security background in a crowd, and it took time to lose that ever watchful look. Mac had it down to a tee. He was now in his sixties, old for this game, but he still had the edge on most and in a surveillance situation there were none better.

"I have only spotted two so far," stated Mac.

"I got one – the stiff in the grey jacket, she is trying too hard to blend," replied Louise.

"The second one is the guy in the red jacket," replied Mac.

"Good eye, Mac. How do you do it?" stated Louise.

"It is all in the walk and the head movement," replied Mac.

"Military men struggle to change the walk they practised for months on end – when they try to, they shorten their stride, but they still can't lose the regularity of the stride pattern. The FSB seem low on the ground; I was expecting more considering the international nature of this conference."

"Maybe they have been prioritised onto something else?"

"Exactly my thoughts. I have a sneaky feeling they are onto us being here in St Petersburg and it is only a matter of time before they twig we are here for this."

Louise ambled her way to the alleyway, shuffling through tourists and businesspeople alike. No one paid her any notice other than to wrinkle their noses at the stench of stale alcohol and piss. It is amazing just how anonymous someone can be in a crowded place. The alleyway was to the right of the conference centre as you looked at it straight ahead. The alley, like most alleys in a city, was full of bins and rubbish and late at night became the de-facto place to take a piss rather than use the facilities inside a pub or club. Louise found a place beside the bins away from the view of any suspecting police if they happened to look into the alley from the street. There was always the chance of security guards making their rounds, but she took up a sleeping pose and like most homeless people sleeping it looked more like a pile of blankets than a person. Louise prepared her Glock in case there was trouble and they had to shoot their way out. Being honest with herself, it would be a total disaster, but in life they had learnt that sometimes shit just happens and it was how you dealt with the tough times that mattered.

As Louise was working the alley, Mac was worrying about their plan to get out of Russia and had an idea he wanted to run with.

"Team, I need 30 minutes, I need to get a couple of things."

"Is it important, Mac? I don't like last minute changes," stated Louise.

"It could be, you need to trust me on this one. I don't like the lack of visible FSB, I think they are closer on our tails than we thought, and we might need an impromptu back up plan. Give me 30 mins."

"I will continue surveillance just outside; I don't need to be in right away anyway," replied Storm.

"Thank you, Zulu 3, Zulu 4 make it quick, 30 minutes tops," stated Louise.

"Roger that," replied Mac.

Mac headed off, having seen a second hand shop a couple of blocks away. It took him three trips to get his purchases back to the stolen car in the multi-storey and stowed properly within the car. It was a bit of a long shot and if they didn't need his impromptu plan B, he would simply leave the purchases in the car park and drive off. He was on edge; all his experience was screaming at him that something wasn't right. He didn't think it was a trap, but something was going on with the local FSB that did not make sense. He suspected the local office knew more about what Adrian was up to than he had revealed during the waterboarding. In retrospect it looks like they stopped the interrogation too quickly. Another couple of sessions would have revealed if he had in fact been the lone wolf he claimed to be.

Bang on 30 minutes, Mac was back in position with a smug smile on his face.

"Back up plan in place in case we need it, and if we don't, no harm done."

"Ok, Zulu 3, time to enter the conference centre. Game faces on, team, let's get this done so we can get the hell out of Dodge."

"Roger that," replied Mac.

FOURTEEN

Inside the venue Dave spotted the package (Dimitri Antonov) surrounded by four very FSB-looking chaps. As a Head of Cyber Security, he would have constant babysitters. Any suspicious behaviour and he would be flagged up the tree as a security risk. It was not a life Dave fancied, constantly under pressure from above to get one up on the opposition in the world of cyber espionage and constantly under surveillance from your own people. In certain Government positions it is like being back in the Cold War, constantly under scrutiny for every aspect of your life.

"Elvis is in the building," stated Dave.

"Roger that, Zulu 2."

Dimitri did not have a social media profile; he was not on Twitter or Facebook or Instagram. Russia had its own versions, of course, so it could firewall its people from the rest of the world. VK is the Russian equivalent of Facebook and if you publish an item on your wall then it appears for you on Facebook. Dimitri wasn't interested and if he was honest did not have the time in his life for the trivialities of what a certain celebrity had for their dinner or what their dog was called. To Dimitri, social media and online games were an opportunity, a way into the person's life, email etc. It wasn't as difficult as people suspected, which was why a lot of companies locked down their laptops and mobile phones so the user could only download security smart applications.

The western hemisphere Governments across the world refuse to allow Chinese manufacturers to provide equipment onto Telecoms networks for a very good reason. It is not hard to take a feed from all of the traffic and push it through your own data centres. The Americans, the British, the Russians, the Chinese have all been doing it for years. That was one of the reasons there was the high-profile defection from America to Russia in 2013. The volume of surveillance on internet and voice traffic is on an unprecedented scale. It is well known that all voice and internet traffic in the UK is monitored by the Government Communications Headquarters (GCHQ) in Cheltenham, UK. They in turn have algorithms running to monitor access to certain internet sites, foreign nationals' phones and all calls to and from. To provide a level of context, the UK trapped 39 billion separate pieces of information in a single 24-hour period. The NSA were caught bugging the German Chancellor before 2013 and they were supposed to be Allies. No, Dimitri was quite happy to avoid electronic communication in his own life. Being Head of Cyber Security meant you were constantly suspicious of everything. If you wanted an offline discussion with someone then you had to leave all electronic equipment behind you. That includes mobile phones even if they are off, as they can still be used as a listening device, computers even while appearing offline can still have their cameras used. Smart TVs were the new one in millions of homes and easy to hack if you knew what you were doing, and the recipient did not have a decent firewall. Dimitri had got to the point where he had built a Faraday cage inside a room within his Government-owned flat so he would talk without the fear of being overheard. A Faraday cage was just a metal mesh incorporated within the plasterwork that prevented electronic surveillance and provided he left all devices outside it he was safe from eavesdropping. He was not naive enough to believe he was above scrutiny.

He had been briefed that he had to go to leave via the front door immediately after his talk where SIS operatives would whisk him away to a new life within the UK. He fully expected weeks of information download to the UK Intelligence community as they made sure they got full use of his experience. He was doing this for a price, of course, and he would need protection for years to come. Russian Intelligence did not forgive nor forget.

He took his four security guards on a tour of the conference centre making sure he talked to as many delegates as he could. A particularly striking young lady in jeans and a t-shirt walked brazenly up to him. His security detail stepped in and holding a hand on her chest shook his head.

"No, it is ok, let her through," stated Dimitri to the guard.

"I am sorry about that, sometimes they are a bit overzealous. I am Dimitri." Dimitri held his hand out to Storm by way of introduction.

"I am Michaela, a cyber security consultant to the UK Power Industry," replied Storm.

"How interesting, it is good to get representation from the UK. Are you one of the speakers today?"

"No, I am here networking more than anything. Do you think I could grab a couple of minutes of your time in private after the speeches, maybe later on over dinner?"

"Certainly, that would be most welcome," replied Dimitri.

"Give me your number and I will text you the reservation details and where to meet me," replied Storm.

Dimitri gave Storm his mobile number and his best smile before wandering off to meet other delegates.

Storm waited a few minutes before texting the number.

"Change of plan, I want you to go to finish your speech and head to the toilets on the LHS of the stage. Wait until it is empty before climbing into the ceiling and dropping down beside a fire exit. Leave by the fire exit and my team will get you there. We can have dinner at your destination."

Dimitri read the text and felt suddenly a bit sick – it was all becoming very real. He started complaining loudly of a stomach-ache. He smiled to himself as the nerves from public speaking would make him need the loo anyway. Despite being a regular at conferences and often speaking, he never found it easy. The dry mouth, the butterflies in the stomach and the fear of standing alone on stage and all the words flying out of his mind like pigeons rising into the evening sky in Gorky Park. He needed the security detail to start to switch off. All he needed was 90 seconds in the toilet and he would be away while they searched the building for him in vain.

"Hi Dimitri, I am looking forward to your talk later on Israeli and Chinese cyber strategy."

"Thank you, Pavel. It is good to see you here this year. The risk is real, my friend, we are seeing increasing attacks over the last nine months or so. Utility companies in particular are under threat along with Telecommunication networks. We have become too reliant on Western architecture. They are jealous of our way of life and will do anything to undermine it."

"That is so true, Dimitri, let's catch up after the presentations and see where we can help each other with shared goals."

Pavel looked nervously at the FSB guards, nodded to Dimitri and walked off into the growing crowds.

Dimitri walked past the exit he had to get to immediately after his talk. He planned his route to the door in his mind, so he would not get lost. He saw a thick-set guard standing at the door dressed in the usual security black. The guard did not look at Dimitri, but you could see him look appraisingly at the four FSB guards, the way two boxers do. There was something about the way he held himself that made Dimitri shiver inside. He wasn't tall but he had an impressive set of shoulders on him. It was more the feeling that death walked behind this person, dressed in hooded cape with a scythe. The room seemed to feel chilly all of a sudden and the hairs stood up on Dimitri's arms. This guard and death had a mutual understanding. It was hard to intimidate someone who did not fear death, and this guy had a look where nothing scared him. It was not so much arrogance as certainty. Certainty that whatever came his way he could deal with it, and not only deal with it but with death on his side he would survive it as well.

Dimitri did not look back – someone of his status would not acknowledge a security guard at a conference centre. He focussed straight ahead and got his head into speech mode. He needed to deliver. He had a reputation to live up to and he was determined that despite what the next few hours would deliver that his reputation in the Cyber Security world would remain intact. He was not be the first person to defect to the West and he certainly would not be the last. He had researched it and the world felt so much more secure in the West. Dimitri took his place to the left of the stage and his guards split, with one guard with him, one on the other side of the stage, and two at the back of the amphitheatre scanning the delegates looking for any immediate threat.

"Ladies and gentlemen, our next speaker is the pre-eminent security expert in our industry and is leading Russia's defence in the dark arts of Cyber security. Please welcome to the stage, Dimitri Antonov."

Dimitri took a quick second to soak in his announcement to the stage, put a smile on his face and walked purposely forward. The words fake it till you make it are so true and confidence in how you will approach the dais in the centre of the stage was so important. He gave a slow purposeful wave to the audience, took five seconds of silence to allow the applause to subside and opened his hands in a welcoming gesture.

"Welcome, colleagues, and thank you for listening to me today. I have a number of topics I want to cover which will take 40-minutes and we will have a 20-minute question and answer session at the end."

With that Dimitri took his slide clicker from his pocket and proceeded confidently through his hour-long presentation and question session.

As Dimitri was going through his presentation, Storm was sat in the audience at the back of the hall, watching proceedings and wishing someone would just shoot her there and then. All this geek talk was completely tedious. She smiled as she thought back to her first assignment as lead assassin.

It was a mission in Africa where they had to take out an African war leader in South Sudan and it went sideways at an alarming rate. They had spent a month dug into a broken-down mud hut on the outskirts of some shit hole town waiting on a specific warlord visiting his family. It would have been easier just to take out the whole convoy with a predator drone the way the Yanks do, but London wanted plausible deniability which meant an assassin team on the ground. At last, the warlord appeared, and Storm had the lead. They had a plan on how to enter the premises, worked up over a number of days. It was action time and, nodding, to the others they took up their respective positions.

Storm left the surveillance position and in a crouched run knelt beside an eight-foot garden wall that surrounded the property. Storm pulled herself onto the top of the wall and rolled over it, landing quietly on her feet on the other side. She took out a guard who came out the back door for a smoke, using her knife, a quick slash across the neck and slowly lowering him to the ground. Just as she did that a second guard came out and just as he took stock of what was happening, Storm launched a frenzied attack, making sure he had to pay full attention to Storm rather than raise the alarm. Keeping him off balance, Storm thrust her knife into the guard's windpipe followed by a stab through the heart.

Entering the utility room and quietly moving about the house, Storm found the warlord sleeping on a chair in the living room. As bad luck would have it, the war leader's daughter came walking sleepily into the living room just as Storm was about to slit his throat. Storm did not kill unarmed non-combatants and with the warlord waking up and raising the alarm, they found themselves trying to extricate the team from the middle of a gunfight against a superior force. Getting pinned down on a hilltop near the town, they had to be extracted by Bravo team of the SAS and that meant a whole load of shit on the flight back to African base camp. The last thing she saw was the smug superior smile on those 22 SAS bastards. They were good, but they were a blunt instrument with no finesse. She still remembered the SIS spook red faced and hopping mad.

"If I had wanted a fucking gun fight followed by a rescue mission, I would have used the fucking SAS in the first place. You are supposed to operate in the fucking shadows, but oh no, you fucking lot operate in broad fucking daylight under a cloudless fucking sky. What a fucking shit show. Get to fuck out of my office, you useless fucking arseholes."

She smiled as she remembered stomping out of the office at Farnborough air strip, raging at how they were being treated when Mac piped up.

"That went pretty well then, anyone fancy a brew?"

Storm still winced at the rollocking they got, but Mac just took it in his stride and started whistling to himself as he does.

As the talk came to an end and the question-and-answer session started, Storm took her leave and headed out the front of the conference centre and stationed herself near the front of the alley in readiness for Dimitri's defection.

Dimitri, meanwhile, took a couple of minutes to milk the applause at the end of his session and with a final wave to the audience exited the stage the way he had come on.

He walked purposefully past his security guard and before the others could catch up headed towards the planned exit door. He went into the toilets beside the door clutching his stomach as he had done throughout the day and smiled ruefully to the guard. The guard took up a position outside the toilet, hands in front of him as guards do.

Hairy Dave saw the package pass him; there was no acknowledgement from Dave. What Dave was interested in was the four-man security team, which was more than anticipated. It wasn't unsurmountable but it could potentially cause a problem. Dave knew the package had a presentation to complete on some geek shit and would then come to the toilet beside the exit door. Dave made sure he was ready with a few minutes to spare. Anyone who approached the toilet in the final 10 minutes was told it was out of order.

Dave had a resting heart rate of under 50, and even with the deadline approaching he never batted an eyelid. It just wasn't in his nature to worry about things; he planned for them, yes, he made sure the plan was as robust as he could make it, and the rest was about trusting your training to react appropriately to any situation that arose. The government had spent an estimated £6million in training him to be the best version of himself.

The package walked past Dave and into the loo. Dave walked over and as the guard took up station outside the loo, Dave shouted over:

"It is broken, mate, you can't use that one, there is another just round the corner."

"Too late, you should have shouted over before."

Dave threw his hands into the air as he walked past muttering to himself about bureaucrats. As the guard turned back to the door, Dave swung round, catching the guard with the taser he had purchased, and he dropped to the floor with a grunt. Dave grabbed his mike and earpiece and dragged him into the toilet. As he entered, he looked at Dimitri and gave him a nod.

"Two minutes, mate, I just need to make sure he remains quiet."

Dimitri suddenly looked pale, the significance of what he was about to do hitting home with a bang.

As Dave duct-taped the guard's hands, and feet to one of the toilet bowls, he looked back and saw Dimitri as white as a sheet.

"You ok, fella? You have gone a bit white. Thirty seconds and we are off."

Dave looked Dimitri in the eyes.

"You are with me now; I know what I am doing."

As they exited the loo, Dave walked straight into the two guards who had been stationed in the crowd during the presentation. The years of training kicked in and before the first one could react, Dave punched him hard in the throat, stifling a cry, and with a follow up uppercut the guard dropped like a sack of potatoes to the ground. Before Dave could get to the second guard, however, he was in the process of drawing his service revolver in Dave's direction. Just as the guard was finalising his aim, Dave rolled across the corridor and came up into a crouch position Glock revolver in hand and fired a shot straight into the forehead of the second guard.

"Fuck, that is going to set the cat amongst the pigeons. Out the door pronto, Dimitri, there's a good lad."

As Dimitri pushed the security barrier to exit the conference centre, he stopped dead in his tracks as he saw an elderly tramp standing in his way.

"This way, Dimitri, I need you to put this on as quick as you can," said Louise.

Louise handed over a disguise compiled of ragged woollen overcoat, hat, grey wig and scuffed up walking boots.

"The boots are too big for me," complained Dimitri.

"That is by design, Dimitri, I need you to shuffle along beside me and drag this shopping cart along with you. The boots are too big to help you shuffle. Try it now."

Dimitri gave his best old person shuffle.

"Not bad, mate, but roll your shoulders a bit, as if you have a sore stomach just roll them in a bit.

"Much better, right let's get moving. Dave, get you at the car shortly."

Just like two aging homeless people, Louise guided Dimitri out of the alley and headed towards the car park to rendezvous with the team.

As Dave went to close the door, he felt rather than heard a bullet just graze the bottom of his ear. He instinctively rolled towards the danger. It was harder for his opponent to re-aim downwards than it was upwards and the fraction of a second gained could make all the difference. Dave frantically scanned the corridor for the source of the bullet. He took aim and fired but he just missed as chips of concrete shot out of the wall as the bullet impacted.

Dave pushed forward toward the source of the bullet. It takes all your training to walk towards trouble when all your instincts are screaming at you to go the other way. Dave saw a head peak round the corner and duck back. Dave suddenly swapped sides of the corridor to give him a better angle and as the head reappeared Dave fired and he saw the tell-tale pink mist that told him he had a direct hit.

Dave walked to the body, saw the guard was dead. Dimitri had been right – death did follow Dave around.

Dave walked out of the theatre, guiding conference goers in a panic over the sound of gun fire before walking purposefully round the corner and heading for the rendezvous at the car.

"Fuck." The team were now in real danger and he doubted the plan of driving to Helsinki would now fly.

The team made their way back to the car, taking the usual security precautions. They did not take detours and the like; however, they did make sure they were not being immediately followed and were at imminent risk of a fire fight.

Mac was the first one back, paid for the parking and got the car into a position of being able to leave immediately. It started first time and was up to temperature by the time the others arrived. Louise arrived first and had a puzzled look on her face as Mac showed what he had left his post to get. Storm and Dimitri were next, quickly followed by Dave.

"I had to take out the FSB guards," stated Dave as he approached.

"Well, if they did not know we were here before now, they sure as hell do now. I said to Louise I think they were pretty much onto us anyway, so I don't think it is as much of a loss as you are thinking. I have a plan B. Hear me out and let me explain before you shoot me down in flames," said Mac in his deadpan serious voice. It was so unlike him that immediately the others stood back and took notice.

Mac outlined his Plan B in as much detail as he could, outlining the positives, the risks and as much of the risk mitigation as he could.

Mac was expecting significant push back and a 'what the fuck is that' from the others, but to his surprise there was only silence.

"Have I lost the plot entirely? Why the silence?"

"I don't like it, Mac, it is beyond our normal risk envelope, but I don't have a better option if I am honest," stated Hairy Dave.

"Fuck, Mac, I hate it, man, I really do; but I think it is the best of a whole load of bad options. OK, let's make it happen," said Louise.

Dimitri just looked from one member of the team to the other as he wondered whether he would live to the end of the day.

With that the team put Mac's Plan B into operation.

FIFTEEN

Josef was growing more and more anxious as he led the coordinated attack of the five houses in St Petersburg. Each house had to be planned separately, and in enough detail, to potentially capture the assassins but not put lives at risk unnecessarily. Josef was a natural planner, it was why he was so good at chess, but when it cut across a time sensitive operation then it naturally caused stress. He could feel his heart pumping faster as Cortisol pumped through his system. His chest felt unnaturally tight and the palms of his hands a touch sweaty despite the war room being cool with air conditioning.

Each attack would have eight specially trained agents, fully kitted out with body armour, helmets and RPK Kalashnikov assault rifles. Four agents would stand by at the front of each property. Windows would be broken, and stun grenades and tear gas would be fired into each room front and back. Four agents would enter from the rear of each property at the same time as the agents from the front and each room would be cleared systematically before moving onto the next one. A standing order of capture if possible was in place. He was pragmatic enough and understood that with trained assassins, this could easily get very messy very quickly and properties could be booby trapped with improvised explosive devices (IED). It was vital that all attacks happened at the same time otherwise news outlets would get hold of it and in the days of camera phones and social media it was almost impossible to fully control it, even in Russia. It was tough being responsible for something but not actually being on the ground. Leadership at moments like this could be tough. To be honest, it was in the tough times you earn your money. Anyone can be a leader on a good day, it was the decisions you took under pressure that make you stand out from the crowd.

Each attack was being streamed live to a bank of monitors set up within the war room in Moscow. Body cam footage provided a real time view of what was happening on the ground. Josef was not convinced it made the stress of leadership any easier to manage.

Each team had conducted as much planning and preparation as they could, the attacks were on houses not compounds and Josef was telling himself that they did this regularly and it was what they were trained to do. Ideally, they would have 48 hours to plan for something like this; however, that was a lifetime when you were chasing highly trained assassins. The lack of planning time did mean additional risks to the team members and he was very much aware of that. It also meant risks to the inhabitants of the houses. These were tourists and this would be a massive international incident as it was. If some innocent teenager or mother died, there would be carnage at a senior level and not only would his career be over but he would probably end up being part of an unfortunate car accident on some remote road with no witnesses, and hastily cremated before someone saw the bullet hole in the back of his head.

Josef smiled ruefully to himself and wandered to the back of the room to get himself a hot black coffee. It reminded him of fishing with his grandfather when he was a boy. His grandfather was a fierce looking individual, very striking features and must have been a hit with the ladies in his youth, although he was never one to tell on those types of things. His grandfather had been in the army during the Second World War and he had a fierce hatred of the Germans. They plundered his country, raped most of the women and stole most of the food. What they had failed to understand in their arrogance was that Russia was a sleeping giant and once the production machine got started it would never stop. Russia still has amazing natural resources, but the German invasion provided a single outside enemy that galvanised all factions of Russian society into a single movement that the red revolution never had. It took time to mobilise armament and leadership, but once it happened the Germans realised to their chagrin that they had awoken a monster. Fighting on two fronts is difficult enough, but when one of them is across a vast wilderness and with the German supply chain constantly under attack by Cossacks on horseback, it was always going to be a tough ask.

On the fishing trips as they sat on the banks of the river his grandfather would occasionally talk about beating the Germans and defending Mother Russia. He used to joke that they could take the artwork and the women, but when they tried to steal the vodka all Russia rose up against them. Josef loved those intimate moments during the fishing trips and his grandfather's stories. He missed the old man. It was his grandfather that had started him playing chess. His own father was busy in the KGB and was very rarely home before they got shipped off to bed and it became part of the bedtime regime to play.

"No, no, no, Josef, you only sacrifice a pawn to gain something of more importance like a rook or a bishop."

"But they are only pawns, Grampa."

"Pawns are important as well, Josef. Remember, Chess is based on war, you do not throw away people's lives unless you will gain something that makes it worth it. That is why dictators can be so dangerous – they have no empathy for the working man. The Tsars became hated as they had everything, and the people were starving. It was the same across the world. Part of a leader's role is to look after his people. If they flourish, so will he. Protect your pawns, Josef, they are how you win."

In a lot of ways his grandfather raised him. He provided Josef with his moral compass, his passion for the people and his steely determination to win. His grandfather never let him win at anything, he had to earn the right to win through planning, hard work and learning from his mistakes.

A shy touch on Josef's shoulder made him turn round to see an awfully young FSB agent standing nervously beside him.

"What can I do for you, young man?"

"Colonel, we have some news just coming in from St Petersburg. That agent that went missing during an unauthorised surveillance visit, it looks like he went to check on one of the cottages we have on our list."

Josef took the information in, paused as he digested it. He thought back to his grandfather and protecting his pawns against unnecessary risk.

"I want to pause the attacks on the other four houses and prioritise this one. Which one is it on the monitors?"

"Top right, Colonel, it is on the outskirts of St Petersburg, a cottage with a large garden."

"Execute top right only."

It took a minute for the command to filter to the team on the ground and suddenly there was movement on the top right video stream. The agents spread out and approached the house, submachine guns on shoulders and walking in a wide formation out of the trees onto the grass. Everyone in the war room seemed to be holding their breath as the team moved into the open. Some would see it as a killing ground and if the assassins were vigilant as you would expect this was a time of extreme danger.

The team picked up the pace and moved swiftly to the walls of the cottage and took out the tear gas and flash bangs (stun grenades). There were three windows to the rear of the property, plus a back door. The team leader stuck a wooden strip to the hinge side of the back door that had plastic explosive stuck to it with a wired remote detonator. As the team leader pressed the button, it was coordinated with a quick machine gun burst to each window. With the single paned glass broken this was quickly followed by the flash bangs and tear gas being thrown through the gap where the window used to be. The flash bang was deafening and was designed to incapacitate anyone in the same room. The flash monetarily blinded you and the bang broke ear drums and caused immediate pain to the extent that unless you were wearing ear defenders all you could do was writhe about on the floor until your senses returned. The tear gas was perhaps a bit over the top, but the teams decided they were potentially up against a highly trained team and wanted every advantage.

It would normally be one or the other, but they could not afford a fire fight and a potential hostage situation as they did not know the whereabouts of the missing FSB agent. Two seconds later and the agents were inside the building, quickly moving through each room, checking cupboards and anywhere a person could hide. The whole operation lasted less than 60 seconds when the screen showed two agents dragging a body from the cottage. The next few seconds seemed to pass very slowly; it was as if time had slowed down.

"Building secure, one person recovered from the scene, no shots fired."

"Fuck it, I thought we had them." Josef banged the table in the war room in frustration.

"Do we know who the person is we recovered?"

"Let me just check to be sure."

A minute passed before the reply came.

"It is the missing FSB agent, Adrian Lahontov."

"Is he hurt?"

"He is dehydrated, Colonel, and has clearly been tortured, but there is no immediate threat to life."

"We need to understand what he knows."

"He is talking to the agent in charge at the scene just now as they put him on a drip and give him a more thorough medical examination."

"I need to know if he saw the assassin team at the cottage and when they departed."

"Yes, Colonel, right away."

Josef made his way to his office to finish his coffee and work out what they needed to do next. It all really depended on whether they were actually at the cottage. If their lead was more than 10 hours they would probably be back in the West by now and out of his immediate reach. With Lahontov being tied up it strongly suggested they were at the cottage and if he was dehydrated, he had been there for a number of hours tied up. He needed to alert the border stations nearest St Petersburg including the airport, although recent mode of operation suggested they would avoid the airport, or they would have left Moscow by plane. He tried to relax his mind, allow his subconscious to take control and work through the information they had, but also what they did not have. He was missing something, some bit of information that would bring this all together, there was something about St Petersburg and why they had rented a cottage. They had to be waiting for something. It could be further orders, another assassination maybe or confirmation that the original attempt had been successful. It felt remarkably like a game of chess.

Closing his eyes, he summarised the events so far to try and create a behavioural profile in his mind. The detailed planning in Moscow to carry out the assassination suggested that they were patient, they were well funded and that they could fit in without raising suspicion in an environment that is well controlled by state intelligence agencies. The ease of their escape from the city before it could be locked down suggested that they planned ahead and did not take the easy, obvious solution. They were confident in their abilities to evade detection and stay ahead of the opposition. The fact they did not head to the airport but north to St Petersburg instead meant they knew it was easier to follow them across the multiple airport hops back to where they came from.

They had strong trade craft from intelligence agency training. The multiple vehicles and where they were dumped, everything wiped down and very little in the way of forensics again suggested a strong Intelligence agency background. Being interrupted by Adrian in St Petersburg, and that they did not panic and just shoot him, showed they could problem solve whatever was in front of them. The bit that just does not make sense is why a team with that level of expertise sits for a number of days in a cottage wating to be tracked. It was totally out of character with everything else they have done. The only conclusion Josef could come up with was that they had orders from up on high and I bet they hated it. Something big has to be holding them in St Petersburg as nothing else made sense. He hated dealing with people that could problem solve; they became unpredictable and more difficult to get in front of, and he was very conscious he and his team up until now had been playing catch up at every step.

One of the Heads of department strode purposefully into Josef's office – he did not knock as he would have normally which suggested something important was underway that made him forget his manners.

"Colonel, reports of gunfire at Kongressnyy Tsentr Petrokongress in St Petersburg, we have at least three FSB agents dead or injured. There do not appear to be any civilian casualties."

"What is being held at the conference centre?"

"That is the thing, Colonel, it is a Cyber Security conference; it should be light touch, which was why we were happy to divert resource to the other issues. It is a conference attended by geeks from around the world to talk about IT."

Josef strode back to the conference room, head down and hands gently clasped behind his back as he did when his brain was whirring with new information. His girlfriend used to tease him about it as she always knew when he was in thinking mode.

"Information please, gentlemen, and let's get it onto the board. We need to determine whether, as we suspect, it dovetails into our current operation. I want FSB to take control at the conference centre and if the local police want to argue, get their Commissioner to phone me directly.

"Ok, what do we know?"

"The conference centre was hosting a Cyber Security conference attended by delegates from around the world."

"Any keynote speakers we should know about? I also want to know what internet chatter there has been about the event – any noise from extremist groups? Cyber security is a contentious issue, ladies and gentlemen, there are always bleeding hearts complaining about personal freedom infringements. Were there any demonstrations outside the venue? What about security camera footage? What would be the possible link with our fugitives and this event; why would a group of highly trained assassins kill or injure three FSB operatives, knowing that we would be all over them like a rash? There is a connection out there and we need to figure out what it is. Time is our enemy, people, let's get it together."

SIXTEEN

Mac got the team to take off their disguises and get back into casual dress. There were fist bumps all round and Mac got the getaway car moving. He headed down the exit ramps with the driver's window down and nodded to the attendant with a broad grin and headed out of the car park towards one of the multiple bridges from the island on which Kongressnyy Tsentr Petrokongress was situated before turning left and picking up the Western High Speed Diameter ring road and ultimately heading towards the E18, which would take them over the border to Finland and ultimately Helsinki. Mac's heart was racing, which was unusual for him. His Plan B was risky, and he was feeling nervous. The drive would normally take just under five hours, but Mac wanted some distance from the conference centre as soon as he could. There were multiple toll booths along the route and that in itself posed a risk. Mac put his foot down and took the car above the speed limit. He needed to get beyond the city limits as soon as possible.

Mac put the radio on. He wanted to know if the shooting at the centre had made the news. Either way, he knew the local FSB would be all over the situation and would be hunting high and low for the perpetrators. Once they figured out there was a defection in play, all hell would break loose. The Russians were not likely to let that one go. They had spent a lot of time getting an edge in the Cyber Security world and that investment in time and infrastructure would need to be protected at all costs.

Mac went through his plan as he drove, looking for ways to bolster their chances of success and mitigate as many of the risks as he could. The biggest risk was the border check point itself. It was about two hours 30 minutes into the journey. The checkpoint would have armed guards and protocols in place to close the border if the order came down from Moscow. It was the biggest weak point in most escape plans. Border crossings were notoriously difficult to navigate and with a Russian defector on the run he suspected it was going to be the most difficult part of his career so far. Mac saw his first sign for toll roads ahead and knew he would soon be passing the entry point to the toll road network. He would not have to stop as this was just an entry point but there would be cameras.

In Moscow, Josef was sat in the war room when there was a knock on the door and one of the senior agents entered looking flushed with excitement. He was tall, blond haired and of slim build. He strode purposefully into the room to stand before Josef, his face slightly red, pupils wide and Josef sat upright in his chair waiting on the news.

"Spit it out, man, don't keep me waiting."

"My apologies, Colonel, I am Senior Agent Rubelov. I have been informed that Dimitri Antonov, our Head of Cyber Security, was the keynote speaker in St Petersburg; the three FSB agents shot were part of his personal security detail, and he cannot be found anywhere within the centre. A full end to end search has been conducted and he is not within the building. He is not answering his mobile phone either. We placed a trace on it and it was found in a bin just outside a car park about three blocks from the conference centre."

"Anything else?" asked Josef.

"Yes, sir, one last thing, one of the local agents spoke to all of the car park attendants and one of them remembers an older large black car leaving the car park with what he thinks was five adults in it. He remembers it specifically because the driver nodded and smiled at him. That was 20 minutes ago."

"Does he happen to have a make and model of the car and maybe a number plate?" asked Josef impatiently. It was like drawing teeth, trying to get all the information.

"Yes and no, Colonel. It was a black BMW 7 series with dark windows – that is why he only *thinks* there were five adults in the car. It was more silhouettes than anything else. It was an older model, Colonel, not one of the newer ones. Unfortunately, he did not get the licence plate number; he did note it was a local registration but that is all. We had no luck with security cameras as it is an older car park and they never got round to installing them."

"Thank you, Senior Agent Rubelov, that will be all."

With that Rubelov turned on his heel and strode purposefully out of the war room.

"OK, gentlemen, what are your thoughts on this new information?"

"It is either an abduction or a defection, Colonel; at this moment in time it doesn't matter either way.

We can find that out afterwards. What we need to do is find the black car and with that we are likely to find Dimitri Antonov."

"I agree, let us find the BMW. There are three main routes, north to Helsinki, west to Tallinn or south to Moscow. They know they are hunted in Moscow so it is unlikely they will head back there, so let's focus the efforts on Tallinn and Helsinki."

Ten minutes later, Senior Agent Rubelov came back into the room.

"Colonel, we have picked up a black BMW 7 series travelling at speed up the E18 towards Helsinki. It was spotted by the traffic cameras entering the E18 toll road. How do you want to proceed, Colonel?"

"Get me a detailed map of the route up to the border with Finland. I also want a conference call with the person in charge of the border crossing at Vaalimaa and our Special Forces Captain within 15 minutes. I don't care what meetings they are in; I want them on a call."

"Yes, Colonel, right away."

Within 15 minutes Josef had his conference call.

"Right, gentlemen, I am going to dispense with the usual round of introductions and pleasantries as this is a national emergency and time is of the essence. The background to this is twofold. General Andropov was assassinated a few days ago in Moscow and we tracked the assassination team to St Petersburg. We were in the process of apprehending them when we found out that our Head of Cyber Security was either abducted in St Petersburg or he is attempting to defect. We have tracked the assassination team heading north to Vaalimaa driving a black BMW 7 series car where we expect they will attempt to cross the border into Finland. Footage from cameras on the toll road confirms what looks to be five adults in the car. It is difficult to tell as the car has blacked out windows. What we need to do is get a plan together and get boots on the ground to stop the car at the border crossing. We know this team is armed and dangerous, so this is likely to get noisy. I have forwarded you all a detailed plan of the E18 route to the border and satellite imagery of the border point itself. What are our options please?" Josef was calm and direct as he addressed the call participants.

"Option one is we wait until they reach the border crossing point and as they hand over their passports, we surround the car with armed agents," stated the Special Forces Captain.

"I run the border crossing, Captain, and although that idea might work, I have to say I am not keen on it – if this gets noisy, we have a lot of innocents in the area. Vaalimaa has more than two million people crossing the border every year and we have queues of cars all day every day."

"That is a good point, Captain," answered Josef.

"Do we have a runoff area we can direct the car to away from the other people? We could have someone out front directing the cars to different queues and when the black BMW approaches, they get directed to a more remote queue." This was from the Special Forces Captain.

"We do, but if these are professionals as you state, then they will realise something is up and we end up back to the same point of potential mass casualties."

"What about the road up to the checkpoint, is there anywhere along the route that we can use to box the car in? We have three vehicles, one in front, one behind and we draw the other up alongside it and all cars reduce speed at the same rate until the target vehicle has come to a stop at a point we want. We put sufficient force in play that they see it is not worth a fire fight. What about this point here? It is close enough to the checkpoint that we would have about 90 minutes to get it set up."

Josef replied, "I like that idea, nice and simple and avoids unnecessary innocent casualties. Is there anyone with a different idea or concerns with this one?"

Silence greeted the question from all on the call.

"All right, we have a bare bones plan. Let's get on with it and get it in place. Captain, you will need more detail to get this to work. I trust you have done this before and know what you are about to commit to?"

"Colonel, we practise this on a regular basis as part of our terrorist threat protocols. I am confident we can make it a success. One question though, if we come under fire how important is the hostage?"

"Alive if possible, for all of them, but I don't want excess risk to your men on the ground so I will leave it in your capable hands."

With that Josef killed the call. This made him nervous, there was a lot riding on this and it was down to a bunch of grunts to make it work.

The SF Captain was called Boris and was glad to be off the call with the FSB seniors; he had total disdain for their fundamentalist attitude. He was a man of the people and the FSB just gave him the creeps. They had their uses, I suppose, but for him they were just geeks that provided the intelligence he needed to do his job. He got three teams of four SF operatives into the air to the border post within a couple of minutes. It would take 30 minutes to get to the post by helicopter from their Operating base. They were stationed near the border anyway as part of a Quick Reaction Force in the event of the necessity to either defend the border from Western Aggression or to be part of an early deployment to pave the way for invasion of Finland. Their job would be to take out the power grid around Helsinki. This job was much simpler but if these were professionals with a similar skillset to his, then the risks were still high. The only way to get a result was to hit them with overwhelming force that they can't see a way out.

Thirty minutes later they were on the ground and he got the team leaders from the other units together to work through the detail and how they would approach it.

"For me, I would have two cars with two people in each, with the other six deployed at the stop point. We would need to be on the kerbside of the car as the chase car would block the other doors from opening on the driver's side. My big concern is if they open fire on the car as it is moving to block them in and I think that is quite likely," said the Bravo team leader. Like most SF guys he was of stocky build and direct in how he spoke.

"I assume the cars we have available are just standard civilian cars and not armoured," stated the Charlie team leader.

"That would be an affirmative. They are government vehicles but just a civilian specification," responded Boris.

"Can we hijack the Engine Management System remotely?" asked Bravo TL.

"My understanding is it is an older style car, so it is not likely. What about some temporary steel plating? Do they have anything on site we can use to shore up the armament? We won't be able to get out of those doors on a stop anyway, so we can add that to the inside of the doors," stated Boris.

"Let me get one of the team on it was we continue to plan," replied Alpha TL. He stepped out of the room to bark an order at two of the SF Operatives that were drooling over the Border Control lady agents.

Five minutes later there was a knock on the door quickly followed by a scruffy looking SF guy entering. "We have found some steel plating that would do the job. One of the guys is just getting some cutting gear to get it to size and we will get it on the inside of the passenger side doors. It means visibility will be impacted but he is going to cut a peep hole. Without it we would be vulnerable to the target car changing speed and direction.

"What about some eyes in the sky?" asked Bravo TL.

"I thought about that, but the car has five occupants and as they near the border they will be looking for any sign we have them under surveillance. It is too risky," replied Boris.

"Let's go through this step by step. Bravo team is in the lead vehicle going slow until they see the black BMW, matching speed until we get within 300m of the stop point. Charlie team and Alpha team are in the chase vehicles, parked up until the target car passes them and keeping a distance until the other cars are in play. Alpha team will move out, overtake Charlie team and work to keep the target vehicle in the box. There are no side roads along the target stretch for them to veer off. We have additional steel plate being fitted to Alpha vehicle which is in the riskiest position side by side with the target vehicle. The seniors' view is we take them alive if at all possible, so make sure the team are briefed. We fire if fired upon and not otherwise. Are we all clear on that instruction?"

"Clear," replied both of the other Team Leaders.

Although they were all of equal rank, Boris had the lead on this operation and that was respected by the other two. They didn't like it, of course, as they would have preferred it to have been them, but they were philosophical. Their time would come.

The three teams headed out to the vehicles to travel to the target site which was two miles to the east of Torfyanovka and five miles from the border checkpoint. They would have preferred to do it further out, but they needed the time to get it set up properly and that meant closer to the checkpoint. The closer to St Petersburg they set it up, the less time they had.

Mac knew the FSB had to be tracking him by now – he had sped past multiple cameras both on the inlet to the toll road and through two toll booths on the E18. Back in his Intelligence days during the Troubles, Mac had carried out surveillance of IRA and UVF activists on the Scottish roads from Stranraer and Campbelltown to Glasgow. They were both smaller ports and in the minds of the terrorists were easier to smuggle through compared with Holyhead.

The roles were reversed in this operation, so Mac bought a map at a small filling station and spent 10 minutes studying it, looking for potential spots the FSB would use to stop the vehicle. He also knew it would need to be near the checkpoint rather than the checkpoint itself to prevent potential casualties. There was one more toll booth to go through before the checkpoint and Mac felt it was important to carry on as normal at this stage.

He set off again and was currently about forty minutes from the checkpoint. Ten minutes later he passed the final toll booth. If the FSB were planning a takedown, it would be within the next few miles. Mac pulled over and looked again at the map. If it was him, the takedown would be just to the east of Torfyanovka. It gave them enough time to set it up with the minimum of casualties. It would either be a box with three vehicles or stingers across the road. Stingers were metal strips easily thrown across the road that would puncture all four tyres on the car. There was a way round them of course nowadays by filling your tyres with emergency foam so Mac suspected it would be a three-car box.

He drove three miles further up the road and then rather than take too much of a risk by driving too far, he took a small road off to the north. It was through heavy pine forest and was little more than a farm track. Mac drove up the track for two miles and found a suitable spot to take the car off the road and into the trees. He took his waterproof jacket, hat and gloves and put them into a rucksack from the boot of the car. He took the Lobaev sniper rifle and placed it beside the rucksack before taking his knife to cut some heavily leafed branches from the trees and covered the rear end of the car, making sure the leaves on the branches were in the same direction as the surrounding trees.

Mac then headed off on foot through the trees in a direction parallel to the E18 main highway. He wanted it to look as if he was taking the natural escape path and was headed directly for the border. He was, in fact, laying down a false trail and that meant he needed to appear to be clumsier than his actual abilities. He left footprints in mud, broke branches on trees and made obvious paths through clearings in the trees. He was not stupid enough to walk along the actual road. In escape and evasion terms it was a big no-no although it was only about a five-and-a-half-hour hike along the road from where he was because it was easy going. It was also the easiest way to get caught. There is no way he would get off the road into the trees in time to not be seen by the enemy chase team.

That meant he had to do it the hard way. The forest was of mixed tree types, dense pine trees intermittently interspersed with hard wood trees like Spruce and Birch. The trees were in general around 100 years old, tall and rangy and surrounded with that beautiful clean forest smell. Unlike the UK, where the trees are planted in straight lines, this forest was predominantly natural, and the trees just grew wherever there was light.

It meant it would take about 10 hours longer to walk the same distance and that was assuming he did not come across rivers that had to be crossed and would mean a diversion until he found a bridge. In Mac's experience he thought he would have about 30 minutes until the FSB would have helicopters and a hunter force in the field to drive him into a carefully laid trap. It was pretty standard escape and evasion tactics.

Mac needed to slow down the Hunter force and other than the false trail the easy way to do that was prepare some traps. It meant the Hunter Force would have to ensure the trail was safe and that took time and effort. The balance he had to think about was did it save more time than the time it took Mac to set the traps. He felt the balance was in favour of setting some traps, so he took his knife and cut some branches into 12 in stakes sharpened into a stiletto spike. He used another branch to help dig a small pit about 40cm square and the same deep. He stored the excess earth in his rucksack pockets before lacing the spikes in the pit. He then did the same either side of the trail so they couldn't just mark the trap and walk round it either side. It was important they spent as much time looking for traps as they progressed along the trail. Mac then used the excess earth from the traps to make false traps. All he did was spread the earth in a rough square and scuffed it up to make it look like he had laid a trap. It would take time to determine if it was real or false and that was important. It also meant Mac did not have to create actual traps each time.

Mac created a number of traps over a 100m part of the trail and then nothing for the next 800m. It was about keeping the Hunter Force on edge. He needed to make them think about their own safety rather than just searching for Mac. To mix it up, Mac also created some spring stake traps. Simply put, he bent supple new growth branches back from the path and attached sharpened wooden stakes to them. He then used para cord to tie them to a trigger. The trigger was the tricky part. It had to be strong enough to hold the branch in place but free enough to let the branch loose when disturbed. If he got it wrong either way, it would be useless.

Mac dug two stakes into the ground either side of the path and placed a trigger twig balanced between the stakes across the path. The trigger twig was made from old wood rather than new, the type that snapped rather than bent. Mac cut a series of notches into it so that when stepped upon it would snap, this in turn freeing the swinging branch. It was a simple trigger and used what was around him. It was simple stuff, but if triggered it would cause significant damage. Mac set the branch to aim for top of the thighs at groin height. Aimed at head height the body's reactions would make the intended victim duck, similarly at calf height the person would jump, especially if they were highly trained, which Mac would expect.

It is difficult to duck or jump at mid height and it therefore had a higher chance of success. Lastly, he disguised the trap so that it would take a trained eye to find it, someone trained in the old school ways of hunting. Mac laid down his false trail for about 45 minutes before backtracking for five minutes, carefully placing his boots into previous boot prints as he walked backwards. It was slow going but he had to hide when he went off the main trail, so the chase team did not know where to start widening their search grid. It was all about slowing the search down to give him time to get out of the search zone. Just as the FSB were looking to find the abandoned car, Mac climbed up into the trees in a wooded area and moved through the branches tree to tree. It kept his feet off the ground; if they were using dogs, they would have no scent to follow and as long as he was careful not to break branches that fell to the ground, the evidence of his passing would be hard to find. It was painful going though, his shoulders and arms had that dull ache and were trying to tell his brain it was time to give up; his face and hands were scratched and stinging with the sweat from all this exertion.

Mac knew it was the right thing to do and forced himself to carry on, ignoring the aches and pains by focussing his mind on the next handhold, the next branch, or the next place to put his feet. Finally, Mac came to the northern edge of the E18 highway. Jumping to the ground and sitting a few feet inside the tree line, he took a few minutes to rest and made sure there were no approaching vehicles or helicopters above before hurrying across the road and quickly stepping into the forest on the other side.

Mac crouched down facing the road and took a few seconds just to check he had not been spotted before climbing back into the trees for another 100 yards or so. It was time consuming, tiring and if he was honest, it was one of his least favourite things he had ever done. He knew this would not stop the pursuit, but it would significantly slow them down. Mac was now heading south for the coast and the Gulf of Finland. It was a rugged coast with trees right down to the sea giving him plenty of cover. From there he would await a pickup from the team. His two biggest fears were helicopters with infra-red scopes and dogs. Both of which could really muck up his hastily laid plan. Back on the ground but still in the forest, Mac got a march on to get as much distance as he could from the hunter force that he knew would be following his false trail by now; every minute from now on counted.

It was hard going but deep-down Mac knew his enemy would never give up. He also knew that the reason the British SAS trained so hard was their amazing ability to get out of a search zone before the enemy had it set up properly. Where he could, he got up to a maintainable jog similar to the way a wolf lopes along without too much effort. Mac knew he could maintain that pace for hours on end if need be. In these situations, Mac forced his subconscious to focus on the immediate task despite his body complaining about his exertions and screaming at him to stop and rest. Through his vast experience, Mac knew he could ignore the messages his body was sending his brain. The trick was to keep the brain busy with other things.

He came across a small clearing and saw it contained dead sphagnum moss. He crouched down and watched the rest of the woods near the clearing, listening intently for the slightest sound that did not belong, a twig snapping, the metallic sound of a gun barrel hitting off other equipment or even the smell of cigarette smoke. After a couple of minutes his senses told him it was safe, and he entered the clearing to gather as much of the moss as he could sensibly carry in his rucksack. It bulked up his rucksack but fortunately there was very little weight in it.

To create some additional room, Mac took out his bag of trail mix and started to munch on it. He needed to keep up his energy levels and trail mix had a good blend of instant energy with chocolate but also longer-term energy with nuts and fruit. If he was to remain sharp, he needed to maintain his energy levels. Mac drank the last of his water and knelt beside a small stream to refill it. It was fast running water and unless there was a dead deer further upstream it was safe to drink and the chances of that were pretty low. Mac took a big swallow of the fresh water and savoured how cold and fresh it was. No chlorine or fluoride to taint the taste the way you did with mains water piped into houses back in the UK. It did make the water safe to drink and the fluoride did help with teeth health, but it did taint the taste of the water.

Feeling better about himself, Mac picked up his rucksack and continued to head south. He followed the same direction for another 30 minutes before changing direction through 90 degrees and heading west. There were two reasons for this. Firstly, it was never good during escape and evasion to continue on the same compass bearing for too long – it was too easy for the Hunter Force to anticipate your route and set a trap up ahead. It was important to keep them guessing. Secondly, he did not want his pick-up team to have to travel too far into Russian territorial waters. They would be in a RIB (rigid inflatable boat) which did have a low radar profile; however, over water noise carries a long way and there was always the risk of discovery. To help the team, Mac wanted to minimise that risk both for himself and the team.

SEVENTEEN

In Moscow, Josef had been anticipating the news that they had captured his brother's assassins and a high-level defector. He could just imagine receiving a medal of honour for this work and another promotion in the pipeline. He had closed his eyes, savouring his moment of triumph as he saw it. It wouldn't be quite as big a deal if they had to be killed during the capture, but it would still help his promising career. Josef had big plans and the FSB was only one step as he followed in the footsteps of other Intelligence services leaders into the world of politics. Like J Edgar Hoover, he had an intelligence file on a lot of the future power brokers. He saw himself as a long-term influencer in Mother Russia and this triumph would push him further along his chosen career path.

His level of anticipation when the video conference unit buzzed and connected was palpable.

"You are calling with good news I hope, Boris?"

"Not quite, Colonel, the target car never arrived at the stop point. We have sent a chaser unit along the E18 up to the last toll booth they passed through. Colonel, there is no sign of the car. We suspect they have pulled off the road somewhere. It looks like we underestimated them, Colonel and they anticipated the stop. I suspect they are holed up in a farmhouse somewhere near the border before attempting to cross away from the checkpoint proper."

Josef banged the table in frustration before replying. "I want them found; we know they were travelling along the E18, so we have a defined search grid. I don't care that the assassins are professionals, they will be slowed down protecting the defector, he is the weak point. I want vehicles all along that route and a search grid encompassing all local farm buildings and warehouses up and running asap. I also want every heavy goods vehicle checked as well."

"Yes, Colonel, right away," replied Boris.

With that Josef stormed out of the war room and stomped back along to his office. Like most narcissists he was happy to blame the special forces for ruining his big moment. How dare they muck up his moment of glory.

Ninety minutes later, Josef had a timid knock on his office door.

"Enter," bellowed Josef.

There was a slight pause as if the intruder was plucking up the courage to open the door.

"We have found the vehicle, Colonel and you are not going to like it, not one bit."

There was a pause before Josef raised his voice in exasperation.

"Out with it, man, it can't be that bad."

"We have found the black BMW used by the targets. It was found some distance up a dirt track and driven off it and into the trees. The back end was camouflaged with branches which is why it was almost impossible to see it driving past. One of the special forces chase cars found some well-hidden tyre marks where the car left the road. They had been brushed over to make them invisible other than to an experienced hunter. The operative followed them 30 yards into the trees before seeing the car. It had been expertly hidden, Colonel."

Boris just stared at him; his eyes staring straight ahead. He had that dead eye look of someone who did not fear death and had seen it up close many times. The agent could almost imagine death standing just behind Josef with his hand on Josef's shoulder in a protective way, showing that Josef was a close ally having provided death with many new victims.

"And eh, Colonel, I am not sure how to share this news, the car was filled with shop dummies dressed up to look like the assassins. With the blacked-out windows all we ever saw were silhouettes and assumed the car was full. We now believe that there is the distinct possibility that the rest of the team plus the defector never left St Petersburg."

Josef felt deflated. How on earth did it fall apart? Just like he was when he played chess, Josef was a bad loser; he hated to be outsmarted by an opponent, no matter their chess ranking. As he contemplated where the search had gone wrong, Josef stomped along to the war room, opening the door sharply and slamming it closed behind him.

"I gave you one job to do, and you allowed yourselves to get blind-sided into thinking the assassins were all heading for the border near Helsinki. Well, I have just been informed that only one of them went that route and the rest of the car was filled with shop dummies. FUCKING SHOP DUMMIES. Let me spell it out for you. I want them dead or alive, I don't mind which. Find out where the hell they are."

Josef turned on his heel, opened the door and sighing to himself exited the war room and went to his office to call the Director. Josef closed the office door and looked around at the beautiful wooden panelling. This might be his last time in it – the Director was not someone you disappointed. Josef was not one for loads of personal effects around the office, but he did have a photo of the President and himself. The only other photo was of his brother and he nodded to it as he promised that despite the setback, he would avenge the assassination.

"Director, I have some disappointing news."

"What is it, Josef? I am just about to brief the President and disappointing news isn't exactly what I was hoping for."

"We failed to apprehend the targets. We did find the vehicle; however, it was abandoned, and we now believe only one of them was in the vehicle as a decoy."

"Josef, fix it." And with that the Director put the phone down.

At the same time as Mac was heading north in a car filled with dummies, the rest of the team plus Dimitri headed towards the train station for the next train to Tallinn. They made a quick stop along the way to create disguises that would allow them to get to there without being detected. Storm completely changed their appearance into goths, all dressed in black with white and black make-up and black long-haired wigs. Unlike most disguises where you just wanted to blend in, Storm was gambling that by turning into Goths they would hide in plain sight. Who in their right mind would dress in that way to hide from the FSB? It was not, however, a universal hit amongst the team.

"Fuck sake, Storm, I feel like a total dick, everyone is staring at us," complained Hairy Dave.

"Suck it up, Dave, there is a fundamental difference in people looking at you and people actually seeing you. The whole point of this is that people only look at the surface and don't see the real you. They are uncomfortable with the whole Goth thing so they will look down and won't engage," replied an exasperated Storm.

"It better bloody work then; I prefer the grey man disguise that no one sees, I really don't fancy our chances of winning a fire fight if we have to battle our way out of the train station."

Storm sighed quietly to herself; she hated it when Dave was on one of his whinges.

"You need to trust me, Dave, I know what I am doing," replied Storm in a calm soothing voice.

"Yeah, Dave, stop being a pussy," chipped in Louise.

"Nice, Louise, just pour petrol onto the fire, why don't you," sighed Storm.

"Any time, my lovely," laughed Louise with a cheesy grin.

Dimitri just looked at all of them in amazement. How could they smile and tease each other when his life was on the line? After a few seconds he realised that their life was on the line as well, protecting him. His decision had placed everyone in danger, and he was starting to feel like a pet poodle in a cage surrounded by hyenas. Dimitri was an office guy and this wandering about with guns was completely alien and quite frankly just a little bit disturbing. He was in awe of the agents protecting him and getting him out of the country. The ease with which they handled a change of plan was incredible and made him feel less afraid than he otherwise would. There was a calm authority about them. Louise still scared him – there was something terrifying about her. Just the way she seemed to see through him. He got the feeling that if he was on the wrong side of her that she would kill him without looking back, no regrets, just another job to be completed. There was a cat-like grace about her, she was supremely well balanced, and she just seemed to see everything at once. Knowing what a potential threat was and what could be dismissed.

Louise took the lead up front, walking about 50 yards ahead of the rest of the team, always looking, checking out everyone ahead and looking for that tell-tale sign of undercover government agent. So far everything was clear. There was an alley on the LHS about 100 yards ahead and Louise was being extra vigilant. It was important if something kicked off that she could cover for the team and buy time to get Dimitri clear.

As Louise approached the alley, she noticed a homeless man dressed in rags at the entrance begging for money. Louise was about to dismiss him as insignificant when something caught her experienced eye. Something was off in the way he was dressed. It took a second or two to place it and she realised he was FSB undercover and more than likely on the lookout for them. Louise now had a dilemma: did she take him out proactively at the risk of creating a disturbance, or did she trust the disguises and bluff it out? Louise surreptitiously kept an eye on him as she ambled passed. Seeing no recognition in his eyes, just amusement at someone that would dress in such an outlandish way, she opted for trusting the disguises – maybe Storm had it right after all. She made a note to pull Dave's leg about it on the train. They were no less than 300 yards from the train station and Louise thought it would be under constant surveillance by FSB agents. Louise slowed her pace to allow the others to catch up so that by the time they were 100 yards out they were back to being a group of four.

Louise started to chat to Dave as they entered the station. The FSB were on the lookout for people that were nervous, so it was important that they appeared self-assured and in control as if they did not have a care in the world.

"So, Dave, are you going to call Sky when we get back? I am sure she could teach you a thing or two," laughed Louise in a teasing voice.

Dave caught on immediately to the plan; they had worked together for a number of years and he could read her.

"I might just do that, seems a likeable young lady and must have a strong core to perform like that on those poles. Mind you, she would need that to spend a night with me."

"She would need glasses to find it first, Dave, I mean all that body hair it would be like looking for a needle in a haystack."

"Not likely, luv, the big fella aint like no needle in a haystack, he is more like one of those poles she likes to dance on."

"Oh, come on, Dave, we are not changing your nickname to Dave the pole no matter how much you beg; any more of it and it will be dickless Dave and we will start telling people about your unfortunate war wound that left you no use to the ladies," chipped in Storm.

"You wouldn't!" Dave put on a show of being shocked by their suggestion. "Anyway, it isn't my fault they called me Donkey Dave at school."

"Hahahaha, that was because you were slow, Dave, not because of your sexual prowess."

They stood in the ticket queue with the banter continuing to flow between the three team members, and Dimitri standing beside them like a priest at a swinger's party, not believing how they talked to each other and moving between intrigued and shocked at the same time. At last, they reached the front of the queue and thankfully it was ticket machines rather than conductors. It was harder to monitor and give a nod to the FSB that someone had purchased tickets to go to Tallinn. Louise bought two return tickets followed by Dave purchasing two and they headed to the platform concourse to find out what platform they were due to depart from.

"We still have 20 minutes until departure, do you fancy a coffee and a cake before we go? I wouldn't mind some time to watch the platform and see how many agents they have looking for us," suggested Louise.

"I wouldn't mind a coffee and a cake," replied Storm.

"Yeah no worries," replied Hairy Dave.

"Dimitri, you are with me and can carry the coffees; Dave, you find a table with a view out over the platform."

"Four white coffees and four Medovik please." Turning to Dimitri Louise said, "I do love a Medovik honey cake, nice and sweet tasting."

"I prefer Praga cake but Medovik are not too bad," replied Dimitri.

"Do you take sugar in your coffee?" asked Louise. "I know how everyone else takes it."

"No, just white, thank you," replied Dimitri.

"One thousand and twenty-five rubles please," stated the waitress.

"You can get your coffees at the end of the counter and here are your cakes."

"Thank you," replied Louise.

Louise and Dimitri took their position up at the end of the counter in the coffee shop, waiting on their coffees.

"What do you do for fun, my friend, when you are not working?" asked Louise.

"I play computer games online mostly. I love role play games where you build your character up over time and you do quests to win additional items. It's a kind of dungeon and dragons type of thing."

"Wow, it must be nice to get some downtime, although I thought you might prefer some outdoor pursuits with you being in an office all day," stated Louise.

"No, I have never really been the outdoors type, my role has always been computers and working on the internet. I started hacking when I was at university, just for fun and because I could, and nowadays, I spend more time on the dark web trying to catch organised crime both within and outwith Mother Russia."

"Oh, my brother does something similar with the UK Government. I never really talk to him much about it but from what I understand he is pretty gifted. I am sure you would like him. He does computer gaming and shit like that as well. Never been one for that kind of thing myself. My downtime is outdoors and competing in endurance events. Each to their own I suppose."

"Four white coffees?" enquired the waitress.

"Yes, thank you," replied Louise who passed them to Dimitri and then took the cakes to the table before sitting down with the team.

"Anything of interest so far?" asked Louise.

"Not as many as I would have expected, if I am honest – maybe Mac's ruse has fooled them better than we could have hoped. According to the platform display, we are on platform 14 and they are going through all passengers before they go through the gates so we will need to be on our game," replied Storm.

"Well, that is just a little bit annoying," stated Louise.

"Let's leave it until closer to departure time as it will place them under pressure to hit the departure time and, hopefully, we'll get a more cursory inspection. I suspect they will come onto the train at least until the border so the more detailed check will happen there," stated Dave.

"Let's get our story straight in case they split us up. We are friends from different parts of St Petersburg heading to Tallinn to party with my friend Maksim overnight. You guys don't know Maksim, but you have been friends with me for years. You think Maksim fancies me cos I am a total babe. We are staying at the Ibis hotel in the city itself as it is only £28 per night and really central. We are travelling back tomorrow evening after the party and once the hangover has subsided. If they ask about being a Goth it is because we love diversity, creativity and individualism. We dislike a nanny state driving uniformity and social conservatism." Storm felt the details were important.

"Five mins to departure, let's head to the platform, team. Dimitri, stick close to me and you will be fine; it will be a cursory inspection at best, and you look nothing like your office-based alter ego. Passports at the ready."

Louise headed off for the platform with the others a step behind. Every fibre of her being was screaming this was so wrong and they would be found out. This hiding in plain sight idea of Storm's was not Louise's idea of fun – she much preferred being in a fire fight where your brain was occupied with staying alive and second to second decisions. Walking towards a checkpoint was torture. Louise slowed her pace down to look relaxed and turned to smile at the team.

"Tickets please," demanded the FSB agent as he looked quizzically at the four friends.

Dave handed over two tickets just a fraction behind Louise.

"You are going to Tallinn just for one night?"

"Yes, babe, we are going to a party. Don't you think my friend looks like a hairier Goth version of Chewbacca?" laughed Louise, using her most disarming smile.

The agent looked up at Dave then back to Louise and handed back their tickets.

"Have a good day," grumbled the guard as he put his hand out to the next person in the queue to reach the platform.

"Let's get to the far end of the train, it means they will have checked most of the train before they get to us and will be a bit bored of the process. Small things can make a difference, and this is the last leg," suggested Storm.

The team legged it down the platform, casually checking the train to see how busy it was and, seeing it reasonably busy, they got to the last carriage and hopped on just as the beeper was sounding to close the doors.

"We cut that a bit fine. It wouldn't have done to have missed the train. Mac would have been furious; you know what he is like," complained Dave.

"We still had 30 seconds; it was all fine. There's a table seat just in the middle. I want the window seat if that is ok with everyone." Without waiting for a reply, Storm hopped into the seat and moved to sit at the window. Dimitri took up a position just opposite, leaving Dave and Louise with the seats on the aisle.

"Oh, thanks for that comment to the guard, Louise, very helpful. Sometimes you are such a cow. Fucking Chewbacca," laughed Dave.

"Hahaha, I just couldn't help myself, we had to appear relaxed and taking the micky out of one of your friends and pointing him out to a guard is an easy way to rise above suspicion."

"Mmmmmmm, it doesn't mean you're not a cow though," grinned Dave.

"Babe, don't you listen to her. I think your Goth Chewbacca costume is kind of cute. I bet Sky would go for it. She might have a thing for guys wearing black lipstick."

Dave just frowned and said nothing in reply.

The team sat in silence for a few minutes as the train left the station. They took stock that they were one hurdle away from making it out of the fire. It was still a big hurdle, though, and the next checkpoint at the Russia / Estonia border would no doubt involve more scrutiny. Mac's progress was key to everything. If they discovered the dummies too early, then suspicion would rapidly fall back on this train and life would undoubtedly get very uncomfortable very quickly.

"I wonder how Mac is getting on?" asked Louise of no one in particular as she sensed the pensive mood building within the team.

"He will be fine; you know Mac, he is a genius at this kind of shit. Nothing scares him. I swear he will never retire; he just comes alive when there is an Operation on," replied Dave.

The team took some time to get their heads into the next phase of the operation and how to get over the border.

EIGHTEEN

As the team were approaching the border, Mac was thinking about finding a camp for the night. He needed to give the team time to contact Edward and get his pickup arranged. Suddenly he heard a scream and instantly knew one of his traps had found its mark. He was hoping it would take around five hunters out of the mix. The one that was hurt and four to carry him out of the woods to a place he could be taken to the hospital back at base. It also meant they were nearing the end of the false trail. Although he had done his best to disguise his trail, he knew this side of the road would be crawling with guards soon enough and he expected drones overhead with infra-red cameras to enable the hunter force to get heat signatures through the tree canopy. They would use those to help coordinate the hunt. There was good and bad news for Mac. There were some 2000 bears and 200 wolves in the woods surrounding the Gulf of Finland. It meant when they found a heat signature it did not necessarily mean it was human.

Mac was now heading along the coastline towards Finland although sticking within the tree line. The last thing he needed was being spotted from a passing ship or worse a Russian Navy vessel. The light was starting to fade so Mac headed further back into the forest and used the remaining light to make a basic camp. He picked a suitable spot in the hollow of the roots of a fallen tree to use that as the basis of his camp. It was only for one night. Ideally in an area with wolves etc you would put a hammock about eight feet up and out of harm's way, but if that was spotted by a drone or helicopter it would immediately be suspicious.

Mac felt on the balance of probability he was under more threat from being spotted from the air than from an issue with a lone wolf. If necessary, he could use the Glock to deal with the wolf. Mac spotted a fallen tree, cut a number of leafed branches from neighbouring trees and used the upturned remaining roots for the branches to lean against. He then used the dried Sphagnum moss over the branches where he would be lying as a layer of insulation before placing turf over and above that followed by more branches. It was a bit rough and ready, but all he was trying to do was reduce his heat signature as much as possible. Mac left one end open so he could roll under the canopy if he heard the buzz of a drone. The reason he did not move in immediately was that his body heat would gradually heat up the shelter and it would stand out from his surroundings. These things only acted as a heat shield for a few minutes.

Traditionally night-time was the time to move about but with the advances in infra-red cameras it was now more difficult if you were being hunted. Mac left off his thermal jacket, hat and gloves for similar reasons. He would put them on if he heard a drone. They would take up to five minutes to heat up and that would buy time for the drone to move off and search another part of the grid pattern. That took care of the immediate aerial threat, which meant he could concentrate in making the immediate vicinity secure from the ground force.

It would be more difficult if the hunter force was made up solely of special forces as they were trained to a far higher level and had superior equipment including night vision goggles. It was unlikely they would deploy that many special forces, but it was possible. It would depend on how badly Mac's team had pissed off Moscow. It was outwith his control so he would just have to suck it up and take his chances. The last thing for Mac to do was gather as many dried twigs as he could find, the type he used to make traps and you looked for to set a campfire. No fire tonight but it did make a good noise trap. You saw it regularly in the movies where a target places something noisy at a hotel doorway to get the heads up someone was going to break the door down so they could make their escape out the hotel room window. Mac spread the dried twigs in a ten-metre circumference round the campsite. All he needed was a heads up rather than a gun barrel in the side of his head before he realised he was in danger. Once the noise trap was in place, he sat down and took some time to munch some trail mix and drink the last of his bottled water to keep hydrated. Take the chance while you can get it was always his mantra as you just never knew when the next time was that he would be able to eat or drink.

Mac determined it wasn't safe to sleep, so he made sure he stayed awake. He was enjoying the quiet you can only experience in the middle of nowhere. City people would never understand it, that silence you got just at sundown. The nocturnal animals were not fully out yet and the daytime ones were heading into hiding to make it through the night. It only lasted about 20 minutes before he could hear foxes screaming nearby – he wasn't sure that was the correct term, but it sounded like a child being attacked. The first time you heard it while on stag duty was nerve wracking. It genuinely sounded like a child or a woman being attacked. On this occasion Mac actually felt it was a comforting noise. It meant the foxes felt safe and that there was currently no one nearby. Celebrate the small wins, he told himself with a wry smile. A couple of hours later, Mac felt a water droplet hit his forehead and held his hand out. Sure enough, it was starting to rain.

Normally he would be cursing as being wet was always a bit of a chore during escape and evasion, but in the current circumstance, he determined it was a good thing. The infra-red lenses on the drones would struggle and improved his chances of making it through until morning without being discovered. As the rain got heavier, Mac put on his jacket, hat and gloves before he moved into his makeshift shelter. The thermal heat signature was no longer his main concern and he preferred to stay dry for as long as possible. No doubt tomorrow he would have to deal with being wet to the skin, but for now he would allow himself to take the chance of being warm and dry.

Mac spent the time thinking through his plan for the morning. He would start to move just before dawn, which at this time of year would be around 5am. It was the time when people were less vigilant so it would give him the best chance of remaining undetected as he moved through the woods to his exfil point. It would be painfully slow as he had to remain as close to silent as he could. At this stage he had no back up and if he came across the hunter force in numbers, he would in all likelihood be captured. The prospect of capture didn't really fill him with joy, nor did the inevitable interrogation and torture afterwards.

Time passed slowly and the night dragged by until about an hour before dawn Mac sat up wide awake in his shelter suddenly, bringing all his senses to the fore. Was that one of his dried twigs that had broken? Was that sound manmade or a creature of the night? Mac caught himself holding his breath – he still did not understand why that was a natural reaction. It wasn't a particularly helpful response. He very gently took his knife out of the sheath on his belt. There it was again, but closer this time, definitely a scuff of a boot. "Bollocks," thought Mac; he was hoping to get through the night without being found. It was only a matter of time before his shelter was seen. He made a small hole with his knife on the side of the shelter to get a view who was within the vicinity of his camp and by now only a few yards away from him. As silently as possible, Mac shifted sideways, freeing himself up if he needed to respond to the threat.

He could feel adrenalin starting to course through his body as his brain took stock of the perilous nature of this change in his situation. He could see the soldier was carrying an AK-74 M, which was a real issue – if Mac took him out with the Glock the sound would be heard for miles around and would flood the area with the hunter force. He had that sinking realisation that he was in deep shit. He could see the target more clearly now in the gloom of the approaching dawn. He looked more like an ordinary grunt than Special Forces as he had no night vision which was a blessing and probably why he had not pinpointed the shelter. There was still a possibility that they would walk on by, but Mac felt the chances of it were slim.

Hope for the best but plan for the worst sprung to mind. It was a bit of a wank senior management phrase, but it seemed appropriate in the current circumstance. Mac exited the shelter, keeping as low and silent as possible, and bringing all his experience to bear he kept the shelter between himself and the hunter. Mac gradually moved back about twenty metres and started to circle round behind the hunter force soldier. Each placement of the foot taken slowly and deliberately being as silent as possible. Each step completed by landing on the side of the foot and rolling back onto the sole to minimise the chances of making unwanted sound. Gentle and slow movements but ready to spring in case he was discovered.

With the light improving minute by minute, suddenly the soldier saw the shelter in his peripheral vision, staring at it through the gloom as if trying to figure out if it was something that belonged or if it was manmade. Deciding it required further investigation he stepped slowly towards it, AK-74M assault rifle at the ready. As Mac was circling to get behind the hunter force soldier, so the soldier was circling to look inside the shelter, both on edge with senses heightened. From the outside it must have looked like the awkward mating dance of some previously unheard-of bird. Mac, with knife in hand, and the hunter soldier with AK-74M pulled tightly into his shoulder ready to fire if required. Mac waited until the soldier dipped his head into the shelter before making his move. Springing forward with as much momentum as he could muster, he knew that by coming in from the side there was no instant killing blow. It meant he had to take the assault rifle out of the picture first to stop any shots being fired and alerting anyone else in the vicinity; he could then react to anything else afterwards.

Mac used his momentum to catch the soldier off balance and slice down hard with his combat knife onto the back of the wrist of the trigger hand, taking away the immediate threat of being shot. As the soldier's hand dropped it exposed his neck and Mac slashed hard sideways catching the soldier at the base of the neck and followed it up with three quick stabs into the assailant's side and puncturing the right-side lung. The neck wound was deep, but it had missed the main arteries, so it was not an immediate killing blow.

The squaddie dropped his rifle and pulled his own knife with his left hand. Mac moved forward to try and land a killing blow, watching the assailant's eyes for that tell-tale sign that he was about to move. Everything was in the eyes; it was the gateway to the soul. The assailant lunged forward, left-handed and Mac reacted with a counter thrust of his own. At the last-minute Mac realised it was a feint and for guessing wrong he took a deep cut across his thigh. Mac took a step back; he had been too confident, resulting in him being a bit hasty and it had cost him. He was lucky the knife wound had missed his hamstring and his femoral artery – the last thing he needed was a life-threatening injury out here on his own.

Mac kept circling his opponent. They were both bleeding, but the soldier's injuries were deeper and bleeding more profusely; by keeping him moving it meant the soldier would slow down faster. They came together with knives and feet flying, everything a blur of kicks, punches and stabs; they were equally matched. The squaddie, however, was younger and fitter, and Mac was looking like he was starting to struggle, the loss of blood becoming a problem and slowing him down. Mac dropped his right shoulder feinting a thrust and attacked with a kick to the knee, he felt it land with a satisfying crunch. That evened things up and slowed the squaddie down as he struggled to put weight on the damaged knee.

He could now see fear now in the squaddie's eyes as he knew he was more seriously injured despite them being evenly matched. The look troubled Mac as people react to fear in different ways. Some run from it and others would use it to drive themselves forward – which one would this guy be? Two seconds later Mac found out: the assailant stumbled, and Mac came roaring in for the kill. At the last-minute Mac realised it was not a stumble but another ruse to draw Mac in and he had fallen for it. As he anticipated a further blow, Mac twisted as far as his aging body would allow just as he thrust his own knife as hard as he could into the heart of the assailant. It was a real killer blow and his assailant slumped to the ground bleeding out. Mac felt an instant glow of triumph which lasted less than two seconds as he buckled forward with the most incredible pain in his stomach. As the pain intensified, he realised that as he was landing the killing blow his assailant had stabbed him in the stomach.

"Fuck, that is all I need." Mac cursed his luck and carelessness.

In the growing light Mac opened his shirt and inspected the damage. It seemed to have missed his vital organs which was a good thing – the peritonitis from any potential puncture of his bowel would have to wait; there was nothing he could do for that without antibiotics. Mac took some duct tape and wrapped it round his torso, sealing up the wound. He pressed hard on it for a few minutes to slow down the blood loss and give it time to clot. Mac then inspected the cut on his thigh. It went deeper than he had first thought. It really needed to be stitched but he didn't have a needle and thread so more duct tape would have to do for just now.

Mac applied a tourniquet using the belt from the dead soldier. He only wanted to use it for a few minutes to see if he could get the bleeding to stop or at least slow down. He would need to regularly release it to prevent his lower leg dying from lack of blood and requiring amputation. Mac limped over to the body of the now dead soldier – he was only a young lad, early twenties at most. Mac took a good look at him.

"It was you or me, lad, it just wasn't your day to come up against me, but you gave it your best shot."

Mac searched him for anything that would be useful. He picked up the AK-74M and a spare magazine, a combat knife and full water bottle. Mac also found a radio dropped during the fight and picked it up – it might just give him a heads up if they found his trail. Mac stripped the young soldier and dressed him in Mac's clothes before dragging him into the shelter and left him there sitting up against the pine tree. It might delay the hunt if they thought they had killed him. He dressed in Hunter force combat fatigues.

Mac limped off in the direction of the border; he had to make the rendezvous point by sunset if he was to get back to the team. The pain was starting to kick in as the adrenalin from the fight left him. He smiled wryly to himself wishing he was in a Hollywood movie – when you got injured, you could just carry on as normal. Pain must only exist in real life and this hurt like hell. The adrenalin might get you through in the thick of a fight, but his body was now telling him to stop, take time to recover, this is bad for you. Being the stubborn fucker that he had always been, Mac chose to ignore it and battle on.

He remembered a spook during the troubles in Northern Ireland telling him he was the most pig-headed man she had ever met. What was a bad thing in one situation was very often a strength in another. There was a time and place to rest up and ten miles inside enemy territory just wasn't it. At most it would be only a matter of a couple of hours before that young lad was discovered dead inside the shelter and Mac wanted a few miles between him and them by the time that happened. He wasn't in the kind of physical shape to lay down another false trail through the trees, so instead he decided to bluff it out and walked in full combat gear as if he was part of the Hunter Force. It also meant that drones overhead were less of a threat.

It wasn't foolproof, and his trail would be open for anyone to follow, not just a semi-decent tracker. It did mean, however, he could move about in the open and that would perhaps balance out his slower movement due to the injuries.

After three hours of movement, Mac stopped to inspect his wounds. His leg was still bleeding although significantly reduced. It was his stomach wound that he was worried about. It did not really matter how you moved, it impacted on your stomach muscles. There was still seepage externally, but it was internal damage that worried Mac; internal bleeding was the silent killer. He was starting to feel the effects of the morning's exertion and that meant due to the blood loss he was getting less oxygen about his body. He had to lay low for an hour or so and give it another go after that.

Getting to the rendezvous on time was becoming less important than staying alive. Despite the warrior voice in his head telling him to keep moving, he knew the sensible thing was to take a recovery 15 minutes. He sat with his back against a tree; he could not eat anything in case his bowel was punctured, but he took a sip of water from the young soldier's canteen. He felt himself growing cold and distant before his hand fell to the ground, spilling the water in a puddle around his knees.

NINETEEN

Josef was looking for some good news – his call with the Director was not one for his highlights scrapbook. So far, they did not have the driver of the car that had been heading north and they did not have the rest of the assassins or the cyber security defector. He had pains in his chest and his stomach ulcer was playing up. Overall, it was one of his worst days ever. He looked around the war room and none of the other attendees would hold his gaze. It was the downside of his high standards style of leadership and the mood in the room was despondent. He needed to inject some energy and bring them back on point. He asked his secretary to buy some pizza and fizzy drinks and about 30 minutes later as it arrived Josef stood up in front of the team and cleared his throat to get their attention.

"We have had some setbacks today but that is all they are. I want to apologise to you all as some of those mistakes were mine and if we are going to bring this to a successful conclusion then we need to put the mistakes to one side and deal with them at the post incident review. I want you to have some pizza and a drink, take 15 mins to regroup and let's step back through it and see what leads we have."

"Josef, the team are tired, they have been at this for days – can I suggest we bring in a couple of fresh sets of eyes and freshen the whole thing up."

"OK, but we need to move quickly, did you have anyone in mind?"

"We have two young agents based here in Moscow, very talented and super keen, a young man called Viktor and a talented young lady called Natalya."

"I will go with your judgement, get them up to speed and we will bring them on board."

Josef gave the team some time to eat the pizza and have a bit of a refresh. Personally, he did not like pizza, it was just Western food for poor people. Instead, he went to the bathroom to splash some water on his face and get some energy back into his thinking. He looked at himself in the mirror and thought he had aged 10 years in the last week, his eyes were bloodshot due to lack of sleep and too much coffee, he had two days' stubble on his chin, and he generally looked like he needed a good wash. His shirt was crumpled and sweat stained and for someone who was normally pristine it was painful to see. He was disappointed with himself and with the team. They had been so close, but that one bad judgement call had cost them valuable time. He walked slowly back to the war room and paused before entering the meeting and pulled himself up mentally to get some bounce back into his voice. He needed to lead by example to get some energy back into the team.

"Ladies and gentlemen, I want to thank you for your efforts so far and in particular for the work in tracking down the assassins in St Petersburg; it was excellent work, and we were a touch unlucky. I have asked for two up and coming agents to join our major incident team. Please welcome Viktor and Natalya, and

I would take it as a personal favour if you could give them every assistance to get them up to speed and to make them feel welcome. Let's start off with a quick recap of what we currently know and our priority lines of enquiry."

Josef pointed to one of the senior men in the room to start off the review.

"Thank you, Colonel. We know that we have a team of four individuals that assassinated General Andropov in Moscow. They drove to St Petersburg and instead of fleeing to the West took up residence at a holiday let cottage on the outskirts of the city. With everything else we have seen this was out of character and did seem somewhat strange; however, we now know they were waiting to help the Head of Cyber Security for the FSB to defect. The defection took place during a Cyber Security Conference and shortly afterwards we believed they were seen in a black BMW speeding north towards the border with Finland and this tied into their perceived modus operandi. The car was photographed with five adults going through toll booths on the highway heading north. We set a trap just to the east of the border crossing point at a stretch of road recommended by the local Special Forces team; however, the car did not appear, and it has since been found with four shop dummies in the passenger and rear seats. The driver of the BMW somehow anticipated what we would do and left the main highway before the trap could be sprung. The driver left the car and is now on foot in the woods near the border. We have a hunter force looking for the driver in the woods; however, as of yet nothing has been found. We have not seen any sign of the remaining three assassins, and it is assumed that they are still with the defector. We don't currently know if they are still holed up somewhere in St Petersburg or if they have fled somewhere else to make good their escape from Russia."

"A good summary, thank you, we need to generate some ideas please. I suggest we leave finding the driver to the team on the ground and we concentrate our efforts on the remaining assassins and the defector. Just a brainstorm please and let's not probe them at this stage."

"Their main means of escape would be planes, trains, cars and buses."

"We also have cruise ships, fishing boats, tankers and leisure sailing craft."

"They could hole up somewhere to let the noise drop. Hotels, B&B, holiday let, camping."

"They could hire a car, steal a car, van, bus."

"They could hitchhike."

"They would need passports and possibly cash."

"They would need to change appearance, something bland and incongruous."

"What about weapons, handguns, knives ammunition etc."

"They would need food."

"They could be injured and need medical attention, hospitals, doctors, nurses etc."

Josef stood back up.

"Excellent, we have a lot to do. Split up the tasks and prioritise exit points from the city and associated border crossings. Can we get CCTV feeds from train stations, bus stations etc both live and recorded over the last 24 hours? I will get in touch with the hunter force and see if we have captured the driver. He may be a fountain of information."

Josef left the team to focus on St Petersburg and headed to his office.

"Get me Hunter Force command on the phone."

Two minutes later Josef was talking to a Major in the Spetznatz special forces command.

"Major, thank you for taking my call, what progress have you made in tracking down the driver of the black BMW?"

"Colonel, it is very difficult terrain and with the rain last night it meant that our infra-red cameras on the drones was ineffective. We brought in additional troops from one of the local quick reaction forces to bolster our own special forces. We had a strong trail heading north deeper into the forest; however, it faded out after a few miles. We put two thirds of the team in the North to flush him out and helicoptered a strike team of snipers further north near the border.

"The Hunter team's objective was to drive him into a trap. Unfortunately, he evaded our hunter force, and it looks like he took to the trees to back out of a false trail. In other words, we lost sight of him. Just after dawn we lost communication with one of the soldiers in the quick reaction force and about an hour ago, we found him dead and hidden in a shelter. He was stripped of his clothing, his gun, knife and radio, which were all taken by the attacker. It is possible the QRF soldier wounded the attacker during the fight as we found a blood trail heading west. We don't know how badly he is injured; however, there was a lot of blood at the fight site. It is difficult to determine if it was from our soldier or the target. In summary, he is alone, injured and still in Russia. He does, however, have a radio, so I suspect he will know we found the body and are closing in on him. If he is injured as badly as we suspect, then he will not get far before he bleeds out."

TWENTY

L ouise was trying to relax. Nothing was more obvious to Police and Border Controllers than a nervous person who would not make eye contact. She closed her eyes to reduce her heart rate when Dave tapped the table in front of her and nodded up the carriage. Louise opened up her phone to use it as a mirror and could see two border control guards making their way down the carriage and checking passports and travel documentation. Everyone was questioned and scrutinised in that totally impersonal way border controllers do.

"Game faces on, folks," stated Dave.

"Come on then, Dimitri, what is your most embarrassing moment you have had so far?" asked Storm.

"Eh well I don't really do much other than work these days," stumbled Dimitri.

"What about a few years ago, you must have done something that makes you wince inside?" asked Louise, following that Storm just wanted the team to be talking.

"I really fancied this girl in school, and she was just lovely, one of those ones all the guys fancied, and she liked me. Well, she lived away from her parents in a local school hostel as they were country folks and the commute to school was too long. One day after school she sneaked me into her room so we could hang out together. I know you will find this hard to believe, but I was the shy type. We were just sitting talking and then kissing and touching when she went to the bathroom and I was looking at her photos on the wall. She came out of the bathroom naked and asked me if I wanted to make love to her, so I stripped off and she pushed me back onto the bed and leaned forward to tie my hands to the headboard. Not that I knew it then, but I have shoulders that are weak and my shoulder popped out, how do you say it, dislocated. Well, I howled in pain and before she could untie me the matron burst into the room with half of the dormitory behind her only to see me tied naked to the bed and the girl standing there with a towel around her. I got whisked to hospital in an ambulance while she got a rollocking."

"Dimitri, you sly dog, it is always the quiet ones you have to watch," teased Storm in her seductive tones.

"Hey dog, I bet that made your reputation at school?" laughed Hairy Dave.

"Passports please," demanded the border control agent as he stood next to the table.

They all handed over their passports and Louise laughed and pointed to Dimitri.

"He is the one you need to watch, sir, he allows young ladies to tie him to the bed and abuse him, such a dark horse. Just don't let your sister anywhere near him. Who knew we had an S&M master in our midst? So, what was your safe word?" teased Louise as she looked back to Dimitri.

Dimitri blushed so red that the rest of the team burst out laughing and that just made Dimitri all the redder.

The Border Controller asked, "What takes you to Tallinn for one night?"

"My Goth friends are having a party in Tallinn, so the plan is to party hard tonight and come back tomorrow once the hangover has lifted. We have room for one more if you fancy it?" queried Storm seductively, touching the guard's hand.

"Unfortunately, I am required back in St Petersburg tonight, maybe next time," replied the controller. "Enjoy your party. I would remember your safe word for tonight, my friend, I think you might need it," said the controller with a straight face but a twinkle in his eye as he nodded to Dimitri.

The team all laughed including Dimitri, although his laugh was just a little bit more nervous than the others.

There was a collective sigh of relief as the Border Controllers continued their passport checks down the length of the train and even more so when they got off the train just over the border in Estonia ready to check passports for passengers travelling the other way and entering Russia.

They had done it, managed to exit Russia in one piece and get the package out at the same time.

"How much longer before we get to Tallinn?" asked Dimitri.

"Oh, we are about halfway," replied Louise absently.

"I can't believe it took 45 minutes to clear border control on the train," complained Dimitri.

"That is actually pretty good, my friend, it can take a few hours through some airports depending on which one you fly into. I have actually flown into Heathrow airport in London on a bank holiday Friday and it took me six hours to get through passport control and customs. That was flying back from Colombia right enough and they are quite strict with that particular country," replied Dave.

"Six hours!!!! Oh my God, that sounds like torture," exclaimed Dimitri.

"No, the torture costs extra," replied Dave with a wink to Storm.

"They torture you at Heathrow in London? What, how?" Dimitri looked at Dave and then Storm and Louise with incredulity.

"Oh, absolutely they have a series of special rooms for it under the baggage reclaim area. The noise of the baggage belts stops people hearing the screams." Dave was loving this.

"Really, that is disgusting, I thought the UK was above that kind of thing?" asked Dimitri.

"So, we don't torture our own people, just immigrants, it is important to make sure they are not a threat to the country. There are just so many bad people in the world. I mean it isn't bad torture or anything like that, it is just water boarding and we buy in SP-117 truth serum from Russia. The UK government would not allow proper physical torture," replied a straight-faced Dave.

"You are kidding right?" asked Dimitri.

"Of course, he is kidding, Dimitri, he is just teasing you because he is a bit of a dick," replied Louise.

"Sorry, Dimitri, it was too hard to resist. The UK is not like the USA who have dark sites dotted across the globe and Guantanamo Bay in Cuba. They are allowed to torture as long as it is not on US soil," replied Dave.

"In Russia they just do what needs to be done, people will tell everything over time. You cannot hold out for long; they have people who do interrogation for a living and really know what to do. SP-117 was developed in the same lab as Novichok. There is some debate over whether it means you only tell the truth, or you just lose your inhibitions and just tell everything. It is not accepted by the courts as evidence but what they do is use it to know where to look to get the evidence. The other good thing is you don't actually remember it being used on you; it wipes out your memory of the event so people never complain about it," answered Dimitri.

"Now that is clever, I wonder if it is more efficient than a polygraph. People now know they can beat a polygraph and history shows it doesn't help with psychopaths who don't believe they have done anything wrong. How interesting, we need to talk more about it, Dimitri, once we get you into the UK. And no, we are not going through Heathrow," said Dave with a grin.

Louise just rolled her eyes and Storm grinned back. Dimitri looked around the team, confused. He was struggling to understand British humour, at least he hoped it was humour.

The rest of the journey was uneventful, the team started to relax as the train stopped at the last station before Tallinn.

"I am going to check in with Edward and make sure the embassy is expecting us. Last thing I want to do is stand in a queue to talk to some jobsworth clerk." At that Louise picked up her phone and wandered up the carriage. Once again, she dialled the number from memory. It was not the sort of thing you stored on a phone.

"Brixton holidays, Sam speaking, how can I help you today?"

"I am interested in a company holiday, perhaps a cruise."

"Do you have a particular cruise in mind?"

"No, but I would like a presidential suite."

"Let me connect you to our cruise expert now."

Edward came on the phone with his implacable Kensington accent.

"Louise, my dear. Is everything going to plan?"

"Not quite, Edward, I'm afraid. We had to make some operational changes. There was a bit of noise when we picked up the package, well that and the potential leak in London."

"And the package?" asked Edward.

"Secure and with me. We are not far from our destination. We should arrive within the hour. Is everything set up at your end? Do you think it is secure?"

"There is a tight circle of people who needed to know, but I kept it as discreet as I could. Edward, as part of the change to our original plan we set up a decoy run up to the original border crossing. I need you to arrange a taxi for one of our party who got separated from the tour. It would need some experienced frog men. The party can be found at 60.505081 and 27.897258. They will be available for pick up from sundown tonight."

"Crikey, Louise, these things take time to arrange and take a lot of approval; what were you thinking?"

"Operational necessity, Edward, you were the one that ordered a last-minute departure from the itinerary and in order to deliver your package on time and in one piece we needed a diversion. This was the diversion. Please don't make an issue of it or be late, Edward and advise the frog men it might be a noisy pick up."

"I will make some calls, Louise, but I will need PM approval for this as looking at the map it is not a place we like to go to." Edward sounded flustered.

"I understand that, Edward, but please remember we don't leave anyone behind. Any answer but yes will not go down well at this end."

"Understood, my dear, I will do my very best for you."

"I will call again once we reach our holiday destination, and the package is delivered. Can you make sure we are expected as I really don't do queues?"

"Certainly, Louise, consider it done."

At that Louise disconnected the call and re-joined the team.

"All set for Tallinn and London is arranging a taxi for Mac."

"Mac is getting a taxi to Helsinki?" asked Dimitri.

"No, Dimitri, it is just a figure of speech. We just mean they are arranging for him to be picked up and delivered into Tallinn."

Dimitri blushed at his naivety and looked to the floor.

"When we get into Tallinn train station it is a fifteen-minute walk from the station to the embassy. I suggest we walk in standard security formation. Dave, you take the lead, Dimitri you walk alongside Storm and I will take up the rear. Keep your wits about you – until we are in the embassy there is still an operational risk."

"I am sure the embassy is going to love our dress sense, Storm. I think we may get some sideways looks."

"You love the attention, Dave; we both know this is your new Saturday night clothes and you are loving wearing makeup and nail polish. Let's face it, you will look a million dollars in your goth get up and navy-blue jacket when you go out with Sky back in the UK."

"Navy-blue jacket?" enquired a puzzled Dimitri.

"Never mind, babe, Dave has a thing for navy-blue jackets. He thinks the chicks love it."

"Really, how interesting. Where would I get one of those?" asked Dimitri.

The three of them looked at Dimitri who sat there straight faced before grinning from ear to ear.

"Just kidding around."

"Good one, Dimitri, you are getting the hang of sarcasm as a sense of humour," replied Storm.

"I am not sure that's a good thing," laughed Louise as the train pulled into the platform.

TWENTY-ONE

Josef was sat at his desk wating on a progress update from either the Special Forces team in the North or the FSB agents focussing on the West when the phone rang.

"Josef, it is Michail. I have some information for you from our friend in London, but Josef, it is time sensitive, so you need to get moving on it. The people you are after are on the train to Tallinn bound for their embassy. They will arrive at the train station shortly. What assets do you have there that are available for immediate deployment?"

"We have local agents and I believe some others off the books that I can tap into if I need to. Leave it with me and I will deal with it. Michail, thank you, it is the first bit of good news I have had in the last 24 hours."

Josef banged the table in anticipation. "I have you now," he said quietly to himself. He stood up from his leather-bound desk and headed to the war room.

"I have just received some information that they are on a train to Tallinn bound for their embassy and will arrive shortly. I want them followed from their arrival at the station and I want the defector eliminated before he gets inside that embassy. I don't mind how it is done but we need him taken out before he gets to the embassy. If the assassin bitch from the theatre is there,

I want her taken alive if possible. Gentlemen, I want a live feed and let us make it a success this time. I do not want mistakes."

The war room became a frantic hub of activity, people walking in and out and making phone calls. At last, there was a buzz of anticipation.

"Colonel, I have the CCTV recordings from the time of boarding the train to Tallinn."

Josef turned his attention to the centre screen on the video wall. It was a full colour feed and was working from five minutes before the train left the station. There was a bottleneck of people passing the security guards and walking up to the train. Josef was watching it eagerly but nowhere did he see the expected team of assassins. He turned to the agent with a puzzled look on his face, the one that said what exactly am I looking at.

The agent took a presentation pointer from his pocket and restarted the video loop. Josef turned back to the screen and he could see the red dot from the presentation pointer circling a mixed group of misfits. Josef subconsciously took a step closer to the screen.

"Is that them there? That group of…?"

"Goths, sir, they are disguised as Goths," interrupted the agent.

"Goths? Who the hell dresses as Goths in the middle of an operation?" asked Josef to no one in particular, his voice giving away his disbelief.

"Exactly, sir. Who indeed? I have talked to the border guard on the train and he remembers them, sir. They were laughing and joking between themselves and very relaxed. There was nothing suspicious about them other than them being Goths. They are booked onto a return train late tomorrow, sir. Apparently, they stated that they were attending a party tonight at a friend's house."

"Thank you, that is very helpful, can you get a still photo of them over to the agents heading to the train station in Tallinn? It should not be too hard to pick them up from the crowd. I am sorry, what was your name?"

"Leon, Colonel. My name is Leon."

"Thank you, Leon. Can you also remind them to be aware that they may well have changed how they look while on the train? They have already shown that they are very resourceful, and we should be extra vigilant."

"Certainly, Colonel, right away."

"Smart chap, that Leon," said Josef to no one in particular.

"Can we get a feed from Tallinn train station CCTV?"

"We can, Colonel; however, it will take time to hack into their system as it is not one of ours. I doubt we can do it before the train arrives. We have arranged for bodycams though, Colonel, so we will have some sort of feed. They work off the local 5G network available in Tallinn. They were getting 500MB per sec during testing so we should get a real time feed. We will also be able to track our agents on the map I am just about to put onto screen 2, Colonel, the one on the right."

"Excellent, is it encrypted? I mean can anyone else track them from the feed?"

"In theory everything is hackable, Colonel; however, the local devices have been deployed with 256bit encryption and they would be months if not years to defeat it and that would only be if the live feed was always available to them. It is encrypted all the way through the internet to servers in Moscow who decrypt it."

"Thank you and in non-geek speak that means what exactly?"

"They can't track our team through the connection."

Josef sighed to himself. He hated dealing with geeks, it is as if they have their own language and looked down on those that don't understand it.

"Let me see, we have four agents at the terminal; how experienced are they in field work?" asked Josef.

"Colonel, the lead agent is very experienced with over ten years' experience in numerous countries all across Europe. The least experienced is just a few months out of the academy, however is showing a lot of promise. They will only watch from a distance and the lead agent will be in charge."

"Ok, thank you. At such short notice we have to use what is available. It is only a five min taxi ride from the station to the embassy or about a 15 min walk through the park – what is the plan? We need to keep this from being a media circus. The last thing I need is Moscow jumping all over me for starting an international incident," said Josef.

"Colonel, we have the train approaching the platform. It looks like platform 2. We have an agent at the head of the platform and one at the exit to the taxi rank and one to the exit that leads to the park if they decide to walk. The third one is in the middle, posing as a passenger looking for their platform."

"They won't be first off and will wait in the carriage until the platform is busy," mused Josef.

Sure enough, on the screen there was no sign of the team until the platform was full of people.

The mood in the war room was pensive as the train pulled into the station in Tallinn and the assassins worked their way through the passengers standing on the concourse looking for the platform their train was leaving from or waiting on friends and loved ones to arrive at the station. They had a team within the station and waiting in vehicles outside. As a backup, Josef had asked for a sniper to be as close to the Embassy as possible. All roads lead to the embassy and it was the sensible play by the assassins. He still could not understand why they had not left Russia directly. Everything else in their plan had been meticulous. The St Petersburg thing just seemed out of place, almost as if someone in their government wanted them to get caught. How very strange, he thought. Josef did not particularly like politics, although he was ambitious and at some stage all roles in Russian Government became political. Josef knew they had a mole within British MI6, and he wondered whether the St Petersburg plot had been part of a masterplan to expose the British as hypocrites on the world stage. There was no logical reason to use a successful assassination team to babysit a defector, which was risky at the best of times.

Josef shook his head to stop his theorising.

"Just remember I don't want the defector to make it to the embassy alive. Take him out. Capturing the girl alive is secondary, but still important."

"Understood, Colonel."

"That's them there." Josef was excitedly pointing to a Goth on the steps of the train surveying the platform before beckoning the rest of the team to exit the carriage.

There was a decided hush in the room as every eye was drawn to the bank of screens on the wall of the war room. You could almost cut the nervous energy with a knife, it was so evident. There was a glow about Josef's eyes, gone was the tired look and the red eyes and in its place was a reddish flush of excitement. Josef loved the chase even more than the actual event. On the screen you could see the queue of people going through the final barrier ticket check before wandering into the centre of the concourse.

"Standby standby, targets exiting the platform," came through the speaker on the centre console of the room.

"Oh, we have audio?" asked Josef.

"Yes, Colonel, the devices do both audio and video," replied the agent.

"Well, that is exciting."

The agent looked sideways at Josef, unsure if he was joking or if he was serious, but decided just to let the comment slide in case he interpreted it the wrong way.

"Targets exiting station to the right toward the taxi rank."

"Roger that."

"Transport arranged, silver sedan."

The four dots on the video screen converged on the taxi rank exit and entered a black SUV vehicle.

"Targets are in a black SUV, repeat, targets are in a black SUV."

The red dots on the screen left the train station on the roads of Tallinn, the video feed showing the back of a car seat.

"Target vehicle approaching stop point."

Just two hundred metres from the embassy the red dots stopped moving and the video feed showed them exiting the vehicle and converging on the black SUV. The SUV had been slammed from the side by an old van. Suddenly the doors of the SUV opened, and a dazed, tall, dark-haired female stood facing the agents holding a handgun in one hand while touching her forehead to see if it was bleeding. Seeing it was, she firmed up her arm with the handgun and aimed it directly at the agents exiting the silver sedan.

"Don't be stupid, you really don't want to do this," she shouted.

"Give us Dimitri and you and your friends can walk away."

The female agent just smiled as the other doors opened on the SUV and and the other two agents exited, keeping Dimitri behind them. They took up a standard close protection formation around Dimitri with the dark-haired agent in the rear, walking backwards. Her gaze never wavered as they moved from the cover of the SUV and started the 200m walk to the embassy.

Within the war room the tension was palpable. They knew this had to be resolved before the entrance to the embassy.

"Take that dark haired assassin alive, I want her alive. That is the one from the Bolshoi." Josef banged the table to emphasise his point.

They could see the foreign assassins move towards the embassy, keeping close to the parked vehicles to reduce the visibility to the Russian agents. The tall dark-haired agent continued to prevent a clean shot at Dimitri. Silently Josef admired the dedication of putting her life on the line for a Russian she did not know and would probably never meet again. The distance to the embassy was now one hundred metres and closing. The assassins had reached the end of the parked cars that were covering their retreat and they paused as they now had to make a last-minute dash for the embassy without any cover.

The assassins paused at the last parked car and Josef could see the dark haired one talking quickly to the rest of them. Suddenly the race was on. Josef's team had under 14 seconds to stop the defector. The assassins sprinting for the safety of the Embassy, still in a formation that protected Dimitri. Josef had his head in his hands when a shot rang out and a second later the dark-haired Bolshoi assassin dropped to the sidewalk. The assassin team turned to see the female lying on the ground. Clutching her side, she looked up and frantically waved them to get Dimitri to safety. Armed British soldiers could be seen at the embassy gates shouting encouragement to the assassins, screaming at them to make it to them so they could close ranks behind them.

"I have a shot on the defector," came through from the sniper.

"Take the shot," replied Josef, struggling to keep the anticipation from his voice.

A second shot rang out on the speaker and a kick up of dust could be seen behind the fleeing assassins. Josef could see the dark-haired female stagger upright and, using the wall for support, making her way to the safety of the embassy. She was clutching her side with one hand while using the other one to move slowly down the building walls, still clutching her gun. The rest of the fleeing assassins were now only 30 metres from the Embassy gates when a third shot rang out and the traitor fell to the ground. The remaining two agents picked him up between them and dragged him by the arms the final few metres and into the safety of the embassy. Josef could see the soldiers stationed at the embassy take the traitor between them and drag him inside the building.

"Any sign of life?" asked Josef.

"That is a negative."

The remaining agents turned, nodded to each other and handguns fully up returned fire and suddenly all hell broke loose. The assassins were making a mad dash to retrieve their stricken comrade when a silver van screeched to a halt beside the staggering female assassin. The side door opened before the vehicle had come to a complete stop. Two burly-looking men in balaclavas jumped out of the van and grabbed the female from behind and into the side door of the van.

"We have the girl," came through the speakers. No emotion, just very factual.

The remaining two assassins emptied their magazines in a vain attempt to stop it from leaving. They, however, could only aim at the tyres as they could not afford to hit their comrade inside the van.

Josef leaned back in his chair and placed his hands behind his head and smiled at the outcome. He continued to watch as the Russian field agents headed back to their vehicle and left the scene. The last thing on the screen was the remaining two British targets aiming their guns at the FSB agents and realising in despair that their magazines were empty. All they could do was glare after them.

"Take her to the safe house near the border. I will get an interrogator to meet you there. I want to make sure we have the right girl before I go to the Director with a victory. Congratulations, gentlemen. You have done well. Time for some well-earned rest. I for one need a shower and a vodka," stated Josef.

The team in the war room looked around at each other. Getting praise from Josef was not a regular occurrence. Josef stood up and turning round he looked at the wall charts full of diagrams and pieces of connecting string, the now blank wall monitors and the members of the team that were jubilant but tired. Success in Russia was understated. They were not American with hugs and high fives, or even the British with their handshakes. In Russia you got a nod at best, not even a smile.

Josef left the war room and walked back to his office along the corridor; at last he had a spring in his step and a self-satisfied glow of success. A small part of his brain was warning they had not yet confirmed it was the right female or that the defector had been confirmed dead, but those details would sort themselves out in the next 24 to 48 hours. The mole would confirm both, but as a backup plan Josef wanted an interrogator to the safe house to make sure the female was in fact the one that he wanted.

Josef entered his office and sat behind his desk, opened his metal filing cabinet to take out a bottle of vodka before pouring himself a large glass. He sat back on his leather chair and sipped his vodka, savouring every drop. He was not a big drinker like a lot of his fellow Russians, but he liked to celebrate the wins. Some people drunk to drown their sorrows, Josef preferred to come out fighting during the tough times and preferred instead to celebrate his successes. As he sipped his vodka, he could imagine his chess board with his rook taking another pawn off the board. Another pawn removed from his path towards his ultimate goal. This one was a pawn from the shadows and that was a bigger victory. As he finished his celebratory drink, he picked up the phone and called an old acquaintance in one of the less talked about parts of the FSB.

"Grigory, it is Josef, who is your most accomplished interrogator?"

"Dr Galina Golubeva, Josef. Why do you ask?"

"I have a job that needs her particular talents on the Russia-Estonia border. I need her to confirm the identity of a young lady we have in a safe house before I parade her in front of the Director. We believe she is the assassin of General Andropov, so it is highly sensitive and very political as you can imagine. Can you free her up for me and get her to the safe house on the border as soon as possible?"

"Let me check what we have her doing, give me a minute," stated Grigori.

Josef could hear Grigory frantically typing away on a keyboard and sighing to himself before eventually responding.

"It will take a bit of doing, Josef, she is in the middle of something in Moscow."

"This has the Director's attention, Grigory, you know what he is like. Is there any way you can free her up? I would hate to pull him into this."

Josef could hear a sigh of resignation on the phone before Grigory responded.

"Of course, Josef. Email me the safe house location and I will get Dr Garina there within a few hours. Josef. You owe me one for this. Don't forget your friends when you are in the Director's seat."

"I never forget my friends, Grigory. Thank you, Grigory."

Josef placed the phone back in its cradle. There was nothing much more he could do in the office and he was not joking when he said he needed a shower. Josef switched the light off in the office and headed down to the garage to get his driver to take him back to his flat. His mind had now moved on to thinking about all the work that had stacked up over the last few days that he had not been able to attend to. Still, he thought this was a very big feather in his cap and a step towards his next promotion. As he sat in the official FSB vehicle on the commute back to his FSB allotted residence, his head nodded forward, and he fell fast asleep for the first time in days.

TWENTY-TWO

Storm and Hairy Dave were sat in the Embassy in despair. There was nothing to be said, so the pair sat in silence staring at the floor. Each one a captive of their own thoughts. Dimitri shot, Louise shot and captured, Mac on his own in god knows where and no idea about his status.

"What a cluster fuck! I knew we should never have agreed to babysit the geek. There are experts in this kind of thing, why on earth did they give that job to us? It is almost as if they wanted us to fail," complained Dave.

"Yeah, babe I get it, I will contact Edward in London and let them know what has happened and make sure they have Mac's taxi lined up. We need to find Louise before they take her to Moscow. They will have her holed up somewhere first though. We need help. I will get London onto that as well," replied Storm.

"OK, I will get us some coffee and some food. I will also talk to the local squaddies to get some ammunition in case we are needed."

"Good shout, Dave."

As Dave headed off in search of coffee, Storm got in touch with Edward. She called the same number as Louise and went through the same recognition shenanigans before Edward came on the phone.

"Hello Louise."

"Edward, this is Storm, we have a situation in Tallinn. They knew we were coming, Edward; they were waiting for us. That leak you thought you had in London is a definite and we got royally fucked by them. Dimitri was shot and died inside the Embassy. More importantly, Louise was also shot before being taken by what we suspect is the FSB. I need her tracked, Edward, to whatever safe house they have her in. So, you can get us some resource to get her rescued?"

"Slow down, Storm. Is Dimitri definitely dead?"

"I know what dead looks like, Edward, and Dimitri was definitely dead."

"That is unfortunate. There will be a huge drama about this back in London. I will do what I can to cover for you."

"I don't need you to cover for me, Edward, what I do need is to understand what you are going to do to help us get Louise."

"Give me five minutes and I will flag it up the chain of command. I will do everything I can."

"Everything you can does not fill me with an awful lot of confidence, Edward. We need action not pretty words. We DO NOT leave people behind."

With that the line went dead and Storm stood there biting her lip, waiting on the response from London.

Fifteen minutes passed before the phone rang and Storm raised the phone to her ear anxiously waiting on the views from the senior team in London.

"Not good news, Storm. George will not sanction a recovery exercise. He will contact Moscow using diplomatic channels and negotiate her release. Louise knew the risks before she took on the mission. She will have to face the consequences of that decision."

"What the fuck, Edward! Who are you kidding, please don't make me come to London and fuck shit up? Just how long does he think diplomatic means will take? Two years, Edward? During which Louise gets tortured and raped and waterboarded!" Storm raged.

"George has made his decision, Storm, and he will not be changing his mind. What I need is for you and Dave to wait in place until Mac arrives and then the three of you will get on the first plane back to the UK."

Storm did not reply and let the silence build. She was furious and was silently shaking with rage. How dare this deskbound upstart leave one of their own behind.

"I take it your silence is agreement, Storm."

"We are going to have to agree to disagree; now I have a coffee and some dinner with my name on it so please excuse me but I have to go."

Storm stomped through the corridors to the canteen in the Embassy. As she walked in through the door, she saw Dave sitting in one of the corners quietly drinking a coffee with a half-eaten sandwich in front of him. Storm walked slowly over to the table but instead of sitting down stood there almost to the point of tears she was so angry.

"I take it from your expression that did not go as planned?" enquired Dave.

"Not here, too many ears and too many spooks."

Storm picked up her coffee, looked at the egg and cress sandwich in disgust and strode out of the room, with Dave following a few steps behind, still munching the remains of his sandwich.

"I have never liked plastic sandwiches you know; these prepacked things just lack flavour, and the bread is always soggy. So, what is up?"

"Edward is a total pussy, and his Director, George, is just going to let Louise hang. They will use all diplomatic efforts but won't raise a finger. You and I have just to hang about here until they retrieve Mac and then get the first flight home."

"What? They are going to do nothing?"

"Exactly that. Nothing. Ivory tower wankers. I cannot accept that, Dave, you and I have to do something. If that was you or me that was captured Louise would move mountains to get us back. I am just not that sure what we can do without a location. How can we find out where they have taken her?"

"Who do we know that could find that out other than spooks? Wait a minute, did you not say Louise's younger brother was into that shit? I am not sure if he is a spook, but he is into hacking or computers and stuff like that? Do we have a way to get in touch with him?" enquired Dave, trying to be the voice of reason.

"I do," laughed Storm; "we went on a couple of dates a year or so ago but I then got deployed and it fizzled out. I never mentioned it to Louise so I would be grateful if you keep it to yourself. Let me see, I have it here somewhere, Jaimie, here we go. It is just going dead, bollocks, looks like this was a dead end."

"Did you enter 00 44 first before the number?" asked Dave.

"Hahahaha, actually no I didn't, let me try again. It is ringing.

"Jaimie, it is Storm, how are you?"

"I am fine, Mrs. This is a bit unexpected; I did not think I would hear again from you. How have you been? Are you back in the real world yet?"

"That is the reason I am calling. We have a problem with an Op and Louise is in some trouble. We could really do with some help. London won't play ball."

"Is Louise all right?

"I can't go into too much detail as it is still a live operation. She was injured and has been taken by the wrong sort of people somewhere. We need your help," stated Storm.

"Anything I can do to help I gladly will, you know that. What seems to be the problem?"

"A Director in London is refusing to set up a team to spring her and is insisting they will use diplomatic means to get her back which will take months if not years. I need you to find out where they are keeping her. Once I know that I can get a local team together to work with me and Dave. We will go in and get her."

"Ouch, Louise will not be a happy girl if she knows you called me. You know how protective she gets. Ok, I have a few questions.

"Who do you think took her?" asked Jaimie.

"FSB."

"Shit, ok, I did not expect that. That makes it a bit tougher."

"Where and when did it happen?"

"Just outside the British Embassy in Tallinn, Estonia around 4pm."

"I need you to be precise please."

"Ok, let me think, we got off the train from St Petersburg at 3:45, walked to the taxi rank and jumped in our ride. We were forced off the road so that would make it 4:03pm on Wismari, number 6."

"Do you happen to know what type of vehicle they used?"

"It was a silver van, about the size of a Ford Transit."

"Thank you. Can I get you on this number?"

"Absolutely. Day or night."

"Leave it with me, Storm. You get your team together and I will do what I do."

"How are you going to hack the FSB, Jaimie?

"Who said anything about hacking, Storm? That would be illegal, and I have a sister who would kill me. Anyway, why would I want to do it again. It isn't as much fun the second time around."

At that the phone went dead and Storm stood there speechless. Hack them again? Like it was nothing. That kid was getting scarier by the day. Storm walked back to find Dave and update him on the call with Jaimie. Surprisingly she found him back at the same table in the canteen eating the sandwich that Storm had walked away from. Dave looked up as she approached the table.

"What? I was hungry," said Dave in a defensive manner.

"You need to get some standards in your life, Dave. That sandwich is gross."

"Food is food, Storm, and beggars can't be choosers."

"It is that kind of attitude which lets you wake up to a howler on a Sunday morning, Mr."

"Touché," responded Dave, looking a bit sheepish and red necked.

Storm spent the next few minutes updating Dave on the conversation with Jaimie.

"We have to plan as if he will come through. We need a team as you and me on our own won't cut it. I wonder how close they are to getting Mac back – we could really use his help on this."

"Let me check with the local spooks on site, they might have something on that as he is supposed to be getting dropped off here. Why don't you go and see if you can get us some body armour and some better armament, and I will go see what they know about Mac."

"Deal," replied Dave with a mouthful of sandwich.

"Dave, sometimes you are such an animal."

"What?" replied Dave looking a bit hurt by the comment.

At that Storm went looking for the spooks at the embassy. That normally meant heading downward to the basement area. Spooks were not the most social of types and tended to keep themselves to themselves. Not only that, but the rooms were constantly locked and only entry using the keypad and retinal scanner allowed any sort of access. Storm found what looked like spook city and rung the buzzer to get some attention. It did not have a sign above the door saying SPIES but she had been in enough embassies to get the general feel of the place. Two minutes later a very pale looking blonde woman peaked her head round the door.

"How can I help you?"

"Hi there, my name is Storm and I just arrived as a babysitter to your defector. Don't worry, I don't want any information about that, but do you happen to know what time our colleague is expected? I need to book flights back to London for us and it would be helpful to understand a basic timeline."

"Let me go and talk to the agent dealing with that particular extraction. Bear with me. Actually, his taxi is currently out to pick him up."

Storm nodded in thanks and turned round to go and see how Dave was getting on with getting some armour and stuff.

TWENTY-THREE

Mac came to with the rain pouring down. A bit dazed he went to sit up and the pain in his stomach and leg came flooding back. He couldn't sit up the normal way and had to scramble on to his side and then all fours to sit up onto his knees. The pain was pretty severe, but the good news was if he felt pain it meant he was alive. Mac checked the wound on his stomach. He needed to check it and make sure it wasn't going bad. He had seen gangrene one time in Africa, and it was something to be avoided.

He took off the duct tape which was like waxing your legs and pulled off all the hair near his wound. He wasn't sure which was worse – the taking off of the tape or the wound itself. He washed the wound as best he could. There was a small amount of seepage, but it was in better condition than he had any right to expect. Mac applied some fresh tape and bound it up as tight as he could. There was no rotten flesh smell and that was positive, but he knew he needed to get it worked on by professionals within the next few hours or he could be in real trouble. Once wounds went bad, they became increasingly difficult to treat and he had no idea what the skill levels of doctors were like in these parts in dealing with stab wounds.

He lay on his side and took down his trousers to his knee. For some reason the top of his thigh was virtually hairless naturally so taking off the duct tape from the cut did not hurt nearly as much. He cleaned the cut, but it was still bleeding and he did not fancy his chances if that continued. Who knew how much damage it had done already? He knew he had to cauterise it. This was going to suck. He had had to do it a few years ago in South America and he could still remember how bad it was. The simplest way was to heat up his knife and apply it to the wound. He could also take a bullet apart and put the powder on it and light it, but he was unsure how easily it would spark when on the wound and he did not have a way of getting the bullet and the casing apart to free up the powder.

The decision made, Mac got some dried grass and some dried twigs together to make a small fire. He did not need much as all it needed to do was heat up his blade. They had been shown how to get a basic fire going from nothing as part of their escape and evasion training. It wasn't a skill he used particularly often, but it came in useful today and five minutes later Mac had a small flame heating up the blade of his knife to a dull orange. Mac dug out a pair of socks from his rucksack before taking a number of deep breaths and placed the hot knife onto the wound. He screamed into the socks biting down as hard as he could and almost passed out with the intensity of the pain. He was not sure if the pain was worse than the hissing sound together with the smell of burning flesh, his flesh. He dropped the knife and took a minute or two to catch his breath before inspecting his handiwork. The bleeding had stopped, which was fantastic, but he now had yet another scar to add to his collection and this one was all his own handiwork.

"I never was any good at art in school. And that is not pretty," he grumbled to himself. Mac gingerly stood up and pulled his trousers back up. He had stopped the bleeding; however, it was scar tissue and could easily start bleeding again if he overdid it. He scuffed the fire out by stamping on it and just had to hope that the hunter force were not paying too much attention. Thankfully there was a light breeze out to sea and the plume of smoke would be easier to hide.

Mac picked up his knife and placed the rest of the stuff back into the rucksack before putting it on his back, picking up his Lobaev rifle and heading towards his exit point. Back in the car park in St Petersburg he had deliberately picked a promontory on the Russian part of the Gulf of Finland as the exfil point. It made life a bit more difficult for him but the frog men team coming to pick him up would be coming from the sea and he did not want them having to come too deep into Russian waters. The Russians did not like that kind of thing and would react hard and fast to any major intrusion.

Mac checked the time; he would love to have said he knew by the stars or the moon or some other astral body, but the truth was he just checked his watch. On a clear night he could navigate by the stars but in Europe there was a lot of rainfall and it was not the easiest nor the most reliable way. Being a touch old school and with the decision to split the team being made last minute, he did not have a GPRS navigation system.

In a hunter situation they could be tracked if the hunter force threw technology at the situation, so old school was sometimes better. Mac took out his map and a compass and calculated he was about 90 minutes from his rendezvous. It was going to be tight. Although he had stopped the bleeding, his leg was still in a bad way and he was favouring his side so a high paced forced march was off the cards. He also had to be aware that they may well have figured out where his exit point is and set up a trap for him, so he was going to have to be careful.

He reckoned he had roughly around 20 minutes to spare, so he put his best foot forward and got up a pace he felt he could sustain given his blood loss and injuries. Mac kept within the edges of the tree line but where he could he stepped onto the seaward side and got up a more consistent pace. He had to keep his wits about him and an eye out to sea in case there were Russian naval vessels looking for him. He did not dare stop and take a rest; he knew he would stiffen up and he might not get moving again. Some painkillers would not go amiss; however, when they had split up, he never took any with him. That was a lesson for next time. He smiled ruefully to himself. He was already starting to think about next time, and he hadn't even survived this one yet.

He knew deep down he was still in real trouble and it was on a knife edge as to whether he made it out of this alive. There was some real benefit to being a stubborn old git and he knew he would never give up. If he had to crawl to the exit point, then that is exactly what he would do. He stopped in his tracks – was that a buzzing noise he heard? Mac threw himself to the ground with an audible grunt and kept his face tight to the ground. Any camera feed could pick up a human face and he needed to make sure his outline was not human shaped. He pulled his knees up underneath him and the pain was horrendous from both his side and the cauterised cut on his leg.

Sure enough, the sound he heard was a drone. He heard it pause in its flight and hover about fifty metres overhead before moving further inland. He was sure that he had been seen, so Mac forced himself into a half limping jog. It might well open up the wound in his stomach, but he would be captured if he did not make the exit in time. It was crunch time and he just had to get on with it. He forced himself to distract his brain. The best way to force your body beyond its natural limits was to distract the brain with something else, anything else. When he was in Northern Ireland, he spent some time as a security driver to one of the Generals and the advanced driving technique for ensuring you could drive safely at pace was to talk yourself through the route, what each risk was and mentally tracking cars nearby, going through junctions without stopping and were those groups of people just people or something more sinister.

Mac started looking ahead, what was over that rise, was that a boat out to sea, could that tree have a hunter force soldier behind it waiting to step out and take him out. Mac paused, gulping down some air. It wasn't that he wasn't fit but with the blood loss there were now fewer red blood cells to transport oxygen around his body, so any exertion was tougher than it would be normally.

He cocked his head to one side trying to trace a sound. There it was again. "Fuck, fuck, fuck," he muttered under his breath. "Just what I need, DOGS."

The unmistakeable sound of hounds in the distance but getting closer. It would not be long before they picked up his scent and the chase would be on. Not only did he need to get to the exit point, but he had to be at least a mile ahead of the hunter force to prevent them taking shots at the Special Boat Service (SBS) team heading to pick him up. He got himself back into that limping jog and tried to up the pace as best he could. His body was running on empty, and he reckoned with the limping jog that he had about 45 minutes left, and he was not sure his body was up to it. The dogs sounded as if they were a couple of miles out, but he could not be sure as the forest and hills could play tricks on you. To be honest, it did not really matter, he just had to focus on getting to the exit point.

He had spent time with the SBS boys in the Iranian Gulf a few years back. A tough bunch of bastards and no mistake. Another scrape he nearly didn't make it out of, but he had saved the life of a young Glasgow lad. Carried him for two miles back to the boat. Amazing how many Scots there were in the UK Special Forces. Mac focussed on making it to the next rise; he was out in the open for the race to the exfil point. The push up the rise was killing his already bad leg and he was really worried the scar tissue would burst open. "One more step, just one more step" he kept telling himself over and over. When he got to the top of the rise, he lowered himself to the ground to scout out the land in front of him and to make a wary check to see if he could spot where the hunter force was. He took a quick 60-second breather and the dogs were definitely closer. That drone must have picked him out. Just as he thought that, he heard a buzzing nearby and turned to look upwards and saw it hovering about one hundred metres away.

He had a decision to make. Take out the drone and definitely be heard, or carry on and make it to the exit point before them. Mac took a chance and stopped at a rocky outcrop, taking the Lobaev off his shoulder and took aim at the drone. He took a few seconds to get his breathing under control and, using the rocky outcrop to steady his aim, he fired at the hovering drone. "FUCK!" He missed. He put another round of ammo in the chamber and took aim again; this time he made an allowance of a few centimetres for the breeze.

He lifted his head to see the drone, but he must have nicked one of the blades as the drone spiralled into the ground. There was no satisfying explosion or burst of flames, but he took pride in hitting it. Just as he was shouldering the Lobaev to get moving, a small piece of rock splintered just above him before he heard the boom of the shot. They must have been closer than he thought. He pushed down the slope towards the exit point and moved back into his jog.

He had about one click to go and would have to wait on the extraction team. The time between the rock and the boom of the shot being so little he knew they were under a mile behind him. He would not have long before the hunter force were on him or they had another drone in the air, tracking his movements. He was stumbling now, his legs full of lactic acid and even his good leg was starting to give out, he was now not lifting his feet properly and stumbling over boulders and shrubbery. The act of pushing himself back to his feet was agony, the stab wound on his stomach burning each time he had to do it. He was hunched over and dragging his injured leg.

He started talking to himself.

"Just get to that tree" or "just one hundred metres more".

"Get a grip, Mac, just one foot in front of the other, one more step just one more step."

He could hear the dogs getting closer and the shouts of encouragement from the Hunter force. He wasn't going to be able to wait on the rocky promontory for rescue – the hunter force would be on him before the SBS team arrived. He was dreading taking to the water. He was a fine swimmer, but he was in no shape to float for 20 minutes treading water waiting for pick up and even less shape to swim for any distance. He looked behind him and could just see the silhouette of the hunter force move over the top of the hill about three hundred metres behind him.

"Swimming it is then," Mac sighed to himself.

Just as he was resigned to the pain of swimming and the significant danger of drowning, Mac heard a voice from 10 metres away that made him jump out of his skin.

"You look like shit, Mac, fancy a ride home?"

Mac turned round and peered into the evening gloom before seeing a heavily camouflaged soldier. He recognised that Glasgow accent. Surely it couldn't be the young lad he had saved from years before.

"Bloody hell, Billy you scared the shit out of me, mate. Let's get a move on; these guys are keen as mustard to take me back to a cell in Moscow."

Billy helped Mac down to a waiting boat carefully hidden on the shoreline. Depositing Mac in the bow of the boat, the SBS lads paddled the boat away from the shoreline before starting the engine and heading off at speed across the Gulf of Finland and into international waters as fast as the RIB would take them. Once they were about a mile out to sea, Billy moved up to the bow of the RIB and crouched down beside Mac.

"How long were you guys in position for, Billy? I wasn't expecting you for another 20 minutes or so."

"When I heard it was you that we were picking up, I felt the need to volunteer for the job. I kind of guessed you might have some company hot on your heels, so we arrived 30 minutes ago to set up a covering fire zone in case you were in real trouble. From the looks of you we arrived a day too late to prevent that. You look like shit, fella, you really do. Why are you dressed in Russian fatigues? We nearly dropped you as you came limping towards us."

"Yeah, I got cornered last night deep in the woods and had to resort to a knife fight. Looks like I am getting older than I thought; the young lad nearly clipped me. For the first time I thought I was in for it."

"We are about 45 minutes from the ship, and we can get the medics to have a proper look at you there. We have orders to drop you into Tallinn embassy as soon as we can."

"So, what brings you guys into this area, Billy?"

"Oh, just this and that, we have some training stuff going on as prep for an Op, but the brass is keeping it under wraps. Op Sec and all that. You know what it is like – they will tell us last minute and we will complain we could have done a better job if we had been brought into the loop much earlier."

Billy looked over and Mac was fast asleep, curled into the bow of the RIB. Must have been a hard few days, he thought, as this guy is as tough as old boots. He was dying to ask what had gone down but he knew he would just get the same answer he had given Mac, "just this and that, mate".

Forty minutes later they arrived at HMS Campbelltown, a Royal Navy Helicopter Carrier stationed near Helsinki and with the job of keeping an eye on the Russian fleet at St Petersburg. Mac was helped on board, leaving the SBS crew to stow away the RIB and their gear. It was a pretty routine trip for them, and they were grumbling about not getting any action. Billy re-appeared and took Mac to the medical bay for a full exam from the resident Medic on board.

Mac entered the medical bay and a young, red-headed female doctor turned and stated in a very matter of fact way:

"Can you strip off please, Mac, and let me get a good look at these wounds."

"Sure, Doc, can you be gentle with me, it hurts like hell."

"It is Lieutenant Commander, and it is supposed to hurt like hell." The doctor cut off the duct tape and cleaned round the wound before looking up at Mac. "You shouldn't play with knives, Mac it is inherently bad for you. I need to flush out both wounds and sterilise them. I am more concerned with the stomach wound. Can you lie up on this bed and turn onto your side." The doctor brought a two-inch scanner attached to a screen and put it onto Mac's side. "Let me just do this ultrasound and see what we have. Ideally, we should do a CT scan, but we don't have one here. Let me see. Ok, Mac it looks like you have been extremely fortunate. Three centimetres to the right and you would have pierced your colon and we would be having a very different discussion about peritonitis. As it is, I can stitch it up and give you a course of antibiotics. The wound will heal within 10 days, but it will take six to eight weeks before it is properly healed deep inside."

"Ok, let's get it done and I can get back to my team."

The doctor injected some local anaesthetic into the wound and went to the drawer to take out a sterile needle and some thread. Without looking up she said:

"Now, Mac, you need to take good care of this. No immersion in water until the wound is healed. These are not the type of wounds you can mess about with. That wound on your leg is no longer a cut but a burn, and the scar tissue will split if you overexert yourself."

"Oh absolutely, I will keep it sensible and let it heal properly. Where are you from, Doc? You have a Scottish accent, but I can't quite place it."

"Oh, I moved about a fair bit when I was small and spent some time working near London before I joined up. It knocks the edges off the accent. I went to Edinburgh University, much to my father's annoyance. Both he and my sister went to a different university in Edinburgh so there is a bit of family banter around which is the better one."

"Edinburgh University, a bit of a posh bird then. I was brought up in Edinburgh, but I haven't been back in years. My dad and I were not that close, and I don't go back if I am honest. My family are down in Yorkshire now. Good hard-working folk in Yorkshire that are down to earth. I like it."

"Oh, my dad lived in Leeds and Bradford years ago before I was born. Worked in a place called Pudsey, I believe. He said he loved it and the people were fab."

"I know where Pudsey is, pretty much bang in the middle of the two cities. Amazing curry houses."

"Right, Mac, that is you all stitched up and just to check, are you allergic to penicillin?"

"I have no allergies other than sticking plaster which just gets itchy and annoying."

"I will use micropore tape then to keep the dressing in place. And please change it every day for the next few days. Keep it clean please and finish the course of antibiotics."

"Excellent, thank you for that, Doc, it is much appreciated."

"Not a problem, and it is Lieutenant Commander."

"Sorry, Doc. Could you point me in the direction of Billy and the guys?"

"Just down the corridor on the right. All the SF guys hang about there."

The red-haired doctor just sighed to herself and mumbled about the intractability of some people and that she was glad not to have to deal with Mac on a regular basis. She knew that he would not heed her advice.

Mac limped down the corridor and knocked on the door of the SF cabin before entering.

"Everything go ok, Mac?" asked Billy.

"Yeah, surface stuff really and got the usual lecture about taking better care of myself."

"Hahaha, got to love them trying."

"Let's get you some food, Mac and then we will hitch a ride with you to Tallinn."

"Perfect, I am starving. I didn't eat last night in case the stomach wound was worse than I hoped."

"We have food all day so what do you fancy?"

"A steak pie would be good if it can be arranged."

"Chef, can we get a steak pie and chips for my friend here and just an omelette for myself, thanks."

"Sure thing, just coming up."

"I do miss a decent chef cooking, Billy. This was a long assed assignment, and I am tired of my own cooking."

Billy and Mac ate their food before heading to the helicopter deck and taking the hour flight to Tallinn. Billy and one other making the ride to make sure the injured Mac made it safely back to the Embassy. Some people find helicopter flights uncomfortable as they bounce about in the air currents, especially flying low over water, but Mac just nodded off, having that ability to drift off anywhere.

Billy just shook his head in amazement at his colleague, but he knew from Mac's appearance and wounds that it had been a rough few days for the aging warrior. He wondered if he would still have it in him at Mac's age to continue in this game and put his body on the line on a regular basis. He doubted it. It took a real stubborn mindset to refuse to give in to the inevitability of time. He smiled ruefully to himself as there was no one more stubborn than Mac and if it hadn't been for that steadfast refusal to give in to pain back in the Iranian gulf then he, Billy, would just have been another statistic on a memorial wall.

An hour later they arrived in Tallinn and landed in the park beside the Embassy with Mac and the two SBS lads entering through a side entrance. As soon as they were inside, Mac went looking for his team. He found them tucked into a small office in the basement. It wasn't really much of an office and in most establishments would have been classed as a box room, but it gave them some privacy to make phone calls. As soon as he entered the room and saw the faces of Storm and Hairy Dave, he knew something was up. He was expecting hugs and handshakes all round but instead walked into a wall of silence.

"Let me introduce you guys to Billy and, I am sorry, what did you say your name was, mate? Both cracking lads from SBS."

"You can call me Liam."

"Cheers, Liam this is Storm and Hairy Dave." Mac turned to his teammates. "What has you guys in such a sombre mood?"

"I will give you a potted history. We got the package out of St Petersburg as we planned and everything was going like clockwork, but Louise had one of her bad feelings about a leak in London, so we substituted the package for our driver on the five-minute ride from the train station to the embassy, and about two hundred metres short of the embassy gates we were ambushed. We exited the vehicle and legged it for the embassy and they had a sniper waiting and took down what they thought was the package. The real package stayed hidden in the vehicle until the FSB left the scene and we sneaked him into the embassy. I have him stashed upstairs without the spooks' knowledge awaiting exfil to London. We haven't told the spooks that it wasn't the package they took out as Louise was worried that someone in London had sold us out. The bad news, Mac, is as we legged it for the gates, Louise was shot, she waved us on to the embassy and as we dropped the package off and turned to go and get her, they grabbed her off the street into a van and took off. We have no idea where they have her or even if she is now in Moscow."

"Awwww, man, I thought we had it cracked. Ok, so what is the plan, what have London planned to get her back?"

Storm and Dave could only look at one another, the words not coming.

Mac looked from one to the other and said, "Spit it out, it can't be any worse than what you have already told me."

"London are refusing to go after her. They want to go through diplomatic channels, but Mac, we all know that means they are going to hang her out to dry and deny all knowledge of who she is."

Mac paused and looked about the people in the room. "So, what are WE going to do about it?"

"With London refusing to help we are flying blind. We don't know where they have taken her. I don't mean to be insensitive, Mac, but how well do you know these guys?" asked Storm, looking at Billy and Liam.

"We go back aways, they are good guys." Mac looked at Billy and Liam. "It is up to you guys; it is highly likely we will end up in real shit if we carry on discussing this, so I will give you the opportunity to head back to your ship."

"I still owe you for a few years back, Mac so if you think you will need some help, I am in. Liam?"

"I was just disappointed that we didn't get into a scrap when we came to pick you up and if I am helping a damsel in distress, I am up for that."

"Hahaha, you need to meet Louise, Liam, I would not mention the damsel in distress thing to her though, she can handle herself just fine and you might just find yourself on the wrong end of her throwing knives," said Dave.

"Thanks for the heads up, I will bear that in mind," laughed Liam.

"What favours can we pull in and make some calls so can get some info on where they are likely to have taken her? Do we know who they are?" asked Mac.

"It is highly likely it is FSB, but we have someone on the case to find out who they are and where they might have her," replied Storm.

"Who do we have with that kind of reach outwith London?" asked Mac in a puzzled tone and looking between Dave and Storm.

"We have a secret weapon, mate. Do you remember Louise had a younger brother?"

"Young Jimmy?"

"Jaimie, yeah. Well, it so happens that Storm here seduced the poor young chap and went on a torrid affair with him behind Louise's back. She still had his number and as he is one of those serious hacker types, he has set about trying to find out where she is."

"He is just a kid!"

"He is older than you think, Mac, and when we talked to him about it and joked about hacking the FSB, he just laughed and said why would I want to hack them again. He has scary talents, Mac."

"Well, who knew? Young Jaimie hacking the FSB, I'll be damned!" exclaimed Mac.

TWENTY-FOUR

Jaimie rented an old run-down warehouse space in the Southside of Glasgow near a place called Nitshill. It looked quite frankly awful on the outside, but the trained eye would have noticed the two external generators in a newly built single storey extension to ensure he could operate independent from the power grid if he had to. He also had fibre broadband from two fully independent network suppliers into the premises which meant he could get one gigabit download speeds. He had a bank of 20 monitors and 10 racks housing multiple servers that he had built and installed himself, together with air conditioning and an uninterruptible power supply (UPS) bank of batteries backed up by the dual generators. In this game, processing power and speed of connection were essential.

He also had separate firewall units running state of the art software that he had part written. He had taken the standard code from a well-known hardware provider and enhanced it. He also had acquired a 256-bit encryptor, the type used by the intelligence services across the globe including the Israeli Mossad. This set up was replicated at key sites across the globe with similar functionality hosted by other like-minded hackers. It was all about masking IP addresses and using poorly secured corporate servers across the world as dummy units, so that it was almost impossible to find the initiating location. If they felt the security services were getting too close, they simply shut a unit down and opened a new one elsewhere.

None of their group had ever been arrested, they were off grid and not on anyone's radar. They had hacked a few larger organisations, but this was not about placing malicious code and then extorting money. This was about industrial espionage, stealing blueprints or ideas and selling them to the highest bidder on the dark web. There were a number of high-profile brands in China and Korea that were happy to pay good money to shortcut the research and development cycle. Most organisations did not even know they had been hacked. The first the company knew about it was when a rival hit the market with new technology. This team of hackers were highly skilled and subtle in approach. It was not about egos and recognition. It was simply because they could.

Jaimie did not want to advertise to his hacking colleagues that he also had various government-related gigs because it would set off all sorts of alarm bells and put Jaimie onto a list which they all wanted to avoid, but this was his sister and growing up they had been through a lot. He owed her big time and she had sent money home to him every month from her Army stuff when he was going through school and university. She never had that chance and he vowed that when she needed him, he would be there for her no matter the cost. She needed him now and although he did not have details of what she had been involved in, it just didn't matter to him. It was time to repay some of the debt.

Storm and Dave were convinced this had all the signs of being an FSB operation. The short turnaround time from the border to the train station meant it had to be a state-owned task – no smaller gangs had the resources and planning ability to react that quickly. That really meant one of the big intelligence services. He frowned to himself as in his mind it also meant they must have had help from someone who had inside knowledge of the Operation. That would have meant London, the team itself or a select few individuals within Tallinn Embassy. The first thing to do was to check the dark web and find out if there were any contracts out to take out the team in Tallinn.

Navigating the dark web was kind of like navigating your way round the London underground without a map. Not the easiest of tasks as navigating it was a bit of a chore, you had to work your way through it in a consistent way, but once you got the hang of it, it wasn't impossible. Time was the biggest barrier to what Jaimie wanted to achieve and he could not be as thorough as he wanted, but sometimes you just had to accept 80% as good enough and move on. Not ideal when it was his sister's life that was at stake. Jaimie always worked through a virtual private network (VPN) connection and the TOR (The Onion Router) browser when using the dark web. The combination of the two meant he had end to end encryption of his data and kept him off the radar of the intelligence services and his Internet Provider.

He made a conscious choice to use a VPN company that uses RAM based servers which by design do not store your data and provide end to end 256-bit encryption. This particular one also allowed him to bypass the Chinese and Russian countrywide firewalls and provide secure and anonymous use of the dark web. These safeguards were important. The dark web is unregulated and is the safe haven for organised criminals, illicit firearms sale, contract killers and cyber hackers. It therefore has that criminal element that could, and perhaps would, try to steal your personal data like banking records, credit card details etc.

The dark web gets a bit of a poor reputation, but it is not all about criminal activity and it is used by journalists, whistle-blowers and activists across the globe to communicate safely without state monitoring and government persecution. Most people are aware of the surface web where normal search engines help you navigate it. There is then the deep web which is thousands of times bigger than the surface web and is used by education institutes, governments, military etc. Lastly there is the dark web, which is a very small fraction of the deep web that is used for more illicit activities.

Jaimie had developed an amazing set of skills very quickly in his teens when Mr MacPherson had splashed out to give him his first computer. He learnt quickly and decided that while hacking was good and also profitable that he wanted more, and progressed from full time hacking to being a consultant training Government cyber security professional across the globe. It was a very lucrative side-line, and it also meant he got to travel to places he would not otherwise get to. He had multiple passports from multiple countries so that his movements were hard to trace. A number of them wanted him to stay on and run their cyber security functions, but that would have meant staying in one place and he would potentially be a target of the wrong sorts of people and that was not particularly appealing.

Jaimie started working his magic on the dark web as that is where he would find black ops or criminal gang contracts to private agencies for off the books stuff that they did not want traced back. Despite the likelihood of this being an FSB operation, Jaimie needed to discount the other easy stuff first. It was dangerous to come up with a theory and only look at evidence that backed up the theory. That was called confirmation bias and was not the way Jaimie operated. It took him an hour to go through the various dark web servers commonly used in Central Europe, but there was nothing of consequence on them for Jaimie's investigation. There was also no dark web chatter on the types of chat room forums frequented by the obvious militant groups. The time element was starting to concern Jaimie. In his albeit limited black ops experience, he had no more that 12 hours before she would be moved and, therefore, he had no more than eight to find her location and allow Storm and the team to put a plan in place to free her.

With the dark web not providing much in the way of information Jaimie turned his skills to the deep web. In a lot of ways this was a tougher task and, in some ways, even more dangerous. It was harder to remain anonymous and under the radar from the top intelligence agencies. He had a number of different security protocols in place including the use of friendly servers across the globe to hide his footprint, and as a last resort he had installed a kill switch. This would only be used in an emergency if he started to see a back trace from one of the intelligence agencies. They were the favoured way to track intruders on the deep web.

Jaimie had hacked the FSB two years previous when one evening he was a touch bored and looking for some excitement. He never stole anything, but just had a look round the architecture. He installed a back door which would allow him to return without the hassle of breaking the significant encryption. As he never went back to it, just lay dormant and undetected. The spooks would look for data flowing out of their network in an unexpected way, so not using it meant it was hard to find. The last time, he got lucky and found a weak link password from someone who should have known better. It was standard practice a few years ago to change out letters for numbers in a name. As a bit of a giggle Jaimie tried Gandalf1234 which failed and was always a bit of a long shot, but he was stunned when he put in G4nd4lf1234 by transposing the "a and 4". Jaimie never understood why lazy people were allowed anywhere near sensitive files.

There was a risk in going back to the same server that there could be a logical trap waiting for him so they could try and back trace his connection. With the time pressure he was under, Jaimie felt he did not have any choice and he would just have to manage the risk. Jaimie went looking for meeting minutes or a special ops folder. The problem was finding the correct folder, most special ops projects were named with some random words like Project Athena or Project Tarantino. Something pretty random that only means something to the select few engaged in it. Jaimie was getting frustrated with how long the search was taking and decided to short circuit the process and use a battering ram rather than trying to be too subtle. He called Storm to ask for some help.

"Hey Jaimie, have you got something for us?" asked Storm as she answered the phone.

"Not yet, Storm, I am calling and asking for some help."

"Fire away, babe, although not sure what help I will be."

"Can you send me over a selfie of you and do you happen to have a name of an agent within the FSB you have had any contact with?"

"I can. Just how exactly is that going to help?"

"I am going to use your email to send the photo to your contact and embed some code in it that will gain me access to the FSB mail server. All I need is for him to click on the photo to view it so it needs to be something he would want to do."

"I can do that. Any specific photo?"

"Yeah, something sexy, hun, so he will leave it open for a few seconds. Oh, and the name or email address of your contact."

"Sacha Goncharov was the name although I haven't ever emailed him. He would recognise my name though. Do you need me to send it, so he knows it is authentic?"

"Hahahaha, oh Storm you are so naïve, I already have access to your email account. You do know what I do for a living?"

"You little creep, are you reading my email?"

"No, you are way too old for me these days."

"Fuck off, Jaimie, too old my arse, you would love for me to ask you out again."

Jaimie had already hung up and set about constructing the code to embed in the photo and getting the right email address. He decided the best thing was just to spam the FSB email server with a number of potential email addresses in the hope of getting the correct one. He did not need this to be subtle, just quick. Hence the term battering ram. Two minutes later a photo came through from Storm and Jaimie whistled quietly to himself when he saw it. She really did scrub up well. Jaimie constructed the email and sent it off to the dozen or so potential email addresses hoping to get one that would work. Jaimie went to make a coffee as he waited for the email system to work its magic and he just had to hope that his code was subtle enough to get past the antivirus detectors on the email server architecture. He was pretty confident as it was subtle code and not based on other coding out in the hacker universe that analysts use to construct their antivirus software.

As he was waiting for the kettle to boil, he was wishing that there were more street cameras in Eastern European cities. If this had been London, he would have been able to secure CCTV footage and get the van details and track it through the city. It was a pity that the team did not have drone coverage or satellite overwatch during the operation as he could have used that. Suddenly an idea hit him. He had bumped into a CEO of an up-and-coming satellite company on a flight back from Jacksonville USA a few weeks ago and this chap had set up a company to take Selfies from space. Space selfie or something like that it had been called. An amazing concept and he was sure he had the chap's card somewhere. He went into his desk drawer and after a couple of minutes of looking through it he found the business card and dialled the mobile on it.

"This is Chris from Spelfie, how can I help?"

"Chris, hi, it is Jaimie Stewart here, we met a few months ago on a flight back from Jacksonville USA. I am not sure if you remember me?"

"Jaimie, how the devil are you? I was not sure I would hear from you, mate. It was a long old flight. How can I be of help?"

"I am on the scrounge for some information. Are you still involved with that space selfie concept that you were working on?"

"It is no longer a concept, Jaimie, it is up and running, we have called it SPELFIE, and we even have an app for it. It is working well, we are just working with some big private sector organisations on covering things like Formula 1, festivals and sporting events."

"Amazing, do you happen to record the images you get from it somewhere?"

"We do for a few weeks just for security reasons and then delete them as we need to comply with the European Data Protection Regulations. You have piqued my interest, mate; how would this be of use to you? As I recall you were into computer networks and stuff."

"Ah well, it is a bit of a strange request really. My sister was abducted off the streets in Tallinn, Estonia yesterday and the local police are struggling to get anywhere. As you know, the first 24 hours are critical and I wondered if you had any satellite footage from yesterday afternoon?"

"Actually, my friend we do. We have access to hundreds of satellites through multiple organisations and we were doing a preparation run in support of a European Athletics event there next month, so I have footage of Tallinn and over into Russia. We are trialling live feeds with a South American organisation who have just launched hundreds of smaller satellites that are more configurable and manoeuvrable than the traditional European ones. The images are pretty spectacular and will be of sufficient quality, I expect, for what you need. We are getting to the point where we can track anyone using wearable tech on a live feed so if you were skiing down Whistler, we could track it via satellite. Jaimie, there is a lot of data here, my friend, and it is protected under copyright etc so I can't just send it to you."

"Ah ok, can we do a screen share? That way you are not sending it to me and I won't get you into any problems with the authorities."

"Give me 15 minutes to talk to my technical support team and get access to the footage. Do you have a specific time of day so we can narrow down the window?"

"I will call my sister's friend and narrow it down as much as we can. I will call you back in 15 minutes. Chis, thanks, mate, it could mean the difference between life and death."

"No bother, Jaimie."

Jaimie put the phone down and dialled Storm.

"Storm, sorry to hound you like a personal stalker, but do you have an exact time stamp on yesterday's shenanigans and more specifically on when the van left with Louise in it?"

"Hey, Jaimie, don't worry about it, babe, let me see, it would be about 4pm."

"Was it 4pm exactly?"

"No, it would have been 4:12 when the van left, local time. Why is it important, Jaimie?"

"No time to explain," said Jaimie as he hung up the phone.

Jaimie was getting excited as it looked like he had stumbled upon a faster way to get the information he needed. The 15 minutes Chris required seemed like an age. Jaimie had another look for the email response, but it had not been opened and he got a number of rejections off the email server for most of the 12 guesses. One had not had a rejection, so the hope was it had found the right person and it was only a matter of time before he had a way into the email system. He was looking for FSB emails originating in Estonia that might highlight the location of where they could be holding Louise. If they had taken her direct to Moscow, then life was about to get a whole lot harder for his sister. Jaimie had never gone through mock interrogations but from what he had seen in the movies it was not something he wanted for his sister. Every hour he was stuck doing this was an hour she was having to endure agony. He checked his watch and time was slipping away. He was already six hours into his eight-hour deadline.

His phone rang just as he was worrying himself into a frenzy.

"Hi Chris, how did you get on?"

"Let me just patch in one of my technical guys, Jaimie and you can tell him directly what you need."

"Hello, John here," came an American voice.

"John, can I introduce you to Jaimie who has a rather unique problem I am hoping we can help him with. Jaimie, John is my Chief Technology Officer and a real guru with the capabilities of the software and the satellite system."

"Let me provide you with a high-level bit of background, John. My sister was in Tallinn, Estonia where she was visiting some friends and it looks like she was kidnapped off of the street near the embassy at 4:12 pm local time yesterday. The local police are struggling, and we have not seen a ransom demand, so the big worry is a sex trafficking ring or some kind of organised gang. We know from the local police that the first 24 hours is critical, and we are rapidly running out of time. What I need from you guys in space selfie is any satellite images you have of the UK embassy at the time to see if we can track the van that took her."

"I am so sorry for your troubles, Jaimie, let me see what we have."

"Can you ping me your IP address, John and we can do a screen share?"

"Sure, let me just text that to you, there you go, should be with you now."

"Got it, if you can just click on accept when the box opens on your screen, I can see what you are looking at."

"Done, it should be coming up now."

"Got it, perfect, thank you."

"We can zoom in on the embassy, and what time did you say?"

"4:12 pm local time."

"Ok, here we go, ah and as if by magic there is your van and we can see if I run the video capture, two men either side of a woman and manhandling her into the van. It looks like there was a bit of an accident or something there as well, as there are a lot of people milling about."

"Can you follow the van as it heads out of the city?"

"We can try, but the satellite images are timebound and we could run out of time. It depends on how fast they are travelling; we might be lucky. Why don't I work on that in the background, my friend and I will come back to you as soon as I have something."

"OK, John, sounds like a plan, can you come back to me asap though as every minute counts and we are already a number of hours since the kidnap."

"I will be as quick as I can and an hour at most."

Jaimie hung up the phone and got a notification through that his email to Sacha Goncharov had been opened and he had clicked on the photo. He smiled to himself and that today lady luck was on his side. Jaimie now had access to Sacha's email and PC and from there he could freely access other parts of the network. Most of it would need to wait as today he needed to search the email system for mails relating to Louise kidnapping. He had a quick look through Sacha's email account but there was nothing of real interest.

Jaimie had two real options. The first was to send a global email attaching the photo from Sacha's email to the rest of the FSB and for each one he infected he would have access. This option was time limited before the security team got involved and shut him down. The other option was technically more difficult as it meant hopping through the network to the email server itself and trying to get administrative access. That would involve breaking a password and it was unlikely to be an easy option like the previous server. He did not have much time left so the emailing the photo option was the best way forward, just a shame that it would burn the access he had for future use.

Jaimie sent the photo out using Sacha's email address and waited for his access to newly infected machines to come through. It did not take long and Jaimie went to work with a real sense of urgency. This was not subtle hacking and once he was spotted by the cyber security team, he would be a target and he would need to shut the whole thing down quickly.

The hour John needed for the satellite feed raced by and when the phone rang Jaimie jumped, he was so absorbed in his work.

"John, how did you get on?" Jaimie could not keep the sense of hope from his voice.

"Good news, we managed to track the van to a farmhouse near the Russian border. I will send over the footage with a geotag of the location of the farm. Jaimie, some bad news, my friend, it is heavily guarded."

"John, you are a legend, fire it over and I will get it to the local police. One quick question, John, if I needed a live feed of the area later today would that be possible?"

"How quickly would you need it as I would need to re-task the satellite. Jaimie, I would need to charge you for it, it isn't cheap, mate."

"How much?"

"$15,000 to task it plus the data storage costs, so $20,000 US."

"Deal, I need it asap so can you set that up for me. How quickly can you do it?"

"It normally takes 24 hours but if I pull in a favour or two from their CEO, I expect I can get it done within an hour."

"John, I can't thank you enough. Once this is over, I will give you some cyber security consultancy for free.

One last ask, is there any way I can get access to the live feed so I can talk the local police through what we are seeing?"

"That will take some time, Jaimie, IT is a bit of a dark art within our organisation."

"I will send you a photo, John, just click on it and I can arrange the access myself, I can have it set up within five minutes."

"That is a deal, my friend, take care of yourself."

Jaimie waited for five minutes for the file to come through from John with the footage. He was blown away by the quality of the imagery. This SPELFIE idea was going to be a big thing.

Jaimie picked up his phone and called Storm's mobile.

"Storm, I have something for you."

"We need something big, Jaimie, every hour that goes past is an hour she is in their hands and they are not the gentle type."

"How about a location where they are keeping her? Let me send it to you and a satellite video feed from yesterday."

"Seriously? You are not having me on, are you? How on earth did you manage that? London won't engage."

"I have my talents, Storm, you know that."

"Shit, kid, that is some serious talent, you are a superstar."

"Well yes I do know that. One other thing, Storm, I have arranged a live satellite feed covering where they are holding her from about an hour's time, I thought you could use some overwatch."

"Jaimie, I think I want you to father my babies."

"Wooooo, steady on, girl, you weren't that great a date."

"Best you ever had, kid, don't forget it."

Jaimie put down the phone, sat back in his computer chair and exhaled with that satisfied glow that he had worked his magic and this time he might be able to repay some of the debt he owes his sister.

TWENTY-FIVE

L ouise took the bullet during the race to the embassy in the stomach and it hurt like hell. She was doubled over in pain as bullets whizzed about her. She waved the team onwards suspecting that once Dimitri was away from her, she would no longer be a target. She was slowly moving down the wall of the building next to her and leaving bloody handprints from the wound.

"Just breathe, dammit and stop being a pussy," she mumbled to herself.

She stopped and forced herself to stand upright; to be honest she just wanted to lie on the ground and curl up into a ball but she would never live that down. She took a couple of tentative steps forward and thought "I can do this, just one foot after the other". As her body got used to the pain, Louise felt more comfortable moving and watched as the team reached the safety of the embassy gates. Breathing a sigh of relief, she turned as she heard a roaring engine and screech of burning rubber. A silver van pulled up beside her, the side door already open and before she could react two guys in balaclavas jumped out before it had reached a full stop. They put a blackout hood over her head and dragged her backwards towards the van. The thing is once you are off balance and moving backwards at speed there is not a damned thing you can do about it. Quick as a flash, Louise was thrown into the back of the van and landed with the heavy weight of her abductors piled on top of her. The engine of the van roared to life and the tyres screeched once again, this time with acceleration too fast for the traction of the tyres. Vans rarely had the traction control that was common in most cars nowadays.

"She is bleeding, a stomach wound. Moscow wants her alive, so we need to get it stabilised."

Louise felt rough hands pulling up her top and moving her about. She winced and moaned as they probed the wound.

"Stop thrashing about like a beached fish and let me check it out."

Louise gritted her teeth and tried to fight off the pain. It was no good, it was too much, and she blacked out in the back of the van. When she came to, she had an instant of disorientation. Where was she and why did her side feel like she had been kicked by a horse? She had no idea of the time nor her location other than she could tell she was lying on the floor of what felt like a van moving at speed. Louise kept still, listening for any clues. Suddenly it came flooding back: she had been shot and kidnapped. They must be out of the city as there was no real traffic noise and there was no way they would get this speed up in a built-up area. That could only mean one thing: she was on her way to Moscow. Well, that was going to be a bit of an awkward situation, thought Louise. It was highly unlikely there was going to be a welcome back party. Her side ached like hell and every time the van went round a corner or over a bump, she had to tense her stomach muscles and that created spasms of pain. Louise tried to relax by accepting the pain instead of fighting it, but with the movement of the van it was almost impossible. She tried to move her hand to the wound to see if the bleeding had stopped but her hands were tie wrapped behind her back. There was nothing to do but try to block it all out until the van came to a stop.

After what seemed like hours of travelling on hard top roads, the van slowed down and turned left onto what felt like a farm track. The van bumped and rolled along the track causing the pain to increase. She hoped like hell they were not on this for hours. Each minute was agony and all she could do was moan on the floor of the van.

"Shut up and stop moaning, I don't need your moans keeping me awake."

With that there was a well-aimed kick that landed a toe on to her thighs.

"Well, that is going to bruise," mumbled Louise.

The guard responded with a follow up kick to the same area.

Louise just grunted and kept silent, having learnt her lesson. They were not in the mood for chit chat or jokes.

Suddenly the van slowed to a stop, one of the guards jumped out and 30 seconds later jumped back in. Louise could only assume they were opening a gate to let the van through. That suggested they were heading to a farm or a forest with a shallow grave. Louise wondered whether they would get her to dig her own grave, maybe Moscow had changed their mind and she was now a liability. It wasn't likely they would do it for her. Louise wondered whether it was on the Estonian or Russian side of the border. Not that it made a hell of a lot of difference as she could not see London mixing it with Russia. No, she knew she was more than likely on her own and that meant trying to engineer a way to escape. She needed to take her time and get the guards to relax around her. She also needed to get a layout of the farm. The other option was to escape when they moved her to Moscow. She had no doubt that would be the end game.

"Water, can I have some water please?" pleaded Louise.

"Shut up and don't talk. You killed a Russian General, Mrs Bolshoi waitress. Oh yes, we know exactly who you are. You will get no favours from us. We have to deliver you alive to Moscow, but they did not tell us you had to be in good condition."

Louise had a sinking feeling, so she was not a bargaining chip for them to get Dimitri back. This was a kind of direct form of extradition. They knew who she was and that meant a cell on the top floor of the Lubyanka prison. A windowless cell with day after day of torture and interrogation until they decided they had all the information they could get and she would turn up dead in a ditch somewhere and classed as a tourist that had been killed by criminal gangs. Everyone would know it was a lie, but the Russian government would just stick to its story and ignore the speculation.

The van slowed down to a stop and rough hands grabbed Louise and manhandled her out of the vehicle. She was struggling to walk upright and paused to try and get her bearings. She got a rough push in her back.

"Get moving."

"Ok, ok. I am moving, all you had to do was ask."

All of a sudden Louise landed in a heap on the floor as a hard wooden baton smashed into the back of her legs just behind the knee and she buckled. Why couldn't she keep her smart mouth shut, she asked herself not for the first time. Mac would have told her it was because she was a wee Glasgow girl and that if she hadn't learnt it by now, she never would. The guards dragged Louise upright and pushed her forwards. She could not see anything out of the blackout hood and even looking down towards the ground nothing was visible. Louise heard the unmistakable squeak of a door hinge that needed some oil and assumed she was headed into the farmhouse. Suddenly she smelt the unmistakable odour of horses and knew instantly that she was headed into a stable.

The tie wraps behind her back were snipped, freeing her hands and she took the chance of rubbing her wrists before her hands were grabbed, tied with a rough rope and hauled upwards. She could only just about manage to stand on her tiptoes which put incredible strain on her wound and that pain made her audibly gasp. Just breathe, in, out, in, out. Each breath was like inhaling broken glass, a real agony of epic proportions. Unless you had been shot or stabbed it was difficult to describe. It was a pain that just wasn't going to subside.

Louise heard the door creak again and suddenly there was silence. A silence so deep it was disturbing. Louise was alone with her pain. She could not see anything through the hood and breathing through it was pretty claustrophobic. The problem with pain was fighting it caused your body to tense up and that emphasised the pain even more. The trick was to accept the pain and try to relax into it. Louise used cooking her favourite meal to distract her brain. A nice fillet steak, double dipped fries, onion rings and mixed seasonal veg. She started by walking round the supermarket and picking out a nice fillet steak. She was looking for a steak that had some nice fat marbling to it – too lean and it would dry out during cooking, too fatty and it was gross – she would look through them all to pick out the best one. In her mind she walked up and down every aisle of the supermarket, picking up the ingredients, smelling them, feeling them and choosing which ones to put in the trolley. Then it was the preparation work, making sure the steak was out of the fridge for an hour before cooking and left to stand for 15 minutes after cooking to let the steak relax and become more tender. All she was trying to do was distract herself from the pain. Every minute she was shopping, or cooking, was a minute free of pain. When she had cooked and eaten the steak in her mind, she started it all over again.

Louise took some time to lower her heart rate and try to expand her senses to the surrounding area. She could smell damp straw and old manure, suggesting the stable had not been used for some time. The silence was all encompassing. There was no noise of tractors or other farm machinery. No 4 by 4 buggies and no farm animals. There were no voices nearby or even at a slight distance. This place was remote and there would be no one calling the police if they heard her scream. She suspected she was imprisoned at an old farm in the middle of nowhere, probably somewhere either at the border or near Moscow. Beneath her feet Louise could feel straw, and underneath that, compacted earth. It was not concrete which, whilst not immediately helpful,

PAWN IN THE SHADOWS

could prove useful later on.

Unexpectedly, Louise was lowered to the ground and her hood removed. The sudden light coming to her eyes made them stream and she had to look to the floor to give them some time to get adjusted to the fact that she could at last see. She took some time to stand in silence and look about. Above her head were numerous wooden beams that were all cracked and split, some were slightly warped in shape and had obviously been in place for tens of years and would remain in place for tens more. The stable had room for ten horses or ponies, with each stall having an independent gate and feeding trough. The stalls were on either side of the centre where Louise had been strung up.

Standing three metres away were two guards, squat but built like tanks, special forces types who did not care what pain they inflicted. They just stood there like they had all the time in the world, waiting. They oozed with the confidence of knowing that they were in control and the understanding that everybody captured breaks eventually, it is only ever a matter of time. They were standing at ease, hands clasped in front of them, silently waiting for the next order. Through a side entrance walked in a quiet unassuming type of man carrying a leather bag. The type of bags used by doctors all over the globe that opened up fully to provide easy access to everything they required. He stood in front of Louise and in English, with a Russian accent, said:

"Take your shirt off, I want to examine your wound and make sure the bleeding has stopped and it is clean. I need to make sure that there is no debris in it, like bits of cloth from your jacket."

"Can I have some water please?" asked Louise in a hoarse voice.

"You, fetch the girl some clean water to drink," ordered the doctor pointing to the guard on the left. The guard left the stables to fetch some water.

"This might pinch a bit," said the doctor to Louise.

He got out some forceps and iodine, and scrubbed the area clean. It stung pretty bad, and it took all of Louise's self-control to not shout out.

The doctor took some time to prod and poke about and took out a stethoscope to listen to Louise's heart and lungs. He placed it on various parts of her chest, both front and back, before grunting to himself, having come to a conclusion.

"The bullet went straight through and did not hit anything important like liver or kidney. It also missed major arteries. You, very lucky lady. I will stitch it up and give you antibiotic injection and you will be fine. You will need to be sensible for a few days until it heals properly. You will have a scar both front and back. I am afraid there is nothing I can do to stop that."

The doctor genuinely looked sorry he could not prevent a scar until he looked more closely at the scars already on her body. Shaking his head in disbelief, he took out a needle and thread.

"I do not have any local anaesthetic, so this is going to hurt."

He looked at Louise who just nodded in acknowledgement of the statement and for him to start the repair work. The doctor took his time and stitched the wounds both front and back before taking a small vial from his bag and injecting Louise with the contents. She assumed it was penicillin or one of its derivatives.

Louise refused to react to the stitching of her open wounds. Just stood there with her face implacable. She was conscious of the Special Forces guards and was not going to give them any hope that she would break easily.

"I have used small stitches to minimise any scarring, but having all those scars already it won't mean an awful lot to you. You did not even wince as I stitched you up, so I can see you are no stranger to the needle."

The doctor leaned in closer and in a low voice only meant for her to hear, said:

"Can I give you a word of advice. Give them what they want. You are not in any condition to take much punishment and it would be shame to see such a pretty young lady dead."

One of the guards stepped forward.

"That is enough, Doc, let's keep the discussion to one we can all hear."

"Thank you, doctor. I appreciate you taking care of my wound." Louise was genuine in her appreciation.

Louise watched as the doctor left the stables and, in the doorway, a middle-aged woman appeared. Stern faced with dead eyes and not a flicker of emotion as she gazed at Louise, standing there with her top off and obviously hurting from the bullet wound. The guard reappeared carrying a glass of water which was placed on the ground near the woman.

"Get me a table and two chairs," ordered the woman. The guard went to an office at the end of the stables and reappeared carrying a small table. Another two trips and there was a chair at each end.

"Please sit and we can have a talk. How is your wound?" asked the woman.

"It is clean and stitched so about as good as it can be considering the circumstances," replied Louise.

"My name is Dr Galina Golubeva of the FSB. I have a few questions for you to answer. I need you to be truthful with me as there are some people here that are not as nice as me and would like to hurt you. Will you answer some questions for me?"

"Of course. Could I have a drink of the water first?"

"Let us talk first and as a reward, if you are truthful, I will let you have the water.

"What is your name, why were you in Moscow"?

"My name is Lynn Mitchell, and I am a reporter for a local newspaper in the UK. I haven't been to Moscow. There has been a misunderstanding. I was on my way to the Embassy in Tallinn when people started shooting in front of me and I got hit. The next thing I know I was hooded and manhandled into the back of a van."

Dr Galina let out an audible sigh.

"We know you work for the British intelligence services, why are you telling me lies?" Dr Galina turned her dead eye stare full glare onto Louise. Studying every twitch and eye movement. Trying to read her the way a medical student would read a patient's notes.

"I am sorry, but it is true, I am a reporter, phone my paper, they will confirm it," pleaded Louise.

"Look, we both know your name is not Lynn Mitchell. We also both know that you put together your back story with some random people answering the phone pretending to be your work colleagues. The whole thing is false. All you need to do is confirm who you work for and all this pain will go away. One simple correct answer and you can have something to eat and a sleep in a comfortable bed. What is your name and who do you work for?"

"My name is Lynn Mitchell, and I am a reporter. I work for a local newspaper in the UK."

Dr Galina nodded to the guard on the right who dragged Louise upright and tied her hands back onto a hook attached to a length of rope and up over a beam in the stable. The second guard tightened the rope so that Louise was back on her tip toes and her upper body under extreme pressure just to breathe as the pain of her wound increased exponentially. One of the guards picked up a metre length of hosepipe and used it to whip the back of Louise's thighs. She let out a high-pitched howl of pain as it landed. Dr Galina nodded again, and the guard repeated the beating a second time. Louise knew they use hosepipe as it doesn't break bones, but it hurts like hell. Not only does it hurt at the time, but it throbs for hours afterwards as it bruises and the affected muscles stiffen. A constant reminder to give them what they want.

"You are being silly. All I need is a simple answer, and we can make all this pain stop. Now, what is your name and why were you in Moscow?"

"I am not sure what else you want me to say. My name is Lynne Mitchell and I have never been to Moscow."

Louise kept her voice neutral and stared at the ground. She did not want to make eye contact as at this stage in the interrogation it could be seen as a challenge to the authority of the interrogator. Out of the side of her eyes she could see the guards watching the scene unfold with anticipation. This was not their first time at this particular rodeo. They were in their comfort zone, telling themselves that it was her own fault, and she was causing the pain to herself and that if she answered truthfully it would stop. The truth was different, of course, and even if Louise was truthful the pain would continue to make sure it was the truth. The pain was excruciating, it was the kind of pain that was all encompassing, nothing else mattered.

Once again Dr Galina nodded to the guard and he set about whipping Louise with the hosepipe. Up and down her thighs and bum. There was no real layer of fat on Louise and the blows pummelled her muscles. Louise refused to let out any more cries of pain and just stared at a point on the floor, inspecting it. Talking inside her brain on what she could see. How much of it could she memorise if she closed her eyes.

"Guard, get a bucket of cold water and mix it with vinegar. Last chance, young lady. What is your name and why were you in Moscow? Guard, get a photo of her over to Moscow and get them onto social media so see what we can get from there." All the time she watched Louise for a reaction. Seeing none, she sighed to herself and left the room.

It was important for Louise to disassociate the logic part of her brain from the pain – it is the only way to buy some time and find a means of escape. Every second counted; every second was a step closer to finding a way out. Five minutes passed with Louise aching from head to toe, she could feel the stitches starting to tear with her stress position stretching her onto tiptoes and the welts up and down her thighs, she could feel her trousers sticking to her legs and knew that she not only had some bruises but there were cuts as well. The guard appeared, carrying two buckets of what looked like water; however, as he came closer, she could clearly smell the vinegar. She was puzzled at the request of Dr Galina until the first bucket hit her and the pain exploded all across her body. It was like electric shocks all over, up and down her body in waves. As the second bucket was emptied it also hit her stomach wound, and despite her best of intentions Louise let out an almighty scream and the intensity of the pain made her black out.

Louise had no way of knowing how long she had passed out for, but as she came back round, she was hit with a wall of pain. The beatings, the stress position and the acid from the vinegar were starting to take their toll. Louise was starting to shiver. Some of it was from the pain and some of it was from the cold. Being wet meant she was at the mercy of the air temperature around her and it was cold in the stables. The shivering only made matters worse, and Louise was in a position where she was starting to wonder whether she could take any more. There was a point in any interrogation where you had to start cooperating with your captors.

Two guards took one arm each and released Louise from the rope and dragged her back to the chair in the centre of the room. Any arrogance she might have displayed at the start of the process was long gone. Dr Galina reappeared, and Louise watched her as she strode into the room. She was not a military type but not civvy street either – she smelled of spook all day long.

Dr Galina sat down on the chair opposite.

"Let us start over, you need to start to work with us, I can protect you from the beatings and get you some food and water, maybe even some clean clothes and a shower, but you have to start to tell me the truth." She placed a plastic bottle of water on the table in front of Louise.

Louise smiled at her. "Thank you," she croaked. The screams of pain had taken their toll on Louise's throat. Louise had to try and build a rapport with Dr Galina; although she doubted there was an ounce of compassion in her, it was better to try.

Louise took some sips of water, taking her time over drinking it and allowing her brain some precious seconds to think.

"I have a bit of a problem with you, young lady. We both know your name isn't Lynn Mitchell and Moscow can only find a veneer of social media. The type of stuff put out to fool the casual observer, but we have experts in this kind of thing. It is quite clear that this is all trade craft, and you are trying deliberately to evade detection. A real journalist would be all over social media. Add to that the fact you were followed from the moment you left the train station – we have video footage of you in Moscow. I just don't believe anything you have told us so far. So, get your sensible head on and let's start over."

Louise sat for a few moments in silence and considered her position. She was not in the greatest of shape and needed to buy some time to find a way of escaping. Normally you are looking to hold out for 48 hours, but that is to let your team get out of the area of operation so any information you do provide is in essence out of date. There came a time in any interrogation to start to come clean and Louise could see that it was obvious they already had a load of information about her and lying any further was just going to result in more pain and the danger of her wound opening up again, or worse it would get infected.

Louise looked up and into the ice blue eyes of Dr Galina. Eyes that pierced the soul and knew your deepest, darkest secrets. There was no warmth to them, just a cold glare. Eyes that had seen the worst the world had to offer and accepted their part in it.

"My name is not Lynn Mitchell as you suspected. I am Erica MacArthur, and I am a freelance assassin. I don't work for any particular organisation but work on a contract-to-contract basis. I was working in Moscow for a number of months and had a part-time job in the Bolshoi Theatre. When I heard the General had died unexpectedly, I left and headed to St Petersburg and then here to get to a safe place. I was heading to the embassy to get a replacement passport as the one I used at the border was a forgery I bought in St Petersburg."

"Freelance, you say. How do you get your contracts?"

"I use the dark web and have a server there that is used by clients. If they cannot use the dark web, then I don't want to know about the work as it won't be genuine. Anyone who is a real player knows the dark web or at least the basics of it."

"Talk me through what you did at the Bolshoi Theatre?"

"I was just a waitress. Not my normal kind of work, but I needed a cover story that would stack up and sometimes you just have to work through the mundane to get the prize at the end. My life consisted of work, eat, sleep and a bit of running in between to keep me sane. I just needed to fly below the radar until my client contacted me with the hit that they wanted me to complete."

"Who was your intended target?"

"The client had not as yet told me. I was still waiting on that information coming through. I suspected it was a criminal gang leader as it very often is. My instructions were to get a job at the Bolshoi and await further instructions. After the General's death I started to suspect that I had been set up as the fall guy for his assassination. I swear I had nothing to do with it."

"What do you mean with 'fall guy'? What is a fall guy?"

"Someone who takes the blame for another person's actions."

"So, you are saying you did not assassinate General Andropov of the FSB?"

"Hell no, I would never be that stupid – why would I want the FSB on my tail from now until eternity? Everyone knows the FSB always retaliates. No, I had nothing to do with that job. Wrong place at the wrong time and just sheer bad luck on my part. There was another waitress there I was suspicious of. Loads of trade craft, you know spy shit. I bet you a million dollars US that she was involved."

"Do you mean Natasha Fyodorova?"

"I think so, I did not know her family name, I just knew her as Natasha."

"Why do you think she was involved?"

"She was always asking questions about the General, when would he come to the Bolshoi. Never socialised with me and the other girls, kept herself apart and was always looking over her shoulder when she arrived at work like she was checking if someone had followed her. I mean that is some real spy shit right there. You know I am right. I have a sense for that kind of thing."

"Very well, Erica, I will talk to Moscow and see what they want to do. You have made the right decision in opening up to me." Dr Galina looked to one of the guards. "Get her something to eat and some more water."

As Dr Galina was leaving the stable, she dialled a number on her mobile phone.

"Josef, it is definitely her; she has admitted being at the Bolshoi and provided me with a name, although I suspect it is just another alias. She has denied any involvement in the assassination and has said she believes it was the other waitress, Natasha Fyodorova. I am not convinced; there is definitely more to come from the girl. Even if she did not do the assassination, she knows a lot more than she claims. How do you want to proceed?"

"Ok, I will continue to question her as you make preparations."

Louise only heard one side of the conversation but suspected she was going to be transported to Moscow. That would be her chance to escape. If they got her to Moscow she was going to be there for a long time with endless interrogations, waterboarding and possible torture. The remaining guard strung Louise back up on the rope and the pain kicked back in. While she had been sitting it had subsided to a dull ache.

"Hey, she said I was going to get food and water. Hey what the fuck, man, I have answered everything she asked. Oh, come on, man, this sucks. Fucking Russki wankers."

The guard did not say a word but casually walked over, picked up the hose pipe and casually used it to whip Louise twice across the stomach, narrowly missing the bullet wound.

Louise refused to shout out and just stared straight at the guard, daring him to do it again. When she got herself free this one was top of her kill list. The guard just smiled at her and arched back to strike her again when the other guard came back in with some food and water.

"What are you doing, man? Get her down from there before the spook gets back."

As the guard got closer, he noticed the two new welts across Louise's stomach and turned and glared at the other guard.

"Sometimes you are such a dick. You just can't help yourself, can you?"

The second guard just grunted sourly and took Louise down from the hook and untied her hands. She collapsed onto the ground, her legs giving way beneath her with all the muscle strain she had been under for the last few hours. There was no help from the guard though, as he just stomped away and stood a few metres away quite clearly sulking that his latest plaything had been taken off him.

The guard with the food and water placed it on the table and walked round and helped Louise to her feet and slowly guided her back to her seat at the table. Louise gingerly sat down and ate what looked like goulash and slowly drank the water. She felt she could win over one of the guards; however, the other one was a lost cause. He liked inflicting pain too much for her to influence. Of course, they could just be playing good cop, bad cop, which was more likely. The good cop just trying to win her over so she opens up and the bad cop showing her what non-compliance looks like.

Louise closed her eyes and started to use her well-honed meditation techniques to switch off the emotional part of her brain. Her mind was currently going crazy, and she needed to slow it down and allow rational thought to come to the fore. The only thing that mattered right now was a plan to escape. She had been shot, her muscles from head to toe totally fatigued and deep in the shit. If she did not get out of this, she faced months of interrogation before being paraded in front of the world's press as the assassin of an FSB General or an execution and a shallow grave. Thinking it through led her to the conclusion that there was no decision to make. It was either escape or she died trying.

The only thing she therefore had to decide was the timing of the attempt and how she could stack the odds ever so slightly in her favour. The best time to escape was during a distraction and just getting some distance between her and the chase team. She knew that if she got away, she could maintain it until she got to safety. It would be better to get away before they started the transfer. She felt instinctively that they would move her in the next few hours to Moscow. It was a stronger environment for what they wanted to do. First, they would knock her down, get her to that place where she felt helpless and despondent. It was all about making her feel desperate and with nowhere to go, no hope of a way out other than to comply with what they wanted. Everything after that would just be a small step on the previous day and she knew she would tell them everything over time. Louise heard some footsteps and opened her eyes to see Dr Galina striding purposefully towards her. Without a pause or even an acknowledgement of Louise's presence, she took the empty chair opposite Louise.

Louise kept her eyes downcast, taking on the persona of the grey lady. Nothing to see here, I am not a threat, you have me beaten. Internally, of course, Louise was biding her time until she could make a move.

"Let's start from the beginning, Erica. I like to make sure I have the details right. What were you doing in Moscow?"

"I don't have much more to add, to be honest. I have told you I was working at the Bolshoi as part of my cover and waiting for my client to provide details of the target. They never arrived and when word of the General's death came down, I was worried I would be a suspect, being a foreigner, and decided to move to avoid suspicion."

"How were you to get your details of the target?"

"Through the dark web. They post a pack on the server I can access and download from there. It is all very electronic these days."

"Who was your client? MI6, CIA?"

"I doubt it, they would use their own contractors and not a freelance. No, it tends to be more organised gangs or wealthy businessmen taking out a competitor."

"Yes, but who was it?"

"That is something we never find out. The whole point is that it is anonymous from both sides, which is why I work that way. If they get prosecuted by local law enforcement, they would try and do a deal to get less jail time. This way they can only compromise the server and it is easy enough to set up a new one. I would never operate these days for someone I knew. Too dangerous."

"Have you ever worked for MI6 or CIA?"

"Certainly not knowingly, not even the FSB. As I said, I work anonymously."

"You must have been trained by one of the big intelligence agencies though. Who completed your training?"

"No one really, I just picked stuff up as I went along, I did not have any one trainer. When I was younger, I had a neighbour teach me martial arts and endurance training."

"Does he still train you now?"

"No, he died a number of years ago, lung cancer. He smoked like a chimney, but he said they did not know about smoking causing heart disease or cancer in those days. I was heartbroken. He was the closest thing I had to a dad; I never knew my own father."

"Interesting, Erica, but I doubt one neighbour taught you how to be a successful assassin and how to use the dark web to get clients. You must have had more professional training. Who was it?"

"Well, that is a bit unfair, I have worked bloody hard to get to where I am. It isn't hard to work out how to use the dark web. I had a friend in school who wanted to be a hacker, so I sat watching him. That is how I tend to learn. I watched him navigate the dark web and just asked lots of questions over a few beers. I learnt fighting while working as a bouncer on the nightclub doors in the less salubrious parts of Glasgow. You don't survive working the doors without a bit of guile and some technique."

"We are leaving for Moscow early in the morning. Get some sleep. It might be the last you get for a while."

The guards manhandled Louise into one of the stable cubicles and tied her hands and feet securely. She couldn't move much but by shifting the stale straw about she managed to get a position where she could get reasonably comfortable. She had very little time to engineer a way out. She lay there remembering her real training…

She was driven by Land Rover and then boat to a remote Scottish Island off the west coast of Scotland. There was no fancy accommodation waiting for them, just a broken-down farmhouse with half a roof and no windows. She met six other candidates and after they made brief introductions they were provided with a bunch of items and told they had four hours to make the cottage wind and watertight. They had two large pieces of canvas, some rope, a combat knife and an axe. They each agreed tasks and set out to get some trees to act as beams for the part of the roof that had fallen in and some smaller ones to provide something to tie the canvas on for the door and windows.

Four hours was not a lot of time as they would have to haul everything they needed from the forest, which was over moorland and a hill about a mile away. The instructors just watched on and took notes. There were no tips or pointers on how to make it work or a better way of doing it. They knew the beams would need to be about 60cm apart as they are in modern houses to support the canvas and make sure it was tight enough not to bow in the middle when it rained. That meant they required 8 beams to get the work completed and two trips to get everything. The hill killed the calf muscles, and the moorland bog killed the thighs.

By the time they made it back to the ruin they were battered, bruised, and disheartened. Louise was the first one up onto the roof without even taking a five-minute rest period. She cajoled the others to get moving as she knew once they sat down the muscles would lock up. They completed the task with a couple of minutes to spare. It was a bit rough looking, and it would not win any architectural awards, but Louise was pretty sure it would do the job. The team were sat on the floor of the cottage looking at each other with that self-satisfied glow of achievement when the Sergeant arrived at the cottage.

"Get onto your feet, who the fuck told you to sit down? You rest when I bloody well tell you to, now get on your feet and follow me down to the beach."

The six bone-tired operators trudged down to the beach just as the wind got up and it started pelting with rain.

"Right, into the water with you and when you get to calf deep, I want you to link arms and lie back in the water face up. The only way you get out of the water is to give up. You walk up to me and tell me you want out. If you do that, we will give you some dry clothes, a hot meal and send you off with a handshake."

Louise would never forget the numbingly cold North Westerly gale battering the beach with metre-high waves. You just had time to catch some air in between the waves. You could not lie back to rest or you could not get air, the constant pressure on the stomach muscles was intense;

as they started to struggle it was difficult keeping their heads above the water. It was one of the most terrifying experiences of her life. The shaking due to the cold water meant they struggled to gulp down air fast enough and the constant waves battering the bodies drained their morale. Hour after hour they lay on the beach before one of the candidates decided enough was enough and stumbled up the beach to get off the programme. Over the following two hours two more candidates decided to leave and the three remaining candidates lay on the beach shivering, blue lipped and thoroughly pissed off. Just as the cold was no longer a problem for Louise and she was starting to feel warm, the Sergeant waded into the water and dragged them up the beach.

"Get your sorry asses up to the cottage and get dry clothes on. When I get there, you better have a fire going and be standing in front of it. MOVE IT!!!"

That was her introduction to assassin school and was only the first 24 hours. She wondered what the hell she had let herself in for and for the life of her had no idea why it was of any use to what she was going to do. Kayaking in storms, running for hours on end with full Bergens, up hills, down hills and swimming, lots and lots of swimming. In between the exercise and mostly when they were ready to drop, they started using different weapons, different surveillance methods, spotting weak spots in perimeter security and how to get in and back out without detection. The view was simple: if you can do it when you are running on empty then you can definitely do it when you are sharp minded and fresh.

The worst task was one where they had 72 hours of constant running, swimming, and carrying boulders, and then being told to take out a target within a posh country house. It had to be completed with a knife and they had to be in and out without detection. The opposition guards had paint guns. If they were hit, then they were out and they failed the task. Making good decisions when you were cold, wet, hungry, sleep deprived and under pressure to succeed was the whole point of the task. Louise always felt she had an element of luck on her side as a storm broke as she was trying to gain entry and the resulting lightning caused momentary night blindness to the security team, allowing her to sneak past without being seen. Sometimes you just got the breaks and sometimes you didn't.

TWENTY-SIX

Josef sat in his home late into the evening enjoying the silence and the solitude. He was just sat in darkness allowing his mind to roam and not be encumbered with "Stuff". He was not a people person, he found dealing with them difficult and frustrating. People were one of life's enigmas. He could not understand why they had made life so damned complicated. He wanted to take another moment to himself before picking up the phone to the Director. He was a difficult man and one who was really only interested in how things made him look. He had no interest in the people who actually did the work, the ones whose dedication made him look good. With a sorrowful sigh he picked up the phone and chastised himself for letting the Director get under his skin.

"Good evening, Director, my apologies for phoning you so late in the evening; however, I have some news."

"Good news I hope, Josef."

"Indeed, Director, we have just carried out an Operation in Tallinn, Estonia."

"I know where Tallinn is, Josef."

"Ah yes, apologies, Director. I was notified by an asset in London that the remaining assassins were over the border in Estonia travelling by train to Tallinn. We intercepted them on arrival and took out the defector and captured the assassin we believe was responsible for the assassination of General Andropov at the Bolshoi Theatre. She was shot during the capture. We have taken her to a safe house at the Border to stabilise her wounds and some basic interrogation before we take her back to Moscow for enhanced interrogation and whatever else you decide."

"When you say took out, Josef, what exactly do you mean?"

"We believe he is dead or at best fatally injured, Director. The marksman had a heart shot and we saw him crumple to the ground before he was dragged into the embassy. There were no signs of life, Director. We have an asset confirming with London to make sure. To be extra cautious we have people in the local hospital admissions checking all gunshot victims that are admitted."

"Thank you, Josef, that is good news. I will brief the President. I am sure he will be delighted with my progress. Josef, do you think we will get any noise from the British or Estonians on this?"

"Oh, the British will complain about it and write us a strongly worded letter, but it will all die down in a few days. The Estonians will just want it to go away. There is no evidence it was us and with the assassin we have captured they will not want to open that particular can of worms in case we parade her in front of the world's press. They won't want to admit responsibility for the assassination of my brother."

"Excellent work, Josef, I know this was a tough one. Where are we with the driver in the North? Any news on his capture?"

"Not yet, Director, the last I heard is that he was badly injured with the hunter force close on his tail. It is only a matter of time before he dies of his wounds or we have him captured."

"Died of his wounds sounds like a more suitable outcome, Josef, we have no need of two captives, one will do just fine. One last thing, Josef, no need to bring the body back. A shallow grave out there is just as good a finish."

"Understood, Director."

Josef finished his vodka and stubbed out his cigar before wandering into his bedroom and falling asleep fully clothed on top of the bed. Exhaustion had finally taken its toll.

TWENTY-SEVEN

Mac had gathered the team in one of the small offices in the embassy. The door was closed, and they were sat around a large whiteboard they had acquired from one of the other conference rooms.

"Storm, could you get young Jaimie on one of those conference phones so we can get some information on layout etc."

Storm dialled Jaimie's mobile number.

"Jaimie's massage parlour, how can I help you?"

"Jaimie, it is Storm, and we are in a conference room with the rest of the team and a couple of guys from one of the regiments."

"Yes, I know it is you, Storm. Who else would be calling me from an Estonian number on an encrypted line?"

"All right, smart arse."

"Jaimie, it is Mac. We have the satellite image of the farm, its location and the access roads. Is there any way you could get us some building plans or a layout within the building? One other thing, did your guys happen to know which building they are keeping Louise in?"

"The answer to both is I currently do not know but I will do some digging and come back to you when I have it. How fast do you need it?"

"Yesterday is too late, my friend so do everything you can for us, matey."

"Laters."

"Let's let Jaimie work his dark magic and see what he can come up with. In the meantime, we need a plan of access, liberation and egress. We need to be in and out without casualties to our side. Remember this is unsanctioned and if we get in trouble there is no one coming to the rescue so let's get it right."

"Billy, do you think we could get the use of that lovely helicopter you guys came in from the ship on?" asked Storm.

"That might be a bit tricky given it is an unsanctioned mission, Storm. I can only ask though," replied Billy.

"What about a training exercise and you guys are doing a reconnaissance visit?" asked Hairy Dave.

"I can only ask; I normally find just being truthful works best and see what options the seniors come up with. If they say no, then you guys are on your own and with Mac being the way he is I don't fancy your chances much. Sorry, Mac, just saying, mate," replied Billy.

"Billy, you go make that call. Storm, can you and Hairy Dave go and sweet talk the grunts and see what kit we can borrow for the mission. Some M16s, ammo, vests and night vision would be pretty handy. We promise to give it back other than the ammo obviously. Oh, and tell them to keep it on the down low, we don't want the spooks learning we are ignoring their order to stand down."

"Liam, why don't you and I have a look at the satellite images of the layout and figure out the best way in and out of this place. Do you think you could get a topographical map of this area so we can see where the hills and valleys are?"

"Sure, Mac. Listen, mate you look like shit, buddy, are you sure you are best placed to do this? If we have to hot foot it out of this place, I am not convinced that leg of yours will stand up to it. If there are only five of us, mate and we have to assume Louise is in bad shape, then you might be a liability to the team," stated Liam.

"Don't hold back then, mate, tell me it as it is. I get it, fella; I was thinking about taking overwatch from Dave and allow him to work with you guys. That way I am far enough from the action to not be a burden and I have already shown I can make my own way back if I really have to," replied Mac.

"Alright, Mac. It is your call. I won't mention it again. Let's get the map up and we can overlay the buildings on it and see what we need to do. We have a main house here and two outbuildings here and here. Normal practice would be to have a detainee in one of those with round the clock guards both inside and outside the building. If the house is big enough it is possible they would have her in there in one of the upstairs rooms. My gut is one of the outbuildings though, as interrogation can be a messy business," stated Liam.

"I hate missions where you can't get some eyes on the ground up front. It makes it so much cleaner. We have trees here and here, and then clear ground all-round the actual buildings. That is a fair size killing ground and we would be wide open for a good hundred metres on all sides. I don't fancy that too much if I am honest. Is that a stream? Looks like a small stream to me although I would normally call that kind of thing a burn." Mac was unsure if Liam would understand the Scots word for a small stream.

"I know what a burn is, Mac, I grew up in the Lake District, we had loads of Jocks there on holiday. Can we zoom in on that with the satellite image?"

"Just a tick, I can but we start to lose resolution, commercial satellites don't quite have the same resolution as the Defence ones. Now that is definitely a burn and runs to within 20 metres of that outbuilding there. That field there, does that look more like a paddock; you know where they exercise horses?"

"You have sharp eyes, Liam, I think you are right, lad. So, there is a strong chance that the building near the burn is a Stable and the burn was their water source for the horses. A lot of farms need their own water source as they are too far from the water mains and it would be a fortune to run it in," stated Mac.

"The stream runs from this wooded hill here and right past the farm. The question is, do we move from the wooded hill and in that way or from the road and go up stream so to speak?" asked Liam.

"Let's get a view from Billy and the team and test our opinion. My view is to come down from the wooded area and cut up behind what we think is the stables, but it would mean a bit of a hike to infiltrate the farm. Exfil would be faster and easier back towards the road, but it is very open, and we would be on the run, so it depends on whether there is a chasing group and how well armed they are."

It took about 20 minutes before, Billy, Storm and Hairy Dave arrived back in the office carrying a bunch of black canvas holdalls.

"What did you manage to scrounge from the grunts?" asked Mac.

"Pretty much everything we needed, Mac, vests for everyone and M16s for everyone as well, ammo but we only got two sets of night vision goggles."

"I will take that. Billy, is there any chance we could get a day scope and a Qioptiq clip on thermal image scope for my Lobaev rifle? That would be ideal. A suppressor as well if you have one?" asked Mac.

"Already requested and granted, my friend. Oh, and we have permission to carry out a training mission for four hours starting at 2am. So that means in, job done and out. We can't be late, or we lose our lift back to the ship, and Liam and I will be in deep shit," replied Billy.

"You are a gentleman and a scholar, young man," replied Mac.

"Hahaha, you crack me up. In reality I am an uneducated council estate boy and proud of it," replied Billy.

"Aren't we all, my friend, aren't we all. Apart from the Ruperts of course," answered Dave.

"Storm, can you give Jaimie a quick call and see where he is up to with the building plans?" asked Mac.

Storm took out her mobile phone and called Jaimie.

"Hey babe, how did you get on with that stuff Mac asked for?"

"Hey Storm, can you put me on speaker, and I will talk to all of you at the same time.

"I have just sent over the plans I managed to get hold of from the local council. They are pretty rudimentary I am afraid they don't have the same planning departments as we have within the UK. Let me just ping them across to you. Right, you should have them right about now. The house itself looks to be stone built with single glazed windows and a tile roof. It comprises two floors above ground and no basement which make sense as it is pretty close to the water table as it is. There are two outbuildings, one is what I would class as a barn and is designated as general farm use and is really just a glorified shed. The other one is classified as a stable and can take up to 10 horses from the looks of the drawings."

"Jaimie, how on earth did you get hold of this, mate, in such a short timeline?" asked Liam.

"Ninja computer skills, buddy, we can't all be door kickers," replied Jaimie.

"Touché," replied Liam.

"We have one hour until wheels up, so let's get some detail onto this plan and get our girl back," stated Mac.

"Looking at the satellite photos, we get a ride by helicopter to this clearing here. From there we move on foot about one klick to the top of this hill. That is about 400 metres out from the farm buildings. I will take overwatch and set up at that point. Dave, that releases you to work with Storm, Liam and Billy to complete the rescue. As Liam pointed out quite eloquently, I am already injured and could jeopardise the mission if I try to kick down doors. From the hill there is a burn that leads to within 20 metres of that building there, which we strongly believe is a stable. Whether it is a working stable or no longer used, we don't know. We clear each building in turn, starting with the stable. One, because it is closest to the burn; and second, because Liam believes it is the most likely place for them to be holding Louise if they are interrogating her, which let's face it is highly likely. After we have cleared the stable, if Louise is not in it, we complete this building here which we believe is the barn and lastly if we really have to, we clear the house and go room to room. I would like to avoid that if possible as it will contain most of the combatants."

"What about comms, Mac? We need some decent comms," said Storm.

"I have that covered as well. It is just some basic UHF comms units with throat mics, but they will do the job," replied Billy.

"Jaimie, the satellite feed will be pretty useless I expect until daybreak, so you can stand down, mate," stated Mac.

"Actually, daylight starts at 3:53 am at this time of year so I won't be able to help with your infill but once you are in position and the sun comes up, I can provide a view of movements outdoors," replied Jaimie.

"All right, mate, a point well made. Jaimie, you can use your mobile to connect with me on overwatch and I can relay pertinent information to the team on an as needs basis," replied Mac.

"Ok, folks, let's open this up to comments, suggestions and concerns," stated Billy.

"We have covered infill and the search plan, what about exfill?" asked Dave.

"We have two options available to us. The easy option is head for the road. It is the fastest, most direct route, and we get the helicopter to meet us at this point here. The danger is if we are being chased and we have an injured Louise to carry then we are likely to be outgunned and in open ground. However, it is still the quickest and easiest option. Option two is we hot foot it back out the way we came in. Carrying Louise would be murder, but we would at least have cover to slow down any chasing group. We meet our ride back where we left it with a maximum window of four hours from boots on the ground to wheels up on the way back," replied Mac.

"The difference in time to exfill would be about 15 mins from option 1 to option 2. In the grand scheme of things, it is neither here nor there as long as we don't exceed the four-hour window. Surely, we are better with the cover. We have to assume they are professional shots and running in the open feels a bit too risky. Just my view," stated Dave.

"Storm?" asked Mac.

"I agree with Dave, option 2 feels like least risk," replied Storm.

"Liam, Billy. Any views from you guys?"

"Option 2 for me. Liam?" replied Billy.

"Yeah I am happy with that. Seems to me like we have a consensus and the basis of a plan," replied Liam.

"I would like to go through timings and who enters which building. The stables in particular has a number of different compartments for each horse so we need to be on the money as we clear it."

"Agreed; Dave, you, Storm and Liam work through the details on how you want to clear each building and then we will go through a final equipment check. We leave nothing to chance on this one."

An hour later, Billy and Liam led the team to the helicopter which had landed near the Embassy in the local park. There might be some noise complaints to the local council about a helicopter landing in the city at 3 am; however, the Embassy could deal with that tomorrow. The pen pushers needed to do something to earn their money. There was no banter or chat, each member of the team was lost in their own thoughts. You could almost physically touch the nervous energy as the team took their seats. This mission was to rescue one of their own and that meant total focus. The consequences of getting it wrong were ignored, there was no time for negativity. It was time for total focus and getting the small details of the operation right and reacting to the unknowns as they happened. You get the details right and everything else flows.

The team took their seats on the Merlin Mk 2 helicopter and seconds later it was in the air and winging it towards their destination.

Within no time the pilot was on comms: "Five mikes to drop off."

Billy turned to the rest of the team, held his hand up with all five fingers and mouthed 'five mikes'. The team all nodded in acceptance waiting on the green light to disembark.

"One mike to drop off."

Billy ensured all the team were aware and the team got themselves ready. They had to assume it could be a hot landing zone and prepare accordingly. Billy, Liam and Dave would be out first and set up a perimeter ready to take on any armed combatants. Sixty seconds later the team were deploying. They set up the perimeter and waited until the helicopter was back in the air before heading off into the woods in the direction of the stables. Billy was in the lead with Liam taking up the rear and the team in the middle, Mac taking up the position of next to last. It didn't take long before Mac was questioning the wisdom of being on the mission. He should have been resting up but instead his ego would not let the team leave him behind.

"I am too old for this shit," he mumbled to himself.

The team walked in formation the mile or so to the ridge near the stables and took stock of the stable's layout, Mac and Billy cresting the ridge and using binoculars to watch the compound.

As they finished their surveillance, they gathered the team in a huddle.

"All quiet in the compound, there are two armed tangos on patrol near the stables. Looks like our suspicion of Louise being held up there rather than in the house itself was right. The best course is to use the stream bed to get close to the building and take out both guards. Mac, you stay here on overwatch and make sure we have a secure exit. Don't let them get behind us and cut us off. Any last minute questions?"

The team all shook their heads to indicate no questions and one by one they headed over the ridge and into the danger zone. Once again Billy took the lead and they wound their way down the hill towards the open ground. The going was slow as they had no idea what improvised explosive devices (IEDs) if any had been deployed, nor if any surveillance cameras with infrared were in use. The best result was to get in and out without detection. They were in a foreign country and if they got caught not only could they end up dead but being paraded in front of the world's press was not going to be much better.

As the team reached the end of the woods, they found the stream they would use for cover. The stream sides were not high enough for them to walk or even crawl, so they had to resort to a slow commando crawl in the freezing water. It was time consuming, and they would lose the cover of darkness quickly. The last few hundred metres took an age. Mac lay on the ridge in the middle of a bush providing overwatch and a commentary of when they were most at risk as the two guards looked out over the fields.

Mac set up an open phone bridge with Jaimie on an encrypted line as they waited on the satellite imagery being useful.

"Everything ok, Jaimie? Anything to report?"

"Satellite visuals are pretty good as we get to dawn. Nothing untoward at the target location so far, Mac. This is probably nothing, but I am seeing a convoy of vehicles on the Russian side of the border. Four large SUV types all travelling at high speed about 30m apart. I will keep an eye on them, but my spider sense is tingling."

"You need to change the movies you are watching, mate. Fucking spider sense. If they were coming here, how much time would it take them?"

"Difficult to tell. It all depends on the border crossing. If we allow 15 mins for the crossing, then anything from 40 mins to an hour. If they each have five armed tangos, then we have up to 20 additional combatants joining this. It could get messy."

"Roger that."

Jaimie was always amazed that these things never fazed the team. Everything was just taken very factually with zero emotion.

Mac relayed the new information to the team.

"We have four SUVs heading in convoy formation to the border from the Russian side. I suspect they are coming to collect Louise, but there are no hard facts.

ETA would be 40 mikes minimum but keep your wits about you as we now have a potential hard stop and an exfil under fire from a hunter group would prove troublesome"

"Understood" came the reply from Billy.

Ten minutes later the team were lying in the stream 20 metres from the stable block.

"Mac, in position. Standby standby."

"Understood," replied Mac.

"Execute, execute, execute."

Mac took aim at the guard nearest the stables and, breathing slowly out to steady his aim, fired a shot and hit his target who dropped to the ground with a thud. At the same time, Hairy Dave took out the second guard who was just outside the house with a similar result. The suppressors did their job and although there were two audible thumps there was not the loud crack you got from normal gunfire. The team were up and moving quickly, Storm reaching the bodies and using her knife made sure they were dead. She did not want more gunfire – although it was suppressed it could still be heard by a curious guard within the house. Once happy both guards were out of the fight, she took up a position at the corner of the stables facing the house, allowing Dave and Billy to enter them. Liam had travelled further down the stream to set up a perimeter watch on the entrance road.

Billy pulled open the stables door with a loud metallic squeal and he winced inwardly at the sound which travelled across the farm buildings with no other background sounds to drown it out. They paused for a few seconds before entering the darkness of the stables. Billy indicated for Dave to move to the stalls on the right. The torches on their M16 rifles on, they searched the stalls quickly but methodically. They had one shot at it and could not afford to miss Louise in case they were keeping her in a box the way the CIA did at some of their black sites. The boxes were deliberately too hot, too cold and too short, draining the resolve of their captives and making them more pliable during interrogation. After three or four minutes of searching, Billy heard Dave mutter a few words.

Touching his throat mike, Billy asked, "Dave, do you have something?"

"I have her, she is in a bad way though, they have given her a real going over. She has a stomach wound from a gunshot by the look of it. I need a few minutes to stabilise her before we go for extraction."

"I have lights on in the farmhouse. We need to get a move on," stated Storm.

Just at that they heard the double tap of suppressed fire followed by Storm saying "contact at the house, one tango down".

"Dave, get a move on, son. I will help Storm hold the farmhouse. This place will be swarming with Tangos in the next two minutes and the exfil to the woods has a lot of clear ground."

"Roger that," acknowledged Dave.

Dave cut Louise free and tended to her wounds the best he could, filling her with morphine from a vial he had pinched from the medic at the embassy.

"You will feel fine in a few seconds, just let it do its job. They really worked you over. Other than your stomach wound, anything else life threatening?"

"No, mostly bruising but I have no idea about internal bleeding. Let's get a move on. They were moving me to Moscow this morning so we could have additional company shortly."

"We are on that already but don't call me shortly."

"Hahahaha, don't make me laugh, it hurts. Your sense of humour really sucks."

"You love it really," commented Dave as he hauled Louise into a standing position.

"No boots?" asked Dave.

"They took them off me when they took a rubber hose to beat the soles of my feet."

"Bastards," muttered Dave as he left the stables to get some boots off of one of the dead guys and giving them to Louise.

"They will be too big but better than walking bare foot."

Louise grunted in pain as she put the boots on her bruised and bleeding feet and with Dave's help hobbled to the door of the stables.

"We have a 20-metre dash to get to the cover of the stream."

Just at that six armed tangos came round either side of the farmhouse and fanning out, having obviously exited through a back door.

Storm and Billy laid down covering fire to allow Dave to help Louise to get to the stream. Despite their best efforts, the tangos opened fire and caught Louise just as she was jumping into the stream, two seconds behind Dave. Dave heard the grunt of pain and the louder than expected splash as Louise hit the water as a dead weight. Dave turned with the dread of someone expecting the worst only for his nightmare to be true. Louise was face down in the stream with little to no sign of life. Dave turned her over and brought her face out of the water and quickly assessed the damage. Shit, he thought, this is bad. There were three additional gun shots in her shoulder, abdomen and hip. The shooter spraying bullets in a line down her torso. Dave felt instantly sick and radioed the team.

"Louise is down, Louise is down. Three new gunshot wounds with heavy bleeding. We need a medivac." Dave had a tone of desperation in his voice and for the first time in a long time he actually felt scared.

"I will be with you in 20 secs. I have a medical kit." Liam was the first to respond.

Sure enough, 20 seconds later Liam appeared at Dave's side.

"Move over, chap and let me in?" asked Liam, and Dave responded by moving over."

Liam quickly assessed the wounds and determined the abdomen wound was the most pressing and bleeding the most. Liam turned Louise and examined her back. The holes were smaller here as she had been shot in the back as she jumped, the exit wounds on the front larger and fragmented. There were only two wounds in the front; the bullet in the hip was still inside and more than likely embedded in the bone.

Liam took out a Stanley knife and two pairs of forceps, enlarged the exit wound and used the forceps to clamp either side of an artery that was bleeding the most. He then took out two tampons and placed them into the entrance and exit wounds on the front and back of Louise's abdomen. The tampons quickly expanded and plugged the worst of the remaining bleeding. Liam turned Louise on her side.

"Dave, I need you to focus and put pressure on the front and back exit wounds. We need to reduce the blood loss."

Liam took out some wadding and a bandage and bound Louise's hip as best he could before turning his attention to the shoulder wound. This was worse than he initially thought and although the entrance wound was high up on the shoulder, the exit wound was lower down. It was possible the bullet had ricocheted within Louise. He suspected it might have nicked her lung, but there was nothing he could do about that here.

Liam touched his throat mike. "Mac, where are we on that medivac, mate. We need it pronto or Louise won't make it."

"Just chasing it up now, Liam."

"Next five mins, Mac."

"Roger that," replied Mac.

"Dave, keep pressure on that wound. I am going to help Storm and Billy. We need a clear LZ (landing zone) for the medivac."

Storm and Billy were pinned down by the six heavily armed tangos that were firing from cover either side of the house.

"Billy, I am going to head left and see if I can flank them and get a better angle than you have here. Mac, I need you to provide me with cover, I will be the rabbit, let's see if we can get you some openings. Take the shots as soon as you have them."

"Roger that."

"Mac, I don't want to be the bearer of bad news, but the convoy is now 10 minutes out."

"Roger that, Jaimie. Jaimie, we have a medivac landing asap at the stables. I need a countdown on that convoy, we need to be out of there before they arrive."

"Who is injured, Mac? Is it Louise?" asked Jaimie, failing to hide the rising tension in his voice.

"We need to keep focussed, Jaimie. Keep an eye on the convoy and give me that countdown. I need five minutes to get from my overwatch to the LZ."

"No problem, Mac," replied Jaimie.

Liam broke left and headed to an old tractor with flat tyres sitting 30m from the side of the stables. One of the tangos shouted a warning and stood up to focus on the running Liam. It was the last thing he did as Mac took him out with a clean head shot and watched in satisfaction as he saw the pink mist rise just before he dropped to the ground.

"One down, Liam."

"Roger that, Mac," replied Liam in a monotone response.

"Keep them pinned down, Mac."

Mac fired shots at the pair of tangos at the left-hand corner of the house and kept them pinned down as Liam stood and in a low running crouch zig-zagged to a point where he could flank their position.

"Cease fire, Mac."

Mac stopped firing and as one of the tangos raised his head to see what was going on, Liam took him out with a quick double tap to the chest. Two quick fire shots in a tight grouping on the chest. Seeing his comrade fall, the last combatant turned and made a run for the safety of the side door to the house. He got no more than five steps when he crumpled in a heap.

"Tango down," stated Mac, still watching for further movement through the scope of his sniper rifle.

Liam casually walked up and fired a kill shot into all three tangos, making sure they were down and would not interfere with the medivac.

"This side is clear. Mac, time for you to head to the LZ and I will head round the back of the house and help Billy and Storm."

Liam made his way round the house and crouched at the last corner. Taking out a mirror, he used it to peer round towards the remaining enemies, taking pot shots at Billy and Storm.

"Billy, Storm, cease fire. I am in position behind the tangos and can take them out. I don't need a friendly fire incident."

"Roger that, Mac, cease firing."

Mac stood up and made his way down the hill to the flat ground and put on as much of a jog as he could with his knife wounds hampering him. He pushed the stabbing pain aside and forced the jog to continue despite every sinew of his being screaming at him to stop. He turned his head, trying to locate the sound of a helicopter, praying it was the medivac and not Russian as Jaimie gave him an update on his headset on progress of the convoy.

"Mac, you are cutting it awful close. Medivac is a few seconds out, but the convoy is less than five minutes. Get a move on, buddy."

As the sound of the helicopter could be heard overhead, Liam crouched down at the back corner of the cottage and turned his focus on the two remaining enemy combatants. He had to take them out before the medivac landed. One lucky shot and the helicopter could be grounded, and Louise's life was on the line. He peaked round the corner and could see them focussed on Billy and Storm. He took careful aim, letting his breath flow out as he pressed the trigger and with a quick double tap to each one, they crumpled to the ground and the fight was over. Keeping his rifle carefully aimed at the downed enemies, he paused for a couple of seconds to fire an extra shot into the heads of each of the stricken soldiers.

Seconds later the medivac circled the stables and landed 50m away, causing a maelstrom of dust and noise.

Billy and Storm jogged to the stream bank and knelt down beside the stricken Louise, and Liam ran to the helicopter to help the on-board medic retrieve a stretcher. As quickly as they could, they got her on the stretcher and onto the helicopter, the medic working frantically to stem the bleeding.

"Hang on in there, honey, keep talking to me," pleaded Storm to Louise.

"Fucking hell, this hurts, mate," croaked Louise.

Mac was last onto the helicopter, limping across the field as fast as he could while Billy and Liam kept a perimeter. They could see the dust of the convoy kicking up as it turned onto the farm track. Mac stumbled and Liam ran to pick him up and help him onto the helicopter with Billy jumping on board. As it took off and headed out over the woods, they could hear the ping ping ping of bullets bouncing off the fuselage. Looking down, Mac could see the tangos jumping out of the vehicles and looking askance at the helicopter moving off into the distance.

The team were looking down at the medic working frantically on Louise and muttering to himself when he started pumping her chest with his hands doing CPR.

Looking at the monitor, Mac could see the heart output had flatlined. The medic spoke into his mike: "I need someone to do CPR." Quick as a flash Storm was doing CPR and pushing hard on Louise's chest. There was still no output on the monitor.

The medic took a syringe out of his bag and filled it with a clear substance from a small vial. "Adrenalin," he stated as he plunged it into Louise's heart directly. The whole team were watching the monitor, desperately wanting to see the regular peaks showing it was working. It showed nothing and Storm continued pumping Louise's chest. In desperation, the medic reached for the defibrillator and placed the sticky pads on Louise's chest, one just above the heart at the right-hand side collarbone and the other on the left-hand side below the armpit. He leaned across and stopped Louise doing CPR, and made sure everyone was away from touching Louise before pressing the button. Again, there was no output, and the tears were streaming down Storm's face. The medic turned up the energy output from the defibrillator and once again made sure no one was touching Louise.

Louise's body bounced with the hit of energy and suddenly there was an output on the monitor. The team sighed a collective sigh of relief. It was close but she was hanging in there.

They were still 15 minutes out from HMS Campbeltown and the medical bay onboard ship which they all hoped would be able to stabilise her before flying her to Germany or the UK for full treatment.

It was the longest 15 minutes of their lives: everyone sitting in silence, watching the monitors, too scared to hope that she was through the worst. They had all lost colleagues and friends over the years, but it never quite prepared you for the next one. Louise lay on the stretcher without a flicker of life, there was no cheeky smile or a thumbs up to say she was still fighting. Mac had his head bowed as if praying, Storm leaned in and all she could hear him say was "Just one more minute, hold on just one more minute". Hearing it hit home to Storm just how fragile their team was. There were never any guarantees of success and surviving a mission. Without really thinking about it, she joined Mac in his mantra "Just one more minute".

Suddenly the helicopter was slowing and circling the ship to land. All the team getting ready to get the stretcher to the medical bay as fast as possible. Within seconds the helicopter was down with a bump. Billy and Liam were out first, followed by the medic, and taking one end of the stretcher with Dave and Storm the other end. The medic holding a drip nice and high to get fluids into Louise. Moving fast though the ship they entered the medical bay and Mac glimpsed the slim red headed doctor that had treated him, only this time all gowned up ready to go to work on Louise. The team were ushered out as the doctor took control and barked orders to the rest of the team in the operating theatre.

The team looked around each other, no one daring to speak when Mac piped up, "How about a brew, Billy, I feel the need of a nice hot cup of tea."

Billy looked round the rest of the team and solemnly nodded to Mac. "This way."

The team followed Billy to the canteen to get some tea, but no one was in the mood to talk, and they sat in silence, heads down, keeping their thoughts to themselves. They were all hoping against hope that Louise would pull through but the moment when her heart had stopped on the flight to the ship had rocked them. A team who normally took whatever an operation would throw at them were for once stunned into silence. As they sat there seconds became minutes and minutes became hours with no information or updates coming from the operating theatre. In some circumstances no news is good news; in this circumstance no news meant bad news, and the longer they waited the less likely it would be the news they wanted.

"I think we need to get some food down us and then we need to head elsewhere as the canteen will be full, and they will need this table," stated Billy.

"Now you mention it, I am a touch hungry," stated Hairy Dave.

"Shocker!!" replied Storm.

"Hey, it takes a lot to keep this bad boy in shape," commented Dave as he showed off his physique.

"I have no idea how you can eat at a time like this," Storm raged and stomped out of the canteen.

"What did I say?" pleaded Dave as he looked round the team.

"Just leave it, mate, she will come round," answered Mac as he touched Dave's arm.

The team formed an orderly queue to get some food, but Mac wandered out to find Storm, which he did up on deck looking out over the sea lost in her own thoughts. Mac limped up and stood beside her.

"She will pull through, honey, she is a tough cookie. If anyone can do it, she can," stated Mac in as calm a voice as he could muster.

"Thanks, Mac, Louise was always the tough kick ass girl that fronted into anything. She just looked so vulnerable lying there and almost grey in colour. It was like a shadow of Louise."

"I know, I felt the same. The grey is down to the blood loss and they will give her a transfusion in the theatre which will help. The bigger question is can they stem the blood loss without compromising her organs and the risk of infection from a punctured bowel. This won't be over today. She is in for a tough fight over the next 72 hours."

"Jeez, Mac, I don't know if I can handle this for 72 hours," replied Storm.

"The only thing we can do is keep busy. We will be flying back to London tomorrow and straight into a debrief with the Spooks in Vauxhall. I am expecting a kicking after ignoring their orders about freeing Louise. This could well end up being my last adventure," stated Mac.

"Don't even joke about that, Mac, you are the glue that holds this team together. We all see you as the founding father."

"Years ago, I was the sex symbol, then the solid team member and now I am the founding father. Wow, I am really heading downhill faster than I thought. I am going to get some grub before they run out, I suggest you do the same. You will be hungry later otherwise and nothing will be available."

"All right, Mac, point taken." At that Storm linked her arm in through Mac's and they wandered back to the canteen.

Mac and Storm joined the back of the queue and picked up some food before wandering over to the table where Dave was sat alone. Billy and Liam had wandered off to join their SBS team and to debrief their line of command on the "training exercise" they had successfully conducted.

"Sorry, Dave, it has been a tough few days, and I am worried about Louise."

"Hey, I get it, no need to apologise. Sometimes my sense of humour gets me into trouble," replied Dave.

"I hope the doc gives us an update soon – the longer this goes on the more worried I am becoming," stated Storm.

"Ditto, this waiting about shit is starting to get to me," replied Mac as he sat down with his food.

"Is that not the doc at the door over there?" asked Dave, pointing to the young redheaded officer at the doorway.

"It sure is," replied Mac, who then stood up and waved to the doctor to come over to their table.

They were all watching the doc to see if they could get a view on Louise's status from her face; however, the doc just looked tired.

"Take a seat, doc, it's been a long day."

"It is Lieutenant Commander, Mac, but yes it has been a long day," replied the doc as she took a seat across from Dave.

"It has been a difficult operation if I am honest and nothing was straightforward. Louise has a punctured lung, a ruptured kidney and spleen. She lost an awful lot of blood, but the complicating factor is a punctured bowel, so we are having to treat for peritonitis as well. We managed to eventually stop the blood loss, but she is by no means out of the woods. We will transfer her to London this morning and she may well require additional surgery. She should have woken up by now if I am honest and the fact that she hasn't is worrying me."

"Shit, doc, that isn't what any of us wanted to hear," stated Mac as he looked down at the floor.

"Thank you for doing your best, though, we genuinely appreciate it. The rest is down to Louise, but she is a fighter, she will pull through."

"I genuinely hope so, Mac, time will tell. One other thing, Mac: when I tell you to rest up and take care of yourself that does not mean start another operation, get shot at and carry a bunch of kit through the woods. I mean it this time, don't do anything else for the next two weeks at least."

Mac looked up and flushed red. "I am sorry, Doc; it was just one of those last-minute things."

The doc just gave Mac one of those withering looks and headed off back out of the canteen.

"Well that genuinely sucks, I know we always worry about how long they are under an anaesthetic, but I just hoped this time would be different. I am totally gutted," stated Storm.

"I think we all are. She is tough as old boots, though, don't give up on our Louise just yet. She has been through a lot in her life, and it is all preparation for a time like this. As long as there is breath in her body that girl will keep fighting," replied Mac.

"You are right, Mac; I think that helicopter ride knocked the stuffing out of me. I mean she technically died twice on that flight back," chipped in Dave.

"But she is still here and still fighting, Dave; if I know that wee lassie, she will come through this and kick our arses for ever doubting her."

"You are right, Mac; I know you are," replied Dave.

The team lapsed back into silence before Mac stated, "I am going for some kip; we will be on a flight back to Tallinn in the morning before getting a flight back to London and Edward is going to be pissed. We will need to get our story straight before debriefing or we could all end up on the dole queue."

Storm and Dave waited for a few more minutes, just chatting about some good memories before turning in for the night.

The next morning the team got separated from Louise – they had to head back to the embassy in Tallinn to pick up Dimitri and get a commercial flight back to London Gatwick airport. Louise was getting an ambulance flight to RAF Brize Norton. The young redheaded doctor insisted on being present during the flight to ensure Louise remained stable although still unresponsive.

At Tallinn Airport the team discussed who was best placed to call Jaimie and let him know that Louise was not in a good way. Storm reluctantly agreed to be the bearer of bad news.

"Storm, have you lost another team member that you need help in finding? It isn't like you to keep in touch," quipped Jaimie.

"Jaimie, are you sitting down?"

"I am, spit it out, Storm what is going on?"

"I know you are aware Louise was injured during the rescue mission, Jaimie; she is stable, and they are flying her home to the UK today, but it was really bad, babe. She lost a lot of blood and was in the operating theatre for over five hours. She should have woken up by now babe and it isn't good that she hasn't. I think you need to make your way to London as that's where they will take her when she lands at RAF Brize Norton."

"Aww hell, Storm, I thought something was off when I didn't get a "we are having a party" phone call last night, but I did not think it would be this bad. I think I am going to throw up. She was always there for me when I needed her, a kick ass big sister was handy. She can't die, she just can't."

Storm could hear the tears forming in Jaimie's voice.

"She is a tough cookie, Jaimie; don't you be giving up on her. Mac gave Dave and I a lecture on it last night. She is a fighter and if anyone can pull through this she can. Get a flight to London, babe, and I will meet you there. The team will be flying into Gatwick airport so we can either get you there or at whichever hospital they take her to."

"I will get you at the hospital I think," stated Jaimie.

"Whatever works for you, babe," replied Storm.

Storm put the phone down and headed back to meet Dave, Mac, and Dimitri just as the boarding call was announced for their flight.

The team took their seats, two on one side of the aisle and two on the other side, with Storm sitting beside Dimitri.

After take-off and the seat belt signs had been switched off, Storm started to ask Dimitri about the potential cyber-attack on the Western financial sector.

"Louise mentioned a big cyber-attack on the West that is imminent, Dimitri. What is that all about?"

"I really need to talk about it when I get to London, Storm; no offence but it is really my bargaining chip to get asylum," replied Dimitri, looking down at the floor.

"That is ok, babe, I don't mind; I am not easy to offend. What I don't understand is that these banks etc are very well protected from a cyber perspective, so why do they think this one will be successful?" persisted Storm.

"Cyber-attacks take different forms, you get the likes of WannaCry which infects your servers and where you store your records, encrypts them and then asks you to pay to release the records out of the encryption. It is just a way of extorting money from you. Kind of like the old kidnapping but instead of a person it is the records you need to conduct your business. Another way is to find a back door into your network and actually steal information like credit card details, personal information and banking records. The companies that are prone to that tend to have internet shops or internet payments and they are not patching their servers facing the internet against known bugs and that makes them vulnerable to hackers who keep up to date with the latest issues on the likes of Microsoft, Cisco, Huawei etc. The big financial institutions employ lots of tools that check every email for known hacking codes and have strong patching policies, so they tend to be immune to that kind of attack. From that point of view, you are right, it would take too long to hack into them if you wanted to steal from them. Banks have protected themselves from stealing for generations. However, what if you did not want to steal anything, what if all you wanted to do was bring them down and stop them trading? How long would the West survive before there were riots on the streets and starving crowds of people storming parliament?"

"Do they have the skills to do that, Dimitri?" asked Storm.

"They do now. This has been years in the planning and infiltrating networks without being detected. Most cyber security departments are looking for people kicking doors down; this was done from within the banks and because there is no information flowing out of the organisation their tools are not picking up the breach. It is also about keeping under the radar of GCHQ and the National Cyber Security Centre (NCSC). They monitor traffic in and out of the UK and are constantly looking for abnormal traffic patterns. All the breaches have been in place for some time. All they need to do is exploit them on the night and wipe the key central servers. When the data is gone the western businesses that reply on those institutions can no longer pay their suppliers, and the food chain, energy chain, all of it grinds to a halt," replied Dimitri.

"You are describing financial Armageddon, Dimitri, the West as we know it will cease to exist. We are geared up for physical confrontation but none of that will matter in this instance. What would you do if we threatened nuclear retaliation?"

"We have simulated that type of response and the current estimate is that with the Prime Minister you have there is a 35% chance of that. Our government is willing to take that chance."

"It could be the end of the world though, Dimitri," protested Storm.

"Just a change in direction and one that Russia believe they would come out on top. Our government have become much more hard line over the last ten years, and they have confidence that can overcome anything the West throws at us. That is why I wanted to defect. I cannot sit by and let this collision course happen. The only way to stop it was to come to the West and help them stop it in its tracks. With my defection, I worry they will bring forward the timetable to try and make it happen before I can get it stopped."

TWENTY-EIGHT

J osef woke up to his phone ringing and a bouncing headache from celebrating with too much vodka the night before.

"What is it?" complained Josef, with a husky throat.

"Colonel, I think you might want to come into the office early. There have been some issues in Estonia, and they have snatched the waitress from the safe house; most of our team are dead. The team we sent to bring the girl to Moscow got there two minutes too late."

"No, no, no. That is a disaster. How could they have been caught off guard?" Josef could not keep the disappointment out of his voice.

"They came over the hills and evaded the security cameras by crawling up a stream bed to behind the stables. We believe the waitress is dead or dying; they were taking a stretcher into the helicopter as the escort team arrived," replied the voice on the phone.

"That is not going to be good enough, we have the driver in the north dead or dying, we have the defector dead or dying and now we have the waitress dead or dying, and we actually have had no confirmation of any of them. Get my security detail on the phone. I want an immediate pick up, I will be in the office promptly, I want every detail you can get me. I need to brief the

Director as soon as I have the details."

"Yes, Colonel."

Josef sighed to himself. Last night had become a hollow victory and he now had to go through all the: we should have, we could have minutiae of how they lost control of the operation. He had one last hope: that he got confirmation of the defector's death. The last thing he needed was that not happening either.

Josef picked up his phone and dialled his contact in London.

"Good morning, Michail, I am sorry for the early hour, I hope I did not wake you up?" asked Josef.

"Of course you woke me up, Josef, it is still early. What is it you want at this ungodly hour, Josef; I hope it is something that could not have waited until a decent hour?" replied Michail.

"I have had a bit of a setback with one of my missions, Michail, and I really need some good news with confirmation of the defector's death. Have you had any news for your contacts in SIS?"

"There is no news, Josef, and I mean zero news. This in itself is unusual – there would normally be some chatter. Your little stunt in Tallinn has them spooked and suspecting an inside mole leaking information. I told you we could not burn my agent, Josef, and that is exactly what you have done. I will now have to go onto radio silence for a few months and let the storm die down."

"Silence is telling, Michail; if he was dead, they would have announced it and started a witch hunt for the mole; the fact they have closed ranks tells me he is still alive and a threat to our plans. That is definitely not good news. I don't understand, as the sniper confirmed a direct hit and saw them drag the body inside the embassy."

"No, Josef, what the sniper reported was a direct hit to who they thought was the defector – nobody confirmed it was the right body we shot," corrected Michail.

Josef sat in stunned silence for 30 seconds.

"You are right, of course, Michail, we assumed that because they had this person in the centre of their guard cordon that it was the defector. They could easily have substituted him for a stand in. Tallinn was all smoke and mirrors.

"Thank you, Michail. Not what I wanted to hear but your analysis was spot on. I am perhaps too close and too personally involved in this one," replied Josef with a hint of exasperation in his voice.

"It happens, Josef, it happens to us all at some point," replied Michail.

Josef headed into the office after being picked up by his security detail, formulating how he could break the news to the Director in the least damaging way. He spent the 30 minutes in the car going round various possibilities in his mind and how he could spin the news to his favour. He hated to admit it to himself, but it looked like he was just going to have to tell the truth. The last few days had been a real rollercoaster and probably the most challenging of his career. He had not even had time to process the murder of his brother, just blanking it all out by staying busy. Never a healthy thing to do, but he owed it to his brother to get payback. If he was honest with himself, he was not sure if it was payback for his brother or just an ego thing for Josef that he could improve his career prospects by being the one to capture the killer.

He entered his office and took off his jacket before making a cup of coffee. He needed the caffeine to stave off the hangover and to sharpen up his mind before calling the Director. He picked up the phone and took a deep breath before dialling the number, not sure whether he wanted him to answer or not so he could leave a voicemail instead.

"Josef, it is a bit early for a call from you, is there a problem?" asked the Director, having been woken up.

"Indeed, Director. The British have stormed our safehouse on the Estonian border and freed the waitress responsible for the murder of General Andropov. The team on site were mostly killed, with the doctor surviving by hiding within the house. It looks like a five person kill team with sophisticated equipment to avoid the on-site security. The team did not really know what hit them. Our convoy we had despatched to bring her to Moscow arrived two minutes too late to intervene. All they could do was mop up and take the bodies back to Russia, so we did not have to deal with the local police. I am as disappointed as you are, Director."

"I doubt it, Josef, this is a real body blow to the reputation of the FSB within the Politburo. Have we had confirmation of the death of the defector yet, Josef?"

"No, Director. After discussion with our station chief in London, it is starting to look like the assassins swapped out the defector for a body double and it is the body double that we killed. The defector is on his way to London alive as we speak."

"Now that is bad news, Josef and is worse for us than the waitress. I have a top-secret cyber operation about to launch imminently and this will cause me a lot of pain. I will have to bring it forward to within the next 48 hours, rather than next week, and I don't know if everything is in place."

"What Operation is that?" enquired Josef.

"That is something you no longer need to know, Josef. I have an exciting opportunity for you. We need a new Chief of Station in South Africa, Josef, so get your bags packed. I will give you two weeks to take some time off and after that get yourself to South Africa."

"I am needed in Moscow, Director; I have a lot of things in the pipeline that have been years in the planning."

"You *were* needed in Moscow, Josef; you are now needed in South Africa. It will do you good to get some time out of Moscow and perhaps rebuild your reputation. The decision is final, Josef."

"Yes, Director."

Josef put down the phone and looked about his office for the last time. He would track down every one of that assassin team. They would pay!

TWENTY-NINE

Jaimie got the first flight to London Gatwick airport from Glasgow and then the express train into London Victoria before making his way across London to St Thomas' Hospital. His sister had not arrived yet, so he left the hospital and went for a coffee and a sandwich in one of the local brasseries. The sandwich was a bit dry and the coffee bitter as Jaimie fired up his laptop and used his trusty VPN over the coffee shop's WiFi to do some work. He never trusted the integrity and security of local WiFi networks as they were inherently insecure. Many guests at hotels across the country get their information stolen including credit card details when they go onto Amazon or Ticketmaster. It isn't that the websites are insecure, it is the WiFi connection out of the building. Jaimie suspected there was a leak at SIS in London and that was how they were waiting for his sister and team in Tallinn. Jaimie was determined to find out who. Jaimie was one of those people who had to finish things – leaving a loose end just was not an option, he needed closure. He suspected he was on the autism spectrum, but he had never been tested when he was younger. With his mum being the way she was, and then foster care, it just did not happen. Looking back, he doubted it would have changed anything.

Jaimie got to work and used an old back door he had left dormant from a previous piece of consultancy he had been asked to complete. He started rooting about and working through email chains and mobile phone records and the local WiFi records. He was looking for a pattern – who was logged onto the network at the same time as the emails were sent, who was in the offices and desks nearby, which switches were they working on within the Local area network. Who had accessed folders on the shared drives? He quickly whittled it down to 30 names which he felt was a decent return for the 90 minutes he had spent working the problem. That was the easy bit, however; the hard bit was focussing that 30 down to the actual mole. He wasn't sure what he would do with the information once he had it, but in his view that was someone else's problem. He had to find the culprit.

He shut down the laptop and paid for his coffee and sandwich before heading back to the hospital and walking up to reception.

"Excuse me, I am looking for Louise Stewart, I believe she was being admitted this morning." Jaimie gave the receptionist his best smile, hoping it would help.

"Let me just check the system for you." The receptionist typed away on the keyboard before frowning and looking up at Jaimie.

"I'm afraid we don't have anyone of that name within the hospital, Mr.?"

"I am Jaimie Stewart; Louise is my older sister."

"Let me just make a call for you, Mr Stewart and see what I can find out."

"Thank you, I appreciate that." Jaimie had a puzzled look on his face as he would normally just have been given a flat, no she is not here.

"Someone will be with you shortly, Mr Stewart. Please have a seat over there."

Jaimie wandered over to a row of plastic chairs, the same ones seen in waiting rooms everywhere, and checked the time on his watch. He was just looking up when a small dark-haired man in a grey suit wandered up to him with a large military type of guy standing just behind him.

"Mr Stewart, you asked at the desk for a Louise Stewart, is that correct?" asked the man in the grey suit.

"Yes, I was told she was being admitted here from a medical transfer flight. She had been working abroad," replied Jaimie.

"Do you have any ID on you, Mr Stewart, something like a driving licence or passport?"

"Why would I need that? I am just trying to visit my sister?" asked Jaimie.

"We have just implemented some enhanced security protocols, Mr Stewart; it is nothing to worry about, we are simply being a bit cautious about who we let know she is here. Now do you have any ID with you?"

"Here you go. I had my passport as ID for the flight down from Glasgow."

"Wonderful, please follow me." Grey suit handed the passport over to the military chap who disappeared and made a phone call whilst looking at Jaimie's passport.

"You are who exactly?" Jaimie asked grey suit.

"You can call me Mr Jones."

"Thank you, Mr Jones, what can you tell me about my sister's condition?"

"All in good time, my dear chap, did you have a good flight?"

"It was fine, just a random flight." Jaimie was getting frustrated with Mr Jones.

The military type walked back up to Mr Jones and nodded before handing the passport back to Jaimie.

"My apologies, Jaimie, we need to be careful in the current climate and we are being ultra-cautious in who we let in to see your sister. I do understand it is a bit frustrating, but it is for the right reasons."

Jaimie sighed before responding.

"I get it, I just want to get some news about my sister. It did not sound too good when I got a phone call from her team to make my way to London."

"I will let you know what information I have, and we will get her doctor to speak to you in person when she becomes available. Follow me and I will take you to her room."

Jaimie followed Mr Jones to the lifts, and once they were inside, he started to talk about Louise.

"Louise is stable, Jaimie; however, she is not improving like we would normally expect. We know she is a fighter, but she should be responding better to the treatment regime she has been on. She has not come round from her original operation and that is the biggest immediate concern. We are hoping now that you are here, she might respond to your voice," stated Mr Jones.

"I am happy to try anything that will make a difference. Can you let the security team know that I have a mutual friend arriving later and he will need to be allowed access to her room?"

"Of course, just as soon as he is vetted by the security team."

Mr Jones guided Jaimie to a corner room that had a few people standing just outside talking in hushed tones.

"Let me introduce you to some of Louise's teammates.

"Guys, this is Louise's younger brother Jaimie, Jaimie, this is Storm, Mac and Dave," stated Mr Jones.

"Hey all, nice to meet you in person, I hope you don't think me rude, but I am anxious to see my sister. I will catch up once I have seen her."

Jaimie nodded to the team and entered the room. Louise was lying on the hospital bed on a ventilator with loads of wires and tubes in every direction with the constant beeping of monitors and the regular whoosh of the ventilator. He had never seen his sister so pale and vulnerable, she had always been a force of nature, someone who would stand in the eye of a hurricane and dare it to try and best her.

"Hey sis, fancy meeting you in a place like this. I am sure you are just doing it for the attention, you know." Jaimie took his sister's hand and just talked, nothing particularly meaningful to anyone other than them. Reminiscing about their mum and the good and tough times of growing up in Glasgow. The tears would not stay back, and Jaimie laid his head on the bed and sobbed. Louise had always been the tough one and the one constant in his life and it looked like she was slipping away.

"Someone did this to you and I don't mean the Russians. There must have been a leak in SIS

(MI6). Someone sold you out either for money or for information. I will find them no matter how long it takes. They are in my world now. I might not be a door kicker like you, but the cyber world is my domain. All I need is a way into MI6, and I will find a footprint; it might be light, but it will be there."

There was no reaction from Louise, not even a twitch, and Jaimie composed himself before leaving the room and rejoining the team.

As he walked up to the team, head downcast, the next thing he knew was a bear hug from Storm.

"Hey babe, I am so sorry about Louise, she is tough as nails; if anyone can get through this she can."

Jaimie stepped back with a sheepish look on his face as he looked round the rest of the team. Storm saw his gaze and shrugged.

"It's all right, Jaimie, they know we had a thing."

"Oh, okay then, no worries," replied Jaimie uncertainly.

"You have nothing to worry about, Jaimie, you dark horse; anyway it's Storm that needs to worry once Louise wakes up," stated Dave.

Just like that the ice was broken and the normal low-level banter resumed. Some people would have found it offensive but in their game, deflection was a very powerful tool. It didn't help longer term and you still had to face your demons, but for the here and now it did its job.

Jaimie watched Mac's face change from relaxed to total focus in the blink of an eye as Jaimie heard the lift doors open followed by a click, click, click from the corridor behind him. Following Mac's gaze, Jaimie looked up and saw a sight that made him smile if only briefly. Down the corridor came Mr MacPherson, his walking stick clicking on the tiled concrete floor.

"It's ok, Mac, he is with me. Mr MacPherson took me in as a kid when my mum died, and Louise went off to training."

With that Mac relaxed and Jaimie walked up to hug the old man who was stood outside Louise's room.

"Hey, thanks for coming, she isn't in a good way, I'm afraid, she never regained consciousness and the longer it goes on the less likely it is that she will. That is her team down there who went in to rescue her," said Jaimie.

Mr MacPherson didn't say anything but gave a quick nod of his head to Mac and the team.

"Let me spend some time with her and you go and spend some time with them," stated Mr MacPherson who then turned and walked into the hospital room, his walking stick still clicking on the floor.

Just at that point the lift doors opened again, and Mr Jones approached Jaimie.

"Not great timing to ask this, Jaimie, but I need your skills for a job. Louise brought me home a cyber expert who has told us of a threat to the UK and I need you to assess if the threat is real or if he is feeding us a line. We have an office just about a mile away and it would be good if you can help. It is rather urgent as the threat is likely to manifest itself in the next 24 to 48 hours if it is real."

"I am sorry, but my sister is my priority just now, if it was any other time, I would of course help," replied Jaimie.

As Jaimie turned away to walk back to talk to Storm and the team, he paused and turned back to Mr Jones.

"To assess this thing correctly I would need access to your tools and systems at SIS. Could you set that up?" asked Jaimie.

"Already done, young man. I have a laptop and temporary pass waiting for us at Vauxhall," replied Mr Jones.

"Let me have a quick word with Storm and I will be with you in two mins. I will get you downstairs," replied Jaimie.

Jaimie walked along the corridor to Storm and pulled her aside from the team.

"I need to go and do some spook work for Mr Jones, Storm, can you look after Mr MacPherson for me please? He means a lot to Louise and me. I will be back later," stated Jaimie.

"Not like you to put work ahead of family, Jaimie," replied Storm, frowning with disapproval.

"There are two things: one is an immediate cyber threat that he wants some help assessing, and the other, which is more important to me, is that someone had to leak your whereabouts to the Russians. It didn't come from the team, so the only other place is SIS and I mean to find out who."

"Wait, how do you know it didn't come from the team?" queried Storm.

"I have ninja cyber skills, babe, you know that," replied Jaimie with a smile.

"You are dangerous, Jaimie; do you know that?" shouted Storm.

Jaimie turned and headed towards the lift as Mac and Hairy Dave looked quizzically at Storm.

THIRTY

J aimie met Mr Jones as he exited the lift and they headed to the SIS offices in Vauxhall. It was a non-descript building, one of those concrete utilitarian buildings from the 1960s. They were not heading to the HQ at Vauxhall Cross. That was more for the administration rather than real life operations.

"Before we enter here, I have a demand. There can be no record of me being here. Nothing can be in my real name and everything gets disposed of before I leave the building. I get to take the wiped hard drive from the laptop with me. If we can't agree on that then I will head back to the hospital," eemanded Jaimie.

"Why on earth would I agree to that?" replied Mr Jones.

"It is quite simple, Edward. I make my living in the cyber world and I do not want to be associated with MI6. I don't want any video or voice recording of me and no footprint of me ever being here. Remember, you asked me to do this; I don't care either way."

"How did you know my name? Did one of the team tell you?" asked Edward, rather annoyed.

"They didn't need to, Edward; this is how I make a living, remember?" replied Jaimie.

"It still feels like overkill, Jaimie, but ok, I agree."

With that, Jaimie donned a black baseball cap and sunglasses before entering the building and being ushered to an office with a table and four uncomfortable orange plastic chairs.

Edward appeared with an old kind of battered looking laptop and a piece of paper with a username and password on it. Jaimie fired up the laptop and logged on.

"So what threat are we looking at, Edward, what is it you need me to assess?"

"Louise took a defector out of Russia for us, a man called Dimitri Antonov. He has told us of an imminent threat to the Western banking sector that would cripple it. This isn't a ransomware attack; this is something destructive that would wipe data. Can you imagine nothing getting paid, no oil, gas, cars? The whole western hemisphere would grind to a halt."

"Ouch, and does this Dimitri know how to stop it?" asked Jaimie.

"He does and we are convinced it is real, but we need his defence strategy assessed. What if he was a decoy and he is really here to open doors to allow the real attack?"

"Ah ok, I get it now. Can I have a few minutes alone with him and we can discuss his strategy?" asked Jaimie.

"I can tell you that, Jaimie, you don't need to sit with him."

"You really can't, Edward, unless you are going to tell me the exact coding they are going to use."

"He is in one of the interview rooms downstairs. Why don't we go down and I can leave you guys alone to talk geek stuff."

"Two points, Edward: the first is the interview rooms have both voice and video recording and that violates our agreement; the second is that geek talk as you call it is the only thing that is standing between you and financial Armageddon."

"My apologies, Jaimie. I will bring Dimitri here."

"Good plan, Edward."

As Edward wandered off to fetch Dimitri, Jaimie got to work on the SIS-provided laptop and used it to hack into the email server, mobile phone records, file repositories and geo location records. In parallel, he opened his own laptop and used his backdoor into the FSB to check out the London operatives. For information to be passed back and forth there would need to be local contact. Working between the two laptops, Jaimie planned to see if he could place someone who was being briefed on the operation internally or who had accessed any of the file repositories. Without both systems it would have been almost impossible to do. They had been clever and there was little to no footprint, but there was just a whisper and that was all someone of Jaimie's skill needed. It might not stand up in court as he could never admit to hacking both SIS and FSB, but what he had was proof enough for Jaimie. He closed his personal laptop down and placed it back in his rucksack just as Edward arrived back with Dimitri.

"Jaimie this is…"

"Hi Jaimie, it has been a while. How is business, my friend?" interrupted Dimitri.

"Pretty good, Dimitri, keeping the wolf from my door."

Edward just looked between the two men with a mixture of amazement and bewilderment.

"I take it you two know each other then?"

"We do indeed, Edward. The top end of the cyber world is pretty unique and there are not many out there with Jaimie's unique skillset," replied Dimitri.

"I will leave you two to talk defence strategies and how the threat will manifest itself. I have a couple of errands to run while I am here," replied Edward, who was looking at Jaimie with a newfound respect before leaving the room.

"Talk me through the details of the threat, Dimitri, and let's see what we can do about it," stated Jaimie.

"There is a dedicated team of hackers based in Novgorod. They infiltrated two large IT outsource organisation that has multiple pan global contracts from Germany, US, Europe, and Asia. Anyone that uses them to support their local area network services are at risk. Within a 15-minute window they will have control of the networks, servers and all electronic storage."

"Wouldn't the local cyber security teams be able to track any information leakage?"

"That is the beauty of the plan, Jaimie, there is no information leakage, they are in the networks, but they are dormant, so it is impossible to track unless they conducted a full security protocol of the entire network – and let's face itm no one does that these days because it is so resource intensive."

"What is your defence strategy?"

"I have a list of IP addresses for external facing routers and firewalls that are the access points to the networks. If we shut down those gateways, then they have no route in. The rest of it is pretty moot as they need a way in to start the malicious code that will wipe out the data."

"That could be a lot of work to shut down those interfaces," stated Jaimie.

"By my calculations, we will need a couple of hundred skilled operatives all working at the same time. If we do it piecemeal, they will realise what is happening and just press the go button."

"Let me talk to Edward and see how quickly we can make that happen. He doesn't fully trust you which is why he asked me to assess everything. Just to make sure it was all real."

"That's ok, Jaimie, I expected it," replied Dimitri.

"I hope to see you again soon, my friend," stated Jaimie as he stood up, picked up his laptop and bag and left the room.

Outside he met up with Edward.

"It is all real, Edward and his strategy to deal with it make sense. The downside is it has to be coordinated and completed simultaneously otherwise they will corrupt the financial institutions you have not managed to get to," stated Jaimie.

"Ouch, that is going to be tough, how do you fancy leading our response?"

"No, I will leave that to you and Dimitri, although I would not let him loose on their infrastructure. He is still Russian, and he is needing money after defecting. I will head back to the hospital in the vain hope that Louise has improved."

"OK, Jaimie, I am disappointed, but of course I understand."

"Save the disappointed talk for someone else, Edward. You and your Director hung Louise out to dry. For the life of me I can't quite grasp why. I think my family has dedicated enough to your spy shit in the last few months, don't you? Now let's wipe the laptop hard drive and I will be on my way," retorted Jaimie.

"I can only say that I did my best by Louise, Jaimie, and I can look in the mirror knowing that I did. George would not budge, no matter what I said. It was out of character, but he has become increasingly out of sorts since he returned from his absence."

"Was he involved throughout the job, Edward?" asked Jaimie.

"No, he had been off sick early on, stress or something. He only came back a week or so ago and his first briefing was after the Moscow part was complete. Why do you ask?"

"Just trying to get my head round everything, Edward. I feel like I am standing in front of a tsunami with a leaky bucket. So much has happened in such a short time."

At that an IT technician appeared, took the hard drive out of the laptop, and placed it into the machine that wiped them. In essence it was a massive electromagnet. Simple but effective. Jaimie took the hard drive, placed it into his rucksack and turned and left the office before heading for the subway to head back to the hospital.

Edward stood staring after Jaimie with a thoughtful look on his face. He had a feeling that he would come across Jaimie again in a professional capacity. He was not sure that would be a good thing. A young man with the skills that he has and with the ability to freelance was a risky business.

Jaimie arrived back at the hospital about four hours after he had left and with a quick nod at the security detail made his way up in the lift and exited at the floor of his sister's room.

He was making his way past the room to meet up with the team congregated at the end of the corridor when he heard a broad Glasgow accent.

"Jaimie, lad, your sister wants a word," stated Mr MacPherson.

"She is awake?" asked Jaimie excitedly.

"Aye, lad, she just needed a bit of a nudge."

"Hey sis, it is so good to see you awake, you had me worried. Thank god that awful tube is gone, scared the hell out of me seeing you like that," said Jaimie emotionally.

"Hey, midget, it is nice to see you. Where did you sneak off to when I woke up?" croaked Louise.

"Oh, I just had some investigating of my own to do and Edward helped me do it."

"Edward helped you? That isn't like him."

"Oh, he didn't know he was helping me, Sis, he thought I was helping him. He isn't the only person that can use others in their games."

"Be careful, Jaimie, he is a dangerous enemy."

"Don't worry, Sis. He doesn't know what I was investigating, it isn't a problem. I need to go and speak to the team outside if that is alright."

"Sure, I am tired, I need a sleep anyway."

Jaimie strode purposefully along the corridor and sat down beside Mac, Storm and Dave.

"She is looking much better, babe," said Storm.

"She is, I am so relieved, I wasn't convinced she was going to make it, she was so pale," replied Jaimie.

"Did you manage to help Edward?" asked Mac.

"Well, we kind of helped each other. I had a task I need to get done and I needed some help of the kind only intelligence services can provide. I know who told the Russians where you would be and helped them arrange Louise's kidnap. I want them assassinated," stated Jaimie with a steady glare to all the team.

"That isn't a job for an active team, Jaimie, I'm afraid. It is too easily tracked, and you would be placing them in real danger of life in prison," replied a voice from behind Jaimie.

Jaimie turned to see Mr MacPherson, who had approached them without being heard.

"I will just do it myself then," stated Jaimie angrily.

"That is not a good idea either, laddie. It is time to engage that supersized brain of yours and stop thinking emotionally," retorted Mr MacPherson.

"He just gets away with it then?" demanded Jaimie.

"Life has a funny way getting its own back, Jaimie, his time will come, don't you worry about that. What you need to do now is get your sister back to Scotland to allow her to recover and leave your revenge mission out of your thoughts. Out of interest, who is this double agent? asked Mr MacPherson.

"Someone named George Henry Williams. I have his security pass photo here." Jaimie showed the photo to the team.

Storm let out a whistle of amazement. "That is Edward's Director, the one that gave us the Dimitri job and refused permission to spring her."

"An inoffensive looking man if ever I have seen one," replied Mr MacPherson.

"I have come across him before, never was a fan. I have to say he was the last person I would suspect of being a double agent. That is a hell of an allegation, Jaimie. You will need strong proof as he is well liked in the echelons of power," stated Mac coldly.

"There is no smoking gun, but there are a number of pieces of a jigsaw that provide a picture of treason. I looked up his financial history and George is massively in debt. It looks like he has a significant gambling problem and is paying out large chunks of money each week to online casinos. We see money entering his accounts every 12 weeks from the Cayman Islands that is reducing the outflow, but he is mortgaged up to his eyeballs and falling deeper and deeper into debt. His kids are at a private school and they opened a court case to recover outstanding school fees. A week later he got money from the Cayman Islands and it all died back down. I tracked George's mobile phone and it has never been in the vicinity of a mobile from one of the London-based FSB agents. However, I also did a query on whether there were other mobiles regularly pinging off the same towers as George and it looks like George has a burner phone. I had an 80 percent hit rate which cannot be a coincidence. That burner phone has been in close contact with FSB agents on six occasions. Four of which have been over the last ten days. Lastly, our friend has a flight booked to Berlin in a few days. A separate flight has been booked in his name from Berlin to Moscow three hours afterwards. The first flight paid for by George, the second flight by an unknown credit card from Eastern Europe," replied Jaimie.

"Money and vice, the two reasons people turn traitor," said Mr MacPherson.

"We need to think through how we deal with this, we can't rush into an accusation against someone of that level. The information obtained by Jaimie, whilst compelling, would not be allowed in a court of law. You need a warrant before investigating and anything Jaimie obtained would be classed as tainted and thrown out by any judge. I doubt they would even get a warrant to do a money trail on someone like George," stated Mac.

"Let's go get something to eat and we can sleep on the information Jaimie got," stated Mr MacPherson.

The team headed out for a burger and to chat through the last few days, including Jaimie's findings. The consensus of opinion was that they did not yet have enough actionable evidence to bring to Edward. With Jaimie's evidence tainted as it was obtained illegally, all they had was which files George had accessed and what emails he had. They could not use any cell phone information as it again was obtained illegally.

"I am worried he will leak Louise's location to the FSB," stated Jaimie. "He has done it before."

"That is a reasonable fear, Jaimie lad. I will take her off grid, somewhere safe. We can take some other steps as well to reduce the risk to Louise. You just get your sister back to Scotland and I will make some calls down here to see what else we can put in motion," replied Mr MacPherson.

THIRTY-ONE

A few days later Louise was released from hospital and the team flew with her to Glasgow airport before changing flights to the Island of Islay. Mr MacPherson had a cousin who lived in the north of the island and who was on an around the world sailing trip, allowing them to take over the house for as long as they needed it. Mr MacPherson insisted she needed country air to recuperate fully and not a flat in the city. They arrived at Ardnave and whistled to themselves when they saw it. Such a magnificent restoration work from what was, according to Mr MacPherson, a total ruin. They would happily retire here. Life seemed so much slower on the islands. They got Louise settled before Jaimie phoned Mr MacPherson.

"That is us settled in Islay, such a magnificent island. How are you getting on in London? Will you be joining us soon? Louise would really value your company."

"I will join you tomorrow, Jaimie, I had a couple of errands to run in London, I don't get down to the big smoke very often and wanted to catch up with someone before I headed back north," replied Mr MacPherson.

Mr MacPherson hung up and put his phone in his trouser pocket. He was sat on a low wall, eating some fish and chips in a suburb of Dorking, which was a commuter town just south of London. There was something quite relaxing about eating fish and chips in the early evening sunshine. He was waiting to surprise someone and was pleased when he looked up and saw a middle-aged man in a grey suit walking up the street towards him. He placed his fish and chips on the wall beside him.

"Excuse me, young man I am looking for some directions," said Mr MacPherson.

"Certainly sir, where are you looking for?" replied the man in a grey suit.

"I am looking for someone named George Henry Williams. Do you know which house is his?" asked Mr MacPherson.

"That is me. Do I know you? I am sorry I can't seem to place you?" replied the man.

"No, sir, you don't know me, but I have something for you from a dear friend of mine," replied Mr MacPherson.

Just at that Mr MacPherson twisted his walking stick and quick as a flash thrust the exposed blade through the throat of George Henry Williams before twisting the blade to the right and slicing the throat through the jugular artery.

Mr MacPherson calmly replaced the blade into the walking stick holder and, picking up his fish and chips, serenely walked onwards, his dark blue cloth cap pulled tight down over his forehead. Like a wraith, Mr MacPherson blended into the neighbourhood and headed back towards Dorking station and the train back to Glasgow.

The best way to reduce the risk is to eliminate it, thought Mr MacPherson as he walked away, his walking stick clicking on the pavement.

THE END

If you would like to contact Kenny MacMillan you can do so at <u>KJMacMillan1968@hotmail.com</u>. I do try to answer every email personally so please be patient. Constructive feedback always welcome.

I am currently working on book 2 of the series. If you would like some insight, please drop me an email.

BV - #0019 - 111121 - C0 - 203/127/22 - PB - 9781914195877 - Gloss Lamination